THE SPOIL

Also by Maile Chapman

Your Presence Is Requested at Suvanto

THE SPOIL

A Novel

MAILE CHAPMAN

Graywolf Press

Published by Graywolf Press
212 Third Avenue North, Suite 485
Minneapolis, Minnesota 55401

www.graywolfpress.org

Published in the United States of America
Printed in Canada

ISBN 978-1-64445-379-7 (paperback)
ISBN 978-1-64445-380-3 (ebook)

2 4 6 8 9 7 5 3 1
First Graywolf Printing, 2026

Library of Congress Cataloging-in-Publication Data

Names: Chapman, Maile author
Title: The spoil : a novel / Maile Chapman.
Description: Minneapolis, Minnesota : Graywolf Press, 2026.
Identifiers: LCCN 2025037272 (print) | LCCN 2025037273 (ebook) | ISBN 9781644453797 (trade paperback) | ISBN 9781644453803 (epub)
Subjects: LCGFT: Horror fiction | Psychological fiction | Novels
Classification: LCC PS3603.H373 S66 2026 (print) | LCC PS3603.H373 (ebook) | DDC 813/.6—dc23/eng/20250903
LC record available at https://lccn.loc.gov/2025037272
LC ebook record available at https://lccn.loc.gov/2025037273

Cover design: Vivian Lopez Rowe

Cover art: Donald Hobern, iNaturalist, https://creativecommons.org/licenses/by/4.0/, modified from original (chalcid wasp); Ralf Hiemisch, Getty Images (color spectrum)

For

Lynette,

Anne, and Marianne,

my mother and grandmothers

If we can furnish accounts no less likely than any other, we must be content, remembering that I who speak and you my judges are only human, and consequently it is fitting that we should, in these matters, accept the likely story and look for nothing further.

PLATO, *Timaeus* (TRANS. FRANCIS MACDONALD CORNFORD)

In fables too, the energies of the gods are imitated; for the world may very properly be called a fable, since bodies, and the corporeal possessions which it contains, are apparent, but souls and intellects are occult and invisible.

SALLUSTIUS, *On the Gods and the World*
(TRANS. THOMAS TAYLOR)

There is no route out of the maze. The maze shifts as you move through it, because it is alive.

PHILIP K. DICK, *VALIS*

THE SPOIL

PART ONE

One measures a circle, beginning anywhere.

CHARLES FORT, *Lo!*

Chapter One

I was reading by the woodstove when I heard my grandmother lift the phone to answer a call almost before it rang. She spoke briefly, inaudibly, so as not to wake my grandfather after his swing shift at the mill. When she replaced the phone softly in its cradle I turned my eyes back down to the open page of my book of Greek mythology. *Night was the child of Chaos and so was Erebus. . . . In the whole universe there was nothing else; all was black, empty, silent, endless.* Until she touched my shoulder to hand me a bowl of warm applesauce and say that Jandine—my mother—wanted to stay with Terry a little longer; she said this like I already knew all about Terry.

To be fair, Jandine probably did tell me.

Eventually I would have an extra hearing test at school, but my ears were not the issue.

After lunch, I closed the back door quietly on my way outside and then sat on the steps to pull my rubber boots on, even though Jandine said sitting on cold cement was an invitation to hemorrhoids. But she wasn't there. So I did it anyway.

The grass in the yard was heavy and wet and I took a shortcut through the garden, over the path between pumpkin runners and cornstalks, toward the line of trees in the distance. In the boundary field I thought I could hear something under the tasseling slap of longer grass against my boots. But when I stopped to listen there was only the sycamore trees of the windbreak ahead, and the evergreens on either side, shivering. I picked my way through the reeds and cattails growing along the ditch, where I felt the shock of cold even through double socks and boots half a size too large; this was the property line, and a sign to turn back. But you know what they say—children feel what they haven't been told. And it was the seventies. Everything bright, but out of focus, as if seen through a haze of goldenrod.

—

I knew to be careful outside anytime I went looking for berries or bottles or owl pellets in the ruins left by old Dutch farmers who retired or died before us, in the outbuildings left to fall down slowly in the fields. Like the empty brooder house, or the old barn, stained with rusty nails in boards turning silver in the weather, where Jandine said I didn't want to be when the roof fell in. But the empty house behind the sycamores seemed different, the house where Mrs. Field had lived, with a dish of peppermints on a table and a rotary phone on the wall, and a wooden front door hidden inside a shady screened porch.

She had sometimes propped that door open with a bucket of river stones. I thought I could remember seeing her there, at the doorway, lifting the bucket by the handle. Though maybe this was just something I'd heard about later, in passing. When she still occasionally came up in conversation.

I thought I'd get to speak to Jandine when she called. Earlier in the day I had lifted the phone to see if the neighbors were monopolizing the party line. Just in case Jandine was calling and couldn't get through. But when the call did come it was so brief that I'd missed it.

Mrs. Field's front yard was nearly gone in the uncut grass, her hedges overgrown, smelling of ammonia, and there were two brindled barn cats lying on her slanted cellar doors, flat and dead in the afternoon sunlight. I stopped short. But they were up and streaking away in the same instant.

From across the field this house had looked as warm as a butternut squash half hidden and glowing at sunset, but up close the paint was cracking away from the wood. And there was a metallic smell, coming from a cast-iron bathtub by the front steps, pulled out of the house and left there by someone who meant to be helpful. Since everybody knows bathtubs aren't safe for older people who live alone.

I climbed the front step to look in through the storm door at an enclosed porch, long and narrow, set up like a galley kitchen with a utility sink, a stove, and a compact refrigerator. Just inside sat the bucket filled with stones: blue-gray, veined with quartz, and smooth. When I opened the door the cylinder overhead wheezed, and after I stepped over the threshold it shut itself slowly behind me.

The air inside was motionless, and smelled of stale broiler pans. The front door proper was locked, but behind a wavy glass window I could make out the shape of an armchair. With blue-and-black upholstery. I probably did remember Mrs. Field, sitting in that chair. Sitting in that room. Maybe wearing a dark plain dress and getting slowly up to answer when we knocked? My grandmother and Jandine and I had been standing outside on the cement steps, looking in through the storm door. *Knock louder*, my grandmother had said. *She doesn't hear well.*

I had been holding some small gift for her. Berries, probably. In a bowl lined with waxed paper.

What I could see of the living room now was dim and indistinct, with a pale shape at the far wall, about the size and shape of the rotary telephone in my memory. Long disconnected, though this hadn't occurred to me until I was standing there, looking for it.

A breeze shimmered through the trees outside and the sheets of plastic nailed over the porch windows rustled, startling me, and when I turned I could see that the appliances had been pulled away from the shingled house wall, so that each rested on one of the support beams visible now as a grid under the linoleum, holding up the drooping floor of the porch.

I took a step backward, without thinking, and my foot split the vinyl and rotten plywood, dropping like a lead weight through damp newspaper. And I was lucky; I'd been standing on a beam without knowing, and it caught me and kept me from falling all the way through. My leg was pinned at mid-thigh in the rotten floor. My foot dangling out of sight, in the root cellar under the house, already numb in the cold.

Unless it was numb because I'd hurt myself too badly to know it yet. By impaling my foot on rusty wire, or cutting myself on old glass, or a hundred other awful things I'd been warned to avoid. I gave my leg a careful shake, to bring the feeling back, to make sure I hadn't gotten snagged on anything down there before trying to pull my leg free. But when I did, my foot grazed something.

I moved my foot again, more slowly this time, and again I felt something there—it was a hand, cupping the heel of my boot, and then another hand closing around my ankle, to get a firmer hold through the smooth rubber of my boot. It wouldn't take much, I knew, to yank me down. I could smell the rot from the floor, and I was breathless, and lightheaded, and I couldn't get a good grip on anything until suddenly I did somehow and then freed my leg, and I hit the storm door, which burst open and then I was out of the house. But my leg felt unfamiliar, and nerveless, and too weak to fully hold my weight.

I heard the bucket inside tipping over, a strange, slow sound, and the river stones spilling out and falling through the rotten floor, and then shattering in the cellar below. And then I was up again and scattering away like the feral brindled cats, running through the field, the ground jolting under a foot I couldn't feel until in the ditch I felt my bare skin being cut by the broken reeds, my boot and sock pulled off and left behind under Mrs. Field's house.

Chapter Two

I would have told them I lost the boot, I would have admitted that I'd gone to the old house, that I'd gone inside when I knew better. I would have tried. But when I opened the back door it was like walking into a different afternoon altogether, where Tineke, my grandmother, was brewing coffee into the big red-and-black thermos my grandfather carried with him to work. Packing sandwiches for the lunch break he would take in the middle of the night. Wrapping a stack of oatmeal cookies and two apples, one red, the other golden, and snapping shut the clips on his big black lunch box.

From the bedroom, the sound of him whistling as he got dressed.

Then the sound of tires on the gravel driveway.

"Jacob," she called. "Ritchie's here."

And then it hadn't seemed important because Jandine and Terry had gotten married, and they came to deliver the news the next day. Terry stayed only a little while before driving back to his home in the north end of Tacoma.

Had I even met him before? I assumed that Jandine would now move two hours south to live with him and I would stay where I was.

"No, pet," said my grandmother, smoothing my hair and then letting her hand linger at the back of my head. "You'll always live with your mama."

Terry's son, Jeff, didn't find out until the day Jandine and I showed up; people did this to children back then. Springing big news, out of nowhere. But Terry's parents, Ursula and Warren, must have known because they were at Terry's house that day to give Jeff and me each a bag of saltwater taffy. They expected him to be upset, but he kept running between rooms to show me one toy after another until he lost interest and didn't return.

"Mandy," Ursula said. "Where's Jeff?"

How would I know, in that big, unfamiliar house?

"Well, go look," she said.

He was upstairs, downstairs, under the kitchen table. Filling the bathroom sink with bubble bath, and later he was climbing up and down the ladder of the bunk beds in the bedroom he would have to share with me, for a while. At the end of the weekend I watched from a little window in the laundry alcove as he disappeared into the back seat of the car when Heather, his mother, came to take him back to their apartment. She didn't turn the engine off, just popped the trunk and watched in the rearview mirror as Terry loaded Jeff's bags and then gently slammed the trunk shut again in a cloud of exhaust.

Jandine said it was best to wait in the house. And that nobody really knew how best to handle these situations.

Jeff was there on weekends, and so were Ursula and Warren, and Terry's friends brought power tools and two-by-fours. New carpets arrived, and oak furniture was delivered. Jandine wore jeans and long necklaces, and she made sandwiches and said funny things while mixing packets of dip into sour cream, while refilling Tupperware bowls with party-sized bags of chips. She asked me to restock the fridge with cans of beer and then to keep Jeff amused, and for both of us to stay out from underfoot.

The wood-paneled rec room downstairs was bare, except for Terry's collection of bar signs, some with in-line power switches that set off optical illusions like white water rapids, or draft horses pulling a wagon. One had an infinity effect inside, with lines of tiny lights extending endlessly backward like a highway leading deeper than just into the wood paneling of the wall. Warren contributed an old barbershop pole he found at a swap meet. It lit up, but the red-and-white stripes didn't turn.

"Just give it a minute," he said.

The bulb inside made a ticking sound, heating up while Warren brought down a miniature slot machine and then a cast-iron gumball dispenser. He tossed a roll of coins at us before going back upstairs for a Bloody Mary. Once the barber sign started turning I had to sit with my back to it while we played nickel slots, because it made me dizzy.

Jeff knew a trick for getting coins back, but when I was out of money he ran upstairs without telling me how to open the machine. I unplugged the hot spinning barber pole, and followed him, for a long time, I followed him.

The center of Terry's house was a two-story natural-stone fireplace wall; on the main floor, Jeff and I ran circuits around it, from the living room around the corner into the kitchen and past the breakfast nook, then around the far corner and through the dining room and back to the living room. We tried to pull the sliding doors out of the wall and lock each other into or out of the kitchen. I didn't see much other use for the pocket doors, since the kitchen and breakfast nook were already tucked away out of sight behind the big fireplace wall. Unless they were for special occasions. Like hiding guests for a surprise party.

The kitchen side of the stone wall had a pair of solid-brass doors, about four feet off the ground, opening right into the fireplace. For cooking in, obviously.

"You can't cook in there," said Terry. "It's impractical." And Jandine agreed with him that the heat would be uneven, and the novelty factor wasn't worth scorching the pans. Which was disappointing. But there was a built-in dishwasher that was much easier to load than Tineke's top loader, which had to be rolled up close to the sink and connected with hoses every time. Terry's house also had a dedicated phone line instead of a party line shared with the neighbors, and a small square hole in the floor of his bedroom closet upstairs; until Jeff showed it to me I'd never even heard of a laundry chute. What a good solution, I thought, and what a perfect hole to climb down through, thought Jeff, who lowered himself feet-first and then swung over to land standing on the washing machine lid, with great effort.

"Did you watch me?" he called up through the chute. "Did you see?"

Yes, I did, but why hadn't Terry put the machine directly under the chute?

"It's easy!" Jeff said. "Do you want to see me do it again?"

If the machine could be moved over a little, then Terry and Jandine wouldn't need a laundry hamper upstairs; they could just drop their dirty laundry down right into the machine, since it was a top loader. As long as they left it open, then the clothes would drop right in and that would be efficient, wouldn't it? All that day I kept asking about moving the machine, including at the dinner table, because I just couldn't understand why—

"Just cool it," Terry said, across the dinner table. "The washing machine is where it is for a reason."

"But what's the reason?" I asked, curious.

"Because that's where it fits."

"But the machine and the chute aren't lined up," I said. "Right now they almost line up, but they don't, so anything that gets dropped isn't going to land—"

"Mandy," he said. He was exasperated. "I told you to knock it off."

I closed my mouth and looked down to my plate.

"It's there because that's where the hookup is," he said. "That's all there is to it."

My mother said, "Don't climb around in there, honey. It's not worth the risk of falling and breaking your neck."

That first year, on days of good weather when the front doors and the windows were left open, breezy cool air seemed to funnel right into the house, tumbling around the atrium where the floors of Terry's sprawling split-level house met—four floors, if you included the attic, and five floors if you included the basement, whose entrance at the bottom of the atrium was usually propped open with a rock painted like a ladybug. The breezes made the crystal globes of the pendant chandelier sway. The intercom system's AM/FM-radio base station was in the entryway, with speaker panels set into the walls on other floors, and Jeff and I figured out that by holding down the Talk button on any of them the microphone would pick up and amplify the sound of air circulating. We tested it, taking turns holding a Talk button down while the other moved through the house, opening doors and windows, listening.

"Hey," Jandine called out from the kitchen, on the day we discovered this. "What am I hearing?"

On Saturdays, when Terry and his friends listened to music through the intercom while painting walls, hanging drapes, carrying and positioning new furniture, and tacking down carpet, Jeff would make a game out of ringing the doorbell, running off, and then slipping back into the house through some other door without being seen. He liked to try to use every door into the house at least once before quitting: front, back, garage, basement, the sliding glass door in the den, and the sliding glass door in the dining room. He knew the doorbell chimes cut in over the music obnoxiously. Which was probably the whole point. As Jandine liked to say, sometimes negative attention was better than no attention at all.

Chapter Three

For years my grandparents had stacked Mrs. Field's firewood, and brought her mail, and turned over her garden when they rented a rototiller for their own. They'd continued checking in on her long after she stopped answering the phone or opening her door, and if the lights ever didn't look right in the evenings they would walk over to see if she needed anything. Which is how my grandmother came to find Mrs. Field sitting in her chair in the living room, an untouched pot of coffee still hot on the burner.

She probably sat down, just for a moment, after putting on the coffee. And she'd been there all through that last day, whenever it was, while we did whatever we'd been doing across the field without knowing she'd died. And eventually my grandparents took on Mrs. Field's property; she had nobody else left to do it.

Mrs. Field had done her own canning, like everyone else, boiling water and sterilizing jars, storing up vegetables and jams for the future. But she had somehow quietly enlarged her cellar, making it bigger than anybody knew, until my grandfather found the piles of spoil dirt behind the house, like a field of molehills. She must have worked slowly, he said, bringing up one bucketful at a time. For a long time.

My grandmother said all the old food in Mrs. Field's cellar had to go before it poisoned somebody. She and Jandine picked a weekend for us to come up and help along with Ritchie Berkenbosch, their good friend and neighbor on the other side.

Ritchie and my grandfather had cleared a spot in the grass to make a fire a little ways from the house. To keep warm, they said, and gave me the job of keeping an eye on it. As they were lifting the cellar doors and laying them flat on either side, I had to turn away from the smell. I tossed green wood onto the fire to fill the air with smoke instead. Jandine and I could hear them down there, with my grandmother, under the house, exclaiming at how far back the jars went, at how many there were, until my grandfather saw standing water in the low places, and said everyone but him had to stay aboveground for the sake of safety.

My mother went back and forth through the garden all afternoon, restless, looking for flashlights, Band-Aids, anything useful. She went out to the road to check the mailbox twice. My grandfather kept handing up flats of jars to my grandmother, who wore rubber gloves as she broke them on a cinder block in a trench that Ritchie kept expanding with a shovel. I didn't see what a terrible day this was for Jandine, but my grandmother must have. She stopped her from orbiting and pulled her close, smoothing down her ponytail and asking her to make coffee and bring it back in a thermos, in case anyone wanted any. Which no one did. But it was a way to be busy.

I had a blinding flash of the obvious only years later, when I realized I knew of course that Mrs. Field had been the mother of my father, who had died right around the time I was born. I knew only very little. Just that the accident happened while he was driving, because of the way it rains, and the way it gets dark so early, and because the roads were narrow and winding and dangerous in the dark, in the wet, in the trees. That he'd long since left off working at the mill and gone to college, then taken a job in town. And that some other future could have panned out, for all of us, but hadn't.

But—her last name? Field?

That's what I called her as a toddler in my yellow corduroy overalls, sitting in the wheelbarrow while Jandine, a young widow, would hang the clean laundry in the yard after we moved back in with her parents. Waving at a woman I might have seen in the distance. *Missus kitty. Missus garden. Missus chicks! Missus field!*

All that time their houses had been so close together, within eyeshot, and Mrs. Field keeping her distance like that. It never occurred to me to think of her as my grandmother. And evidently she hadn't wanted me to. Maybe it was just easier for everyone to call her by this new name. But Vandervelden was her surname really. The same, of course, as mine.

So much faded and useless food. Such a waste. At dusk Ritchie emptied a last wheelbarrow full of trash, still trying to distract us by gently lobbing things into the sparks of the fire. Bowling gutter balls with wood scraps. Pitching strikes with balls of old twine, though everyone was tired and must have felt more disgust than sympathy for the woman who'd done this much extra work and then left the mess for others to clean up. I didn't see my lost blue boot until it left Ritchie's hand and landed in the fire, and then I held my breath and waited to see if it would burn, my pulse getting loud in my ears, beyond which I could faintly hear Jandine coughing delicately.

"Jesus, Ritchie," said my grandmother. But he'd already lobbed another handful of scraps onto the embers, hiding the boot from view.

My grandfather snapped a padlock onto the cellar doors and came to stand beside him. Their overalls were streaked with dust, their steel-toed boots gray with cobwebs. In the firelight they both looked even bigger and more solid than they did in regular clothes—they were big men to begin with, both sandy second-generation Dutch farmers, with massive hands and ruddy cheeks. Both sturdy enough to moonlight as pulp-and-paper-mill workers on top of their fields and farms. Until their knees paid the price of standing on cement for so many years. Until all the sawdust they'd been breathing started to catch up. But in their denim bib overalls they were as rectangular and tall as doors.

Jandine was thinking out loud about dinner plans and speculating about how late Barter's Drive In would be open. Maybe she should leave now to get there in time to pick up some hamburgers? But the air stank of burning green beans and nobody answered. My grandmother was leaning on the metal rake with both hands, firelight coming and going across the lenses of her glasses while we watched Ritchie lift another jar from the wheelbarrow, filthy and misshapen. I saw him glance down at it in surprise, a moment before my grandmother seemed to come out of her reverie, and she said, "Hold on there, Ritchie, let me see that one . . ."

He'd already almost let go. He tried to stop himself, but the jar rolled off his fingers and fell just short of the fire, hitting the dirt with a dull thump.

"I'll get it," I said, because I was closest.

"Leave it be, pet," said my grandmother, while Jandine stepped closer and rested both hands lightly on my shoulders. Before my grandmother could sweep the jar into the fire with the rake it made the sound you get from tapping a stubborn jar of preserves against a wooden butcher block. The hollow rush of a vacuum seal breaking. The glass cracked, and out came a gush of dark jelly, and a clot the size of a peeled beet that rolled to the edge of the embers and began to smoke.

Left in the broken glass were a handful of bent nails, tangled wire, and a filthy silver coin. When the smell of it all caught me in the face I ducked my head and clapped both hands over my burning eyes, but it did no good.

Jandine took me by one arm and my grandmother by the other to carry me over the sharp reeds of the now-dry ditch, through the garden, back toward their house. My eyes were streaming, and I kept stumbling, losing my footing, until my grandmother said, "Hold your breath," and they dunked my face briefly into the rain barrel at the side of the house. The cold, silky water slopped over the edge, drenching my pants and shoes. I had no time at all to check for green lacewings or anything else that might have been floating in the water.

My grandmother said, "Once more—and open your eyes."

"Hold your breath," my mother added, and they put my face

back under. Then I was out again and they were pulling my coat off, working together while I stood like a stunned doll being undressed in the cold.

Ritchie and my grandfather had by then caught up.

"Is she okay?" said Ritchie.

"She's okay," said my grandmother, touching my hair.

"The stink of it!" said Ritchie. "What in the world?"

My clothes were wet and I could feel water sliding through my underpants and down both legs to pool in my shoes.

"I mean, really," said Ritchie. "What was that?"

My grandfather picked up my coat.

"May have to burn that," said my grandmother.

"Sorry, kiddo," my grandfather said to me. "We'll find you another nice new jacket."

My grandmother looked into my eyes, then up my nostrils.

"Did you breathe anything?" she said.

I was fighting back nausea. The burbly kind you can't talk yourself out of.

Suddenly my mother said, "We need hamburgers!"

When nobody said anything she repeated herself. "We need hamburgers," she said. "I'll get hamburgers, and some cheeseburgers, maybe a couple of hot dogs. . . . Mandy? Do you want a chili dog?"

"Maybe ease up on that, Jandy," said my grandfather, with a big hand resting on my back.

"Sorry, kid," said Ritchie. "Sorry that you got a face-full of something so rotten. I can't even begin to guess what kind of a god-awful—"

I heaved a mouthful of hot water onto the grass.

"Would you ever stop talking, Ritchie," said my grandmother, "and give her some peace in which to vomit?"

And then I was sitting watching them all from a hard chair at the kitchen table, wrapped in a flannel nightgown and a chenille blanket after being soaped and rinsed with hard well water in my grandparents' bathtub. There was a shimmer moving across Jandine's cheeks—a puff of face powder like mica—as she leaned down to ask me a question.

She had her town coat on. Her hazel eyes were flecked with gold, like the flakes I'd spent all that summer picking out of a mountain of sand my grandfather hauled home and dumped onto a tarp to keep me occupied. For the work of which Ritchie offered me a wide shallow pan he'd used at the river when they had looked for gold together, so many years before, when they were young men panning for mineral riches of their own.

I turned my head slowly, looking for the gold flakes lined up in baby-food jars on the windowsill of the mudroom. My own gold flakes were floating there in tap water beside the jelly jars of herb cuttings Tineke was always propagating in water. I could see Ritchie leaning over the utility sink and looking at his hands under the yellow light bulb, lifting one to tentatively sniff and then washing again with the big cracked bar of castile soap. Cold water throbbing up from the well to hit the bottom of the sink with an unbearable sound like a big match striking, a match that was always striking, never catching fire, and there was something else nearby invisibly burning in the compost bucket by the back door. The smell of wet coffee grounds, grapefruit skins, and broken eggshells trailing an alkaline film while the residue of what had been alive in them kept burning off into the air and disappearing up an endless chimney.

My mother was speaking loudly. "Something to eat," she said, "but what else? Can you think of anything?"

She touched my face gently, with the back of one hand.

"Mandy," she said. "What are you hungry for?"

I blinked, and saw her there.

She said, "Maybe a milkshake?"

Something turned over in my throat. She set a little bucket by my feet.

"If you think you can throw up, don't fight it," she said. "You'll feel better after."

—

If this were a movie, three elders might have watched my mother drive away before closing the blinds and turning to look down at me with concern. My grandmother might have stepped into the role of a knowing ancient, pulling up a chair with purpose as she spoke. Or it could have been Ritchie, not because his Calvinist wife knew that malevolence swirls everywhere without mercy, but because Ritchie himself was attuned to the mystery of this world. And of course my grandfather, who did the work of three men every day, he would have taken steps to flush out whatever had been hidden in that jar and then bury it again deep. But this is a memory, and not a movie, and it doesn't matter how much I wish there had been some obvious sign. As it really happened, my grandmother leaned down, as Jandine had, and looked into my face.

"You all right, pet?" she asked.

I could hear the drip, drip behind her. The sound of the tap not fully turned, and drops of water hitting the nickel sink first like a yes, then like a no. Back and forth, and neither answer correct.

Jandine returned with a vanilla milkshake and some magazines, adjusting the bedside lamp so that I could sit up reading, if I wanted. I wanted her to stay. But with a bolus in my throat and a ringing in my ears, I couldn't say so.

She saw, though, and she said, "Do you want me to read to you?"

She sat in the chair beside the bed, took up a magazine, and read the editor's note out loud: a description of the cosmos as a library full of keys, or books, or both, quoting Einstein maybe? I would later recognize the magazine she held as the first issue of *Omni*. Which I long thought I remembered as a blue void with red letters and two red eyes. It's actually a blue road, with red taillights. I only noticed my mistake years later, while packing up everything in Terry's house, including the magazine and the rest of what had been the occult library of my childhood.

By morning I felt an ache like loose baby teeth, everywhere. I tried pressing my head, with both hands, on the freeway back to Tacoma. Just to relieve the pressure.

"Are you carsick?" said Jandine, pushing a plastic bag at me, and I shook my head, no—but the shaking movement was too much. I braced with one hand against the glove box while she pulled off at the next exit.

"You need to eat," she said. "You didn't have enough breakfast. Or dinner."

She coasted to the grassy edge of a parking lot and I opened my door, leaning out to dry heave. The interstate was so quiet, after. Just a few cars passing, barely visible on the other side of the trees.

"Let's get some air," said Jandine.

I put my feet on the ground and stood, but as I moved away from the car I either felt or heard something drop out behind me and unfurl like a loose bundle of silk on the pavement. I was afraid to look back. I took a few more steps, and it dragged along, and as the breeze picked up I felt a sudden terror that the wind would fill what I couldn't see and lift me away into the air.

"There's a Denny's," said Jandine.

Whatever was behind me swung out of sight as she took my hand and we walked across the parking lot, through glass doors into a restaurant filled with steam and sound, and the smell of coffee burning into molasses at the bottom of a dozen glass carafes. I said yes to a stack of warm bland pancakes with extra scoops of butter and a glass of 7UP, extra ice, please, thank you, and then I rested my forehead on the paper place mat.

"She's carsick," said Jandine. The waitress brought some saltines. By the time I walked out, whatever was with us couldn't move me so easily. But I could still feel it riding behind like a parachute, or a life raft, something packed up small that would open if triggered.

Terry's driveway was full of cars and the house was vibrating with music when we pulled up. Jandine had to park on the street. All the activity was in the basement, where, by removing the iron handrails, Terry and his friends had gotten a pool table down the stairs along with an eight-foot dry bar and matching barstools.

Jeff was jumping from the stairs into some beanbag chairs, grazing the wood-paneled ceiling with one hand before landing.

"Mandy, try it!" he said. But my head was still queasy. Head, ear, jaw, whatever.

Terry was showing Jandine the score-keeping beads hung between the pendant pool table lamps, sliding the beads back and forth with the tip of a pool cue. Jeff pulled me past a new brown leather sofa and bulky console TV from Warren's shop, to show me chalk lines on the new carpet marking the doorway of his future bedroom. By the time I got away Terry was positioning the wrought iron banister back in place while another man held the impact driver, ready to sink a dozen big bolts loudly back into place.

"Hold on," said Terry, when he saw me lingering by the bottom step. "Mandy, did you want to get past?" And he lifted the iron railing away so that I could escape back upstairs to hide in my room. Even from upstairs I felt the grinding of the bolts. And the jump of the subwoofer, as they listened to an Eagles album. But not just that, because whenever someone flipped a record over, in the gap of quiet there was still something wrong.

Soon I heard Heather honking from the driveway, and then the other car engines starting one by one as Terry's friends left. Then the quiet click and roll of the pool balls as Terry racked them, over and over, so that Jandine could practice taking break shots, while they talked in the tones of ordinary conversation.

Chapter Four

After school I opened the front door with my house key, locked it behind me, picked up the mail from the floor, and called Jandine at work on the kitchen phone to say I was home. After getting settled at the breakfast table, with my homework assignments spread out, I couldn't seem to concentrate. I kept noticing how quiet the house was.

My grandparents' house could be plenty quiet, too, especially when my grandfather was working swing or graveyard, but this was a different feeling. Less natural. I kept reading, but not remembering what I'd read, until finally I rested my head on the table. I must have dozed because I popped back into sudden wakefulness when I heard someone step out of hiding downstairs and then stand, waiting, at the bottom of the stairs.

I listened hard, watching the numbers turn on the stove clock. When I was sure I wasn't imagining it I called Jandine, my fingers catching in the slow rotary dial while I tried to quietly unbolt the back door with my other hand. When she answered I whispered into the phone that I'd heard an intruder in the house, but then I was afraid my voice had carried, and I dropped the phone and ran out to the backyard. But the backyard was fenced and lined with trees and I didn't feel safe there either, so I ran down the shallow steps to the side yard and around to the front of the house, where I waited, coatless and shivering, while Jandine drove home in a hurry. She pulled into the driveway, left the car running, and told me to get in and lock the doors and to lean on the horn if I saw anyone coming or going. And then she did what nobody should ever do and went into the house alone. But she didn't find anything out of place. Nothing but the phone in the kitchen dangling off the hook, beeping.

I don't know why I didn't call 911, or why she didn't. Or

why she went through the house by herself. Unless maybe she hadn't quite believed me?

"Is this what you were reading?" she said, holding up the library book she found next to my homework, with a cover illustration of a skull-headed horseman in a forest. She pulled out a chair and sat across from me at the kitchen table. She reached her hands out, and then folded them over mine, and she waited with me in the quiet house, trying to hear whatever it was that had frightened me so badly.

"I don't want you to take this the wrong way," she said. "But I think you freaked yourself out."

"I heard something."

"Yes, but if you're thinking that you're hearing something in the house, then you're going to hear something in the house."

"But I wasn't thinking about hearing anything in the house until I did."

"I don't mean that you *want* to, but if you *expect* to, then you will."

"How do I stop expecting it when I already know something's there?"

She held up my book. "Maybe stop reading nightmare books, for a start," she said. "And next time, try walking out to the entryway and looking downstairs. Because seeing nothing there will make it go away."

"Make it go away?" I said. "Make *it* go away?"

"Not *it*," she said. "I mean the fear goes away if you know you're alone in the house."

"You don't believe me," I said.

"On the contrary," she said; she was smiling. But gently. "I completely believe you heard something. But I also believe your mind can play tricks on you."

I was looking down, still listening to the house around us with half of my attention.

"Mandy," she said. And she waited, until I looked at her. "You know there's no such thing as ghosts, right?"

I didn't answer. She squeezed my hands, hard.

"People don't get stuck here after they die. They move on. And they don't come back to visit."

After coming in from the cold my clothing had begun to ache, and I couldn't concentrate on what she was saying and whatever might be downstairs at the same time.

"There's nobody else in the house," she said again.

"You don't hear anything?" I said.

"Mandy," she said, with an unfamiliar edge of impatience in her voice. "Please give this a chance. Because we live here now and we're not going anywhere else."

I shut my eyes. Suddenly Jandine reached across and touched the inside of her wrist to my neck.

"You're burning up," she said. She pressed the cool back of her other hand against my cheek. "Oh, Mandy," she said. "You really have to start telling me when you're sick. Okay?"

"Okay," I said. "I feel sick."

"Mandy," she said, getting up to find the yellow pages. "Don't make things harder than they have to be." And while she looked for an urgent care clinic nearby, I burst into tears.

The unfamiliar doctor checked my ears, eyes, nose, and throat with a piercing silver penlight and sent us to a pharmacy window. It was evening by then, and dark, and on the way home we stopped at a drive-through so that I could take the first dose of antibiotics immediately with food.

Jandine shook two red capsules into my humid hand as we waited in the car for chocolate milk and a molten apple-pie pocket.

"They smell weird," I said. "They smell like chicken shit."

"Good," she said. "That tells us your nose isn't stuffed up."

But nothing could have made me laugh just then.

"The sooner you take the first dose, the better," she said, passing me the carton of chocolate milk, and then at home she drew the shades in my room and leaned under the bunk to tuck me in. I saw the gold of her necklace glinting in the shadows, and then I slept.

Jandine took a day off work and then two more half days, waking me every so often for bowls of soup, or tumblers of acidophilus milk and red capsules. By the time I got out of bed on my own I found midday sunlight filtering into the atrium at the far end of the hall, and the phone from Terry and Jandine's bedroom sitting on the brown carpet outside my door. She had taped their work numbers to the handset. So it was a work day, apparently; I'd lost track. At the end of the hall I put a hand on the iron railing and leaned forward over the atrium, listening. The house seemed empty, but I couldn't see enough to know. Just the stairs going down and part of the entryway, then the lower stairs, and one corner of the den, far below, by the locked door that led to the garage. On my way down to the kitchen, I saw, as if for the first time, just how big the fireplace wall really was. It filled the whole center of the house, and would easily conceal anyone or anything that might be standing there, on the other side.

I'd known this, of course. Jeff and I chased each other around those blind corners all the time. But I'd never felt it. Now the fireplace wall seemed to weigh everything down, cut everything off. There was a deadened quality in the air that made it suddenly acutely obvious that someone or something around the far corner in the living room could move when I moved and remain unseen, by keeping the fireplace wall between us. And downstairs, I realized, there was a smaller version of the same kind of blind spot in the guest bathroom, which could be entered either from the guest room or from the den, and if you were on your own, you could never be sure if there was someone ahead or behind, stepping out of sight. The kitchen, at least, had the back door as an exit strategy and the phone in case of emergency. So I was there, drinking flat cola and fixing a plate of buttered toast at the kitchen counter when I realized I was hearing a small, intermittent crackling sound from the intercom speaker in the entryway.

Jeff and I had been so rough with the intercom master station that by then it only picked up a couple of FM stations clearly. One of these exclusively played the kind of music piped in from concealed speakers in the long, empty hallway leading to the distant public restrooms at the Tacoma Mall. It was the same music Ursula liked to listen to in the car, and Jeff loved to make fun of it, and he made fun of the station's TV commercials, too, which were long, and eerily quiet, seemingly without any music . . . or maybe with music too low or too hypnotic to remember . . . an empty patch of blue sky, and then a gull, coasting on a sunlit breeze, while a voice from somewhere offscreen repeated: *KBRD . . . FM 104 . . . as beautiful . . . as a bird . . . in flight . . .*

The other stations were there in the static, like small bumps as I turned the dial, but I couldn't get to them. So I turned the radio off and went back to my bland breakfast alone in the kitchen.

Once I was settled in my usual place at the table, I looked up, and saw—even though I'd already known this, too—that the imposing angle of the corner of the stone fireplace wall made it impossible to see both of the doorways into the kitchen area at the same time. It was unsettling enough that I went back out to the entryway to put the beautiful music on, with just enough volume to cover the sound of the house, but not the slam of the garage door and the tapping of Jandine's clogs on the slate floor later when she came home on her lunch hour to check on me.

Jandine slid open the kitchen door, dropped her burgundy leather purse onto a chair, and said, "How do you feel? Why are you sitting in the kitchen with the doors closed? Nice music, by the way."

"There was a draft," I said. Because she had not believed me, before.

"Sweetheart," she said, "just turn up the heat if you're cold. Don't be uncomfortable unless you want to be uncomfortable." And she hugged me into her silky work blouse and corduroy blazer.

"Do you have to go back to work?" I asked.

She took a seat at the table and propped her chin on her hand. "I have to go back for a couple of hours. And—today's Friday? Jeff's coming. Be sure to tell him you're not contagious."

I said, "I don't think the bug in my ear is contagious."

"Just make sure he knows that," she said.

It was lost on me at the time that she had skipped her lunch to drive across town to sit with me for fifteen minutes before turning around and going back to work, only to repeat the drive again at quitting time in rush hour traffic. But I would understand the feeling of going back and forth years later when I found myself driving across a different city to check on her, thankful that my job was flexible and that I could.

Jeff leaned on the doorbell while Heather waited, her car idling in the afternoon dusk. She'd probably have taken him back if she'd seen my sick day nightgown and bathrobe.

"What's wrong with you?" Jeff said.

"I'm not contagious," I said. "Look at this." I turned on the radio, let go of the tuner dial, and we watched the needle drift back through static to rest on the endless orchestral music.

"It's your favorite station," I said.

"That's K-bird!" he said. "Why are you listening to K-bird?"

I pulled the step stool to the entryway so Jeff could find something better to listen to while I made mini pizzas on English muffins in the microwave.

"It's broken," he said. But he hesitated.

"What?" I said.

"I just hate K-bird so much," he said, turning the radio off.

We were peeling melted cheese from paper towels when Jeff

stopped again, staring at me. “Did somebody just get home?” he said.

Some time after the sun had gone down we heard Terry’s car in the driveway, and the garage door opening and closing. He came up the stairs and paused in front of the closed sliding door. He was carrying an armful of rustling paper bags of fish-and-chips for dinner, and when he came around the corner he nearly dropped them.

He said, “Why are you two sitting here in the dark? You nearly gave me a heart attack.”

We’d been at the kitchen table for at least an hour and a half by then, listening, only looking up at each other when we thought we heard movement, to see whether the other had also heard it. Sometimes we looked up simultaneously, meeting each other’s eyes. Whatever we were hearing seemed to move sporadically, at long, irregular intervals, too slowly to be sure we weren’t imagining it. But it felt like we were not alone in the house.

We’d stopped talking, stopped even whispering, too afraid of missing any sign of movement, and by the time Terry got home we were both staring dully down at the tabletop. Jeff’s face was streaky when he looked up, his lashes stuck together and dark with tears. He pushed back his chair and reached for Terry’s arm, crushing his face into the sleeve of his coat. But a moment later he was running down the stairs to greet Jandine at the door to the garage.

Terry handed me a bag, squinting as he noticed my bathrobe.

“Are you feeling any better?” he said.

“I’m not contagious,” I said, and then Jeff ran back into the kitchen, having just done a quick change into his pajamas now, too.

We should have told him. Terry had installed burglar bars on the windows and floodlights in the back and side yards, and if he thought there was an intruder, he’d have turned the place upside down, baseball bat in hand. I don't know why neither of us said anything. But maybe after the lights were on and the dinner bags were being torn open, it had seemed less real, the way these things always do. It was Friday night, and even though I was still sick and already tired I wanted to watch the variety shows I'd watched with my grandparents every week. Jandine and I settled down in front of the TV in the living room while Jeff and Terry went downstairs to watch shows with plots, with car chases. They couldn't miss an episode, or they'd never catch up.

On Saturday night, Jeff and I unrolled our sleeping bags in front of the TV in the rec room, on a patch of carpet between one end of the pool table and the long curve of the dry bar. Because we could watch *Love Boat* and *Fantasy Island* down there, or not at all, since Terry and Jandine would be in the living room, with blender drinks, until *Saturday Night Live* ended.

Jeff and I fell asleep with the TV still on but I woke later with Jeff huddled close. Most of his face was tucked into his sleeping bag, except his eyes. When he saw that I was awake he whispered something.

"What?" I whispered back.

". . . Under the pool table," he said.

"What's under the pool table?" I whispered back.

"Something. Standing there."

I said, "Standing? Under the pool table?"

"I don't know," Jeff said, eyes filling with tears. "I can't explain."

I sat up, and I turned my head, and I looked behind me, into the darkness. I didn't see anything there.

"Okay," I said. "Let's go up."

We stood and scooped at the bedding and then we went single file in the half-light, him first and me behind with my hand on his shoulder, navigating the narrow space between the pool table and the dark leather couch. I hadn't seen anything, but that didn't matter, I still couldn't bring myself to look down at our bare feet, passing so close to the shadows under the pool table. Which is why I accidentally stepped on a corner of Jeff's sleeping bag. He dropped everything and ran, fumbling for the doorknob at the top of the stairs while I grabbed what I could and ran up after him. We put our sleeping bags on the bedroom floor upstairs, instead of going to our bunks, so that we could share the one pillow that hadn't been dropped and left behind in the basement.

In the morning I tried to ask him what he'd seen. But he said it had been nothing, just a nightmare about nothing. I wanted to know if he meant the kind of nothing we had been listening for on Friday afternoon, or nothing he wanted to talk about, but his eyes started watering, and I didn't press.

Chapter Five

I kept to the kitchen when I was home alone. Leaving the radio on helped, and I listened to the soft background static between the fuzzy stations while I did homework at the kitchen table. Sometimes a quick burst of the afternoon news would break in, or a few organ tones and the crack of a baseball bat from the Triple-A stadium a few miles away. Stray signals now and then didn't bother me. But it was distracting when voices briefly materialized with the gritty quality of a broadcast sent from a ship in the middle of an ocean, or from some distant moon, or some other decade.

Traffic report at the top of the hour: Construction continues on northbound Interstate 5, with delays expected for the next three days at least. Two lanes open on the viaduct this evening, then down to one lane over the weekend . . .

I could feel the cuffs of my pants and my socks, still damp and cold after walking home in the rain. I wanted to change into something dry. But I didn't want to leave the kitchen, and the thought of climbing up the stairs to my room seemed like so much effort. I wondered how long it would be until Terry or Jandine got home. Lifting my gaze from the table to check the clock took a lot of energy, but I did it, looking up just in time to hear that muted and familiar *crack* from the intercom again. An impact in the distance, held aloft in the static.

But that didn't seem right; it was raining pretty hard for a game at the Triple-A stadium down the road. Maybe it wasn't the sound of a bat connecting with a ball, maybe it was something else, in which case the roar in the background probably wasn't a crowd of human voices from the stands of a stadium, either. Suddenly the static seemed abrasive. I made myself stand up and walk across the kitchen, past the awkward corner of the fireplace wall, and I slid the pocket door open and turned off the radio. The sudden quiet was such a relief. At first. Until I realized that under the sound of the radio it felt like there had been something else happening.

My hand felt heavy, uncoordinated when I reached up to turn the radio back on. I moved the dial away from the pseudo ball game, and I kept the dial moving, ready to stop for any music or news or ads that came in clearly and didn't collapse back into static. Something—normal. I didn't care what. Then I would go upstairs. Because I thought I might be sick. Some local afternoon show was almost coming in:

A Good Samaritan saw brake lights in the trees shortly after nine p.m. Earlier that evening, the couple had watched the local news, they ate dinner together, and had a normal evening, if it's even possible to say so now . . . just a basic Saturday evening for almost anyone . . .

There was something behind me now, on the stairs leading up from the den. Someone moving very slowly. My hands felt fluttery, inexact, like when you have to get the key from your key ring into the lock of your front door so that you can open it and step inside and shut the door and lock it safely behind you. And turning to look behind you will only slow you down.

If I didn't turn my head, if I didn't look directly, if I didn't acknowledge whatever was there in any way, then somehow I knew I would be allowed to just go back into the kitchen, as if nothing were wrong. This was as clear in my mind as a contract. But now I couldn't even find the beautiful music. Just distorted fragments.

Go ahead and say it: If I've never been given the details, it's for the sole reason that all three of them decided—

I felt so much pressure to get the needle into some pocket of clear sound—but I didn't want to hear this, whatever it was.

Maybe I could make it to the kitchen, maybe I could get the back door open in time. Maybe I would have the advantage of knowing the yard and could make it to a neighbor's front door before being caught. I didn't know which neighbor's house to head for. The closest? The most likely to be home? The most likely to answer? Terry's house faced away from the rest of the block and we barely knew anyone else on the street. These thoughts passed through my mind in a second or two, including that there would not be time to call Jandine. I hunched my shoulders against whatever would happen. When I let go of the dial, the needle slipped back and settled into the rut of the beautiful music on its own.

I stood staring at the dial as the music floated out from the speaker. It felt like a trick. But the station came in clearly. I slid all the room control switches to the down position, so that the music bloomed from the wall speakers on the other floors.

A fragile equilibrium had been set. I went back into the kitchen, slid the flimsy pocket door shut behind me, and returned to my homework. I unbolted the back door, just in case I had to run. But otherwise, I behaved normally. As normally as possible. Even though the wooden pencil kept sliding between my fingers because my hands would not stop sweating. I couldn't finish the math, but I didn't look up again or allow myself to react to anything more, until Jandine came in from the garage that evening, carrying a rain-spotted cardboard box full of Shakey's pizza.

In the car the next morning I asked Jandine if she could pick me up from the library on her way home that evening. I had reasons prepared, including that it wasn't much farther from school than walking home, and on a route that was busier, probably safer. I said there was a reading club and extra credit. I said a few things like that. Every persuasive reason I could think of.

"Sure, but you know I can't be there until after five," she

said, with mild exasperation. "Once you're there, stay there. Wait for me in the library foyer."

"Perfect," I said, unbuckling my seat belt, "that's great, thanks."

"I'll pick you up at five twenty—here," she said, handing over a fistful of the coins that accumulated in the cup holders of her car, writing down her work number, knowing I couldn't remember it. "Go straight to the library and call me from the pay phone as soon as you get there. Don't forget."

I did call. But then I lost track of time, and so I wasn't standing in the brightly lit library foyer at 5:20 as planned. When Jandine parked and came in she found me at a reading table between Section 110: Metaphysics and Section 130: Parapsychology and Occultism. I was bent forward over Konstantin Raudive's *Breakthrough: An Amazing Experiment in Electronic Communication with the Dead* when she put a hand on my shoulder and I looked up, startled, to discover that an hour had passed since I'd last checked the wall clock.

"What's that?" she said, in a low library whisper.

"It's miscellaneous," I said, flipping the book. "For school."

Did I want to check it out and take it home?

Actually, no. This was just the first relevant book I'd found; I would need to return the next day, and every day after that, to keep looking.

Reading tables, book stacks, a restroom, a drinking fountain, and my pockets filled with trail mix. Other people around. All was well. I tried to remember to look at my wristwatch, but Jandine still sometimes had to come in to collect me from the corner where unexplained phenomena and unsolved mysteries overlapped.

I missed Bellingham. I missed having my hair rolled up for home permanents, and the crinkle of unfolding Butterick sewing patterns, and the sounds of fabric being sliced with sharp sewing scissors. The sound of my grandfather parking outside on the gravel driveway. At Terry's house there were no apple trees, no windfall apples to scrub and peel and core, no cinnamon applesauce by the fire, and no fire. Instead we had ashtrays full of low-tar cigarette butts with names like Now and More. The throb of the basement stereo speakers, and a kitchen that smelled faintly of celery salt, Bloody Mary mix, horseradish, marinade, and freshly ground black pepper.

I looked in the periodicals section of the library for the magazines Ritchie used to give me after he was done with them, magazines like *Beyond Reality*, and *FATE*. But the library in Tacoma didn't have them, and the librarian couldn't think of anything similar. My grandparents mailed letters to Jandine every week, with notes for me written on the pad of letter paper kept in the drawer under their telephone, one side from Tineke in ballpoint ink and the other from Jake in dark pencil with a sketch of a bird, a clover, a cat. Or the title of a paperback from Ritchie, maybe the latest Erich von Däniken book, or more magazines whose back pages advertised sea monkey colonies, pyramid power amulets, or correspondence courses in hypnotism. They never mailed me those books. They carefully added each to the brown paper bags of reading material being set aside for me in their garage, tucked safely under the hanging bunches of garlic and onions. *To ward off vampire stories, ha ha!*

At the library I found books about psi experiments, and premonitions, and attempts to catalog dreams of disasters before they happened. Herds and flocks who navigate by instinct, and schools and shoals who move like single creatures. The collective consciousness of insect colonies, and the language of bees. The orange tomcat who woke his people when their house caught fire by pestering the woman, who fed him in the kitchen every morning, instead of the man, who would have groggily put him out through the window, as he did every night. In which case the cat would have lived, but the humans would have perished.

"Smart cat," said Jandine, when I told her about these things. "I understand your interest."

—

I brought home book after book about unexplained events, including anecdotes collected from anonymous sources, from people who knew they weren't crazy but also knew they wouldn't be believed when they described flashes of impossible insight or dreams predicting disaster. Amazing examples of dogs who could diagnose diseases, track the missing, or locate the dead. Pictures of astral calendars and henges and granges and ancient religious sites in underground caves. Rediscovered memories of the soul family you live many lives with. The apparition of a loved one at a moment of crisis, and the tunnel, of course, the tunnel and the white light beyond.

When Jeff was there I would set these aside. If the TV was on there might be something for us to watch about Bigfoot, or about UFOs, mysterious disappearances, lost treasures, amnesia, the Bermuda Triangle, Atlantis, hypnotism, curses, miracle cures . . . but there's wasn't much talk on TV about astral families, even though separations and divorces and custody arrangements were always in the air now among Terry and Jandine's friends. And gradually somehow I would only see Tineke, Jake, and Ritchie once a month, and then half a dozen times a year, and eventually even less.

Chapter Six

Warren gave Jeff and me each a small metal safe with locking tumblers, a keepsake from a local bank, and I filled mine with cones of strawberry incense from a gas station, Zener cards, tarot cards, and inkblot cards that also came from Warren in a boxed set of ESP games he'd originally given Jeff, but that had to stay at Terry's house due to Heather's new zero-tolerance policy for anything occult, weird, or potentially satanic. She didn't know that we did ESP testing regularly.

Terry's house faced an empty athletic field nobody ever seemed to use. Jeff and I took turns in the cold sunshine, on the front steps, one of us staring at an image on a card while the other wrote down any feelings about whether that image was a star, a circle, a square, a cross, or a wave.

"Do you want to go inside?" asked Jeff, eyeing the ski hat I'd started wearing, pulled low against a chronic earache.

"Not really," I said, mixing the cards for another round. "Do you?"

The instructions said random guesses should result in 20 percent correct. We always did a hundred cards per session. Otherwise the math would overwhelm me.

I said, "Are you being precognitive this time, or clairvoyant?"

"Precognitive," he said, so promptly that I assumed he remembered the difference.

The number of correct predictions either of us made would dip lower and lower the longer we kept at it, which the instructions said was normal. Because getting tired made it harder to exercise psi abilities. It happened regardless of who was looking at the cards and who was writing down predictive guesses. But sometimes, when we scored the columns of guesses after each round, I noticed stretches near the end when Jeff didn't get any right at all, not even by chance. It seemed like it should mean something, though I didn't know what, and I pointed it out because it was weird, and interesting. He thought I was being critical. But I wasn't. Maybe it had to do with the receiver (him, in those cases) but it was equally likely to be with the sender (me), or with both of us. But he would quit, if I mentioned it. The higher his scores were, the more engaged he was. Which gradually turned the whole thing away from an investigation into what was possible, and into a balancing act of keeping him interested.

"Let's try with clairvoyance instead," I said. He slumped, letting his head fall back against the wall. "Or we can just stop," I added, shuffling the cards to put them away.

"No," he said. "No, just tell me what I'm supposed to do."

"Don't guess what's on the card," I said. "Try to guess what I'm seeing."

He turned around so that he couldn't accidentally see anything. And I tried not only to see the symbol on each card as I turned them over, but to send each one out into the air, toward him.

When we compared afterward, I said, "You got thirty percent right."

"That's a good score, isn't it?" he said, with more interest again.

"That's amazing," I said. "I think."

"I'm psychic!" he said.

"Lucky you! Just don't tell your mom," I said. Because I understood that it wouldn't be funny if he repeated it to Heather later, out of context.

Chapter Seven

Construction on Jeff's new bedroom downstairs had been slow while the contractor friend who'd been doing Terry a favor got divorced and sorted out custody of his three kids, instead of working overtime. But then in one quick weekend Terry finished staining the shiplap walls an oily walnut color and bought new furniture to match. By Sunday night the new room in the basement was ready.

Jeff hadn't gotten to pick out anything. He stood looking in from the now-finished doorway, plucking at the hem of his shirt. Pinching it, and releasing it. Pinching, and releasing, and watching as Terry kept opening and closing the door to the closet, testing it, because hanging and balancing a door was a lot harder than it looked. But this door was perfect. The walls in the closet were as dark as the walls of the room, and at the back there was a small plywood panel, like a half-sized door, with a brass latch.

"What's that for?" I asked, but nobody answered.

Terry opened and closed the closet door again.

"Where does that little door go?" I said.

Jandine tried to plug in night-lights, to brighten the room, but since there weren't enough outlets she took me with her to Kmart, but the only battery-operated lights they had were baby bedtime toys or camping lanterns. Since neither was quite right, she got both. And some pale flannel sheets that would be easy to see when the room was dark.

"Does Terry actually like that room?" I had asked.

"Of course he does," she said, absently. "It's the bedroom he wanted for himself when he was Jeff's age." But she was distracted by two comforters: The yellow probably matched better with the brown carpet, but maybe Jeff would like the blue instead? She took both to the register, opened Terry's checkbook, and was already writing the date as the cashier began to ring up one thing after another after another.

—

Jeff was already worried about spending the night in the new bedroom when Heather dropped him off the next Friday afternoon. "You should stay down there, too," he said. "It will be fun, we don't have to sleep in the new bedroom. We'll watch TV." He was talking fast. "We'll put sleeping bags by the TV. Please?"

"Just stay upstairs," I said. "You still have the upper bunk."

"I can't," he said. "My nightmares don't matter. My dad and your mom . . ."

His face looked hot. "My dad and your mom—they're going to force the issue!"

"Okay," I said, quickly, before he started crying. His hair was damp. I realized suddenly that he was sweating. And also that he'd never complained about moving downstairs. Somehow I'd let myself assume it was all right, while at the same time I had known he must be dreading it. We had both treated the new room like a hypothetical, even while it had been taking shape in the corner for months.

"Force the issue?" repeated Jandine later. "That doesn't sound like Jeff. It must be something he heard Heather say."

Maybe Jeff hadn't complained because he recognized that he was stuck with the new bedroom. Because once decisions were made, things stayed in their places, in Terry's house. After a painting or a mirror was hung, it never moved. If some potted cactuses from Ursula were placed on the end table in the living room, where they scratched anyone who tried to open the drapes, they would remain for decades, even after they were dead.

In practice, Jeff and I kept doing pretty much what we'd been doing anyway, sleeping upstairs on Friday nights, and downstairs on Saturdays. I pretended that I wasn't afraid to see the bedroom door standing open, and the dark interior of the room beyond, and we didn't talk about the muffled feeling in the basement or the way that even with the TV volume turned up we sometimes couldn't make out all the words. Or the powdery look of the semidarkness, and the haze that hung near the ceiling, like layers of atmosphere around a mountain when you fly past in an airplane, a haze you could clearly see if you leaned down from the top of the stairs to make sure the rec room was empty before going all the way down.

But we did adjust around the way the rec room felt. We would sometimes change the channel, by unspoken agreement, when something we were watching didn't seem right. We stopped bringing our big bowls of microwave popcorn downstairs. After a while we didn't bring drinks down, either. And since neither of us wanted to be left alone, if one of us needed the bathroom on the nights we slept in the basement, we both went up. These adjustments were as close as we got when we were down there to acknowledging that something wasn't right. Maybe because children didn't work things out for themselves in horror stories, back then. We just buckled down. And when sometimes on a weeknight Jandine would ask me to go down to the workroom for a jar of pickles or a bottle of wine from the extra refrigerator, by myself, I did it. Without acknowledging how much I dreaded it. I could do this as long as there were other people awake and alert in the house, and as long as the lights were on, and as long as I only had to go as far as the workroom near the foot of the stairs. I would prop the basement door open, and as long as I kept moving, without looking up, it was doable. Even though it always felt like something would happen. If I took too long, or if I looked directly at whatever seemed to be there in the darkness, behind the bar, or under the pool table, or in Jeff's room, always around a corner, out of sight.

The workroom was small and lined with particleboard pegs holding drills and sanders and saws, with an outside door to the backyard, belowground, at the bottom of a cement stairwell. The extra refrigerator was in a corner beyond the furnace, and to look inside I had to box myself in between the open refrigerator door and the cinder block wall behind the furnace, cutting off my view of the workroom and the door I'd come in by, as well as the locked door to the backyard steps. It was an awkward, tight space, and there would have been no room to react, if I'd ever heard anything. And every time, just before shutting the refrigerator door, I half expected something bad to happen. But when something did happen downstairs, it didn't happen to me, but to Jeff.

"Do you think it's a ghost?" he asked. "Here, I mean?"

We were watching one of the Friday-afternoon talk shows in the living room before Jandine or Terry got home. The guest was a psychic medium whose gift was to bring messages back to the living, but also to help the dead move on. In the middle of the afternoon, in daylight, for Jeff it was somehow all right to ask a question like that out loud in the living room.

"No," I said.

"But maybe it's a lost soul who hasn't gone into the light," he said.

It had never seemed human to me. Whatever it was.

"I believe that's what we're sensing here," he said, in the language of the psychic on TV. A few minutes later, during a commercial, he got up and went to rummage through puzzles and board games until he found Jandine's old Ouija board, next to the Scrabble and Monopoly boxes.

"No way," I said.

By then I'd read all about the ideomotor response, but I'd also read stories about people who truly believed the Ouija board put them in touch with something real. And I did not want to be in touch with some real thing in the house.

"But Mandy," Jeff said, holding the board with both hands, like an offering.

"No," I said again.

He looked as sincere as one of Ursula's angel statuettes from the Franklin Mint, but he sounded a little . . . rehearsed?

"Please," he said. "When you said you wanted to do psychic tests, I did them."

"That's true," I said.

"And you took my bedroom," he said. "You displaced me."

I couldn't answer this.

"You took my bedroom," he said again. "So help me make this right. Help me put whatever lives in the basement to rest."

"Nothing lives in the basement," I said.

"Except me," he said. "Because you're in my old bedroom."

We set up the board in the den.

"Hello?" he said. "Hello?" Then, probably because we'd been catching parts of *Smokey and the Bandit* on cable for weeks, he added, politely, "Over." And we waited.

It wasn't smooth, like in the stories I had read. But we felt something?

"See," he whispered, watching the planchette.

It felt like an air hockey table, nothing special at first, just a totally inert surface, until you drop a coin into the slot and then a cool, lifeless breath flows out against your fingers, with a little humming sensation that means the table is ready for play.

"What's your name?" asked Jeff. "Over."

The planchette suddenly felt heavy against the board. It gritted a little, moved forward, and stopped with the clear center of the planchette directly over the letter Z.

"Wow," said Jeff.

Then we watched it jerk slightly away. Then back. It wasn't moving freely, but it seemed to go back and forth, by a fraction, between blankness and the letter Z.

The word *Goodbye* was printed in one corner of the board, where it had seemed like a fancy decoration. But now it looked like a good way to hang up.

"Let's say goodbye," I whispered.

"We just started," he said, incredulous.

"But it's tired—that's what the Zs mean."

I did not believe this. But I hoped Jeff would.

"Oh," he said. He became even more formal. "Goodbye for now," he said, enunciating clearly. "We'll try again, friend."

The ingratiating way he said it—*friend*—gave me a cramp in the gut. But the planchette didn't react. It just kept slowly touching and retouching the same place, Z-Z-Z, until we forced it over to the *Goodbye* corner.

I lifted my hands away instantly. And Jeff started turning it into a story, right away, as if the board had told us to get some sleep in a friendly way, like a cartoon. But I was filling in different gaps, having read *On the Beach* by Nevil Shute, with people in Australia who wait for the cloud of radiation after a nuclear war, knowing the rest of the world is already dead but unable to ignore a few telegraph signals that keep arriving in Morse code. Random strings of letters with an occasional word or two, offering just enough hope that a crew makes a one-way sea voyage, through an unpopulated world, and what they find at the other end is an empty room and a telegraph key near an open window in a dead city. And that's what I felt from the board.

By Sunday morning I was a little more sure that Jeff had been moving the planchette. Mostly because it had been pressed down so tightly, and he was desperate to be right. Whether he knew it or not, he must have been doing it. Because whatever was there, it wasn't going to talk through a game manufactured by Parker Brothers, was it?

"One more time," he'd said. "Please?"

On the other hand: Maybe Jeff really needed this. Maybe a message from the board would make him feel better.

I wanted him to feel better. And if my own subconscious contributed, without me moving the planchette consciously, I could probably live with that. If it meant Jeff could go back to Heather's feeling better about the room.

I-I-I

V-V-V

Jeff was doing the talking again, looking down at the board with intensity. And I was trying not to think about whether either of us was moving the planchette.

"Do you have a message for us?" he asked.

I-I-I

V-V-V-V-V-V-V-V

"Ivy?" I said, interested now despite myself. "Or maybe Ivan?"

A wrinkle crossed Jeff's forehead.

"Ivy, do you have a message for us?" he said.

I-V

I-V

"Four?" I said. "Is that Roman numeral four?"

Was I conversing with my own unknown self?

"Four?" asked Jeff. "Four what?"

We waited, staring down at the heart-shaped planchette.

The planchette suddenly released from the board—it was light and unattached now, and it drifted halfway to the next letter, which was *U*, and stopped.

"Four *U*!" he said, lifting his hands away. "For you! I asked it, do you have a message for us? And it said, for you. The message was for *me*!"

He touched the planchette again, but of course it was just plastic.

"Ivy's message was for me," he said, in tones of satisfaction.

"Say goodbye," I said, with my fingertips still in place.

"I don't want to say goodbye."

"You have to say goodbye after talking to . . . It's like hanging up a phone. You have to."

"No," he said. "That was a message for me. Not for you."

I slid the planchette to *Goodbye* without him. Then I put the board and planchette into their flat cardboard box and returned them to the shelf of puzzles and games.

Jeff looked pleased, I saw, and a little secretive.

"What's in your hand?" I said.

"Nothing," he said, which always meant something.

"If you don't show me your hand, I'll tell your mother," I said.

In his palm was the tooth he'd lost recently, and it looked

so . . . terrible, really. A broken little thing, with a trace of blood in the hollow center.

"It's time to give Ivy something," he said. "A gift of friendship."

"Please don't," I said.

"I'm going to give this to Ivy, instead of selling it to the tooth fairy," he said.

He carefully wrapped the tooth in a tissue and tucked it into a small wooden box from Warren, formerly part of an old shoeshine kit. At which point I decided that when Heather picked him up I would hide the Ouija board for good.

"I'm going to add something from my dad and your mom," he said. "Since they live in Ivy's house."

I shook my head, and let him make his decisions. He added a brass wood screw from Terry's toolbox and a big safety pin from Jandine's sewing kit. And then, according to Jeff, the box needed something from Ursula, too, for balance, since the box had come from Warren.

"But they don't live in Ivy's house, do they?" I said.

In the guest bathroom Jeff found one of Ursula's metal nail files and poked it in under the tissue. And then he said, suddenly, "What about my mom?"

"What about your mom?" I said, warily.

"If this is to protect people—"

"I thought you said it was a friendship gift."

Abruptly, his hazel eyes began filling with tears. He dashed them away with his wrist. "I want to include my mom," he said.

There were the photos in a photo album from before the divorce. Jeff peeled back the clear protective vinyl and tried to pry one of the pictures up with his bitten little fingernails.

"If you leave a blank spot your dad will know something's missing."

"Nobody looks at these anymore," he said, without looking up.

He carefully lifted a photo of Heather in front of an unfamiliar yellow refrigerator, sitting in a kitchen chair with Jeff, a baby on her knee. He looked at the photo for a long moment, and I assumed he wouldn't give it away, not after holding it like that. But he moved to add it.

"You're putting yourself in, too?" I asked. Not because I thought I knew what it meant. Just because I was surprised.

He looked at it again, and then before I could stop him he carefully tore the photo, placing only Heather's half into the box. He didn't seem to know what to do with the other half, though. In the end he put himself as a baby into the box, as well.

"We should add something from your grandparents, too," he said, and I knew then that he would just keep adding more layers, more and more, while the original idea got further and further away.

"They don't live here," I said. "In *Ivy's* house."

"So we're giving it things from my family, but not from your family?"

He was just chasing ideas. Making them important because they were his own ideas. First the box was a gift, then a protection offering, and now an obligation that he was going to resent. And I wasn't going to give him something to complain about, so I unbolted the garage door and nerved myself to slip between Jandine's car and the wall, past Terry's 1968 Buick Electra, all the way to the shadowy far side of the garage where bunches of garlic from the farm hung above the freezer. Even though it meant passing Terry's fishing poles and nets and the dark rubber waders dangling from the ceiling. I climbed onto the chest freezer to snatch down one of the papery bulbs, because although Jeff was just making up rules for this box of bullshit, and it wasn't real, Jake and Tineke had both worked in the garden and they'd be covered if it somehow was real. And in the back of my mind, I thought maybe I should add something for Ritchie? But no. Because it was silly. And anyway he'd driven the rototiller.

Who or what was Ivy anyway? There was no Ivy; whatever was in the house didn't have a name.

We thought we had been moving around quietly, but the sound of the garage door being unbolted must have carried. Jandine was at the top of the stairs when I came back in.

"What are you up to?" she asked.

"Nothing," I said.

"Would you be a sweetheart and get a bottle of wine from the fridge?" she asked.

"Now?" I said.

"Thanks, honey," she said, drifting away, back to the living room with a drink in her hand.

"Dinner in ten minutes," she called out over her shoulder. "Jeff, is your bag packed?"

Jeff appeared and wordlessly held out the open box for the garlic, tucking it into the tissue with the rest. Then he waited, still holding it open.

"What about you?" he said.

I did not want to contribute anything. But he stayed like that, waiting, and I checked my pockets, and found nothing I was willing to give away. From the coffee table in the den I picked up some small thing from Warren. A refrigerator magnet, in the shape of a horseshoe. I put it inside, and Jeff closed the box. And then his face fell as he seemed to realize it didn't matter. That it was just a box of junk, after all.

"Do you want to bury it in the yard?" I asked.

"No," he said. "I need to think about how to give it." And then he hid the little wooden box under one of the end tables by the door to the garage, where he sometimes stowed his school bag on Fridays after getting home. Then he went downstairs with me, to collect a bottle of wine.

Chapter Eight

On Friday my teacher took our class on a field trip to explore the rocky shoreline and have a brown-bag lunch on the deck of some retired people she knew who lived in Gig Harbor. We spent an hour or two on the beach, searching out creatures from our spring science unit. Crabs under rocks and clams under perfectly round air holes in the sand. Barnacles, obviously. Leathery kelp. There were also flossy yellow cigarette filters, and beer caps with pictogram riddles inside, and plenty of tumbled beach glass.

"It's amber!" said someone, holding a piece up to the light.

Jandine said, to me, "You know that kind of amber comes from broken beer bottles, right?"

She was chaperoning us that day along with half a dozen other mothers, but she'd driven separately, and when the rest of the class headed home on the bus she and I would continue north to the farm so that Terry and Jeff could have the house to themselves for the weekend. They would play pool and then they would sleep downstairs, Jeff in a new sleeping bag that looked like a giant bag of Doritos, clearly a bribe, and Terry in Warren's army-surplus bedroll, which was a gross, grub-shaped cocoon with a Band-Aid-colored interior of pilled flannel known as the fart sack.

I turned over a flat stone and found a dark-veined leaf stuck to the underside, but it wasn't stuck, it was embedded—a fossil. I was thrilled and I held it up while our teacher asked leading questions about sedimentary layers. Everyone looked for more fossils and the chaperone mothers made them return each rock to its place afterward.

For lunch we met our host and hostess, who smiled in the background as we left our sandy boots on the deck outside their house. We'd been told to each find something from the beach for show-and-tell, which was great as far as I was concerned. But later, when we were standing in our rain jackets and saying goodbye, and thank you, our teacher instructed us to leave all the found objects on the edge of their porch. The couple would enjoy looking at them for a little while before presumably sending them back into the water at high tide.

I could not believe my ears.

"Do I have to do that?" I asked my mother.

"Just put it down in front, when you say thank you," she said, and then turned away. She had her big purse with her that day, as always. That night, in my old room at the farm, I found the fossil on the nightstand.

In the morning, my grandfather and Ritchie showed me how to power a light bulb using a raw potato as a battery, smoking their pipes, chuckling over the project. We were sitting at the picnic table out back, looking at a two-page ad of Natural Science Book Club choices, with my fossil as a paperweight and the potato as a reading light, helping Ritchie choose three books (a value up to $67.50) for only 99 cents each. But the math was complicated. Because the color-photo books each counted double.

"That right there," said my skeptical grandmother, "that right there is how they get you, Ritchie, and I hope you know it."

"But how can it possibly be a trap, when I want to know more about these fascinating subjects anyway?" he said, and winked at me.

"Because you think you know what you're getting," she said, "but here for example you'll pay for three books technically but you're only getting two. And," she said, looking more closely, "look, you're committing yourself to buying three more over the course of a year, and those will be more expensive, I'm sure!"

"True," said my grandfather, who had discussed this already in the car during their commute to and from the mill in Anacortes. "But look, Ticky," he said, "future books are available at handsome discounts. It says as much, right here: *handsomely discounted*."

"I'd need proof of a future handsome discount."

"And all this time, I thought being handsome in the here and now was good enough," said my handsome grandfather, smiling from behind his pipestem.

"Savings range up to thirty percent and occasionally even more," I read aloud.

"Rit-chie!" said my grandmother. "Jacob, help me, what's sixty-seven dollars and fifty cents minus thirty percent? Because that's what he'll be on the hook for next time."

"He'll be on the hook for at least forty-seven dollars and twenty-five cents," said my grandfather.

"It's an investment," Ritchie answered. "An investment in the future!"

"Plus the two dollars and ninety-seven cents for the first batch," said my grandfather.

"That's fifty dollars and twenty-two cents in total," said my grandmother.

"Yes," said Ritchie. "For six very special books!"

"Five books," corrected my grandmother.

"Probably four books," amended my grandfather. "If we assume the next batch also includes a few handsome photo books."

"Which, again, is how they get you," said my grandmother.

"A shipping and handling charge is added to all shipments," I said, quoting from the order form.

"Does it tell how much for the shipping?" asked my grandmother.

"No," I said. "But there's a Bonus Book plan with savings up to seventy percent off. They send those automatically. You don't even have to ask."

"That's criminal," said my grandmother.

"Terry joined a club like this for music," I said. "He gets records in the mail and it's not criminal."

Jandine was in the house, on the phone with Terry.

"Well, Mandy," said Ritchie. "I don't recall if I have yet

heard your vote for which three books to order, or which two books, as the case may be."

But I could not make the decision. I kept rereading the titles and descriptions, but I couldn't retain the details, forgetting each by the time my eyes moved to the next on the list.

"Cross out one you don't want," said my grandfather.

"The math puzzles," I said promptly.

He had a pencil stub in his shirt pocket. "Cross it out," he said again. "Then it's easier to see the rest."

I looked to Ritchie.

"Go ahead," he said. "It's your own magazine."

I flipped to the cover; it was one of the issues Jandine had bought me the night we emptied the cellar.

I barely remembered to look over at the house on the other side of the trees; I no longer felt a pull from that direction. When we left it was the potato light that caught my interest, still lighting up one corner of the carport on Sunday when Jandine started the car and backed us out.

My ultimate book choice votes had been:

Earth's Aura

Mechanics of the Mind

Ten Faces of the Universe

When we got home there were empty pizza boxes and an open two-liter bottle of pop on the kitchen counter, but no Terry and no Jeff. No notes, and Terry's car wasn't in the garage.

"Let's hope they're doing something fun," said Jandine.

They'd followed the plan, unrolling the sleeping bags in Jeff's new bedroom, with the door open and the rec room TV on for light, but when Terry woke in the night and went upstairs for the bathroom, half asleep, he may have forgotten the plan and gone back to his and Jandine's room, from force of habit. Or maybe not, to be fair, maybe Jeff woke right away and reacted before Terry had a chance to return. However it went, Jeff was suddenly awake and found himself alone in that bedroom, zipped into a new sleeping bag and surrounded by the comforters Jandine had picked out. He probably tried calling out for his dad, but the stifling acoustics would have swallowed his voice. He'd gotten splinters in his fingers, from feeling along the unfamiliar walls, looking for the light switch. He'd tripped and fallen between the pool table and the dark leather couch, and then he ran up the stairs as fast as he could. Who could blame him for panicking when he couldn't get the basement door open, or for screaming until Terry came to open it from the other side.

Ursula found three red marks at Jeff's nape, leading down to three deep scratches under the collar of his pajamas, probably from trying to get out of his zippered sleeping bag while half asleep. His thumb must have been in his mouth when he ran into the basement door because he bit down hard. More than hard enough to break the skin. And of course Heather was incensed.

Maybe it wouldn't have happened if we hadn't gone out of town?

Jandine shook her head. "I'm sorry that he got hurt, but at least this way they know he did it to himself."

She meant I might be blamed, if I'd been in the house at the time?

"It's a moot point," she said. "Since luckily those bite marks match his own tiny teeth."

Many years later, while clearing out the Tacoma house, among the many photo-lab envelopes of pictures that had never made it into albums I found the roll documenting Jeff's injuries. I knew what I was looking at right away, even though the marks were worse than I'd imagined at the time. The scratches on the back of Jeff's neck were the nasty kind, with swollen red edges. In the pictures of his hand the individual teeth marks were clearly visible, and definitely child sized, exactly where you'd expect them to be if his thumb had been in his mouth when he ran face-first into the door. There was even a blank spot for the missing front tooth that had been tucked away in his impromptu offering box since the week before. I wondered who took the pictures, and then I set them aside with other keepsakes I thought he might want, or would at least want to throw away himself.

Chapter Nine

The following Friday afternoon I skipped the public library to wait for Jeff at the house, but Heather never dropped him off. On Saturday morning Terry pushed his ball cap back and knelt to remove the training wheels from the purple Huffy one-speed bike he bought and taught me how to ride, so that I could go out with Jeff, who already knew how. There had been no pavement at the farm, just gravel driveway and a county highway with poor visibility, and the Huffy was my first bike. He watched as I wobbled across the driveway and the empty boat pad. The weather was bright, harsh, cloudy; it's the angle of the sky that far north that makes the sunlight seem so painful.

"Where's Jeff?" I asked.

"Stay out of the street," said Terry. "Keep doing what you're doing. You've got the hang of it now."

He went into the house and I kept riding around the perimeter of the huge driveway, in and out of the cold shade of the garage. But Jeff did not come that weekend, or any other weekend for a long time, because Heather had been upset about more than just the scratches. She didn't like the Ouija board details she got from Jeff, and whatever he said about the Zener card testing made her think I was trying to hypnotize him. But finding the wooden box among his things after Jeff came home with the scratches and the bite mark . . . I've tried to imagine that. Finding a scuffed wooden box, probably stuffed into his backpack by Terry, and opening it to find a big purple-veined clove of garlic, Jeff's still-bloody front tooth, and several sharp metal objects stuck to a magnet—a pin, a nail file, a screw—all of that would have upset her, but then, underneath all of that, the photo, torn in half.

But it was Jeff who wanted that photo included, it was Jeff who took it out of the album and he's the one who tore it . . . not me. Definitely none of it had been my idea. I never touched it.

"Okay," Jandine said. "Okay, but the more you say, the less she'll believe you. We'll just make sure that she knows it's Jeff's collection. That's true, isn't it?"

"We used your Ouija board," I said.

"Oh, everybody has a Ouija board," she said, dismissively.

Terry did not appreciate the guilt-tripping phone calls from Heather. As for the box? He didn't find that one bit odd, not one bit. "That's what kids do," I heard him say on the phone. "It's a time capsule, or something."

But Heather had a voice that carried.

"Time capsule?" she said. "No, Terry. It's a box of pins and needles stuck to a torn-up picture of my face. Can you explain that?"

"Get him to explain it," said Terry. "And be happy he wants a picture of you."

Heather's voice lifted up and out of the phone handset in the den, all the way across the room and up through the atrium.

"Happy? With a magnet on my face and his baby picture torn up? Do you honestly think that's funny?"

"Jesus," he said. "Calm down a bit."

Which was probably the wrong thing to say.

I'm sure she was genuinely upset. But Jandine used to say that Heather would drag anything into a fight, because she hated Terry and had no choice but to stay in contact with him. It was complicated, the way Heather had loved Terry, and then hated him.

She expected me to apologize to her, to Ursula, and to Jeff.

But Terry told me not to listen and that I didn't have to apologize to anybody.

Without Jeff, the weekends seemed like longer versions of weeknights, like we were waiting for something, and then even dinner trailed off, as if Jeff was the only reason we'd ever sat down together. Terry started taking his plate out to the living room to watch TV. Jandine never seemed to be hungry, and I started to sit down with a plate at the kitchen table by myself, earlier, at the hour of the day that Tineke used to call supper. Sometimes I sat up for a while with Terry and Jandine in the living room, but I spent most of my time upstairs, in the bedroom that had been Jeff's and now was mine, where I had a hermit crab in a terrarium, and a few too many guppies in a ten-gallon tank under a shelf of Natural Science Book Club choices arranged in alphabetical order.

At the library, I figured out certain subjects were too hard to get out of my head again later and to drop a book at the return shelf and wash my hands in the restroom if I got the feeling I didn't want to keep reading. Like for example when precognitive dreaming leads to psychic tips during searches for missing persons, which leads in turn to those unfortunate people whose dreams or visions or intuitions connect them mysteriously to the minds of serial killers, which wasn't so hard to avoid when there wasn't much about the subject on the shelves, the way there would be after Ted Bundy was arrested and tried and convicted, after Ann Rule wrote the book about him. After the term *serial killer* became so familiar from newspapers and the evening news. But it had always been there. That awareness of shadows concealed among the trees, waiting in parking lots, potentially lurking in every park, every public restroom, along every route you might take home, even long before we learned that Bundy had been a student at the high school whose grassy field sat across the quiet street from Terry's house.

In one book I read about a scientist who made a vaccine breakthrough using the blood of horses, then casually gave the order to bleed the healthy horses to death rather than go to the small trouble of retiring them out in a pasture somewhere. That's what I would always remember, not his name, or even which vaccine, but only the horses, and the question of what kind of person does a thing like that by default. Luckily it had been old news even then, so he was probably already dead. But I had wanted him to pay, I wanted everyone to repay everything owed after opening books that appeared perfectly normal only to find photos of baby macaques, alone in bare glass cages, separated from their mothers so researchers could measure how they suffered, and observe the permanent damage done to them. To find out anything at all about the mysterious nature of perception, I would have to choose carefully, and avoid reading about the brain. Because of what the research entailed. Even the anecdotal stories in which nobody was harmed intentionally were full of electrocutions and steel rods through eye sockets, and ancient skulls bearing the holes of ritual trepanations, done slowly.

I tried to describe this to Jandine, this balance of somehow avoiding the information I didn't want, while needing to check to see if I'd been right to avoid subjects like trichinosis, and eugenics, and cattle mutilations and Nazi occultists. At some point she asked if there really was an after-school reading club? Or whether I just didn't care to be alone in the house.

"I don't like being alone in the house," I said.

She turned over one of the books I'd been looking through, but she didn't open it. "Tell me about what you're looking for. Not just what you're avoiding."

Pets who save their owners' lives and owners who save their pets' lives and lost pets who find the way home over hundreds of miles. The Nazca Lines in the Pampa Colorada of southern Peru depicting giant birds and other creatures, and the silhouettes of horses etched into the white chalk under green English hills. I told her about the talking mongoose named Gef on the Isle of Man who claimed to be eighty years old, but I left out the stories about reincarnation, and the persistence of soul families, and anything else related to the afterlife.

It took me a while to see that blowing, ragged canopies were killing trees in our neighborhood that year. I didn't know until the tent caterpillars themselves started dropping out by the thousands. I stopped riding my bike, or walking outside. Even in the car, with my eyes closed and the windows rolled up and the radio on I still recognized the dusty, overpopulated smell coming down from the trees, and I couldn't get out of the car until she'd parked in the garage, because I couldn't bear to put my feet down on the cement of the driveway, knowing I might accidentally walk over some of them.

I hung a blanket over the lower bunk, like a four-poster bed in a ghost story, so that I could curl up inside with my clock radio and my reading lamp from the farm, which put out a hot, metallic smell, like cotton from the clothesline being ironed. At night I fell asleep listening to old-time radio plays, with news and weather at the top of every hour, including morning dew points, station identifications, visibility at the airport, the Dow being up or the Nasdaq being down, and a word from our sponsors followed by calls from our listeners. If I woke up in the middle of the night, I would sometimes have to get out of bed to crack my door and listen for the sound of Jandine sleeping and Terry snoring in their bedroom down the hall, and if I could hear that they were alive I could usually go back to sleep.

When Jeff started coming back again for weekends he had a short buzzed haircut and three fading scars on the back of his neck. He did not completely ignore me, but that's how I've always remembered it feeling. And when the exterminator trucks drove through slowly, shooting gray powder into the treetops, Jeff and a group of neighborhood boys I didn't know followed behind, riding their bikes through the acrid clouds and shouting.

PART TWO

By operating in this way, they gradually heat the apparatus of the art, on a rounded furnace, in a crucible arranged on steps, and gold is produced.

ZOSIMUS OF PANOPOLIS, *Collection des Anciens Alchimistes Grecs, Vol. 2: Comprenant, Les Œuvres de Zosime: Texte Grec et Traduction Française, Avec Variantes, Notes et Commentaires* (TRANS. CHARLES-ÉMILE RUELLE)

Chapter Ten

When I was deciding where to apply for grad school, I told Jeff that Las Vegas was at the top of my list. A few months later he was incredulous when I chose the extremely decent offer from UNLV's English department over a slightly better-funded one for an MA in research methodology in Chicago, so I told him, again, why UNLV had been my first choice from the start.

"And you think that's a wise decision?" he said. "Studying *The X-Files* in Vegas instead of doing something that might get you a job someday?"

"That's not what I'll be doing there," I said.

"It sounds like a bunch of bullshit to me," he said.

He sometimes summed up my liberal arts education by saying I had majored in underwater basket weaving. He assumed it was easy to dismiss whatever I had done there because the school didn't give letter grades, when in fact the paper copy of my detailed transcript of narrative evaluations weighed so much I had to use reinforced envelopes to mail it with my grad-school applications.

I'd done extra coursework, like independent studies in language and history and the history of written language, because I had wanted to know more about language and perception. But too many of the programs where I might have studied this explicitly had minimum GRE requirements in quantitative reasoning that I couldn't meet. Not with my math deficits. I'd done well on the verbal assessment, though, and well enough on the analytic, so I'd found a solution. And now here was Jeff, shitting on my plans.

I should have just ignored him. But I couldn't help sending him press releases from UNLV's website, as if more information might change his mind not just about my plans, but about everything we disagreed about:

April 9, 1997

Bigelow's Chair of Consciousness Studies Established at UNLV

A $3.7 million gift from Robert T. and Diane Bigelow will fund a new academic position in the College of Sciences at UNLV according to UNLV President Carol C. Harter. The Bigelow Chair of Consciousness Studies will initially be filled on an annual basis by distinguished visiting science scholars. The new position was recently advertised in several national academic and scientific publications.

"The students and faculty at UNLV are extremely fortunate that concerned citizens like Robert and Diane Bigelow take an active interest in the sciences and provide funds to bring the finest quality scholars here to teach," said UNLV Provost Douglas Ferraro. The new gift is a continuation of Bigelow family gifts in support of the Sciences and Health Sciences colleges at UNLV.

"We are very interested in seeing the disciplines of physics, biology, and chemistry—empirical scientific investigations into the natural laws of the universe—applied to the study of consciousness," explained Robert Bigelow, president of Bigelow Holding Company. "There is a lot of important research by clinical biochemists, neurobiologists and others who are trying to understand consciousness. Our goal is simply to help scientists unravel some of the mysteries of consciousness and ultimately benefit mankind."

According to Warren Burggren, dean of the UNLV College of Sciences, a very small percentage of colleges and universities offer similar programs. Those that do include Duke, the University of Kentucky, Northeastern, Virginia Tech, Carlton College, and Seton Hall. "Some very serious universities are engaged in the scientific study of consciousness, but not many. So the Bigelows have presented our students with a unique opportunity. It is definitely a prize for UNLV."

Years earlier, I'd heard Art Bell on the radio interviewing Dr. Dean Radin, when he was director of the Consciousness Research Lab at UNLV, which is what put the school on my radar. Terry was also in the habit of listening to Art Bell's broadcasts from Nevada in the middle of the night, for the weird news, Iraq War updates, and UFO reports, and when I told him and Jandine where I was moving he didn't seem particularly surprised. I didn't say to Jeff, *Your dad doesn't think I'm stupid*. I just sent him more links:

July 3, 1997

UNLV Hires Consciousness Studies Chair

A professor of psychology at the Institute for Transpersonal Psychology in Palo Alto, Calif., has been hired as UNLV's first Bigelow Chair of Consciousness Studies, President Carol C. Harter announced Thursday.

Charles T. Tart will assume his duties in UNLV's College of Sciences this fall.

The Bigelow Chair of Consciousness Studies was established and funded by a gift of $3.7 million from Robert T. and Diane Bigelow of Las Vegas. The chair will initially be filled on an annual basis by distinguished visiting science scholars.

"UNLV is about to begin developing a program in the fascinating area of consciousness studies, and we are most fortunate to have a scholar of Dr. Tart's considerable experience and reputation in the field to guide our efforts," Harter said.

Tart, who has been at the Institute for Transpersonal Psychology since 1994, also served as visiting professor at the California Institute of Integral Studies in San Francisco (1994–95) and professor of psychology at the University of California-Davis (1966–94), where he is now professor emeritus. He is a senior research fellow at the Institute for Noetic Sciences in Sausalito, Calif., was a lecturer in psychology at Stanford University (1964–65), and an instructor in psychology at the University of Virginia School of Medicine.

May 20, 1998

1998–99 Consciousness Studies Chair Named

The University of Nevada, Las Vegas has named Dr. Raymond A. Moody, a psychology professor and researcher, to fill the Bigelow Chair in Consciousness Studies during the 1998–99 academic year, President Carol C. Harter announced today.

Moody, who holds the Ph.D. in philosophy from the University of Virginia and the M.D. from the Medical College of Georgia, will begin his teaching position in UNLV's College of Sciences in August.

"UNLV is fortunate to have a scholar of Dr. Moody's caliber join the faculty for the coming academic year," Harter said.

Provost Douglas Ferraro noted that Moody's research and writing on near-death experiences should be of considerable interest to students and to audiences at his public lectures.

The Bigelow Chair in Consciousness Studies was established and funded by a gift of $3.7 million from Robert T. and Diane Bigelow of Las Vegas. The chair is filled on an annual basis by distinguished visiting science scholars.

A former forensic psychiatrist at Central Georgia State Hospital, Moody currently conducts research at his personal research institute, The Theater of the Mind. He has held professorships in philosophy at East Carolina University and West Georgia College, and a visiting professorship at the University of Virginia.

He has published several books, including *Life After Life, The Light Beyond*, and *Laugh After Laugh: Humor in Relation to Health and Illness*. He has also published in professional journals regarding near-death experiences.

I thought the amount of money pledged might impress him, or that the credentials of the scientists might matter, since Jeff considered himself a realist and a skeptic. But I privately knew he was neither skeptical nor realistic. Ironically, I was the one asking at least somewhat empirical questions, while his ideas about reality were so dogmatic and dismissive that it sometimes seemed like he was on autopilot. It felt like I'd been waiting years for him to be present, in the moment. For him to actually meet my eyes again, really.

Then I thought, Fuck it, and forwarded him a barrage of emails. I asked if he was getting paranormal investigations confused with parapsychological research, adding a link to FAQs about parapsychology from Dean Radin's website. I pointed out for Jeff's attention that the group of scientists who authored the FAQ answers were drawing on experience and expertise and credentials from many disciplines, including but not limited to physics, statistics, math, and chemistry, as well as anthropology and psychology, and that their bona fides were included. But I don't know what he thought, because he never acknowledged what I'd sent.

I felt lucky that Dr. Moody had stayed longer and would still be at UNLV when I got there, and though I'd missed the class he taught about grief and spiritual experiences after the 9/11 attacks, I could get a head start on books for his public lecture series. But I couldn't find the fall schedule, only the list of past guests, like Dr. Elisabeth Kübler-Ross, who wrote about death and dying, and Edgar Mitchell, the astronaut who had done precognitive testing in space. At the new-student orientation, in August, I was surprised that none of the grad students in my cohort knew about the research in consciousness studies, even though it was covered in the local and sometimes even national news. The English department didn't keep information handy about events in another college, and someone suggested I call Dr. Moody's office to find out about the lecture series. Which was how I learned from the person who answered that the Bigelow donation was being redirected, away from the visiting-scientists program and the public lectures, into scholarships for students in the College of Sciences. I stayed in Las Vegas, though. Because that's how things went, before the internet became what it's become. Back when there was so little real-time information on which to base life's big decisions.

I was teaching two classes and doing freelance editorial work for a real estate agency on the side when I realized I was paying too much in rent, in fact more than I would for a mortgage. So I started looking for a house (*because you—yes, you!—can have a home in the sun*), and when I first came to this complex it was to see a different unit entirely. But Paloma, who would be my neighbor for a long time, caught sight of the real estate agent and me going into that other unit and decided I looked nice enough, and quiet, so she came over to tell us about the vacant unit next door to hers. A big town house, at the end of the row, standing empty for a year.

"I've got the spare key," said Paloma.

"You're a doll," said my Realtor. "But I have to do it by the book."

It was hot and we all stood in the dappled shade under a big mimosa tree full of hummingbirds, waiting for the code for the lockbox. When the front door swung open the rooms inside were airy, full of indirect sunlight, and twenty degrees cooler than the air outside. In the kitchen I opened the back door to the walled patio, and a cross breeze stirred all the curtains at once, as if the house had been waiting.

The house was in escrow when Terry died, unexpectedly.

Jandine moved down to Las Vegas to be with me, and for a year we lived in the town house, along with Jasper, the last of Terry's cats. I was no longer teaching as a graduate assistant, just freelancing, and Jandine and I could put on swimsuits and hats and go over to the pool whenever we wanted. We'd sit on the steps in the shallow end and then relax on the chaise longues under palm fronds that rustled overhead in the faint breeze.

"This feels like a vacation," she would say, gazing at the other residents, mostly solitary pretty girls in their early twenties who were flipping through summertime novels and glossy magazines. We didn't stay too long, not during the heat of the day. But sometimes we went back later to watch the sunset.

"This feels like a vacation," she would say again, looking at the sky. And she would glance down at her bare wrist, as if checking a watch. "It's getting late," she would say, like someone ready to stand up and go.

"It's not that late," I would say.

But after a few minutes she would say, "It looks like they're closing up. Should we go?"

Sundowning, it's called. Agitation late in the day. In this case literally at sunset, and I'm sure Jandine would have made a joke about this if she could have. One of so many things that might have been grimly funny, if the timing had allowed.

Eventually I knew we'd have to figure out next steps, including where she might want to live, but there were too many other important matters to attend to first. And so the shipping container full of furniture and boxes from Tacoma would sit in storage for a few weeks. Or a few months. Because I was overwhelmed with Jandine's Medicare details and finding her a doctor who was accepting new patients, and by things like figuring out how to refill Medicare prescriptions from out of state with no apparent primary care doctor. There was Social Security, too, and banking, and all the other reasons for getting a durable power of attorney. I didn't see at first how carefully she was sweeping the laminate floors and the kitchen tile. How many times a day. Sweeping, and then sweeping again, and then carefully emptying the dustpan into the kitchen trash as if this routine mattered most of all.

Once I noticed this we started going out in the afternoons, not just to the pool but to walk around malls, or big air-conditioned thrift stores, and while I shopped for pretty new summer clothes for her on one side of an aisle she would simultaneously straighten the hangers on the other side, moving at the same pace. Sometimes holding up a garment that was especially pretty, or especially unflattering. The Tacoma coffee maker was long gone but she found a secondhand replacement in the housewares section, and after that she made coffee every morning. She would rinse the carafe and dry it with a dish towel, mindfully. Sometimes asking me, brightly, where to put the coffee grounds? I would point to the trash and she'd bang the gold filter cone against the side; then wash it at the sink, dry it with the dish towel, and reassemble the coffee maker.

"All set for the morning," she'd say, hanging the towel on the oven-door handle. But an hour or two later I would hear her back in the kitchen, sweeping again, making another pot of coffee, following the routine, so I started putting decaf in the coffee canister because I wanted her to be able to sleep at night. The gold filter disappeared and I started buying paper filters; she must have thrown it away. I only realized when I found the carafe full of silt.

One morning I saw her take a dish towel and snap it lightly in the air before turning back to the sink.

Tineke used to shake out towels just like that. She was

afraid of spiders on clean linens from the clothesline outside. I'd seen it a thousand times, but I'd forgotten it, somehow.

Jandine had quit cooking years before but at my house she started looking for flour in the cupboards. She floated raw eggs in cold water, then cracked them into a separate bowl before adding them to the mix. Because Tineke always said to check eggs twice. Never to eat floaters. Which made Terry laugh out loud.

"What's for breakfast?" I asked.

"How about a Dutch baby?"

That used to be a birthday breakfast or a holiday brunch, a special treat. A custard pancake puffed up in the oven and topped with cream. I didn't have the ingredients, so what landed on the plate was just a regular pancake. But it was a good sign. We went to the farm sanctuary on the edge of town for two dozen eggs at a time, nestled in shredded newspaper in brown paper bags. We'd also buy some hay and carrot sticks, all proceeds going to the sanctuary, and Jandine held her palm flat, fingers out of the way, while the horses nickered and the donkeys pushed closer, their babyish ears standing up with curiosity. While feeding them, Jandine would occasionally glance in the direction of the chickens.

"The henhouses aren't open to the public," I would say.

"Good," she said.

I knew the memory that put her off, because she started recounting it. Something about looking down and seeing hundreds of dark fleas bouncing up her white socks, from where they'd been hidden in the hay, on some day when she'd been wearing a skirt.

"I'm itching just thinking about it," she said, lightly rubbing her arms. Then shaking her head. Then telling me about the fleas again, a short time later, as if for the first time, and rubbing her upper arms vigorously, as though warding off a chill. She rubbed her left arm in particular for weeks after that until her skin was raw and looked like a scrape.

"Does it hurt?" I asked.

"No," she said, a little surprised to see anything there at all.

After the biopsy she couldn't remember to leave the bandage alone, so we switched to long-sleeved blouses while we waited to be told she had basal cell carcinoma with multiple centers, maybe from past sunlight streaming through a driver's side car window. The skin-cancer center was the same I would go to for the basal cell spots on my own arm and my back, years later, and it somehow already felt both anonymous and familiar, that packed waiting room. After her Mohs surgery we sat across from a woman with big soft waves of hair, smooth yet windblown. It was the hairdo of Jandine's dreams.

"Excuse me," Jandine said. "I'm sorry to interrupt you, but I just have to say this—your hair. It's beautiful."

"Oh, thanks, honey," said the woman, smiling back at her. "You're sweet." Her voice was heavy, and slow and friendly.

"It's gorgeous," said Jandine, and next she would ask a question, to prolong the exchange. "Is your hair naturally curly?"

The woman laughed. "Oh, no—I work hard for this."

Jandine gave a soft answering laugh. "With hot rollers?"

"No, I sleep in foam rollers, the big ones. It drives him crazy," she said, gesturing at the door where her husband had disappeared a moment before, and then her face looked more tired than all that smooth silky hair might suggest, from a distance.

"Goodness," said Jandine. "Every night?"

"Not every night," said the woman. "I set it and then it has to last, especially when we travel." She hesitated briefly. "We're going to the airport after this. We have to go home for a funeral."

I broke in gently then, saying, "I'm sorry to hear that," and I hoped Jandine would be able to tactfully leave this woman alone now.

"My stepson," the woman added. "Fifty-one years old. Here

we are, everybody so worried about his dad, and then suddenly out of nowhere he's dead of a heart attack. No warning."

"Today?" asked Jandine, unsettled.

"We're flying today. Just making sure he's okay first before we get on the plane."

Jandine said, "I'm so sorry."

I was thankful she could still read the moment.

"Life is cruel," Jandine continued, and she meant this. Really meant this. There were so many moments of clarity.

"Yes," said the woman. "Life is cruel."

Jandine looked down at her hands for a moment. And then she looked up and leaned forward again in her chair. "But I just have to say this—your hair. It's so beautiful."

I had debated over ordering some small cards I'd seen online, printed with messages like: *Please don't be offended, my mother's intentions are good, but her memory is not.* I'd seen them while trying to find a medical ID bracelet appropriate for someone with symptoms of dementia, meaning it should be both impossible to get off and discreet enough for everyday while also looking clearly medical just in case, god forbid, she might ever get lost. It happens. Certain alerts in the news about older people who've gone missing—you can tell, by what's being said. The time of day they were last seen. What they were wearing. There's something about the tactful arrangement of the information, including the urgent need of medical attention, that makes my blood run cold, imagining Jandine slipping out and walking so purposefully that nobody would question seeing her walking away into the heat.

The woman looked at Jandine, and then at me, and I compressed my lips and tried to convey everything wordlessly. Always wordlessly. Without making Jandine feel ashamed.

"Thank you, honey," the woman said. "I appreciate it." She gave me the same small smile in return, and went back to the magazine.

In a few minutes I would take Jandine with me to the restroom and then find different seats, facing the other way, so that she wouldn't see the woman's curls. Otherwise I knew she would compliment the woman again: *Your hair. I just have to say this. It's so beautiful.*

It was eerie, the repetition, so eerie to watch her approach strangers with kind intentions again and again, using the same words. To know that she meant them just as sincerely, every time.

Jandine's arm was healing fine, the scar looked great, and we were in and out of the exam in under ten minutes. The woman with the big soft curls was gone, on her way to the airport, but the room was the same. That feeling of so many people suspended in the quiet filtered sunlight. Before we got out the door to the parking lot Jandine stopped, bending down to squeeze the knee of another stranger. An older man, wearing a ball cap emblazoned with *Retired Navy*. He wore a thick, miserable-looking square of gauze taped over half of his face, held in place under his glasses. Startled, he had to crane his neck awkwardly to look up at her with his good eye.

"Hey, sailor," she said. "Are you winking at me?"

I cringed, trying to whisk her out the door. But the man was smiling broadly.

"I sure am, sweetheart," he said, patting her hand. "And it's awfully good to see you."

Chapter Eleven

I replaced the guest room box spring with a bed board, to make it lower and safer for Jandine, and we went to the building-surplus store down the road for a bed frame with a center support. We didn't find one, but I did get a Nalgene mixing bottle for hummingbird nectar, and Jandine wanted a coffee cup with a daisy on it. I'd already turned over the next day's newsletter copy to the office, leaving us time to wander.

The man standing behind us in line looked down at what I held.

"Heck," he said, "I'll bet you gals are spending more on gas to get here than you're saving on that stuff!"

I would let Jandine handle this kind of thing.

"Good thing it was on our way home, then!" she said.

"Let me guess, you were almost home, but then you felt the steering wheel pulling the car into the parking lot," he said. "I get it! I understand."

"That's what women drivers do best," said Jandine.

The girl at the register was ringing up a shopping basket full of individual PVC pieces and I watched her manually entering price after price after price into the register.

"And now you get to bring home more stuff you don't need," said the man.

"A place for everything and everything in its place," said Jandine.

I didn't want to chat with him, but I felt a pang of gratitude when strangers treated Jandine the same as anybody else. Gratitude when she got to be like this, in the world.

"That's right," he said. "But how come you don't have anything? It looks like your daughter's the one getting everything today."

I demurred noncommittally.

He said, "Women can justify shopping better than anyone else I know."

Jandine seemed happy enough but it killed me a little, every time I thought of her internalizing all the old chestnuts about women drivers this, and women shoppers that. But the time for me saying something to her was already in the past.

"It was nice talking to you!" she said, when we were finally leaving.

"Stay out of trouble!" he said to her. And to me, a brief glance and half a nod. Recognition.

"Do you know him?" asked Jandine in the parking lot.

"No, but it seemed like you knew him," I said.

"He did look familiar," she said. "But I have no idea what he was talking about!"

We caught up on things like haircuts for her, and dental appointments, and I booked her an eye exam with a computer-assisted vision test to avoid pressing her to decide whether lens A was better, or lens B. I discreetly let the staff know about her cognitive trouble and then checked in with the doctor in the hallway. Because Jandine knew, of course, and it crushed her to be reminded, especially in public. What need could there be, to ever make her feel that way.

I asked the eye doctor not to dilate her eyes because she was already a fall risk, and told him she might not be able to answer right away if he asked her to make decisions. He didn't seem to know what I was talking about when I mentioned the computer-assisted vision test. I said I'd seen it in his ad.

"Oh that," he said. "That's really just for children."

Jandine was indeed hesitant, not wanting to offend him by saying that one of the test lenses he'd given her to look through was better than the other. It's confusing, I know, for someone who hasn't been around dementia yet. But it's also not all that fucking hard to figure out.

He snapped the lights back on abruptly and Jandine sat blinking. The whole room felt like he'd ended the appointment even before he said she needed progressive lenses.

"I don't think progressives are going to work here," I said, because I'd read that they made people dizzy at first and I was worried she wouldn't be able to adjust.

"I suppose bifocals could work," he said.

But I thought she might try to wipe the lines away. Because I had a ceramic stovetop and for weeks she scrubbed at the heating elements under the surface until I bought a big wooden cutting board and covered them up. But then I worried she might turn on the burners and start a fire.

"Then she needs two pairs," he said. "One for distance, one for up close, and she can swap them when she needs to. You can do that, can't you?" he said, to her.

I included her in the conversation. I presented it as a practical issue. I tried to explain to him that we could barely keep track of one pair of glasses, and two would be impossible because it would be hard to know which pair was which, or when to switch them. I didn't say there was no chance she would remember that she even had two different pairs, let alone navigate between them.

She was so affable, and yes, two pairs would be impossible, she agreed; she didn't want the extra complication of keeping track of two pairs! She was amazingly willing to go with the flow. But I could tell she didn't like the doctor, particularly, and I loved seeing this. Anyway: Progressives were obviously out, but he obviously didn't agree, so I was just trying to salvage the appointment to avoid starting over entirely at another optometrist's office. I appealed to his expertise, shamelessly, for her sake: We just needed his opinion and his help. In a situation like this, even though it wasn't ideal, if she could only have *one* pair of glasses, with a *single* prescription, which did he think would be better? Distance? Or close-up?

"If you're ruling bifocals and progressives out," he said, "then she needs two pairs. She'll just have to remember to use them both."

I rephrased: Which correction did she need more?

"Both," he said, "she needs both."

Despite increasingly wanting to put a foot up his ass, I asked him which prescription was stronger, the distance, or the up close?

He said, "If you expect your mother to be able to see, she needs both. I don't know what else to tell you."

I already knew we would have to just order both pairs so that she could decide between them later, at home, which was inefficient and more expensive than necessary but still better than more pointless discussion with a moron. But there he was, at the door, poised to go already. Standing like a caricature of a doctor, conveying to us that we'd been wasting his time.

I couldn't explain anything to him, and I knew we were easy to dismiss, but still, I said, "This is going to happen to someone you love. And when it does, I hope you really feel it."

"Oh, yes," Jandine added, "I hope so!"

After he stepped out, leaving us to make our way to the optical counter on our own, Jandine pulled a subtle face, and whispered to me, "Was that the doctor?"

"Yes," I said.

"I could be wrong," she said. "But he seemed like a real twat, didn't he?"

Chapter Twelve

One year after Jandine moved in, I began to slowly gather information about memory-care residences. We visited the first one together; she hated everything about it so much that I went to the others on my own. One had a car chassis with comfortable seats in a grassy courtyard where residents could sit when it wasn't too hot, so that everyone could feel like they were on their way somewhere. The people there seemed to like that. But the monthly fees were dizzying, and I believed she would live a long time and that the money Terry left would have to last. Eventually I found a place that was a little less expensive because it was a family-owned assisted living and memory-care facility combined, where they celebrated everything, all the time. And where, until they were bought by a corporate entity, everything seemed about as good as one could hope.

When I took Jandine there for lunch one day we sat at a table of mixed memory-care residents and assisted living residents. I'd curled her hair, and she looked so pretty. After lunch a man in a blue tuxedo jacket played oldies on the piano in the activities hall, and she seemed like a visitor or a volunteer enjoying the show from a folding chair in the first row.

Even if I'd gotten us both out of the house every afternoon there were still so many hours when Jandine sat alone downstairs in front of the TV, waiting. She must have been bored, and I worried that she might be losing ground quicker that way. I didn't want to squander her time. Her attention. I knew she would be happier around other people, instead of waiting all those hours while I was working, only to then do the same routine things we did every day. So while memory care was not an easy decision, the people in the memory-care residences I'd visited had fuller lives than she had with me. Music, activities, parties. Friendships and flirtations. A certain generational connection.

The man in the blue tuxedo jacket kept playing, and Jandine knew all the words. She sang out loud from her seat while I spoke to the residential coordinator about the timeline for moving in.

When the day came I wanted Jandine's new room at memory care to feel familiar. I paid a mover to bring over the dresser she'd been using, filled with bright pretty clothing we'd found together in thrift stores, along with her cedar-lined hope chest, which I put at the foot of the bed with some of the same sentimental souvenirs she'd always kept inside. Old greeting cards and letters, empty bottles of perfume, name tags from her past jobs. So what if I didn't understand why she kept so many vintage Avon and Tupperware catalogs, or the extra buttons from sundresses she sewed for me a lifetime ago. I tucked these ephemeral treasures under an afghan Tineke made, and I left the chest unlocked so that the staff or I could get a few items out, any time she wanted something familiar.

Holy shit: what a mistake. As soon as she was alone the first night she must have started taking everything apart, opening drawers and scattering her clothes, pushing some so far under the bed that the staff had to pull them out again with a broom. She hid little items from the chest all over, behind furniture, in her shoes, in the pockets of coats hanging in the closet. She threw the empty perfume bottles away, or someone else did, because I never saw them again.

I put her clothes back in the closet and took most of the ephemera home. But regardless of how much or little there was to work with, she did this again and again—strewing and hiding with the kind of attention she couldn't bring to very many other tasks by then. I didn't actually see her doing it, but I could imagine all the activity like a film running backward. There was only one item I destroyed when it reappeared, an awful Polaroid photo of me in my old bedroom after the bunk beds had been replaced by a full bed, two adult-sized nightstands, and the big dresser, all from a set chosen by my mother and father before I was born, kept in storage in my grandparents' garage before being loaded into a U-Haul and driven to Terry's house. By the time that photo was taken the runners had cracked off the drawers and I had to pull so hard to get them open that the handles had popped off and disappeared into the shag carpet. My clean clothes were piled at the foot of the bed. I could go on about how uncomfortable the room was, and how often I stubbed my toes on the bulky furniture, hard enough to fracture a bone once. I didn't grasp then how bad it was. But I wish someone had noticed that their house was an overstuffed death trap and helped me fix it.

I had only left that photo in the hope chest thinking I might be able to ask her a few questions, sometime. Like why did I end up with so many castoffs and clashing colors and hazardous inconveniences? Did you notice I slept like a mouse in a permanent heap of clothes? But when I saw the picture reappear one day, propped casually on her dresser, looking almost normal, I didn't bother, I just took it with me and ran it through the shredder at home.

She had never liked talking about the past, I knew that. But after she moved to memory care she would sometimes shut down like she'd caught me trying to pick a lock in her mind, even when we weren't talking about anything, really. But then one time, apropos of nothing, she said, "The cats, you know, in winter they slept down there, too. They slept in the furnace and we could hear them screaming at night."

I said, "The cats slept down there, *too*? You mean, with Jeff?"

She said, "You know what's worse than three cats screaming in a basement?"

I shook my head.

"When they stop. That's worse."

I knew that feeling. That listening, in the quiet after.

"And then the main floor," she said, matter-of-factly. "I would have the vacuum going, and he would just be standing there. Beyond the entryway. Watching me."

"Who, Terry?" I asked, a little confused or a little surprised—but evidently I was too interested and she turned her head away again.

"Look at that!" she said, suddenly pointing at the fig tree a few feet away from our bench in the inner courtyard. "Do you see that?"

"See what?" I asked.

"Those little birds!"

She couldn't conceal it quite as easily as before. All the moments when she deflected conversation away.

"I hated it," she'd said a different time. "My neck, my back." She gestured. "But this is so nice." We were sitting on the bench in the courtyard; it was easier, sometimes, for her to sit facing forward, side by side. Easier than facing another person directly. She greeted people warmly as they walked past and I couldn't tell if she knew the people she spoke to or not, and it didn't seem to matter. But I wanted to know what she'd hated. And about her neck, her back. It would be time to go inside for dinner, soon, and I didn't want to push her, so instead of asking I tried to stay neutral, as patternless as walking on the sand randomly to avoid alerting the sandworms underground on Arrakis.

"It wasn't so obvious then," I said, about nothing, about everything.

"Well," she said, slowly. "I wouldn't say obvious."

"Did—" I said, but then I stopped myself; sometimes the past tense alone was enough to put her off. She was looking at me, waiting. Squinting slightly. I'm sure we looked like visitors, like family members waiting to see someone, enjoying the courtyard, the green grass, and all the figurines of rabbits and kittens and robins in the flower beds. It wasn't worth pushing. Because you can't argue with dementia. The moment at hand is the only moment, but even that's not fixed.

"Isn't it pretty?" I asked, pointing to a hummingbird feeder hanging in a slender peach tree, right across from us. A sapling, like the fig tree. The afternoon sun made the red acrylic glow like stained glass, casting a tinted shadow onto the cement walkway below.

"Very pretty," she said. "We had one. But it wasn't as beautiful as that."

I didn't remember a hummingbird feeder. Terry fed other birds, but he didn't want to attract ants and wasps and there hadn't been a hummingbird feeder at the farm, either, just lots of tubular flowers for them. Yellow bells. And honeysuckle. But that wasn't the point. What mattered now was that she was willing to let something here be more beautiful than something she'd lost.

She pointed out the sunlit jewel of the hanging feeder to an aide who was leaving after her shift, who then stopped to look where Jandine was pointing. She came over to squeeze Jandine's hand and hug her.

"Everybody just loves your mother," she said to me. "She looks forward to seeing you, and you're so good about being here. She always knows you're coming. Don't you, Jandine? You always know your daughter is coming to see you."

Jandine looked happy. And I was grateful and am grateful still to that woman, who stopped to look at what Jandine was pointing out, even though she'd had a long day and was on her way home. Not everyone is kind. But so many were.

Chapter Thirteen

We took regular evening walks until almost the end of her life. Until she fell a final time and then everything changed so quickly. But up to that point whenever we stepped out of her residence she would take a deep breath, and say, *It's so nice out here.* Or, *It's like a vacation.* I'm not sure the inner courtyard and paved paths were ever what she expected to find, but she never seemed disappointed.

Our circuit included a pretty area behind the residential buildings, landscaped to soften the look of the tall stone property wall. We could see roofs and trees on the other side, where there must have been backyards, one with a grapefruit tree that bore fruit all year. One of the branches hung over the wall, onto our side. The grapefruits there were a little too high to reach and somehow this delighted Jandine, every time.

"Look!" she'd say. "I guess nobody brought a ladder."

I tried not to listen for oracles in her words. Tried not to hope she might still somehow convey things that she'd never told me, or at least acknowledge the fact that she hadn't. I know that's how it's done in movies: Those who are older, or unwell, or who see differently and can't give a straightforward answer for whatever reason will offer up uncanny clues and indirect allusions. It's not that I don't believe in oracles, of course I do, I know oracles and enigmas abound, but they have to come from strange, unfamiliar sources. And so to make someone close into an oracle is to make them strange to you. In those years I was walking with my mother in the courtyard at twilight, not listening for coded messages from another plane. I'm sure there were moments when she did make statements of manifold meaning, but if so, and if I remember, then time will be the distance needed to make it strange, and I don't want that to happen, either.

The night Jandine died I was sleeping on the floor next to her bed. She'd been dying, peacefully, for days, and it was late when she decided to go. I think the sudden quiet in the room after the end of her labored breathing must have been what woke me. When I opened my eyes in the darkness there was a feeling of suspension, of stillness, and I got up and sat in the chair by the bed, listening, and then removed the safety locks and opened her bedroom window. We sat like that. Until it felt like time to tell the night nurse, and ask her to let the good people from hospice know.

It took an hour, maybe, for the hospice nurse on call to arrive and certify her death, and then another hour or so for the people who came to transport her body. I sat with her while all the quiet details fell into place around us. The hospice nurse, whom I'd come to know and liked a lot, told me that it would be better for me not to be in the room when the mortuary staff came. Then, more plainly, she said I would regret it if I was there to see them taking her away.

I said I couldn't leave the building as long as Jandine was still there, and the other night nurse, whom I also liked, said there was a model room in the same hallway, behind a door I had never noticed. It was unoccupied and fully furnished, kept ready to show potential new residents and their families.

"You're tired," the night nurse said, and it was true. "Lie down and sleep a little. I'll let you know after they've gone."

She woke me gently around dawn. I looked into Jandine's room again and left her things as they were until I could return to collect them. And then I found myself standing outside in the empty parking lot, with my car keys in my hand, watching the sun come up. Watching the planes in the distance. That's when I caught my tired brain putting it all in good order so that I could tell Jandine the best version of the story of the night she died.

I believed she would be whole again after everything, somehow. But until that moment I didn't know how much I had believed that I would see her again here. In this life. As if she'd been suspended in the air on a flight she'd boarded years ago, and she'd only been stuck in transit, held up somewhere because of this illness. And now it had run its course, but she was gone.

PART THREE

I am inclined to think that Chalcidius rightly divined what Plato was imagining—a feature of his model which it would not suit his purpose to mention as a third ring. It is rather the trace left by the "carrying round" of a meridian circle, namely the surface of the sphere considered as symbolising a motion.

FRANCES MACDONALD CORNFORD, *Plato's Cosmology: The* Timaeus *of Plato, translated with a running commentary*

Chapter Fourteen

Las Vegas is a city of builders, and nice surplus from commercial projects often gets donated to charity shops. Which I check out frequently, now that I'm catching up on things. Like recaulking baseboards and replacing broken grout and crossing DIY projects off old to-do lists that keep surfacing as I sort through piles of old mail I've been ignoring for too long. The salvage shop is like a lottery; if the right materials appear, I buy them and then I'll deal with the relevant project.

That's as far ahead as I can plan.

I really don't know how I got through these past several years.

After Jandine died I thought I'd find myself catching up on all the deferred priorities. I planned to tackle the old boxes from Tacoma first, so that I could finally clear out my garage. But it doesn't work like that, apparently, and now that I'm halfway to the first anniversary of her death it feels like I've done nothing at all. I've heard all the advice, about using a bold black marker to write a date on storage boxes and commit to throwing them out when the date arrives, in six months, or a year, if you haven't needed the contents by then, which I personally think is bullshit, as is a lot of the standard advice about grief, though it's equally well-intentioned. Like that someday my memories of Jandine won't center on what she went through at the end of her life. I appreciate the impulse. But frankly forgetting the terrible, fucked-up, unfair hand that she was dealt would also mean forgetting the way she handled it with so much grace.

Anyway.

I thought I'd read somewhere that periods of official mourning should last a year and a day. But now I can't find anything to back that up. Just that a loved one will visit you in a dream within a year and a day of their death, or they never will. And that an escaped medieval serf would be free after a year and a day. And that Sir Gawain beheads the Green Knight with the stroke of an axe while agreeing to let the knight cut his own head off in turn a year and a day later.

For some reason I thought I remembered more positive examples.

The Green Knight leads me to Cú Chulainn, with a nearly identical decapitation story, and from there to Gauls and Celts who embalmed the heads of enemies in cedar oil or pine resin. So many kings beheaded in defeat: The head of Conaire Mór drinks water and keeps talking; the head of Fergal Mac Maile Duin is given tributes including seven cooked pigs, and also keeps talking. . . . An AI overview includes the owl and the pussycat, something to do with the way owls appear to turn their heads all the way around. In cedar trees, or in pine trees.

The owl and the pussycat: Their journey lasted a year and a day, didn't it?

I have to stop myself from scrolling on my phone like this before I'm even out of bed.

Jasper is awake so I take my pills and give Jasper her pills, always careful to keep them apart—hers are in a translucent red bottle as bright and beautiful as a healing charm in a fairy tale or the red pill that comes from Morpheus—and then I get myself together so that I'll be sitting in the office chair in the room down the hall when the machinery on my brain's factory floor starts up for the day. Because if I don't provide myself with the props of a proper routine, whatever I happen to be doing when the lights come up is what I'll still be doing hours later, with a degree of hyperfocus almost beyond blinking.

I keep Terry's jade desk clock in my home office, letting the hourly chimes remind me to stand and stretch, and drink water, and have some lunch. I can hear a plane coming down over the house, and Paloma's dog barking in the patio next door: Funny how the barking and the wind and the planes overhead and the grit thrown against the window didn't even register until now. But that's the Adderall, obviously. The magic of selective tuning in and tuning out. Which I generally appreciate most as the effects are wearing off, and suddenly I can't stand the shadows of the planes, or the urgent barking of dogs in patios along the alley who barely get to settle down before the next plane comes through with a terrible rushing sound overhead.

Jasper is nearly deaf and noise doesn't trouble her sleep. But there's a hitch in her breathing and a green tinge in her fur. Fucking mulberry pollen. Even when the windows are closed.

New windows, by the way. Still paying them off.

Meanwhile Jandine's expensive air purifiers are still buried somewhere in the garage.

I should also get the mail. Except that's not critical. Also, the wind is unpleasant.

Another plane passes over the house, loud enough to shake the windows.

I have ambient earplugs somewhere but I haven't used them since Jeff stopped staying here when he occasionally visits Vegas; yesterday he texted before getting on the freeway back to L.A., saying he'd been at my door, ringing the bell, wanting to say hello and yet getting no answer. I must have been out for a walk, and I'd missed his texts at the time, but Paloma says she saw him.

Her big sunglasses are the sporty wraparound kind, better for windy days than her usual glamorous Sophia Loren frames. These match her fancy red T-shirt, with the words *Fallen Angel* in cursive across the front.

"He was parked in the fire lane and I said, 'Excuse me, how shitty are you going to feel when somebody needs an ambulance and your car is in the way?' Which by the way I've said to him before."

"He's not a good listener," I say.

"He heard me," she says.

Back inside my cool shady house, the lovely bronze corydoras are swimming up and down inside the long acrylic aquarium in my living room, because when the barometric pressure changes they swim up and down the tank walls, up and down, expecting rain by tomorrow.

My phone notifications have been turned off since Jandine died. I guess I could turn them back on. I guess I could try doing that.

I mostly only watch the kind of paranormal shows where the investigators stay on location around the clock for a few days, because obviously by the end it would be a challenge not to have genuinely weird experiences of some kind. But not in asylums or prisons. Tonight I'm drinking wine on the couch with Jasper while a small team of analog-friendly investigators draw straws to determine who should sleep on a cot in the dry swimming pool of a shuttered luxury hotel when a text from Paloma makes me jump slightly: *The pool opens this weekend, get yourself a damn UV swim shirt this year if you don't want to die early*. She includes a thumbs-up emoji and for some reason also the nail polish one.

I will, thank you, I reply.

And read your HOA newsletter calendar.

I will, thank you! I reply.

You're welcome, she responds, with prayer hands. Unless they're high five hands.

Paloma says I need exercise and that I should swim laps but she's also quick to point out that I have to avoid the sun and also that I'd better never swim solo, because she hopes she won't have to send me a violation letter nor see me die needlessly due to stomach cramps or other preventable reasons that happen to dumb shits who don't use the buddy system. I appreciate her practical concerns. Despite the fact that my own reservations about swimming alone lean more to featureless shadow people tossing wired appliances into the water or piranhas waiting in the overflow drain, and/or all the other twists of fate that nobody who arrives after the fact would ever believe, unless, like me, they've also watched too many scary movies, maybe out of a need to condense all the formless free-floating horrors of the world into something distinct enough to confront. She's right about the swim shirt, though; it would make getting myself out the door a little easier.

Chapter Fifteen

Every morning I work on pulling together Las Vegas–themed content for a free newsletter directed at people who believe they'll get to retire someday. After I send what my boss calls Daily Desert Dispatches (triple *D*s, my coworkers and I call them), others add everything you need to know about *how to buy and sell real estate in the golden Southwest . . . either for you and your family to enjoy . . . or to flip for profit . . . or to enjoy now and use for passive retirement income in the future*. Or whatever. It's not the worst kind of bullshit daydream, given that there's no actual real estate changing hands. Just paid subscriptions and seminars, which do in fact contain useful information. But the information isn't the point, either, I don't think.

I suspect readers want to pay because it helps them believe they'll get to use the info someday. And anybody who wants a refund gets one, though surprisingly few ask—which I would feel conflicted about if it wasn't so easy to click a bright-red button and *Send Your (Emailed) Letter to the Editor HERE*. To those who write to say they're on the fence about a paid subscription, I send "welcome" links to copywritten pages full of promise and possibility and paywalls. To those who just need advice about ending abusive time-share memberships, I send "e-introductions" to my boss's "panel of experts"—a rotating list of advisers who presumably pay commissions for referrals, but I wouldn't know, because the marketing and money details are not my responsibility, I just do the parts that I do, and then I'm done for the day.

I don't know how they make enough money to sustain this. But they do.

Perhaps I spend too much time and energy on miscellany. Like the emails from a reader I've heard from every week, for years now, who always signs off with a first initial and a last name after a cordial if formulaic reply to some daily dispatch, always concluding with the question: How much does it cost?

Thank you for the interesting info about Hoover Dam today—how much does it cost?

In the past I tried to answer: *Hoover Dam is free to visit . . . if you're planning to visit southern Nevada, here's a link to a recent Daily Desert Dispatch about some of our partners offering customizable guided day trips. . . .*

It surprised me somehow to never get a reply.

I appreciated the photo of a desert tortoise today—how much does it cost?

Every desert tortoise in the state of Nevada is a beloved natural resource protected by law. But while it's unlawful to touch a tortoise in the wild, here are links about making a donation or even adopting one of the thousands of tortoises who can neither be taken out of state, nor reintroduced to . . .

The mail bag takes up a disproportionate amount of my attention. Like the daily recurring email that says, simply, *Do you like enema?* I thought it was funny the first time, but then it started to give me the creeps. Until one of my more seasoned coworkers said, *You know that's spam, right?* Which in fact I did know. But still: There's something eerie about them.

What I want are emails from readers motivated to share useful, usually catastrophic information, who are happy to be published. Recommendations, ratings, cautionary tales; I keep them in a folder along with the evergreen tourist topics I can use in a pinch, if necessary, in case I fall behind.

We don't pay them. But they get bylines. And links they can send to their friends and to their adult children.

Some of these readers are expressing needs far beyond what they say they're writing about, and they don't just want answers. They want somebody else in the world to feel bad about something that they can't change. They want to vent about gambling (*you glorify an activity that destroyed my daughter's marriage*); about smoking (*shame on you—the cigar bars—hookah lounges—you treat vaporing like candy for children*); about alcohol and legal pot dispensaries (varied and sundry concerns); even wedding chapels (*bachelor and bachelorette parties and venereal disease plus the secret history of divorce needs to be told—why don't you ever tell that side of things?*). It's not always irritable, sometimes it's just needlessly intense. Like a recent reader who confused Area 51 (off-limits) and AREA15 (day passes available). Or the ones who sometimes want to pit motor homes against mobile homes, for some reason.

Today a reader sends a warning: Due to drought, the roof rats in Las Vegas have concentrated minerals in their teeth that are sharp enough to chew through wood, drywall, vinyl siding, even concrete, and for this reason our readers need to be aware that they cannot safely store paper currency inside the walls or ceilings of their homes without first installing hard metal sheathing as a ratproof security measure. The letter writer adds that a soft metal lining is no longer good enough. Because if those teeth can get through concrete, they can obviously chew right through gold or silver or even copper. *Believe me*, the reader wrote. *I know because forty years of my savings was gone when I needed it, including the precious metals I thought were protecting me.*

My coworkers in the Arizona office wouldn't gravitate to this kind of warning. But I like it as a parable on the absurdity of living in this environment as casually as we do. And for the everyday pageantry and power Las Vegas has when it comes to adding a louche sparkle to situations that don't actually sparkle at all on their own: *I was completely broke*, for example.

I was completely broke . . . is the end of the line, at least for the moment. Whereas *I was completely broke . . . in Las Vegas* is a different story.

Rats got into my house and ate my cash

becomes

Rats made off with a fortune wrapped in gold that I kept hidden in the walls of my desert home . . . in Las Vegas.

And so: There was a time when Jandine and I had the chance to lean back in lounge chairs by the pool, watching the line of distant airplanes waiting to land, knowing they were full of people who were feeling lucky. The heat would rise from the cement pool deck after the sun went down, and the cicadas in the silk tree would go on and on, and Jandine would point languidly up at the palm fronds moving overhead, asking me if it was getting windy. While in unrelated news, a colony of roof rats was nesting up there, rustling around to get at the ripe palm fruit.

But she wasn't well. She suffered for a long time, and then she died here.

Preceded in death by two husbands, Jandine retired to the desert, where she enjoyed live music and sunsets by the pool. She died in the company of family . . . in Las Vegas.

It's dusk, in those memories, and so hot. The cicadas were so loud. I was grateful for the time with her. And I was overwhelmed. I remember thinking, How much longer? How much longer can we do this? It was a real question, but one I did not want answered.

Chapter Sixteen

When the storage container from Tacoma was unloaded here, it took less than an hour for my open living room and dining area to be filled up with the oak dining room table, eight matching chairs, the hutch, and the liquor cabinet. Why did I let that happen? How did I ever think I could absorb so much stuff? Even some furniture that was supposed to be donated in Tacoma ended up here instead; my heart dropped when I saw the massive oak bedroom set emerge as the shipping container emptied, with a yellow carbon copy taped to the headboard from the charity that had declined to haul it away. Somebody had underlined the reason in blue ink: *Furniture donations must be in good salable condition. All drawers must glide.*

The bureau and headboard were so heavy and so tricky to get up the stairs that the movers wanted to remove the railing on my stairs, and I was about to say no when they tilted it again and somehow found an angle that cleared the corners with only a slight scrape to the ceiling. The house was built in 1978, after asbestos was prohibited in new materials for popcorn ceilings, and I chose to believe that mine were safe.

Letting it all in was a bad decision, of course. But then again Jandine seemed so much more comfortable in rooms filled with familiar heavy oak furniture, and I was glad about that.

Anyway.

Today I need to do a water change for Pinky, my crown-tail betta. I should get started before I get pulled into thinking too much about anything beyond the present moment.

Only once I'm siphoning Pinky's gravel do I realize rogue bubbles from the airstone in his five-gallon tank have caused a small, nearly invisible trickle of water down the back, and that accumulated damp has already swelled the grain of the oak end table where it meets the smoked-glass top. I hate to disrupt Pinky, and he hates it, too, but I've had a better spot in mind for him for a while now anyway, so I lift him out carefully, in a new baggie so that I can siphon his tank water into a food-safe bucket, relocate the tank closer to where I sit in the evenings, then put back 80 percent of his bucket water and add a gallon of clean dechlorinated water. While he's getting acquainted with his new views of the room, I drag the heavy old end table out to the patio, then the one that matches it, as well.

I thought it would make me feel better. But seeing the oak table frames outside in daylight is painful. It's physically painful. There are scratches in the wood and humiliating stains that show in the sun, and one has a gauzy corner underneath, like a spidery egg sac tucked into what had been a safe dark place right in the middle of everything until now.

I try to find a charity willing to pick them up. I make a good faith effort, but one asks for photos by email first, and another puts me on a waiting list with the caveat that their staff aren't responsible for loading anything heavy into the truck. The tables are too heavy for me to lift on my own. But more than that, I'm not sure they'll be accepted if a truck ever arrives. They sit out in the patio for a couple of days while I screw up the courage to carefully remove and wrap each smoky glass top in cardboard. Once they're sealed with moving tape, I write dire warnings in black marker to prevent an *Omen*-style beheading if anyone gets too close. The night before the next bulk trash pickup I drag the oak frames and wrapped glass tops out into the alley, one at a time, where I leave them with the bins. When I check in the morning, they're gone.

Chapter Seventeen

I should not shop on my phone after I'm already in bed. Not even for important things like UV-protection swimwear, not even with amber night mode, because it's not just the light, it's also the scrolling that makes it so hard to fall asleep even after putting the phone down.

But then I feel or hear a glancing whine bounce past my head and I'm glad I was awake because a mosquito needs a blood meal before it can reproduce and I can't stand that. Or the idea of anticoagulant saliva. They're one of the few creatures I can bring myself to kill preemptively.

I check the popcorn ceiling with a flashlight and I check the curtains, too. Maybe it wasn't a mosquito. But the expectation keeps me awake and finally I go out to the garage for a high-velocity fan, some netting, and a handful of zip ties to make a mosquito trap. If there's one here the airflow will pull it through, into the netting, where it will quickly dehydrate and die.

"Mosquitos?" says Paloma, when I see her. "Not this year, not that I've seen. Why?"

She wears a turquoise scoop-neck T-shirt with the words *Tempus Fugit* glinting across the bust; it's weird how often her bedazzled T-shirts echo the names of old *X-Files* episodes. "Fallen Angel." "Young at Heart." "Nothing Lasts Forever." "Squeeze."

"Are you sure you didn't watch *The X-Files* on TV?" I ask.

"No," she says, "I told you, I get my conspiracy theories from the news. Where was the mosquito? Inside your house?"

Belatedly I realize she'll probably just blame my fish tanks, despite the fact that there's too much surface turbulence for mosquitoes to breed. Due to the filters. And the airstones.

"Never mind," I say, "I'm sure it was nothing."

"Listen," she says. "Get more exercise and then you won't

hear things that aren't there. Exercise improves circulation. Is your blood pressure still high?"

"Not really," I say. "Actually, yes, it probably is."

"High blood pressure will make you hear bugs," she says, "everybody knows that. And you'll see bugs, too. So get some exercise."

Instead of exercising I go back inside and get a five-dollar bottle of chardonnay from the fridge to join Jasper, who's watching the female bettas, floating like murderous darts in their thirty-gallon sorority tank. I put the wine in a terra-cotta chiller between the couch cushions and hide my phone under the throw pillow. Designating places for things like phones and keys—I wish I'd always known to do this for myself.

Jasper settles onto my lap, and suddenly tomorrow is Easter, according to the local evening news; a pathway in my brain flickers forward to seeing Jandine for brunch tomorrow morning in the decorated activity hall at memory care, four miles down the road. Where they celebrate everything, all the time.

I have plenty of shows to catch up on, and bottles of wine, as well, now that I know the phone won't ring, because Jandine can't fall, and will never hit her head again or suffer another seizure, and I don't need to be sober in case a night nurse calls from memory care, handing the phone to an EMT to tell me which hospital they're taking Jandine to. I won't be getting out of bed to drive alone through the dark city to any one of the ERs in the valley whose locations and layouts all blend together now because I wasn't taking in the bigger details, just following one urgent sign at a time, into dark parking lots, toward the whooshing automatic doors of late-night entrances.

Sometimes on these shows people encounter good things: a lady at night who resembles a great-grandmother whose photo they didn't see until after . . . a paramedic on a deserted road who keeps you awake but then disappears once the real paramedics arrive. But the majority are negative. A rental house with bad vibes, but the storyteller can't afford to break the lease. A hotel suite where newlyweds have a shared nightmare about the room catching on fire. I like this particular show because at the end of every episode the experiencer is given the opportunity to go back to the location in the company of a medium, a paranormal investigator, and the spiritual adviser of their choice. Some say they won't go back under any circumstance, but most say yes, and this keeps me watching.

I would not go back. I'm too afraid of stirring something up again and bringing it home, like a burr picked up in a field and carried into the house by accident. I don't know what it was, and I don't expect to, and I don't want to encounter anything like it again. But I still, every once in a while, have a dream that feels like the field under a towering sky, behind shimmering trees. They might look different, these dreams, but the arrangement is always the same. The proportions, the directions. The weight, and the shimmer, and the damp, and the fear of what's underneath.

None of this is about my grandparents' farm. Because there was nothing scary on their side of the trees. The new owners of their property run it as a berry farm, as they have for many years, and the last time I was in Washington I drove by the house and found it brightly lit, and well taken care of. The little cherry tree in the front yard was bigger than I remembered, and on the day I passed it was heavy with ripe fruit and filled with an aura of songbirds.

Instead of Easter brunch I could go to the pool. Why not. Swimsuit, sun hat, sunscreen, and then I'm ready: Is it this easy for other people? You just decide to do something, and then you do it? If so, then your life must be marvelous.

I'm letting myself in through the pool gate when a jingling dog collar and whiff of cigarette smoke alert me that Paloma is nearby, and when she sees me she pushes her large sunglasses back onto her stylishly cropped hair, squinting, and I don't begrudge her the life she lives but I always know that she is older than my mother ever was, because Jandine was only seventy-three.

I can't imagine I might some day end up older than that.

When Paloma shifts Pepper to her hip I can read her shirt: *Irresistible*. I hold the pool gate open for her, but she stops.

"Mandy," she says. "Happy Easter. What are you doing? Are you going swimming without any protective layer?"

"I don't have a swim top yet," I say. She reaches out to tweak the brim of my sun hat and I flinch, and then I regret it, so I say, "But I ordered one."

"You're as bad as my friend," she says. "You haven't met her, I know. She's reclusive, but her house is at the other end of our row. She's the squamous cell carcinoma friend I told you about. You'd better go take a look at her, take a look at your future—I hope you know that your hands are literally broiling in the sun when you get behind the steering wheel of your car. And pool water is a giant magnifying lens. What do you say to that?"

"I don't have squamous cell." My voice sounds petulant.

"Lucky you," she says. Now she's holding Pepper against her shoulder like a baby being burped. He contorts to look at me, warily, and I feel a pang, because when an animal doesn't like you, it's either because you're a bad person or because you're sick. Everybody knows that.

"Anyway," she continues, "the plumber got the hand dryers installed, so thank goodness nobody can blow up the crappers again like last year."

"What?" I say—dammit; I don't need to hear about HOA violations. But Paloma collects them like some people follow true crime.

"Please, Mandy, read the newsletter," she says. "Flushing paper towels, exploding the pipes. It's the kids." And then, without modulating her voice, she adds, "Kids with parents who either don't or can't read the signs I posted about what not to flush. And I'm sorry, but I'm not going to print bilingual signs."

"But," I say, but then I don't know what to say about the

fact that Paloma, who is from Cuba, and who speaks in Spanish half the time on her phone on the other side of the patio wall, says no to printing signs in Spanish for the Spanish-speaking neighbors. And the moment passes before I say anything.

"I'm sure it was a mistake," I say, lamely. "The flushing and the pipes."

"Oh, honey," she says, shifting Pepper again, settling in, and my heart sinks. "See those cameras in the pool area?" She points, until I look. "People understand that they'll get caught doing the crazy stuff they used to do out here, so now they do crazy stuff in the toilets instead. Somebody went into the men's bathroom and pissed up the wall. Probably somebody who's been pissing in the pool all along."

"How do you piss up a wall?" I ask.

"You don't believe me?" she says. "TK caught the same guy on tape earlier—right into the water, like a fountain at Caesars. No shame at all. Son of a bitch—we took away his pool key but somehow he still gets in." She shakes her head. "These people are your neighbors," she says, as if I have any say in it.

"Yours, too," I say, mildly offended.

"I know!" she says. "The men are bad enough, but the women are just *filthy*."

"I know a lot of filthy White people who don't follow rules," I say, belatedly trying to reply about the signs. "I mean, I just want to point that out."

"Mandy," she says, "I don't care who it is. All people are filthy. You're so innocent, I know it's not you doing it. But what we find in the sinks—you wouldn't believe me even if I told you."

This is what happens, I can't stop my brain from cycling through vomit, tampons, clumps of pubic hair trimmed from bikini lines—why not do that at home? And dirty diapers. Dirty *adult* diapers? I adjust the brim of my hat, in an effort to get the miasma out of my head.

Paloma watches my face. "Everything you just imagined," she says. "I've seen it. All of it. Right there in the pool restrooms."

"Okay," I say, trying to wrap things up. What would Jandine say? "At least the pool is clean. And most of the neighbors are nice," I add, wondering if the other people in the pool can hear us. The man swimming laps in a Speedo and goggles, and the pretty girl in a white one-piece, languidly rinsing off in the shower alcove in the shade of the clubhouse wall.

"I know," she says. "The neighbors are nice people. But as soon as you're not looking, they'll shit in the sinks."

On that note she leaves the pool area. The water still looks pristine, but she's sort of killed my trust in the hygiene part of the social contract.

I turn to pull a chaise longue more deeply into the shade of one of the sun umbrellas.

The girl standing at the lip of the pool's deep end is watching me while she twists up her long slick hair. She'll probably dive into the pool right under the black-and-white *No Diving* sign as soon as Paloma is out of sight, but now, as she's still slowly knotting up her sun-streaked hair, she turns her back to me and I see that where it isn't covered by her swimsuit, her spine bears a thick vertical scar, with a corset-like pattern of smaller stitches on either side. An old scar. She must have been young, I guess. And that must have been a hell of a surgery.

The girl executes a splashless little dive and stays under for a long time, breaststroking along the bottom in her white one-piece. Like a vintage Bain de Soleil ad under the sparkling surface, swimming toward the edge of swimming pools that aren't real anymore.

A little bird flutters over to the oddly exposed trickling pipe of the hot tub and it hops, hops, hops for little sips of chlorinated water.

I feel so tired. At least this little bird has access to water. It's better than nothing, isn't it? Even though it's hot. And chlorinated. What's the bright side? That it's better than sewage? The bird hops, looks up at me, looks away, and then aims a squirt of sandy poop into the hot tub. I leave the pool enclosure with my ridiculously colorful towel still thrown over my shoulders, hoping not to let Paloma see that I am leaving already.

In the coolness of the living room I'll go looking for a movie I think I remember watching all the time, years ago, but can never quite find. The archetype of a syncretic seasonal celebration with buttercups nodding in the background all day, and neighbors dancing in a circle after dark at the center of a village where summer visitors ignore their intuition, giving every strange encounter the benefit of the doubt right up until the night of the bonfire.

Chapter Eighteen

It's getting harder to tune out the garage. Whenever I think about it, I can feel my blood pressure rising. If I think about it too much, my pulse starts to flutter at the base of my throat. That's what my beta-blockers are for. I don't know where to start, and I don't see how I'll ever manage to finish clearing it out, when even the idea of the looming bulk of everything out there has this much power.

I do know however that I won't make any progress out there today if I spend any more time looking for the old episode of *Space: 1999* that I hazily remember, in which the crew of Moonbase Alpha are drugged by something—an outgassing of alien spores? But I keep looking anyway. Because that's what today feels like. Albeit with zero of the euphoria I remember. Maybe a better comparison is the couple in the *X-Files* episode cold open who are starting to hallucinate in their motel room, because in fact they're being digested by the massive underground fungus in a field they visited earlier in the day, and never actually left. No euphoria there, either, come to think of it.

It's okay not to know, if you're the one trapped in that field. If you really can't change what's about to happen, I mean. It's taken a long time for me to come around to this conclusion, which I probably should have just accepted the first time I heard it, while holding my mother's hand, as I was weeping against the reptile window of the pet store and seeing through the glass that the snakes I loved were preparing to swallow the mice I loved. Preparing to swallow them whole. And that one was already carrying a mouse-shaped bolus in an otherwise slender body.

How long will the mouse be alive? I managed to ask.

Jandine promised me that the mouse did not know what was happening, and that almost immediately, it wouldn't feel anything.

But how do you know?

I know, she'd said. *Shock is nature's way of protecting us.*

I don't know why I remain like this, at the desk, planted in my chair, unable to do anything productive. I can feel that time is passing. But it also doesn't seem connected to me. And yet I avoid looking at the clock and I keep my eyes away from the time display, because I know I'm not going to change what I'm doing. All I'm capable of is poking around online, until eventually I'm watching the episode, and near the end, I discover that I was wrong. There were no blissful spores. It was an artificial intelligence. Not a fungus. But there are pedestals that look a little like mushrooms. And only as I'm watching the episode do I understand that it has haunted my entire life, including the mistrust of bliss, and the way the personalities of crew members change, and the desperation of Martin Landau, the shock when he lasers the beautiful Servant of the Guardian in the face—which he did to save the crew—but more than anything it's the sight of her lying on the floor with her face plate gone. An android, with human eyes, staring up from the deactivated circuits: I don't know that I've always remembered this image until I watch it unfold. And it's further complicated by knowing, consciously or not, that the role of the Servant of the Guardian was played by the same actress who would play Maya for the rest of the series, Maya, my favorite, with alien eyebrows and auburn sideburns and the ability to take the form of any animal in an emergency. That's my 1970s childhood in a nutshell: seeing something confusing that changes you forever and that you may never see again and might not even remember until now, I guess, when it's possible to find almost anything online. But you can't look for something you don't remember. Until you remember it without knowing. Not unless you catch hold of some small corner of the memory, distorted, like a dream.

When the episode ends I realize that the ceiling fan in my office, behind me, out of sight, needs rebalancing. I knew this at the end of last summer. But by then Jandine was already dying.

Still, I should have remembered to dust the dirty blades before turning it on today.

It's an alternate measure of time. From turning off the squeaking fan last year, to hearing the sound again now. According to which nothing that happened in between actually took place.

I need to either find Jandine's air purifiers or give up on them and buy new ones, because now Jasper's breathing sounds even more ragged than yesterday. If she's sick, that's my fault.

I hate myself on days like this.

I need to take care of myself; it's a thought that makes me pause, hands over my keyboard. Did I wake up feeling so awful that I forgot to take my pills this morning? It's possible. It's late enough now to take a second dose, either way. And it's an odd kind of relief, to know I'm not just lazy, or careless, or stupid. As I believed about myself for years. And after I take the pills, I will make myself go out to the garage.

Chapter Nineteen

I only went looking for help when Jandine was living with me because I thought antidepressants would help me hold down my job, and with it the flexibility I needed to work from home and hang on to my insurance—the kind of garden-variety stresses that everybody has to manage sooner or later.

"Well," said the doctor, "what you're describing doesn't sound like depression to me. Not alone, anyway." He asked questions, and scheduled diagnostic tests, and later, when he said that I had attention deficit disorder, I didn't believe him because for starters I have the energy of a lizard. If I'm left alone in a cold corner, I won't move again for months.

"Don't get hung up on the hyperactivity aspect," he said. "Girls and women are often diagnosed with inattentive types of ADHD."

But in retrospect it explained everything. And got me thinking that everything could have been different, maybe, if somebody had noticed it earlier. But Jandine was struggling herself, and had been struggling for such a long time, and I don't see how she could have recognized that I was struggling, given the time, given the era. We know more, now. We can get a little further toward comparing subjective experience. If nothing else, there are handy metaphors now, like the ones that might explain ADHD to newly diagnosed children: Your brain is a sports car—with bad brakes. Your brain is a jet plane, flying high into the clouds—but you don't have any landing gear! Alarming, but weirdly vindicating. I've heard people say ADHD is life in hard mode, which I get though I don't play video games. But many adults don't come across these descriptions unless they have children who have just been diagnosed, and then the realization settles into place.

I think of it like this: Your car has a stick shift but the gears are soft and mobile, and sometimes your steering wheel rotates the full 360 degrees. The brakes are inconsistent, the bolts that keep the driver's seat from sliding are loose, and obviously there are no seat belts, but since you've never driven anyone else's car you don't know that it's not this way for all the neurotypical drivers on the road. After a few crashes you might start to figure it out, with the help of a reasonably good mechanic, if you can find one who'll accept your insurance. By then it will be too late for a lot of whatever you wanted to do with your life. But you can still take care of yourself, and better late than never. You can try to prioritize sleep, and reassess the booze, the sugar binges, and any other self-medicating habits, trading them in for brain-healthy supplements and prescribed medication—not that you have to take it, or take it forever. But do something, because there's more at stake than how shitty you feel on a given day. The consequences for people whose ADHD goes untreated will break your heart.

For me Adderall revealed the disadvantage of having been unable to see or touch or understand the disadvantage itself—the invisible *Matrix*-ness of it—so profoundly that it reordered most of what I thought I knew about myself. And so, I will keep paying the high-deductible prescription co-pay every month, and the out-of-pocket fees for monthly medication check-ins. If it were to ever come down to deciding between paying the mortgage or paying for the Adderall refills, Adderall would have to come first. Because I can't pay the mortgage either if I can't work.

TL;DR? Be kind to yourself and don't put sugar in the gas tank.

Also, keep your garage in order. Don't pile up storage boxes you can barely get around, because if you pull something heavy down on top of yourself in an extremely hot garage and knock yourself out, there's a good chance you'll die there. Especially if you live alone in the desert.

I can feel the difference in temperature, not just in degree but in kind, between the bright patio full of plants with their very slight humidity and the hot stifled overwhelm inside the garage. There are two small steps from the patio down to the cracked cement garage floor, and whenever I reach for the switch to turn on the overhead light, I brace myself against the crowded airlessness and pressure.

When I first saw this house, I thought the huge garage was a good thing. But now I can barely remember the version of myself that expected to be able to use the wide surface of the work area against one wall, where the previous owner had obviously hung tools on the pegboard, to see them and find them whenever you want them. The outlines where those tools once hung are still visible. Or, they would be, if there weren't old moving boxes stacked in the way.

It's a normal wish, to want to walk into the garage and find something that should be easy to find, without having to sidestep around containers and boxes that have been here so long now that I don't even know what's inside. And that I can't seem to do anything about. A few times, I've made a little headway, clearing an area, ruthlessly sorting and donating and discarding, but somehow, to my horror, it actually felt worse to see a little improvement than none at all, because the enormity of everything that had been left unaddressed would suddenly take on texture and fine detail. A little improvement made it clear that I can never fix this.

I know it's bad math, a bad calculation of time and effort to look for one thing at a time, spending so much more energy to avoid addressing the bigger problem. But it's all I have the energy to do. Especially toward the end of the day. In the heat. And so instead of taking it all in, I step around one thing at a time, like the dainty, empty, impractical jewelry cabinet on Edwardian legs that had been Jandine's, wedged in between storage containers and a pile of extra travertine tile from when I had the kitchen floor replaced, tiles I wish I could stash out of sight, under the deep built-in shelves, for example, to forget about until the day I might ever need matching tile in the future. But I can't, because that space is already full. Full of what, I don't know. To get a look, I would have to move both cars to the parking lot, and shift aside everything else that's in the way. And then figure out what to do with whatever's there now before sliding the heavy stone tiles into that space, one at a time. It's the work of a full day, and maybe just another exercise in futility, if whatever is back there is something important enough to also keep. Which is why I end up just stepping over and around the sharp, hard corners of the stacked tiles. Carefully, because if I dislodge them, I could break an ankle. Still, in the short term, it's simpler. It's what I can do, on my own.

There's just enough room between things to slip over behind the shrouded Buick, where there's a narrow strip of exposed cement floor. From there I can still get to the overhead shelves, or the most recent half dozen storage cubes balanced on the boxed appliances Jandine accumulated. I hadn't known where else to put the cubes, on the day I brought them here, after she died, and they're still full of her clothes.

I have a feeling that the expensive HEPA units Jandine ordered from QVC back in the nineties might be among those unopened boxes of appliances, as if the movers might have consolidated like with like, approximately. But once I pull the likeliest-looking box loose, I can see from the label on the vintage box that it's an old tabletop fan from the farm. Since I can't shove it back into place, I have to leave it on a pile of black trash bags full of blankets, or bedding, or who knows what. Sidenote: I wish I'd known to use clear storage bags and clear plastic totes to pack up the Tacoma house, instead of the opaque cardboard and plastic ones that now fill the built-in floor-to-ceiling shelves on all three walls of the garage. I'll eventually have to drag each one of them out to the patio, just to see what's inside.

Is it possible to have too much storage space? The original owners of every end unit like mine got to choose between a fireplace downstairs or an extra closet upstairs, where the chimney would have been. My house has the extra closet.

Pepper barks behind the patio wall next door. A plane

shakes the sky, and then the contents of the garage vibrate all around me.

Somewhere close by, under the shelves or behind the piled boxes, there's a heavy-duty storage tote full of Jandine's jewelry; so much yellow gold and cubic zirconia, so many birthstones and other gemstones. There are years of gifts from Terry. Some silver from the mine where Jacob and Ritchie worked when she was little. I'm pretty sure her wedding ring is in there. The first one. I'll move her jewelry indoors when it turns up, probably one freezer bag at a time, but I don't know what I'll do with it after that. There's no rush. Out of everything here, Jandine's jewelry is the least likely to be damaged in the heat, the most likely to look exactly the same in a hundred years as it did when the movers put it wherever they put it, and it's probably slightly safer out here than in the house, since no burglar is going to dig into a Jenga pile of new but outdated smoothie makers and low-fat sandwich grills, multipurpose choppers, handheld mixers, and so many waffle irons. But I'll still have to unpack each of them, at some point, before getting rid of them, because Jandine hid cash and other valuables in so many places.

Sometimes I find boxes she packed herself, toward the end. Even a box full of forks and magazines feels like a relic of her life and a schematic of the day it was taped shut. Today I open one that holds half a dozen hairbrushes, which I'm happy to donate, until I realize how many loose strands of her hair are tangled in the bristles. And something else rolls in the bottom of the box: an old Revlon lipstick. A familiar dark-green tube that I once believed was real jade when, on cold windy days, if she couldn't find the ChapStick in her purse, Jandine would stop in overcast parking lots to gently tilt my face up, and dab just a little of this or some other lipstick from her purse onto my lips. *Do this*, she'd say, pressing her own together.

I don't know why she kept this tube with nothing left inside, when even the name of the color is worn away. But I'll keep it, too, because otherwise it's just another piece of trash in a landfill. This pretty thing, that lightly touched my mother's face, when she lived.

I will need to change everything now. Won't I?

I will have to let so much go.

Including the metal fan from the farm. I know it will find itself in a retro room soon enough, in some other house, maybe full of other vintage treasures. But it's hard to add it to the bag of donations in my car, knowing that a stranger will probably just throw away this original box whose corners Tineke so carefully reinforced with strapping tape over the years, probably as they boxed it up for storage in winter.

The ephemera is the hardest to part with. Because nobody else will want it. I make the decision, though. And then I've had enough for one evening.

Chapter Twenty

When I wake up on my own before the alarm I sometimes find myself in a moment of complete silence, too complete to be real. Because the faint ringing in my left ear that I've had forever isn't there. Then gradually—I say gradually even though it happens quickly—the sound of the world returns. The sound of muffled heavy equipment. It must be the water company getting started at the far end of the alley, cutting down through the new asphalt again for yet another wasteful broken sprinkler pipe. I can almost feel the vibration underfoot when I put my feet on the floor; I hope I didn't miss a note from the HOA to move my car to the parking lot or else be boxed in.

There are so many rules, so many instructions that half the time I don't even know I'm breaking.

From my big bedroom window overlooking the alley I see nothing going on, and from the guest room window there's nothing out front, either. I can feel it, through my bare feet, though it's not exactly loud. It's not coming from Paloma's place next door, I don't think. Would a TV even carry like that? Downstairs my front door is still bolted, the chain still in place, and nothing looks out of place in the living room, and the patio door is locked, too.

I guess I thought it might conceivably have been Jeff, down here listening to something on headphones loud enough to carry . . . but that's ridiculous. He doesn't have a key at the moment.

There's nothing unusual in the kitchen, except the old fan whirring quietly on the counter. Which is wrong—I did unpack it, just to see it again, but I turned it off last night. I would never leave that thing running, for fear of Jasper getting clipped or cut. And for fear of the old wiring. I was sure I had left it unplugged, but it's definitely on now, and stepping into the kitchen is like walking into a convergence zone, with the whirring fan blades in the center, pulling in other sounds from the air-conditioning, from the airstones in the aquariums . . . There's a weird echo in the kitchen that makes the fillings in my teeth vibrate as soon as I step onto the tile floor.

I turn the fan off and as the blades slow down suddenly everything I could feel hanging in the air falls apart so abruptly that I look to the floor half expecting to see something hazy settling, like dust. But there's nothing. Just the sound of Jasper's water fountain, a faint shushing that rises and falls as she leans in to drink copiously.

In the silence after, I feel like there's something obvious I'm missing.

And now I'm going to have to check the whole house, to restore my peace of mind: It's something I used to have to do when I first moved out of Terry's house in college, when I realized I could see into all the corners of my various dorm rooms and later apartments whenever I wanted to, if I felt uneasy. I rarely do this anymore. But if ever I feel compelled to make sure I'm in the house alone I start from the blindest corner, working outward, so that if something's here, or someone's hiding, they'll be swept out, instead of being pushed deeper into the house.

I'm sure there's no intruder hiding in any of the closets, or behind the shower curtains, or under the beds or behind any doors but I check under the dining room table anyway. I open and check the seldom-used powder room/guest bathroom, and the closet under the stairs, because if you're going to bother to check at all then you have to check everywhere, otherwise later, in some quiet moment, you'll start thinking about the places you missed. Behind the couch, against the wall, where no adult human could reasonably squeeze, but that doesn't matter. Under the couch, under the kitchen sink, because the thought of someone folding up to fit into any of those increasingly unlikely spaces carries its own horror, that I will nonetheless have to treat as possible, otherwise, again, I will not be able to sleep tonight, hours from now, lying in bed, when I think:

Yes, but did I look under the bathroom sink? Did I look in the kitchen cupboards, which are not really big enough, but then again, what if? *What if?*

I do all of that and then I remember to take my morning Adderall. I should have taken it first, before doing anything else. I know it's important. And yet I can still be distracted and forget about it, so easily.

I delete emails to the editor while waiting for the tea kettle to boil. Delete, delete, delete. When I hear the kettle in the other room shut itself off I see movement from the corner of my eye—something about the size and color of a modest green pumpkin seed pops into the air above the sixty-gallon fish tank and careens diagonally across the ceiling of the living room—but of course that's impossible. When I check the shadows under the potted majesty palm where I saw it land there's a gleam in the loose soil. Bronze, hard shelled. A beetle, maybe? A June bug? A quick moment later there's just a small rolling under the crumbling surface, bright, dark, then nothing.

And then at midmorning I leave my desk to walk across the grass to check the mail, where I discover a postcard reminder that I'm now two years overdue to have my eyes checked. I call the office as I walk back to my door, instead of putting it off. Which is another thing I wish I'd always known to do. Because just getting myself onto the appointment calendar is a minor victory.

I describe the movements across the ceiling.

"The doctor's going to want to take a look at that right away," the receptionist says. Which means I'll have to pay for an exam without dilation, because there's nobody handy to drive me home after. "Hold a moment?" she says.

When she comes back, she says it again; yes, if possible, I should come in today.

I can't settle down anyway. So yes, I'll come today, and thanks very much.

While updating my patient forms I let them know about Jandine, so that they can update her file. I mean, close her file. Too many reminder cards still arrive for her, and the only one I'm sure I did respond to was the summons for jury duty.

"Any flashes of light?" the doctor says.

"Some," I admit. "In the lower left. Some in the upper right."

She looks into my eyes.

"Good news," she says. "Your retinas look fine."

No wonder the receptionist made room to see me so quickly, if the flash on the ceiling might have sounded like a detaching retina.

"Welcome to midlife," the doctor says, and points to a wall chart to illustrate how the fluid in my eye was doing what they all do when the inner eyeball starts to lose volume and sag away from the outer.

"That's the good news?" I say.

"It's not uncommon," she says.

The anatomical chart on her wall shows a cross section of the brain, including a shape like a stylized Egyptian eye right in the middle under the corpus callosum. A hieroglyphic like that in the midbrain can't be an accident, can it? We all have retinal cells buried deep inside the skull, vestigial light-sensing cells that never see the light of day—unless you're a lizard with a literal third eye covered by a scale, under which those extra retinal cells are still actively tracking sunlight. Lizards, and some bony fish. Or so I've read about.

"Any other questions I can answer?" she says at the end.

I would love to know if the types of bony fish with vestigial third eyes might possibly include small armored catfish like my little bronze corydoras. They're completely armored; does that count? If the internet holds an answer to this question, I haven't found the right combination of search terms to find it. But I can't think of the right way to phrase it.

Instead, I say, "How high does my blood pressure need to be to damage my eyes?"

"How high is it?" she says.

I read the numbers to her from the notes I keep in my phone; she says that if I have any more light flashes, she'll give me a referral to a retinal specialist. A new one, because Jandine's retinal specialist has retired.

"I'm sorry to hear about your mom," she says, before leaving the exam room.

"Thanks," I say, but then my throat squeezes shut and I can't continue.

"My mother died a few years ago," she says. "But when her Christmas cactus bloomed this year, my first thought was to call her. It's not like I ever forget she's gone. The whole reason I have her cactus is that she's gone. But I still have those automatic thoughts."

I'm nodding, and I'd like to say that I know what she means. But I can't speak because of the lump in my throat.

On the way home I pass bright-green signs for an estate sale to be held this weekend. And that's the way of it. Always a tide of people coming, and a different tide of people going out, leaving so much behind.

Chapter Twenty-One

The heat catches me by surprise, as it does every year, and suddenly I want to finish a project I set aside last summer: drilling a hole in the side of a mini refrigerator (unplugged, yes) to pass a silicone line of tubing through it, curling the excess length on the shelf inside, and then anchoring both ends of the tube inside the big tank, with one end attached to a pump in order to circulate aquarium water out of the tank to be cooled inside the fridge before it's returned to the tank, to bring the water temp down. I run the air-conditioning in summer, of course, but all my generations of bronze catfish seem to feel the fluctuations. And I've read that it's the fluctuations that can do them harm. But I can't justify buying the kind of chiller that reef-tank keepers use to preserve their delicate saltwater fish, and anyway I have too many tanks for a single chiller of that type. If it works, I can add lines in and out from every tank, adding more holes in the sides or the top as needed. Avoiding the coolant, of course, and the wiring.

And then it's not that I want to keep the fan from the farm, it's more the question of whether or not I could put a rubber mat underneath to absorb some of the vibration. The question is a good enough reason to leave the house, even just briefly, to check the surplus store, where I don't find a mat but I do find a roll of spongy underlayment that's worth a try. The girl at the register is calculating a discount for somebody by hand with a calculator. I would freeze up, if I had to do that, especially with people waiting in line.

I should probably put the underlayment back and just go home to finish the next day's dispatch. I should have sent it before leaving the house.

The man who talked to Jandine is here again, hanging around by the register—how long ago was that? Years ago, by now. He looks thinner. Older. Though I can't tell how old he is. Only that I'm closer in age to him than I am to the girl at the register, which means we're both from a time of shared inconveniences, from an analog world, where you wait in lines when delays pop up in your path. Maybe he works here. Volunteers here.

I miss the seventies. I've been thinking this a lot, lately, though I don't really know if it's true.

He points at the items I'm waiting to pay for, and says, as if we'd been having a conversation, "Yep, nobody can justify shopping like women can . . ."

What is it, exactly, that I think I miss about that older world? When it was standard to have to listen to slightly greasy male blowhards? And to be nice, perpetually. Jandine would have touched his shoulder and invited out the best in him. I doubt I ever saw someone part from her company feeling worse. How many people can you say that about.

I say, to him, "My mother would have agreed with you there."

For some reason, he drops a bit of the bullshitty demeanor, and says, "You know what, I come here a lot, too. Can I tell you what I found here once? I found two brand-new stair lifts, right over there, lying under some boxes of Pergo. You know, the rail and motorized seat you can install in a stairway to help seniors or anybody with limited mobility. They're safer. They prevent falls."

"Good find," I say, though I know absolutely nothing about stair lifts.

He says, "They were brand-new, and you know, those things can cost around six thousand dollars apiece. Apiece! One of them wasn't even opened. I asked how much they were and the guy here that day told me three hundred bucks."

Now he's animated from within, and I think, Maybe you just genuinely never learned how to talk to people. To women. So maybe it's okay that you keep trying, even though the effort makes you weird and abrasive?

He says, "I bought both, took them home, and my wife sold them on eBay for fifteen hundred dollars each. Local pickup only."

"That's great," I say, meaning it.

"She did the computer part," he says. "She made that part look easy."

"Were they heavy?" I say.

"Pretty heavy," he says. And falls quiet.

"Well, that was a good catch," I say. "That's the fun of it."

"That's right," he says.

I notice then that he doesn't have anything in his hands to purchase.

"Are you waiting with a question—you can go ahead of me," I say.

"You go ahead," he says, "I'm just waiting for somebody to help me load an oven. Listen to this," he says. "It's a fifteen-hundred-dollar range, brand-new, but the ceramic cooktop is cracked so I'm getting it here for fifty dollars. I'll get a new cooktop for a hundred bucks, put it in, good as new."

"Is a ceramic top hard to replace?" I ask.

He wiggles a hand in the air, and I'm not sure I'd want to be the neighbor sleeping next door to a house full of his replacement wiring. I don't mess with the electrical DIY projects. It would be too easy to electrocute myself whereas an average plumbing fuckup most likely can't kill me.

"I used to flip houses," he says. "Now, it's kind of a hobby."

I'm suddenly jealous; I wish I could spend my time doing that. Or maybe I just like the idea, from a distance.

"Well, if it keeps you out of trouble," I say, channeling Jandine. But did that sound condescending?

"That's right," he says. "It's good to stay busy."

And then I feel the crushing burden of the need to stay busy. To do something that adds up to something, even if in the end it adds up to nothing. And I think, silently, I hope you don't get sick, I hope your wife doesn't get sick, I hope you get to keep doing what you're doing forever if you like doing it. Even though I never expect to see you again. Maybe that was the real thing, with Jandine: She had endless opportunities to feel good about people without the burden or responsibility of really knowing them.

"See you around," he says, after my turn at the register.

Surprisingly, I do see him around. Right here, in my own complex, and I cringe a little when I see him in the alley with the woman I assume is his wife. They stop for a word with Paloma, then keep going.

"Jesus, no," says Paloma, "Stacia's not his wife, don't be disgusting. He's her son. He's got a unit over by hers. You never saw TK before? Usually he comes and goes, but this time he'll be here for a while. Doing handyman work. He and his wife were snowbirds, they drove from Idaho every year." She watches them go. "I can see how you might not recognize him," she says. "He's lost, like, thirty pounds."

I don't want to know any more. But I hear myself saying, "Is he sick?"

"Yeah," she says. "And a widower now."

I sigh.

"She was nice," says Paloma. "One of those things. One minute she's fine. Then she stands up and blows an artery and that's it. Nothing anybody could have done."

TK and his mother turn the corner, out of sight.

"Did she know he was sick?" I ask.

"She died before he got sick," says Paloma.

"That's good," I say. "At least she wasn't worried about him at the end. And he doesn't have to wonder now if his illness was causing her any extra stress."

"I guess that's one way to look at it," says Paloma. "Okay now, go away, sweet pea, you're depressing me."

"I'm depressing you?" I say. "Are you serious?"

She just pats my arm in a way that I guess seems sincere before taking her little dog inside.

Chapter Twenty-Two

The desert sky is amber. Smooth and hard as ceramic glaze.

Today's high: 112. A dry heat.

Every afternoon I collect the mail, always taking the same route to the community mailboxes, always keeping to the path in case of superheated dog shit hiding in the grass; that's a mistake you don't step in twice. The cicadas move as a group, from tree to tree, and today they're drilling into the air from the big mimosa tree by my front door. As I pass they all, to a one, fall silent.

There's no sign of Paloma, who sometimes holds court outside in the late afternoons. I see a young couple floating together in the shallow end of the pool, the woman holding a baby steady in a tiny inflatable ring. And one of the pretty young women who come and go at all hours, propped in a chaise longue, reading. For a moment I feel her gaze on me rather than on the book in front of her, and then her face dips back down to the page. I remember living like that. Shift work, maybe. Idle afternoon hours. Sunlight, a book, and all the time in the world.

A few years ago, on a day like today, I might have been helping Jandine down the same broad steps, holding her hand for balance as we descended into the shallow end of the pool.

The mother adjusts a small sun hat to better cover the baby's face. The young woman with the book is watching me again, and I look away from all of them.

A long time ago I must have read somewhere that our brains record every moment of our lives, storing memories we're not aware of in such high definition that they include details we didn't notice at the time, if we could just access them. Probably in Ritchie's pop-science books. And I still, in some way, believe it's all there. And that the right stimulus—maybe the light touch of a faintly electrified probe—could let you walk through any moment of the past all over again.

Without an index, though. So it would be like spinning a roulette wheel, and everybody knows roulette is the worst odds in the house.

At the row of steel-reinforced mailboxes I hear a small sound close behind me—it's TK, but I jump anyway, a reflex. He doesn't look like the HOA handyman right now, more like an off-duty semiretired neighbor in a microfiber guayabera shirt. He shrugs one shoulder up toward his face in a shorthand acknowledgment of not being able to lift away his mirrored sunglasses—Paloma probably told him that mirrored glasses give me the creeps. But in fairness I said that before I knew about his light sensitivity. His headaches and other medical issues that Paloma says are not exactly cancer, which is more than enough detail to pass along to me, a stranger.

He's holding something awkwardly but carefully in front of his chest.

"Mandy," he says, "I'm really glad to see you." He lifts his closed hands. There's a flicker behind the mirrored lenses as he blinks.

"Look," he says. He parts his hands and something quivers between them—he's got a baby bird, greasy and out of the nest too early. When it sees us it opens its mouth wide, the fragile head tipping backward under the weight of an oversize beak.

"I think it's hungry," he says. "Is it hungry?"

"It's a starling," I say. "It looks hungry to me."

"I found it right in front of your place," he says, letting his hands close gently. "I guess it fell out of the *pine tree.*" We both know this means it fell from a nest in the eaves over my front windows where he's technically supposed to exterminate everything, per the HOA rules, since the association owns the roofs that connect all the town houses. Ordinarily no bees, no birds, no nothing is allowed to live up there in peace, but I noticed that instead of clearing out that area he just keeps spraying this year's nesting-season droppings off my window screens. Not as a favor to me, I'm sure, but so that Paloma won't tell him to destroy the nests.

"Paloma saw me with it just now," he says. "She told me to kill it. But she knows I can't do that."

I groan, inwardly. Of course I'll take the bird somewhere, that's not the problem, I just don't want to be complicit with him about anything. That's why I haven't remarked on him spraying the window screens. I haven't thanked him. Because he's weird in the way of a friendly neighbor who might even so be the first to call the tow truck if your car is briefly parked where it shouldn't be. He lives in an end unit like I do, and over his slump-stone wall I've seen that where I hang tomato planters he's got what appears to be a poison trap for wasps. I'm afraid of wasps—but wasps are also the world's babies. That's the hard part of it all.

There's a troubling smell over there. It must be the lure in the trap. A smell like rotting meat, and this somehow passes for normal.

"Put it in here," I say, taking off my sun hat so that he can set the bird in carefully. Because, as Jandine would have said, you can always help the fellow creature right in front of you. He does and then lifts his sunglasses and wipes his forehead with his forearm, and I resist the urge to tell him to go wash his hands before touching his face. Out over the grass behind him I can see two, then three hummingbirds hovering in the sultry air around the silk tree. The HOA forbids bird feeders. Too messy. But because my hidden hummingbird feeder is disguised in a hanging planter, only the hummers know where to find it.

My focus is waning, after a bad day yesterday, and bad sleep last night. I say, "The veterinary hospital on Flamingo can send it to a wildlife rehab."

He puts his sunglasses back on, and says, "That's perfect. Thanks."

"No problem," I say, and turn away.

"Wait," he says, "Will you have to pay—do you need money?" He's reaching for his wallet and suddenly my eyes are stinging, not because he wants to save the little bird now scrabbling at my fingers, but because it's so much like what Jandine inexplicably started to say again in the months before she died, falling into some partial memory loop from long ago when I was a teenager and she would stop me on my way out of the house. Standing in the doorway of her room at memory care, she would reach for a purse she hadn't carried in years. *Do you need money? Here, wait, let me give you something—take five dollars, put it in the gas tank.*

I say, "They appreciate a donation, but it's voluntary."

"Here," he says, "I'm happy to pay," and he tucks some bills under the hat.

"Go swimming or something!" I say, because I have to leave now to catch the clinic before they close.

I don't look back until I am unlocking my door with one hand and stepping into my house, careful not to crush the hat. TK is gone, but as I lock the door behind me it seems again as though the pretty girl in the pool area is tilting her face in my direction.

On my way back from the veterinary clinic, I pass a gas station where I remember filling up the car with Jandine in her early days here; I remember, suddenly, that while I was paying at the cashier's window, I turned back to find her trying to pay at the pump with some card from her wallet. Any card. Probably a players-club loyalty card from a casino, and in any case, no longer a credit card. It's understandable. The force of habit.

Let me get it, she had said, laughing, even though I had told her to stay in the car, please. Back when I thought it worked that way.

What if she'd gotten out and stepped in front of a car? Gotten hurt, somehow? Anything could have happened to her then. I was probably impatient, exasperated, worried. When all she wanted to do was to help. To fill the tank because, as she said, I was always the one who had to drive. Leaving out all the years in which she of course did all the driving first.

Later I see TK alone in the pool area after dusk, lining up the chaise longues. Emptying the coffee can that the die-hard smokers keep in one corner as an ashtray. I'm not watching on purpose, but I think he glances in my direction more than once, probably expecting an update about the bird; I doubt it will survive, but who needs confirmation of a thing like that.

Chapter Twenty-Three

The washing machine has a mildew smell from last night's laundry, which I accidentally left sitting in the stiflingly hot uninsulated garage. So I add more Dr. Bronner's Sal Suds and run another cycle, and maybe all of this is my first mistake of the day. Because failing to take my morning pills before trying anything else leads inevitably to destruction.

When the wash cycle ends I'm somehow still in the garage, still looking through the stackable storage cubes that have been sitting here since the day I packed up Jandine's room at memory care. I still haven't managed to donate her soft clothes, or her bright-teal bedding. I kept that as a consistent color for her sheets and blankets; I thought it might make the bed recognizable for her, even if the place felt unfamiliar.

I don't know why I keep expecting this process to get any easier.

There are half a dozen hotel-sized bottles of shampoo among her things. Sweet and light. Provided by the hospice nurses. They're in a plastic bag that I cannot bring myself to open, because I can tell they still smell of orange blossoms and baby powder. So instead I lift her hot rollers and add them to the latest charity-donation bag. Not so long ago these rollers were ticking, expanding, warming up at memory care. I brought bars of the dark chocolate she liked, and we were watching TV in her room, black-and-white classics on a cable channel, Jandine humming, tapping her foot while I combed out her dark-blonde hair before rolling it up in sections. Dinah Shore. Peggy Lee. *You know all the words*, I say, *I'm impressed*.

Oh, she says, *let me tell you—*

I hear a rapping on my closed garage door, and TK's voice calling my name.

I hesitate before I push the button and see his shoes, his socks, his shorts, utility vest, etc., up to the mirrored sunglasses and cap. He takes off the sunglasses and stows them away in his pocket. I see how his clothes shift. He's lost weight even in the last few weeks. In morning sunlight he's got a faint line connecting his eyebrows; have I never seen him without one pair of glasses or another?

"Hey," he says. "Didn't you say you could use some help getting rid of things? Taking stuff to the Goodwill?"

I never said that. The garage is not yet in a state anyone can help me with. His eyes move over all the boxes; he's the type of person who will probably never find himself living in a mess like this. He must have heard from Paloma that I ought to clear a few things out. Of course. That makes sense. Now I'm sure she sent him. I might appreciate that, but it's still humiliating.

"Thanks," I say. "Maybe some other time."

He says, gesturing at the boxes, "Sentimental value. But it's surprising how much you can let go, when the time comes."

I say, "Yeah, I know. I'm still waiting for the right time to come."

He says, "I had to get rid of all my dad's things. He had so many old woodworking manuals, just dozens of them, full of corny jokes. What was I going to do with them?"

"I don't know," I say.

"People used to have less," he says. "It was simpler."

His eyes sweep to the back of my Subaru.

"Still got the sink out here?" he says.

I'd forgotten he was there at the surplus store when I bought it. Because when he's not here, he's there, hanging around. I can't help but pop the hatchback of my wagon and uncover the marvelously gleaming cast-iron kitchen sink: It's beautiful. It's also really heavy. I might do a lot of stupid things around the house by myself, but there's literally no way I can even make an attempt to move this without the assistance of at least one other person.

He whistles, but I can't tell whether he's just letting things seem like they matter, or whether he actually believes they do.

"Nice," he says. "Everything you need, already attached.

Do you want a hand getting it into the house? I can help with that."

Bless him, I guess. But I am not in the habit of letting anybody into the house, and it would take time to clear the way now. Also, there may be an HOA issue over the number of my fish tanks inside, and I don't want to hear about it later. Though maybe if he just sees the kitchen, and doesn't see the living room . . . maybe I can figure that part out.

I say, "Thanks. Maybe another time. Thanks."

"Okey doke," he says. "Well. I'm looking at a surgical procedure sometime soon, so let's see if we can't get that sink moved before I'm off my feet for a little while."

"Thanks," I say. I feel awkward. "I know you have people, but if there's anything I can do."

He nods. Waits a beat. "Any word on the little guy?" he says. "That little bird?"

"No," I say, against a rapid flutter in my ears like a small separate heartbeat hanging in the air behind me. My pulse reacting, because the odds against that bird are so high that when they asked me if I wanted a postcard to let me know the outcome, as a token of thanks for the donation, I said no, no thanks. But today, I say, "The staff at the veterinary clinic seemed to think you found him in good time."

He nods again, and slips his sunglasses back on. He raps my car with his knuckles, and then he's off to the next stop on his circuit, giving a wordless thumbs-up as he goes.

It's hard to explain all the reasons I'm slow to donate everything without it sounding like a conversation you might have in line at a thrift store with a nice older lady in a gray sweater covered with cat hair who admires what's in your shopping basket, before mentioning that she's buying the blue candle in her basket because of the angel she sees attached to it. Agreeing with a thing like this in principle is easy, because there's so much more in heaven and earth, Horatio . . . And yet it's something different to stand in the daylight, two strangers looking at an actual stub of pale-blue wax. I understand this, even when it's my turn to play the part of the lady in the gray sweater.

A minor procedure, he said. But that's not how Paloma describes it.

"He's got a nonmalignant brain tumor," she said, "whatever that means."

I should take better care of myself. Everyone should. Even if it's impossible to change the path of whatever's coming for you.

Dear Editor, If I am legally blind can I still obtain a Nevada driver's license?

*Probably not, but you *can* get a state-issued Nevada ID card from the DMV without a vision test. Here's a tip: Go to the website to make an appointment in advance, to avoid waiting in long lines. ~~I did this when my mother needed a new ID, because by then she couldn't sit in a waiting room without getting agitated.~~ Remember that along with all the necessary documents, anyone applying for an ID card must be physically ~~and cognitively~~ able to sign their own name. ~~I didn't realize my mother couldn't sign her name anymore, or that I would know to put my hand over hers, so that the weight would help steady her hand. In the end she signed her name accurately but only because I knew the cursive loops of her signature by heart.~~*

I defrost a UFO in the microwave for lunch—that was Jandine's term for leftovers you don't recognize. An unidentified frozen object. Today's UFO is solid and gives me time to get a water sample from the betta sorority tank in the living room, but under the canopy I find neon-green scum gathered at the waterline. Bastard pollen again. I try to net it out while the beautiful, bad-tempered betta girls circle, expecting to be fed bloodworms, and Cupcake, the alpha female, watches for any chance to jump up and bite my wrist, my fingers. Because she's naughty. When she tries, dust scatters out of her cellophane-colored gills and glitters down through the water.

In the medium tank I find Goldie with his mouth to the

surface, gasping, and I don't know whether it's the pollen to blame or whether he's sick, but I have a two-gallon hospital tank running in the kitchen. I transfer him carefully, with a net and a bowl from the quarantine bucket of equipment I keep for when a fish gets sick. They always get sick suddenly. Their lives go by, so quickly. But maybe he just needs a break from the mulberry dust, or maybe he's just morbidly constipated, either of which is my fault—it's hard not to overfeed him, because he's the last of his cohort of five colorful male guppies who hustled together all day, every day, parting only to sleep at night in different favorite places. The other four are gone, but he still looks for them in the mornings. He needs companions and I'll get some—but right now the sight of Goldie panting in the water and the sound of Jasper's raspy breathing make me ashamed enough to go back out to the garage to make a better effort to find the air purifiers. If I don't find them today, then fuck it, I'll finance a really powerful big one and get rid of the others whenever they finally do turn up.

Again I lean into the shadows behind the shrouded Buick, this time reaching up to check a hanging shelf overhead. I'm squeezed into the narrow space between the driver's side door and the unstable ziggurat of storage cubes, one foot poised over an old wooden stool, and I think to myself explicitly: This is a bad idea. And then I put my foot down on the wooden stool anyway and it skids out from under me and disappears under the Buick.

I try to stop myself from falling but the silky car cover slips away like a tablecloth in a magic trick and I land hard on the cement floor. When I open my eyes I'm on my hands and knees, in the dark, behind the car, and everything around me is buzzing. I shift my weight; at least I didn't break my kneecaps. So that's good. And I didn't knock any teeth out. Also good. So I might be stupid, but today I'm also lucky.

As I slowly get to my feet I realize my palms are skinned and my knuckles are scraped, but neither look too bad in the shadows. Not until I flex my hands, and the scrapes abruptly fill with blood. Great: Keeping my hands entirely out of the tank water will be a huge hassle for a long time, but then I stop worrying about my hands as a new pain jolts up and down both legs.

In the half bathroom off the living room I shuck off my pants and find rows of welts rising under the skin on my legs. Above one knee there's a knot in the shape of a right angle from something I must have hit on the way down.

I can feel a headache starting and there's a ticking feeling inside one ear which is in itself not exactly painful yet. But it's a reasonable guess that any new ticking sound inside your head is not great news. I find the rubbing alcohol and start the tedious process of picking grit out of my skinned palms with tweezers. Best to get it over with, my grandfather would say, stopping to take a pocketknife out and carefully remove whatever splinter or foreign object I'd picked up. He would start with the magnifying lens, which he called the loupe, and he'd ask me, *Is that right there what you want to get rid of? Are you sure now? Because you know I can't put it back if you change your mind later. . . .*

That must be why, for years, I've half thought that to be looped in on something meant I would be made privy to some important detail, about which my opinion mattered. Which seems like it should be more exciting than being added to an email thread.

An hour or two later I finish the bowl of cold microwaved leftovers at my desk. That UFO was a dud. Just a big lump of acorn squash. Did I really cook this, at some point, and freeze it? My hands are so jangled that I drop the bowl on my way back down the stairs.

I'm grateful Jandine didn't remember the times she fell. Grateful for the small shitty mercy that the more her nerves and sense of balance betrayed her, the less she seemed to feel the injuries afterward. I had hoped that at memory care she would be safe, and watched over. But those occasional falls were hard to prevent. Sometimes she would smile across the breakfast table at memory care with a bruised eye socket the color of an overripe plum, fading backward into green for a week or two, and even though she didn't seem to notice her own reflection, in the last year of her life I took the wall mirror away so that she wouldn't catch a glimpse. The mirror is still hanging on the far wall of my kitchen, tilted up at the ceiling. Just one more among the many things I intend to donate back to charity, sometime soon.

Chapter Twenty-Four

I can't find a position in the office chair at my desk that doesn't aggravate the bruises on my legs, and I hate the feeling of scrapes on my hands reopening as I type. By late afternoon I'm back out in the garage, wanting to get rid of everything I see, including fallen boxes I didn't know I'd pulled down with me. One is so heavy that I couldn't shove it back up to the shelf even if I wanted to, so I drag it through the patio to the kitchen and leave it next to the latest pile of donations, which now includes the old fan. Of course I'm going to look inside first, but I like seeing it piled near the trash because whatever's inside tried to break my neck.

I've been saving a documentary about the Great Sphinx of Giza to watch, but Jasper keeps returning to the foot of the stairs, yowling up into the void. The vet says her thyroid levels are a little low, and older cats just do this sometimes, and her hearing isn't good, and cats can get dementia, too, and hearing loss and dementia go together, just like they do for people. And as the world recedes, they feel stranded.

Jasper is still yowling so I pause the documentary to bring her to the couch, but a moment later she runs to the kitchen to dig her soft little claws into the cardboard box. It probably smells like the Tacoma house. I rewind the documentary and listen again: the Sphinx is not a built thing. Solid stone in that place was cut away to reveal it. The Great Sphinx is living rock, still attached to the ground, which is why it wicks groundwater up into itself, which causes it to deteriorate.

After it's over, I get up to address the box that Jasper keeps returning to. When I cut the tape there's a round stamp on an inner flap listing the kind of freight-class and edge-crush info that Terry would have understood. It's a nice box, actually. Inside I see layers of Bubble Wrap around what look to be photo albums?

No, unfortunately. Not photo albums. Somebody's old stamp

albums, maybe. As I'm pulling the wrapping away, in a blinding flash of the obvious I suddenly recognize my collection of *Man, Myth & Magic* magazines, in a set of binders designed to transform all the individual issues, over a hundred of them, into a fully illustrated encyclopedia of this mysterious world.

I'd taken it so seriously, then. Carefully reading each issue, and then rereading it, until whenever I might get the next issue. I'd mailed away for the binders, but even though the instructions explicitly said to remove the covers of the issues before assembling them I didn't, because I didn't want to mutilate them. When I open the top binder now I see the familiar cover of the very first issue, looking up at me, a blue background with the words *Man, Myth & Magic* emblazoned above a grinning face painted by Austin Osman Spare. It's so familiar—so eerily alive that I don't understand how I didn't always know it was there, all these years.

I turn the pages, reminding myself of the contents, from Abbots Bromley through to Astrology but I stop when I get to the start of the second issue because something doesn't look right, and doesn't feel right. I thought I remembered the back covers having perforated subscription cards to detach and mail in, but there are no perforations on these, just dashed lines showing where to use scissors to cut a subscription form out. But we'd been sitting at the kitchen table. I had carefully detached the subscription card while Jandine painted her short neat fingernails with mauve polish. She then handled the card carefully, noting the preprinted address on the other side, somewhere in the UK, and I remember this, but the small print here says to mail payment to an address in New York.

I unwrap and look into the other binders, but only half the issues seem to be here. I had them all, though. Didn't I?

Are these not mine?

I feel the way I've sometimes thought my mother must have felt, early on. It must have happened to her again and again, and she probably didn't tell anyone. They come and go quickly, those unsettling moments. When you're sure of something, but then realize you must be wrong. There's an explanation of sorts on the last page of what's here, the inside back cover of part fifty-six:

> We regret that weekly sales of *Man, Myth and Magic* have declined to a level where we cannot continue weekly newsstand or subscription distribution.
>
> Recognizing that this will disappoint our readers, we have made arrangements whereby you may purchase the remaining 56 parts of the encyclopedia in the form of 13 fully bound book volumes, each containing 140 pages. We are pleased to be able to offer these bound volumes to you at a special price of $39.00 inclusive of shipping and handling.
>
> To apply please complete the form below, detached, and send it with your remittance to:
>
> Man, Myth Mag.
6 Commercial St.,
Hicksville, New York 11801
>
> As stock of bound volumes are limited we suggest you apply quickly.

I remember now that I had flipped back and forth between that note on the last page and the boilerplate inside the front cover of this and every other issue, opposite the bios from contributing historians, journalists, professors, and experts, with author portraits of white men and occasionally a white lady or two. There was always a binder in the boilerplate, stamped with gold, and a *foundation reader subscription offer*, good for twelve issues, which hadn't made sense to me when there were a hundred more to collect and I wanted them all. I wanted the binders, though, and I'd been saving up. I had $10.75 tucked away in my combination safe by the time the end came. I knew I wouldn't be able to get the rest of the money together before the limited stock disappeared. I don't know why I didn't ask for help or barter against future birthday and holiday presents. Or how I put it out of my mind, that these issues had been abruptly cut off at issue 56 out of 112, the full set sliced right in half.

But why are these binders made of red plastic? I think I'd been expecting brown binders, appropriate to a personal library, and I'm about to lose a few hours, a few days, maybe more than that looking online, trying to remember why things look so different now than they do in memory.

I had been so disappointed. I remember that now.

I'm turning slowly through the pages when I catch a smell, almost nice, but not entirely nice. It's not perfume, but it reminds me of the Christian Dior perfume I loved later, years after I had loved these magazines; maybe the pages got spritzed and these were old molecules, degrading in contact with the paper. That bottle had been beautiful, a deep blackish purple, and heavy in the hand, with the name, Poison, in gold letters. I'd loved it partly for that weight in the hand, and that color. And the name. The last time I saw it at a perfume counter, years ago, the bottle seemed the same, but the formula inside was not.

These pages have been sealed away in darkness for a long time, and now that they're open and exposed to the air their faintly liquor-like odor is changing, expanding, like ripe plums in the hold of a wooden boat after you lift the hatch. Or the almost floral odor lifting from a bucket of opaque aquarium water after I swish a dirty filter, a smell of algae that stays on my hands for a day or two, no matter how much I wash them.

The air-conditioning unit overhead somewhere on the roof kicks on, just like it does a hundred times every day all summer. The cold hits the back of my neck like a metal pin piercing the base of my skull so precisely that it doesn't even hurt. But I'm queasy, and dizzy, and my skin goes instantly into a cold sweat.

I want to put the binder back into the box and get out of the path of the cold air. But when I move my head I hear and feel a loud crack, too much pressure on some small component that's been keeping my skull attached to my spine this whole time. It makes my ears ring, with a set of loud, ascending tones that feel almost electronic, and that look like lines of light over the floor of the living room, stopping at the baseboards and sinking like water at the edges of an infinity pool. Like the old bright opening credits of some familiar show that I can't identify, disappearing under the bottom of the screen. The smell from the binders is too much now. I close my eyes, and I'm slow to open them because I'm pretty sure I'm about to discover that I just had an aneurysm and possibly that I'm dead.

When I do look around, the lamps in the living room seem dim. In fact everything looks more amber than it should. My pupils look even in the mirror over the sink in the guest bathroom. But the burnish is persistent over everything, like the golden tint on a pair of warm-brown sunglasses. Easy, actually. Comfortable. Too comfortable.

Fucking hell.

I drag the box of magazines out to the patio even though my legs hurt, even though the scrapes on my hands crack open around the healing edges. I leave the binders splayed open in a fresh-air quarantine against whatever mild hallucinogenic mold I just inhaled and whatever else is in there with it. The spores and face huggers and other contaminants that should be easy to prevent, if I could just exercise a little common sense.

Late that night I wake to the sound of the kitchen window screens shifting in their frames and the patio wind chimes touching. The house is quiet, the TV off, having gone into power-saving mode. I take Jasper upstairs with me in the dark to the window in the big bedroom, where I can look down through the mesh patio sun cover to see if I'm imagining it, or whether a prowler really has come over the wall to quietly pry at the back door. I pick up the big flashlight I keep by the bed, plenty heavy enough to tear through the sun fabric and do some real damage to anyone below. The light is on down there, triggered by the motion sensor. The hanging plants rock in a warm breeze, and the wind chimes are moving softly, but there's nothing strange, nothing but the plants moving, and the cardboard box with the open red binders and all the pages fluttering back and forth, back and forth, as yesterday's heat rises from the cement to set everything in motion.

Chapter Twenty-Five

I wake up wondering whether the MM&M issues were even still available on newsstands when I first found out about them; the internet says I wasn't old enough to be getting them in real time. So the notice about ordering those complete sets must have already been old, the magazine already discontinued in the US before the night Jandine brought me the first one. She must have found them somewhere—I don't know—a head shop? A crystal shop? The university was right there in town, after all, and Fairhaven College was pretty hip. I genuinely remember a first-grade field trip to an art building on campus some early June afternoon, before we moved to Tacoma. The grass was green and glorious, the trees in bloom—ornamental plum trees? We walked through an exhibit of papier-mâché statues and paintings that included at least a couple of nudes with pubic hair that hung like clusters of grapes right at eye level for a class of seven-year-olds. I'm sure there were places to buy water pipes, and incense, and surely occulture-related books and magazines. She may have bought a big stack of them someplace. Or maybe they'd come from Ritchie to begin with. They were probably doled out to me, already a foregone conclusion that the set would never be completed the way I expected, and I never could have been a foundation member, even though the offer had seemed ironclad and reliable in perpetuity. Like a contract to be cryogenically frozen after your death, and looked after, until a future when old age would eventually be cured.

I don't realize there's a problem with my ear until I try to sit up in bed.

By the time I get to the bathroom it feels so much like there's a moth fluttering against my eardrum that I try to check with two mirrors angled to reflect each other, but I have to give up because the effort makes me dizzy. I call the ENT doctor's office but the soonest they can squeeze me in is over a week out. I'm dismayed—but I'll take it, I'll take the appointment, I find my insurance card, I read out the updated number, and so on. Because I can exert focus when necessary.

Amazing, that I was still in their system. The way old information hangs around like that.

By midmorning I'm squinting at the computer monitor and so distracted that I can barely work. If this gets any worse I'm afraid I won't be able to drive.

"Please," I say on the phone when I call the ENT's office again. "Is there a cancellation list? Can I be added to that?"

The receptionist gives me the admonition about seeking emergency care if in fact this is an emergency, which I don't interrupt because obviously that would be counterproductive but the words do tumble out of my mouth and whatever I say about a foreign object seems to strike the right balance between fitting me in versus advising me to hang up and seek help at the nearest emergency room.

"Let's see," says the receptionist, typing. "Doctor likes to keep a few spots open . . . Can you come in early Thursday morning?"

In the intervening days my ear ticks almost constantly, but irregularly, and it's maddening. Antihistamines don't seem to help and neither does a neti pot, nor steam. Nor a beeswax ear candle, and neither does a silicone suction bulb for pulling mucus from a baby's nose, the kind I get at the dollar store and use to get suction started in the gravel vacuum tubes when I clean the bottoms of the tanks. Nothing helps. I pinch my nose like I'm adjusting my ears on an airplane and feel pressure in the ducts of my eyes, which is repulsive, but nothing changes the twitching, echoing fullness in my ear.

Maybe I did bump my head?

Maybe dust from the box caused a reaction?

It could be anything; we have no idea of what's swirling

around us, all the time. I hate the garage and everything in it. I'll end up hating the house and hating myself. I don't mean that. But also I do mean it, completely, and I also hate the mattress, the pillow, all of it. Everything. I look up new mattresses online and then I look up auditory nerve spasms, eustachian tube dysfunction, even the possibility of insect larvae trapped in ear canals. Which is a mistake leading to search results that can't be unseen. The only thing that makes me feel a little better is rewatching the moment in the M. Night Shyamalan movie when a sinister breeze ripples through a park and a lady on a bench draws a long hairpin ominously out of her chignon. Because that's how it feels: The moment of the last straw is approaching, and she's going to stab herself, or someone, or something, and whatever she'll do next, I get it and I could also be driven to stab myself in the ear. I can live around a lot of distractions, and most of them won't kill me, but this is different. This is physically inside my head, and already, in only one day, or two days, however long it's been, I would do almost anything to make the trembling stop.

After he examines me, the ear doctor smiles and says, "Your ear trouble will go away on its own when the weather changes."

"Oh my god," I say; I'm clutching the paper on the exam table. So that I don't lose my mind here. "Please. I haven't slept in three days."

He says, "Antihistamines will help with that."

I want to keep this exchange light because respectfully I know how trivial a flutter probably sounds in the grand scheme of maladies, and also because he was looking at my medical history and my list of current prescriptions.

I say, "Is it possible to get a shot of Botox for this? In the ear?"

"I don't think that's the first solution to try here," he says.

"I'll pay out of pocket," I say. "If the insurance is a problem, I'll pay."

"The antihistamines should help, if you give them a chance. I want you to try a twenty-four-hour allergy pill and a steroid spray. Do both, every day."

I'm about to rattle off some things. That's what happens.

I say, "Do you know what a hornworm looks like? Those bright-green hairless caterpillars? They ripple when they're just about to pupate into moths. That's how this feels. Like there's a nerve being touched by something that's rippling and fluttering."

"Well," he says. "It's not a hornworm."

"I know," I say. "But that's how it feels. As if there's something alive in there."

He lets that hang in the air for a moment before he answers.

"It's not a hornworm. But you're under a lot of stress, I think," he says.

"I'll sign a release," I say. "If you could perforate my eardrum. Just a tiny nick."

"Your resting heart rate was ninety-three here today. Your blood pressure is pretty high, too. If you don't get that under control . . ."

"My mother died," I say. "I was her caretaker. I'm taking beta-blockers now."

"I understand," he says. "That part will get better, I truly hope. But if you don't get that blood pressure under control you risk doing yourself real damage. Come back in three months if your symptoms don't improve."

He seems slightly embarrassed for me. Maybe that's nice?

I say, "Is there something you'll be willing to do in three months that you can't do today?"

He says, "They're printing your prescriptions at the front desk. In the meantime, let's hope the weather changes."

At the checkout window I'm given a generous prescription for top-shelf antihistamines, a month's worth of generic Valium, and a full-size sample of a new over-the-counter steroid sinus spray, plus a reminder card for a three-month follow-up appointment. The last thing I need is a prescription for downers and I'm sure I can get the condescension elsewhere without another two-hundred-dollar out-of-network specialist co-pay for the privilege. But I take the card anyway and I'm polite because it's not the fault of the person at the desk. And every day that passes I remember more clearly that Jandine was gentle with others not because she was submissive, but because she assumed the pain of everyone was radiating everywhere like infrared beams we can't see. I'm not as kind to strangers as she was. But I try not to take my problems out on other people.

There's a bowl of little Dum-Dum suckers. I find a butterscotch one, and maybe that will help equalize the pressure.

We spent so much time in medical buildings. In waiting rooms, and at checkout desks. Standing in elevators with other people who also have problems of their own, so many strangers Jandine could still read so well for so long.

While I wait for the elevator I check my phone to see whether or not I can put mineral oil in my ear. I don't know why, but it has suddenly started to seem like a good idea. Because what if it's a tick? Literally a tick?

For so long I thought Jandine didn't stand up for herself because she wouldn't say no to her unpredictable work schedule at a retail job that made her knees ache and her feet hurt, and didn't pay enough, and carved into her days without leaving her enough time or energy to do much else. She used to tell me, sometimes, about the women who came into the store to talk to her about their problems. So many problems. So much unhappiness. I wanted her to quit the job, or at least feel like she could tell all the sad customers whose names she didn't know that she wished them well, but couldn't stand in one place and listen, because of her knee and because of her supervisor, and also, just because. I wanted her to ask for a more regular schedule so that she could have days to herself without worrying that she'd be called in to work unexpectedly. Or to at least say no, when called in unexpectedly. What I wanted for her wasn't what she actually wanted, but all that time I thought I was helping by telling her that she deserved to be treated better, that she didn't have to jump to help out, that her time was valuable.

I'm guessing everyone probably has a person who thinks they're being supportive but who doesn't listen. Someone whose frustration isn't helpful. Even if the intentions are good. Because the frustration can undermine you. Can make you feel like shit.

Anyway.

Where was I?

Oh, yes—Jeff. In the car, as I'm opening the steroid nasal spray to get the first dose into my face as soon as possible, my phone dings out a text from him.

Hey how's it going? Got plans for Mem Day?

Did you see this article I sent about UV light healing some skin cancer?

Amazing—pls take a look this time.

For a nanosecond I had thought he was checking in to see how my doctor's visit went. But of course not, because I don't tell him anything anymore. I drive home carefully, taking surface roads, avoiding the freeways. I'm excruciatingly careful. Preoccupied, because I don't know how I can live with this. My ear. Whatever this problem is.

When I get home the patio is warm and green, and striped with light. The temperature is all right, the sun fabric must be working, but I am so distracted by the fluttering in my ear that I overlook the box of binders still sitting outside and I almost walk right into it. What am I doing? What will I do if I trip over it and break an ankle? Or a wrist?

It feels like everything's a stumbling block. I can't open a cupboard or a drawer without something tumbling out. Just like Jandine, always working around too many dishes in the drying rack, always pushing the vacuum cleaner hoses back into the hall closet. Everyone has days like this. But she had so many.

I wish she'd gotten to hear someone impartial say: You have a neurodevelopmental disorder that sometimes makes you feel paralyzed, especially when you're under pressure. I wish she'd gotten to hear about emotional dysregulation, difficulty prioritizing, trouble getting started with a task, or trouble seeing a task through to the end. And to hear about time budgeting. Impulse control. Sleep and mood. And to have someone with some authority impress upon her that not sleeping well, not eating well, not reducing stress, and not remembering to exercise would make it feel worse than it had to be.

The sun fabric over my patio doesn't change anything in the one strangely cool corner of the patio where the air doesn't move. The corner where there's always a handful of small flies slowly moving in the air together, rotating like a mobile in the devil's nursery. This year, hoping to deter them, I hung a clear bag of water with a penny in the bottom. I also put up two USB desk fans from the dollar store plugged into solar panels. But the flies don't react to anything outside their turning gyre. I can't watch them now. They make me dizzy, there in the slatted shadows, turning.

I spend the rest of the afternoon on the couch, flat on my back, with a warm compress on my face and my sinuses full of steroids. I wish I could change everything. I wish I didn't have to get up in a little while to send dispatch copy on the subject of why my boss loves the time-shares everybody loves to hate.

I wish for the life I assumed I would be living by now, back when I was a kid. In which today I should be in the cool quiet of a vast library, situated at the crossroads of the world, struggling toward something worth struggling to understand. Old scripts, maybe. Like cuneiform, or hieroglyphic, or runic. Working without urgency. Imagine getting glimpses of how the world must have been long ago. Not too much, though. Just enough to feel the mysterious weight of time.

As if he's reading my mind, Jeff sends a text: *Questions? Problems?*

He's quoting the vocational counselor at our junior high school, who said this over and over with a rising inflection for at least twenty years of ninth graders. *Questions? Problems?* When I took the aptitude test, the results suggested I could be a newspaper reporter or a teacher, both highly unlikely, since both require getting things right instead of looking for the unexplained mysteries of the world. I don't remember what Jeff's results said. By then, I doubt he'd have told me.

I start to answer Jeff, then I erase and don't bother.

I couldn't see the point in telling Jeff about the ADHD. He thinks I'm a total fuckup, and having an official reason would only make it more official in his mind.

I've missed my afternoon pill. But if I take it now, I'll have trouble sleeping tonight. And if I don't sleep, all will be lost tomorrow, so either way, it feels like I'm screwed.

Chapter Twenty-Six

What will I do if the trembling never stops? Or what would I do if it suddenly stopped? Can I live with the idea of something inside my skull, lying dead behind my eardrum? Or something merely dormant? I'm turning the possibilities over as I open another of the fallen boxes. I'm more careful this time. Inside are sewing patterns in paper envelopes, sewing machine bobbins full of thread. There's also a cache of moot warranties for appliances bought thirty years ago, and a clear plastic archival folder displaying a little undershirt and matching pair of my grade school underpants, from a set embroidered with the days of the week, neatly folded with the embroidery showing topmost. Folded the way Jandine folded and aligned everything from fabric to shelf liner to wrapping paper on presents. Always with a kitten or a heart or something sweet wherever your eye falls first. There's also a green baby bootie with a white ribbon for a baby's ankle. My ankle.

I flip through the warranties; could any of them still be useful? Should I mail them to whoever lives in Terry's house now, just in case they haven't replaced everything yet? Anonymously, maybe? But I guess that wouldn't really be anonymous. There's a vintage-looking catalog: *Cheer Up with NuTone built-in intercom-radio systems.*

I flip through a few pages; it's a compulsion, I know.

New—walls act as infinite-baffle for finest sound.

I recycle or donate almost everything but I can't donate one bootie alone, so I have to throw it away. Right? And the underthings. What am I supposed to do with them? It's not productive but I feel like I can't slow down, not with the ear ticking and ticking, so I open the next box and stuff these unsolvable things inside to be dealt with next time and I flatten the empty box, but before adding it to the recycling I lay it down as a little cushion under my bruised kneecaps, and I take a look under the Buick. There's an air purifier under the car, lying flat in the original cardboard box. Motherfucker. I push it out with a golf club, and drag it inside and insert the various filters. I plug it in, and then I'm out of energy. I lie back down on the couch, and the discomfort in my ear adjusts, distantly, like an air bubble floating in the little window of a spirit level.

Jasper appears at just the right moment. I lift her featherweight body and she curls up on my neck, and the small sound of her quiet purring is conducted up through my jawbones and into my sinuses in the form of benevolent white noise.

The doorbell rings pretty early. I hate it when the doorbell rings. I'm still on the couch and I roll back over, but as soon as my left ear is against the cushion the trembling of the nerve inside is amplified so much it's nauseating—I've read that in some cases of demonic oppression—not that this is relevant—some afflicted persons can hear the many muttering low voices of demons through their pillows. I get up and check the peephole and discover that apparently I must have ordered a new mattress, which I find on the front doorstep compressed into a smaller box than I would have thought possible. What is wrong with me? Who has the energy to make a return? So I'll keep it. Which, by the way, is a form of the ADHD tax levied on life in general.

The box is just manageable enough that I can slowly cartwheel it upstairs by myself. The harder part is to slide the old mattress down the stairs first, and then wrap it in plastic, because otherwise bulk pickup won't touch it. But I manage. I always manage somehow. Then I lean it against the patio wall, to wait for the next bulk pickup day.

The sight of the mattress against the wall is hard to bear. Everything is, I mean.

Later when I glance out the window above the kitchen sink I'm startled to see the mattress there, shrouded in translucent plastic and dreaming inwardly in the evening shadows. It reminds me of *A Nightmare on Elm Street*, the scene in the high school English class and the final girl who is so tired, trying to stay awake at her desk while someone reads aloud from *Hamlet*, and something drags itself along audibly in the hallway beyond the classroom. And then her dead friend is there, wrapped in translucent plastic, and the voice reading *Hamlet* slows down . . . *I could be bounded in a nutshell and count myself a king of infinite space . . . were it not that I have . . . bad dreams.* But it's not real. Not even when the dream itself is real.

I look down and I can't unsee the state of my sink. Almost certainly the 1978 original, with white enamel chipped down to the metal in places. The faucet is newer, but full of mineral buildup, and even after soaking it in a bowl of vinegar the sprayer holes are still half blocked with calcium that makes the water hiss. How can I complain? I've been so lucky. I found this house at the bottom of the market, and I work for people who made money during the financial crisis, at a job that has been recession proof, at least so far.

Suddenly I've got a flatheaded screwdriver in one hand and a mallet in the other and I'm tapping out the border tiles around the sink. I always knew I'd have to do this, sooner or later, and I couldn't stop now if I tried.

By midnight I've removed the border tiles and disconnected the garbage disposal, the drain, and the hot and cold waterlines, and taken out the clips that stabilize the basin. Moving the garbage disposal unit is the most awkward part. And then the old sink comes out so easily. Even with the faucet still attached, it feels impossibly light. Only a shell. I leave it with the mattress, quietly, so as not to bother Paloma, even though her bedroom is at the front of her house, and even though she says she's proud of sleeping like the dead.

With a flashlight I look through scrap wood in the garage for bits of old two-by-four, short pieces I don't need to cut, not at this quiet hour of the night, then I wedge them into the sink cabinet for support, in case the counter isn't strong enough to hold up the new cast-iron sink on its own.

I wake on the couch; I'm still dizzy despite the fucking useless antihistamines so I don't want to use the stairs more than I have to. Or at least that seemed like a good reason to sleep here last night. When my phone moves I see multiple missed calls and then a new text arriving from TK.

Today I can help in the kitchen if that works for you?

Followed by another: *Your sink I mean, of course.*

My stone patio walls are high enough that he can't know I just took the old one out. But the timing is weird, isn't it? I have to say yes, I think. Even if the red guppy's hospital tank on the kitchen table is too complicated to move out of sight. At least I can shift the buckets of dechlorinated tap water under the table and cover the bucket holding detritus and a fuzzy layer of the kind of fluffy biofilm that fish keepers in the online forums call mulm, suctioned from the bottom of the sixty-five-gallon tank, which I still need to check with a magnifier light, because I found a tiny cory in there. I can't bear the possibility of tossing any others out into the heat to die in the tomato plants.

I know TK is doing me a favor. Before his brain surgery. God almighty, what's wrong with me?

I see that Jeff texted again about coming here for Memorial Day: *Okay unless I hear otherwise from you by midweek I'm going to assume we have a plan.*

For a moment I want to throw my phone and then I consider the two types of embarrassment: whether it's better to take the single unpleasant marshmallow now and get it over with by letting TK in to help move the sink, or deal with a bigger pile of shit marshmallows all weekend if Jeff turns up and sees the hole where a sink should be.

My ear is beginning to tremble . . . It must have been quiet when I woke and yet I didn't even notice. Now I want to scratch all my skin off—perhaps the trembling is somehow related to my blood pressure after all.

Thanks, I reply to TK. Too late I realize I should have added, *Come by in the afternoon*, because he texts back instantly: *Great, I'm at the garbage door if you want to let me in.*

"Fuck," I say out loud.

Garage door, he clarifies.

I put my bra back on and try to look like these aren't yesterday's slept-in clothes, and swallow an Adderall and tell myself that this is normal life. This is how acquaintances and neighbors behave; you invite other people into the house even when you feel terrible. Maybe especially when you feel terrible? Maybe this is how other people get through the various ways there are to feel terrible.

After I pop the hatch the sink looks much bigger than I remember. Bigger and heavier. And the tailpiece underneath is longer than I remembered, which means we'll have to lift the whole thing even higher before we can lower it into place.

"I changed my mind," I say. "I don't think we can do this."

"Only one way to find out," he says.

I go first as we lift and carry, because I don't want him walking backward. Because I'm not strong enough to stop the sink from crushing his legs if he stumbles, and I won't be able to stop the tailpiece from stabbing him in the femoral artery like a vintage-oilcan spout, like the floating silver sphere in that movie—*Phantasm*? It could happen. People fall all the time. I hit my bruised legs against the side of the sink with every step.

We get it all the way across the patio and up the step and into the house, and then we manage to maneuver the sink up to rest against the counter. I'm sweating, and afraid I'll lose my grip. All the bandages on my fingers are gone, I don't know where. But we manage to lift the sink just high enough to gently set it down into place.

"See," he says. "No problem." But he's winded, too. And we're idiots.

"I don't think the tile is strong enough," I say. "Do you?"

He presses the counter, bearing down, and this makes me wince.

"Seems fine to me," he says.

We shift the sink a little, to align the tailpiece into the trap below, and when we stand back it looks absolutely beautiful. Gleaming white enamel. An immaculate new faucet. The sloping porcelain sides are so smooth and so clean.

He says, "Makes everything else seem sort of new again, too, doesn't it."

Maybe I will never stop wanting to wrap the corners and edges of everything with foam, after realizing that everything would be dangerous to Jandine, getting up in the night, losing her balance. Maybe I won't unlearn years of making sure her pant legs wouldn't trip her, years of making sure the rubber soles of her shoes wouldn't catch on the transition strips between linoleum and carpet. There was so much to guard against. And yet I somehow didn't remember well enough that TK is fragile, too, and that I should not have let him help with this.

I should be able to ask Jeff, shouldn't I? Instead of being judged?

What will I do, later? If I ever really need anything?

"Thank you," I say, but TK brushes this away.

"Let's hook this sucker up," he says.

"It's okay, just leave it for now."

But he's already sliding underneath the sink. And I'm worried that we dislodged the support braces when we lowered the sink, and that it won't take much to crack the tile around the hole and drop all that cast iron on top of him.

"Please come out," I say. "I don't trust the braces."

"They're fine," he says, his voice bouncing off the rough underbellies of the double sink basins. I hear him tapping the wood, demonstrating. "I'm almost done."

But he's not almost done. My pulse is stirring in the center of my left ear. My blood pressure, tightening around whatever else might be there. His elbows move as he tightens the collar to connect the tailpiece to the trap.

"Almost done," he says again. "Do you want to bring over one of those buckets and we'll make sure it doesn't leak?"

"Hold on a second," I say, "those are aquarium buckets . . . Let me find something else . . ."

I get the little wastebasket from the guest bathroom, and when I come back he's still lying on his back, stretched out on the tile kitchen floor with his head propped at an uncomfortable angle still inside the cabinet, staring up at the flange and hole where the garbage disposal unit will lock back into place when we're done. I wait, but he doesn't seem aware of me.

"Everything okay?" I say.

What's he staring up at? The light fixture over the sink? I look up, too, and notice the shadow of a dead fly inside the glass cover. And everything here has that feeling, I know. The shelves of speckled cookbooks. The medicated hospital tank, still cloudy with doxycycline. If I'd known he'd be down on the floor I would have swept and mopped. But there's never enough time to do everything.

He lifts a hand and starts absently turning and turning the white PVC collar above the P trap again. He's overdoing it, I think? The sink shifts and then it shifts again.

"That's tight enough," I say. "That's tight enough, isn't it?"

I sound deferential and I hate it.

"It's fine," he says. Attempting to be cheerful. "A longer outlet from the disposal would be nice, but I don't know if we want to bother, I mean, it's so dang close to being long enough . . ."

I see the sink jerk again.

"TK," I say. "Stop."

He says, "These braces are fine—just fine—"

One corner of the sink slips, but slowly, so slowly that I doubt my eyes until a counter tile cracks with a glassy snap.

A line of grout falls from somewhere and hits his shoulder, which finally startles him.

"What was that?" he says, in surprise, swatting it away.

I drop what I'm holding to grip his work boot with both hands and pull with more strength than I have, tipping backward as he tries to slide himself out from under the sink, like a mechanic from under a car. Three of the braces hold and one does not hold; the one that fails is the one he kept tapping to show me that it wouldn't budge. The tailpiece shears off above the P trap, leaving a sharp edge that might have caught him in the face, or maybe in the throat. Or maybe not. I'm sprawled down hard, still clutching his boot. When I let go his heel hits the floor like a deadweight and he stays down, still not moving, still staring vacantly up.

"Hey, are you okay?" I ask.

He doesn't blink. Something's wrong. The hole in his ear looks dark, too big, maybe, and I realize thick-looking blood is slowly pooling in the hollow, and that, too, I'm not sure I'm really seeing. Not until more blood drops to the floor, leisurely and horrifying.

"You're all right," I say, in an effort to sound calm. "You're all right, stay there. I'm calling 911."

I feel compelled to narrate what I'm doing as I feel around for my phone.

"I'm finding my phone and I'm going to call 911."

He still hasn't said anything, hasn't looked at me, even as I check his pupils, and check his other ear for blood as I'm scrambling to unlock my phone with one hand while also gingerly tucking a dish towel around his head, because I'm afraid he might be bleeding underneath from where I can't see. His scalp feels too warm, the skin too thin. His eyes flick to my face and this startles me.

"Don't move," I say. But he does move. He struggles to sit, and then to stand up, and I give up trying to make him stay down and just try to prevent him from knocking his head on the lip of the counter on the way up. In the process I drop my phone and it clatters onto the tile.

His big work boot comes down on top of it and I hear the screen cracking under his heel. Then he bears down, and it cracks again. When he moves away the screen is crushed. I can't even try to dial now that the display has gone. Funny that I never realized I might ever wish for the old buttons.

"Give me your phone," I say, with my hand out.

He's gone over to the cookbooks on the shelf like he's looking for something hidden behind Jandine's brown-and-yellow Tupperware entertaining guide, which is full of recipes for Jell-O salads and fancy pork chops. I keep it only because the margins are still so full of Jandine's neat handwriting.

"What about the others?" he says.

"What others?" I ask, confused, because I'm afraid for him but also now afraid of him. He's reading the spines like he's searching out beads on an abacus that I can't see.

"The recipe book in which . . . a goat?"

"No," I say. "I don't know."

". . . A billy goat steps out for the guests . . ."

"I don't know about a billy goat," I say, and this is like a dream in which the one task you need to accomplish is the one you can't get anyone to notice. I'm moving now to the back door to get Paloma's attention over the patio wall, or I'll—what will I do, if she doesn't hear me?

"Aspic," he says, not reading, just talking, pushing one book back and pulling another forward. "Rémoulade," he says. His ear is no longer bleeding, at least, though there's a spill of red on his collar.

"Those are old," I say.

He says, "How about an open-faced cold-cut sandwich with a dill pickle. How about two scoops of horseradish and mayonnaise."

Is that supposed to be dirty?

"Hey," I say, sharply, because this is my house. "Give me your phone."

He turns away from the cookbooks. "I don't feel too good," he says.

I pull a chair out for him. He sits and then says, abruptly, "You should get rid of this book, Mandy, and that one, most of them, because you don't want them. You don't want them. They're fine—I'm sorry," he says, just as abruptly. "Keep them. Don't listen to me. There's just an awful lot of gelatin, in there."

He gets up and moves to the back door, unsteadily. His shirt is wrinkled, damp across the back, and when he moves his sweat smells like the interior of an airtight kitchen canister that's been sitting on a thrift-store shelf for a long time. I'm trying to remember the three things you're supposed to ask someone who may have had a stroke. Do they smell toast burning. Can they say something out loud in a complete sentence. Which he just did.

"Do you smell anything?" I say, but my voice seems inappropriately faint and artificial.

"Can you open the door for me, please," he says.

The third is to smile. To ask them to smile. But I can't make myself ask him to smile, so I gingerly open the door and then I pull my hand back out of the way. He leaves without shutting the door behind him, weaving through the patio, out through the garage, turning sharply to walk around the house like he's following an invisible line painted on the ground. I follow at a short distance and watch him walk stiffly across the grass common area. It looks like he's going directly for the door of his town house until he swings wide in a detour and disappears around the corner, probably to his own garage door. Before he's out of sight I start pressing Paloma's doorbell, and then I realize my own ear is quiet, and that the air seems raw, and painful. When I check I find a trace of blood on my fingers, and I shudder, and I don't think about it, I can't think about whether this is his blood, or whether maybe I was right and something did burst out of my ear and flutter away during the chaos. I should go back to that ENT. I should ask him what he sees now. Or maybe not, since whatever might have been there would be gone.

“Honey,” Paloma says, as she comes back from checking on him, when she sees me peeking out through my front door. “Come to my back door. Stacia’s always looking out that front window and I don’t want her to think we’re gossiping.”

By the time I get to her kitchen table she’s handing me a glass of rosé even though it’s barely one in the afternoon. “He said he’s fine,” she says. “I know, men always say they’re fine right before they drop dead. But in this case, he’s already under a doctor’s care. So I don’t know what to tell you.”

I say, “He was bleeding from his *ear*.”

“Are you sure?” she says. “I looked and I didn’t see anything.”

“There’s blood on my kitchen floor. Go look. And he wasn’t himself.”

“What did he say?”

“Strange things,” I say. Because I’m not sure how to convey it.

She says, “You know, normally he’s already maybe just a little bit strange.”

“He talked about an old-fashioned sandwich,” I say. “And a dill pickle.”

“That’s your reason for wanting to call 911?” She wrinkles her nose.

“It was the way he said it.”

“Always trust your gut,” she says, lifting Pepper up to her lap, “but also, don’t jump to conclusions. You should tell Stacia if you notice anything strange with him in the next few days.”

“Paloma,” I say. “He hit his head. He broke my phone and wouldn’t let me call for help. Or at least he wouldn’t let me use his phone.”

“Listen,” says Paloma, “you did your due diligence and I think you can let it go. And by the way, how would you feel,” she said, “if one of your neighbors kept insisting that you hit your head and you’re not all right, even after you say you’re fine?”

"Did he say he's fine?" I say.

"I don't know," she says. "I mean, he's got the . . ." She motions to her head. "I don't know whether to pry, or give him the privacy."

On Jandine's behalf, I learned to ask for help using red flag words so that others would take us seriously. Words like *seizure*. And *concussion*. Otherwise it's too easy to be sent home with Tylenol instead of being given a CAT scan. I have no idea if what I saw was a seizure, but I say it anyway.

"Please," I say. "Please tell Stacia to say he had a seizure on my kitchen floor."

She picks up her phone, reads a text, and says, "It's okay. She's taking him to the ER."

"A seizure," I say. "Tell her that I saw him having a *seizure*."

"Okay," she says, and she does it. And I go home to clean up the drying blood from the floor. And then I'll go out for a new phone. But before I do either I get an old phone from my drawer full of old phones of the past that I don't know what to do with, and I charge it up enough to take a picture of the blood on the floor and one of my shattered phone screen, too. Just in case anyone ever needs to see proof.

That evening I use the jack from my car and more pieces of scrap wood to raise the sink just enough to reposition, rebrace, and clip the new sink to the counter. I have to add a little extension to make up for the broken part of the pipe, but then it all seems to fit, so I put a bead of silicone around the edge, and call it finished.

Chapter Twenty-Seven

I text to ask him if he's all right later that evening, and again the next morning, and the next afternoon, as well, but he doesn't reply. I know it's not the correct impulse but by the next day I feel the need to say out loud again that I asked him to get out from under the sink. And that he wouldn't listen. Because I feel responsible. I find myself checking from the upstairs window first before I go out to collect the mail, because I don't want to run into him by accident, and when I see Paloma making the rounds I intercept her.

"Listen," says Paloma. "They're not going to sue you."

"Are you saying they might?"

"I said they won't," she says. "And don't blow up my phone worrying. He's okay. He's out and about. He's fine."

But that seems even weirder. How can he be fine?

"What are your plans this weekend? You should do something fun," Paloma says.

I stare at her.

"Memorial Day," she says. "Try to relax a little."

Time got away from me; I forgot to tell Jeff not to come. It's a maneuver I'm familiar with, the way he puts the onus on me to beg off and to let him make other plans, knowing I'll be too disorganized to reply in good time. He'd be fine if I canceled, of course. But I feel obliged to hold up my end, as if it somehow seems simpler.

It's not, though. It's a lot of work. I don't just have to clean the house, I have to move things around, because he takes up a lot of space. Even Jasper's food dishes have to be tucked out of the way, because he'll kick them over, accidentally, and send kibble across the floor and then walk away. I used to have a beautiful deep-green rice bowl, something that caught Jandine's eye in a thrift store. A bowl of perfect proportions, with a hollow interior so pleasing that I tried to find more to match online. There were no identifying marks except the word *Germanium* on the bottom, which was not a brand, as I'd assumed, but seemingly a type of glaze. Jeff broke the bowl. It happened after Jandine died, and I was upset. He didn't apologize but he gave me an ugly floral replacement. *Geraniums*, he'd said. *I thought they were your favorite.*

I'll unpack the binders of *Man, Myth & Magic* because if he sees them boxed up he may well assume they're his, I don't know why this happens, since he still says he doesn't want anything from the Tacoma house, and yet will sometimes also claim keepsakes that were mine before he and I ever met. Objects, mostly, but even something as little and as dear to me as the funny episodic bedtime story called "Mushroom Family" that my grandparents used to tell me, and that I picked up again and told him when he couldn't fall asleep. Even that morphs into something he somehow remembers as a story his grandparents told him, a story that therefore belongs to him. It's not worth fighting over, but I know the mushroom family sprang from the plant atlas on the bookshelf at the farm, from categories like Carrot Family, who carried lacy green sun umbrellas. Mushroom Family balanced suitcases on their heads, and came to visit on rainy days. Their lives were always made up endlessly out of things that happened the day before. Like dreams are.

I use the shop vacuum to decontaminate the issues of *Man, Myth & Magic* so I can put them on a shelf where he won't even notice them. Except as background clutter.

So many of these pages are familiar as they ruffle past, and I remember individual details as I glimpse them. Like that corner houses were considered unlucky, a detail that stood out to me as sinister because Terry's house was on an isolated corner, but that evidently I forgot by the time I bought this corner house. The whole entry about houses rings a bell, and I turn off the vacuum. My memory runs alongside as I read, like a horse galloping apace at dusk while my childhood self watches like a passenger in the back seat of a car.

I probably don't know how much of what I take for granted about the world came from these pages or was corroborated in them, then buried over the years until I barely remember where the associations came from first. Like the way potential charms of protection are everywhere. Like single shoes. Whenever we passed a single shoe lying by the side of the road I would point it out, and Jandine would often say, *Oh, that's sad*. When I asked why, she said, *Because it can't do anybody any good now, out in the open like that*. This magazine encyclopedia is where I discovered that single shoes or boots serve as protective amulets when they're intentionally left behind in old walls and foundations and hearths, bricked up, plastered over, never to be removed. Everybody knows the trope that renovating an old house can stir up bad energy if the work isn't done respectfully. I wonder how often that kind of trouble begins with old shoe swept aside by new owners who don't realize what they're tossing into the trash.

Chapter Twenty-Eight

I don't see TK around the pool environs or the parking lot or the mailboxes, so I step outside to collect the mail, none of which looks important. Coupons, a free neighborhood newspaper, notice of the next HOA meeting. A credit card offer for Jandine. Her name is still taped inside the mailbox next to mine, where only the mail carrier can see. There's also a renewal notice for the joint safe-deposit box we opened when Jandine first moved here. That was the kind of errand we did a lot of, when she first got to Vegas. Funny that I'm so nostalgic for crossing things off a to-do list while crossing the valley in my car to keep appointments and run errands, with Jandine singing along to oldies with KJUL FM on the radio.

I check out the yard and estate-sale listings in the free paper and the public safety page, though this neighborhood rarely gets any marks on the smudgy four-color newsprint crime map. Not like others in the zip code where terrible things are marked by yellow dots, black triangles, and purple crosses. But this time there's a red star for assault and battery in what appears to be this complex.

The Sinatra station is playing on the other side of my patio wall, which usually means Paloma is in the alley, with her garage door open, talking to people and promoting the general welfare. I take the paper out to show her, though she must already know. As my garage door lifts I see her standing in the lane behind our town houses, turning away from TK and Stacia, who are out on their evening walk—dammit. I roll the paper up and drop it in the recycling bin as I step out.

Stacia nods at me tightly and she's perfectly polite though she doesn't say a word. TK doesn't acknowledge me.

This is such a pisser. Even Pepper retreats against the hem of Paloma's cobalt caftan. But at least he looks like he wants to get away from all of us equally.

"Hey," I hear Paloma say. "Teddy. Are you okay?"

I look up just as she snaps her fingers in front of TK's mirrored sunglasses. There's a trickle of blood slowly tracking down his face from behind the lenses, but if he feels it, he doesn't wipe it away.

"Teddy," says Paloma, feeling her pockets for a tissue, not finding one. "Lay off the Coumadin. Talk to your doctor, for god's sake."

He doesn't react, and we watch as they start making their way home.

"That didn't look right," Paloma murmurs.

Does she mean the eye bleeding? Or the motionlessness?

"I saw something on the crime map that didn't look right, either," I say

Paloma picks up Pepper, her face flushing with the effort. In her low smoker's voice, she says, "Yes, Mandy. I would have told you. But I haven't seen you since it happened. Your blinds were shut and I don't like to wake you, with your strange hours."

Yes, I know; she says it often enough.

I shift a little so that she won't be looking over my shoulder into my open garage door, at cardboard boxes and storage containers and toolboxes piled like sandbags around Terry's Electra. They're not too untidy. But they're a lot.

The sun is setting, but Paloma still reaches out and tugs me more fully into the shade, because Paloma never forgets. I sigh, inwardly.

"Down there," she says, indicating the other end of our row of town houses. "My friend. You know. The lady with the squamous cell skin cancer. A man tried to break into her house."

I feel a sick thud behind my ribs. "Really?"

"She heard something, she looked out, and saw somebody in her patio."

"Did he get in?" I say. I do not want to ask the obvious questions.

Paloma looks pained. She strokes Pepper. "Well, no."

"She's okay?"

"She tried to slam the window but it got stuck. She's younger than me, but she's not as fit." Paloma moves her shoulder, unconsciously. "She should have replaced that shitty aluminum window a long time ago. She's got scratches, all here," she says, touching her forearm. "And her hand needed stitches."

Paloma's bright clothes and manicures and pampered little dog don't soften twenty-five years as a cage supervisor in a downtown casino. But she's rattled. "You know what?" she says. "I think she's got a bite mark on one of her fingers. But she doesn't want to talk about it."

I don't know what to say.

She rubs Pepper's ears. "She didn't call 911 at first. You know what she did?"

I shake my head.

"She called her doctor's office, got the answering service, and left a message," says Paloma. "She wasn't thinking clearly. I hope it doesn't cost her that finger." She reaches into the other pocket of her caftan for her cigarettes, shifting Pepper out of the way, an unresisting little burden on her hip. I watch her hand, the greenish-blue veins running under her turquoise-and-silver bangles, wondering which of the unknown woman's fingers had been hurt. Paloma slips out a cigarette and holds it away from the dog. "I saw her hand," she says. "It looked horrible."

Pepper squirms, his golden ears quaking.

"Did she see the intruder's face?" I ask.

Paloma shakes her head. "I said, 'Please tell me you grabbed something and hit him good. Tell me they got the DNA.' But she said there's none," says Paloma. "She didn't want to call Metro, so I did."

"She lives alone?"

Paloma nods. We both fall quiet, looking around at all the familiar sights of our alley, the open garage doors, some kids throwing a ball to one another, a lady walking her two dogs. Wordlessly we move a dozen paces closer to the end of the alley, where we can see across the lawn to the row of town houses on the far side, where TK and Stacia each have a house, as does her shut-in sister. Which is her term, not mine, for pretty, ladylike Loretta, who rarely goes out anymore.

They are still making their way along the path to their front doors, passing the impatient guy who drags his little poodle mix out to pee before his shift dealing table games. He's always in such a hurry, rushing the dog, usually sucking down a cup of coffee in his dress shirt and emerald green cummerbund and bow tie. But even his crankiness seems benignly familiar compared with whatever Paloma just described.

Paloma says, "This sounds nuts. But I think in all the chaos—I think she bit herself. That could happen, couldn't it? In the chaos?"

Pepper whines softly, straining up with his bug-like face and flickering pink tongue.

"The screen was still on the window," says Paloma. "The screen was totally intact. So it kind of couldn't have been anyone outside. Right? Not if they didn't get through the screen."

"An accident, maybe," I say.

"I feel like I should post signs on the mailboxes to let people know. But I don't know what to warn people about. And look," she says, her gaze still on Stacia and TK. "He shouldn't even be outside. He's got surgery the week after next. But when I told Stacia what happened she was afraid to go out alone for the mail."

I say, "I thought he was looking better."

"You think he looks better?" she says. "Better than what?"

I think of his stale good humor, but then about his boot on my phone. Suddenly the heat and weight of the air are too much. The sun is nearly down but the pavement is only just starting to release the stored heat of the day in waves that I can feel crawling up my calves. The asphalt under my sandals is almost soft enough to press something into, like a bottle cap, or a coin, or four little paws. No wonder Pepper didn't want to stay down there.

"Mandy," she says. "The other day. When he was in your

house. Did you think he might do something weird? Something violent? Is that why you were upset after?"

I start to say no, but that's just a reflex. "It was weird," I say. "Yes. It was weird."

She says, "I've known Stacia such a long time."

"Do you really think . . ." I say. "I mean, what are we talking about?"

"Honestly, I don't know," Paloma says.

She takes a drag of her cigarette. The heat never puts her off.

"When she said she saw a man standing in her patio—I can't believe I'm saying this. But right away I thought of him. It's not because he's a creep. He's not a creep. I don't know why."

I can't imagine the strain she's felt, the effort of pretending everything is normal when talking to him. And looking Stacia in the face and wondering what she thinks.

"Well," I say. "Be careful, Paloma."

"I'm okay," she says. "I have Pepper as my alarm system. He barks like crazy."

I nod politely, as if I don't already know this.

"Plus I keep my late husband's pistol by the bed," she adds. "And I'm between you and my neighbors on the other side, so nobody gets into my patio unless they come through yours. So you should be careful, Mandy. You're on the corner. Don't cultivate bad luck."

This makes my skin tighten.

"I always lock up," I say. And then, unnecessarily, because I already know the answer, I say, "You said your friend lives in the end unit?"

"Yes. He came over the wall." And then, scrupulously, she adds, "Whoever it was, and whatever happened, somebody must have gotten in over the patio wall."

I excuse myself as Paloma waves to the lady with the two dogs. I go back into my garage and hit the button to close the garage door. It's much hotter in here than outside but I am gripped, absurdly, with the need to know before dark that I have spare flashlights handy. A spare by every window. Because cell phone flashlights don't carry far enough.

Terry and Jandine had everything they needed, but because they could never find anything they bought more. Dozens of flashlights, extras everywhere, but everywhere is the same as nowhere in a moment of need if you can't find one, and now it feels like I'm in that position. I lock the door behind me and double-check the front door. I close the downstairs blinds more tightly but then of course I'm compelled to check all the windows.

To be clear, I don't think anyone is hiding in my house. But if I feel anxious then checking will help, reasonable or not, so I start with my walk-in closet, new cell phone in one hand and a broom handle in the other, poking behind the clothes to make sure I'm truly alone. Except for Jasper, brave Jasper, little cowlicked tabby cat who follows me endlessly from room to room on her ancient legs. I look under the beds, in the closets, every available space, even those filled to capacity with cardboard boxes. In each room I close the blinds before I poke into the corners; I don't want to be observed as I check like this for observers.

Even though, again: I don't really think I'm being watched.

But what if? Paloma is right, the end units are more vulnerable. This may be a well-established oasis, full of bright grass and pastel landscaping rocks, with an azure swimming pool and mature shade trees. The original owners may well maintain an emotional investment in the property and the deed of my house may say Paradise, Nevada, but in reality of course there is danger all around us in the desert darkness, shifting and shimmering with an emptiness that isn't empty at all.

Chapter Twenty-Nine

By the time the sun is up the next day I'm already prowling around the house. I should have installed new security bars on the patio door by now. TK had offered to go with me to the architectural-salvage place, to see if by chance there might be some that could be made to fit well enough to drill into the wall and anchor in place. I can't believe the memory of that offer now.

But who could? There are documentaries, podcasts, true crime shows about precisely this feeling. *When did you know something was wrong?*

But do I know there's something wrong?

Paloma's friend didn't specifically say it was TK in her patio. Or that whoever it was actually tried to get in. But a gut reaction is usually the correct reaction. And looking in windows is super creepy. Especially after climbing a patio wall to do so—holy shit. He climbed over her patio wall?

Did she say he was looking in the window, or did I infer that?

I've let so much slide. I barely know how to listen to my gut at the moment.

I hear more birds outside.

The window salesman had jumped up and down on some sample glass, to show how hard it would be to break, and in exchange for signing a payment plan to cover so many thousands of dollars I was promised the silence of a tomb as well as nearly the safety of one. It was a trade-off, because the security bars that had been on the old windows wouldn't accommodate the wider sills of the new windows and had to be scrapped.

I'm distracted by what the birds are doing. And what the cicadas are doing. And I'm wondering whether or not cicadas aboveground can still hear the pulse of the trees among whose roots they lived for a decade and more. Whether what they're broadcasting now is that pulse, or a memory of that pulse, or something else.

Actually, history shows that tombs are not very safe.

Terry's wind chimes touch lightly in the breeze.

Terry would have told me to get the security bars done. Like the ones he put on the old house. He saw projects through, which was why the neglect after he died was so shocking. Our yard (his yard) had borders that were neat, tight, scalloped, pristinely maintained. Yet he never made us stay off the grass. He walked across it all the time, dragging the hoses, moving the sprinklers. My mother said he had wanted to be a veterinarian. I understood nothing about adult life, about marriage, divorce, remarriage, or why Terry spent so many hours moving and repositioning hoses and sprinklers for the lawns, the azaleas, the ornamental plum trees, the roses that bloomed around the front steps and obscured the entrance eventually. The miniature spruces that would get too big and crack the sidewalk.

One bird here sounds like an electric stapler: *thatch-thatch-thatch!*

If I don't take some amphetamines soon this day will never come into focus.

My ear is quiet. Isn't it?

I can sleep upstairs again. And when Jeff is here for the weekend I won't have to explain to him that I'm sleeping on the couch for fear of losing my balance in the hall near the top of the stairs, especially at night or first thing in the morning, before I'm alert. So that's good, because he fills every room with chargers of one kind or another and I cannot stand blinking lights while sleeping. Maybe because mitochondria need total darkness at night. I just want to be able to live a calm life and learn how to make interesting nontoxic 3D submersible aquarium hardscape backgrounds. Is that too much to ask for?

I know. I'm making things too complicated, when supposedly all you need is clean Styrofoam and one of the many aquarium-safe spray paint types. But I don't want to make a mistake and accidentally do more harm than good.

Instead of getting the house ready for Jeff I spend the morning opening closed spaces filled with hot, dry, noncirculating air, where smaller boxes are stacked in the closets, pushed under the beds. Because unless I keep the air moving my house starts to smell as if an element of the Tacoma house is still in the cardboard: naughty cats, deodorant soap chips, dusty wall-to-wall carpet, and a buttery odor of worn-out flannel bedding. I pull at a box on a shelf in my closet. It's heavy and shouldn't be sitting up that high. Toes get broken that way. What am I doing? I don't want to sort through any box small enough to leave in place, not at the moment.

I wonder if Jasper could tolerate a dog. A small dog trained to rip out an intruder's throat.

I can hear too much of the world through the double-paned windows—the shifting screens, the chimes touching, the air moving around the corners of the house. Someone could almost be working through the locks on the back door and I might not hear it over the sound of everything else.

I never saw the King Tut exhibit in person but in this box under old paperbacks by Ray Bradbury and Frank Herbert and John Keel I find a book Warren picked up somewhere when the exhibit was in Seattle. He'd given Jeff a glossy black Frisbee with a gorgeous reproduction of the eyeless golden mask, and he'd given me this, to add to my occult library.

There are so many stories, about the explorers of the past, digging down, opening and violating graves. I look at the pages now and think: what a bunch of creeps. I don't know how the paradigm could have been otherwise, given the nature of this world, but of course that's because I'm downstream in history.

It's hot already on the westward-facing side of the house, and I'm looking for a doorstop so that if in fact I can't stop myself from sorting boxes in the hot closet then at least it can't swing shut when I turn away and little Jasper cannot accidentally be shut inside when I'm distracted. Did the builders forget to properly insulate that side of the house or something?

One of our cats once knocked Terry's handheld sander off the workbench in the workroom at the old house and the sander ran against the concrete floor until the motor burned itself out. Imagine being locked in a dark room with the noise and scorched smell of the motor destroying itself. The cats were howling. It could have started a fire—it could have killed us all in our beds.

Terry said it hadn't caused a fire, had it?

Jandine was angry at Terry for his cavalier attitude about killing us all in a fire.

And Jeff told his mother about it.

And I learned to worry about what happens when you leave rooms unattended.

I can't find my pills, that's the real story here; I should always keep my prescriptions in the bedside drawer. But it's more reliable to keep the pills in the kitchen, next to the caffeine. I go back and forth on this too often. And now I don't know where the pills are. In the bathroom? Actually they're in the kitchen, but not with the caffeine. It's infuriating; I have no idea how this happens, or why I just spent an hour looking at pictures of King Tut, instead of getting myself in order and getting some work done.

Actually, yes I do; yesterday I picked up the pills with the intention of putting them away in my room before Jeff gets here, because I don't want to discuss my pharmaceuticals with him. But I must have put the pills into a different kitchen cabinet instead during a moment when I was on autopilot without knowing it. And so it goes. I push Jasper's place mat and saucers under the kitchen table, and put the special kidney-protection prescription food into a heavier bowl. To make it harder for Jeff to accidentally send milk or broth flying across the tiles.

The kettle heats with the lumbering sound of hard tap

water. All steamers, irons, kettles, humidifiers here do the same. Calcium and magnesium corrode the faucets and fixtures. Little rocks precipitate out, and they rattle and hiss. They catch in the screen in the spout of the kettle, and today I remember to shake them out, into the planters. And while I'm out there, doing this, I try to think about what to do in the short term about the fact that TK knows I don't have security bars on the patio doors, even though I also can't think about what this means.

In the Ray Bradbury paperback, I find an ADHD parable in a story called "The Scythe." A man and his wife and children run out of gas at the end of a long road near a farmhouse surrounded by ample wheat, and once the engine dies, they have nothing. They've been displaced, maybe by the dust bowl, and he's too proud to ask for help at the only house in sight. But the children may starve if he doesn't. So he goes to the house, alone, where he finds the farmer dead, laid out in his best suit with a single stalk of grain clasped in his hands, having left a letter bequeathing the fields and the work and the house to whoever stands reading now, and after the man buries the farmer he tries to live a normal life in the farmhouse with his family. He tries to accept this moment of unexpected grace. But he can't rest. Soon he takes up the scythe he finds leaning in the corner and steps out into the field to cut the grain and then soon he no longer needs to stop for anything because he's in a state of hyperfocus that neither requires nor permits him to do anything other than whatever he is doing in the endless entrainment of swinging the scythe.

Today in hyperfocus my path through the grain is clear and easy to follow and it doesn't matter that anything I manage to cut through today will just reappear overnight. I go deeper into the field anyway, endlessly remaking a path as if it's always been there, in part by opening the books as I find them and watching the words spring up again as I read, so familiar, but I don't know how familiar until the instant just before I reach the end of each line. The man who works the field eventually comes across three ripe heads of grain that are also the lives of his family, ready now, and waiting among countless other lives also ready to be cut down. He falls to his knees in time not to cut them. But this was always going to happen. Remember the farmer, who worked and worked until he must have encountered and cut down the stalk of his own life at the ordained time, and then went home to dress for his own burial knowing that someone else would take up the work after him because the work will never be finished. And even while you know this, you will still work yourself to death.

This ADHD parable is perhaps not ideal for the kids.

But it's helpful when you look up in the middle of a day to find that you've shifted so many storage boxes around in the garage that you can't easily get out from behind the Buick, though it wasn't your intention to come out here to look for anything. Especially not in the awkward place behind the Electra, where you've already fallen once and where you were lucky not to hit your head last time. But this is how it happens. No time is passing, until you blink and the plants out on the patio are already in shadow. You still have work to do, work that you didn't do earlier because you were doing—whatever it is that you're out here doing instead of the work that pays the mortgage for this house. The thing is, I know there's a boxed-up reverse osmosis filter out here somewhere. And I'm having a moment of clarity in which I can admit that I will never get around to installing it under the new kitchen sink. It seems important that I find the RO filter and donate it to a distribution center where the belongings of people like me, who don't have family, will be dispersed back to the rest of the world. Now, before I change my mind.

My plan for the day had been to turn my attention to making sure I have enough evergreen copy in the folder on my desktop in case I fall too far behind on any given day and can't engage my brain in time to meet a deadline. The people

I work with don't seem care too much which properties or lifestyle topics I write about, for the most part all they want from me are 250 to 500 bona fide words a day about Las Vegas, or other places in southern Nevada, plus an appealing photo (and not too professional looking, either), with a subject line intriguing enough and also simple enough to compel some fluctuating percentage of the readership to open the email. Because, luckily for me, Las Vegas is where enough search terms intersect and recombine to catch the eyes of the mature visitors who are also the ideal readers. Not the kind of visitors doing searches for pool parties or half-price show tickets or celebrity DJs or spa packages, but people of semiretirement age seeking snowbird destinations with good weather in winter, a lower cost of living than wherever they live now, no state income tax, convenient RV parks, and a choice of oncology centers. And so on. My job is to catch the eyes of those who might slip into reading about shopping for condos in which to escape the winter months in Ohio, or Michigan, or Washington, almost anywhere, even though they aren't actually shopping. People who aren't yet retired but also aren't who they used to be, and who want something new. Something to do. Somewhere to go. *Something.* Even though half don't know how or whether they signed up for the free mailing list some will still convert to the paid subscriptions. And plenty of others will unsubscribe. But others linger. They neither open the daily emails nor unsubscribe, and when periodic calls go out for legal purposes they don't opt in. Which leads me to sometimes wonder how many have died. How many inboxes are filling up with marketing emails and with spam and notifications of various things that will slowly, over time, dwindle down to almost nothing, as the people who would have had to click to continue receiving are no longer there to click on anything.

It's funny; in the Keel book from the box I just found, he mentions the story about the farmer and the field, by Bradbury. He doesn't name it, but he describes a story in which plants are screaming as the farmer approaches to cut them down with a scythe. It's not technically inaccurate. And yet, described like this, it's not at all the same story, I don't think.

Where was I? The evergreen folder? It lives on the desktop, next to a folder of doomsday info about an animal sanctuary I've picked out for Jasper in the event that she outlives me, and the phone number of a local fish store offering tank-breakdown services that would include absorbing my cories and my bettas and my guppies back into their community tanks. I've included instructions for how to pay those expenses. Because the important lesson for me from the farmer in the ADHD parable is that he knew the work would get done somehow, including the work of burying him, but that there was nobody to see to his final day but himself.

Chapter Thirty

I wake up cautiously, and then in my hand the new phone shivers with a text from Jeff: *I'll let you know when I hit Barstow.*

I make a last-minute attempt: 95 *plus degrees at dawn, record high today, if you want to reschedule.*

He answers, right away: *WTF why don't you want me to come?*

Then he texts again: *Did you see the link about sunlight for healing skin cancer?*

I type: *Fuck you.* And then I change it to *Thank you.* But I don't mean it and can't stand the way it looks so I delete it and then I get up and I shred an armful of notices about property taxes and a stack of old insurance statements for my mother that say, *This Is Not a Bill*—what do most people do with these things? I shred until I need to get oil for the shredder, and this makes me feel better. Until I find an old paper prescription from the years of hand-carrying paper prescriptions back and forth due to no refills on Adderall by federal law, paper prescriptions which expired in seven days if I didn't get to a pharmacy in time, where someone would check the watermark and ask for my ID while I would ask, always politely, when they could fill it. Soon, if it was in stock, but they couldn't give out information about inventory, because Adderall is a federally controlled substance. Nor check inventory at other locations, for the same reason.

Thank you, I would say, *I understand, but do you have a general sense that it might be in stock this week? If you were me, would you try to fill it elsewhere?*

Many people were professional and kind, offering to tender the prescription back legally so that I would still have whatever was left of the original seven days to drive around and try elsewhere. I must have done that but then given up; the seven-day period probably got away from me once I ran out of the Adderall that helped me do things like fill prescriptions on time. Luckily the neuropsychiatric clinic could rewrite it, for a fee. Which made sense. ADHDers probably tripped over the seven-day stumbling block all the time before electronic prescriptions were mandatory. But imagine going to pick up a refill of your blood pressure pills and being asked to put your arm in a blood pressure cuff at the register, and then being told that you're too stressed out and they can't legally give you the refill until you sit still and breathe and demonstrate that you can bring your blood pressure down on your own. And I know: If it was that simple, you probably wouldn't need the pills. I know, believe me.

In that box of mingled papers and old bills and expired coupons I also find shopping lists in Jandine's writing, work notes in Terry's writing, and, surprisingly, something in my grandfather Jake's writing; it's a list of quantities delivered from the farm to the butter-and-egg company, graded by class, and I recognize *rots*, but what are *blanks*? I put these aside and the crosscut shredder keeps scattering little shards of everything else, blue for banking, red for past-due bills, hard to sweep up, and what's the best way to recycle them? Or do they just have to go to a landfill? I keep meaning to look this up.

I work, I make lunch, I feed the cat, I feed the fish, I check the water parameters. I look at the pool from the window; I watch for TK. Gradually the day gains a bit of focus, but repeatedly I will look down and find that I'm holding something I don't know what to do with. The cracks in my fingertips are darkened with tannins from the blackwater aquarium supplies I'm experimenting with and my skin looks like the crackle glaze in pottery class in school so long ago, or the craft projects of tearing up masking tape to cover an empty wine bottle with uneven pieces before rubbing it with shoe polish to make it look like an ancient vase.

I'm holding a little vintage-looking red spiral notebook filled with pages and pages of Scrabble scores and checkers scores that already didn't mean anything five minutes after a game ended. The pens that wrote those numbers are in landfills, the pencils ground away to sawdust. Jeff and I will never sit down to any game again, because neither of us would actually want to.

The last time we went to a movie theater together was a long time ago. I was home for a weekend from college, and he'd still been in high school; I'd heard about a movie based on a Philip K. Dick novella, which turned out to be *Total Recall*, perfectly and exactly of that weirdly tinted moment poised between the eighties and the nineties. The lurid violence made Jeff laugh, and so did the scene when Schwarzenegger tries to get through customs in a disguise that malfunctions, his lifelike mask of a woman with red hair opening like a puzzle, the wig falling away, the head and neck sliding apart to reveal his face. He lifts it off and slides it back together, tossing it at the agents pursuing him, like an art thief throwing a marble bust at museum guards. One catches it, and they're gazing down in confusion when she opens her eyes, smiles, and says, *Get ready for a surprise. . . .*

If I had a fireplace I could burn the notebook. I'll shred it, I guess. Since it feels wrong to recycle something that looks so much like a code book for breaking a cipher of some kind.

I'm about to change the bedding in the guest room when I realize I'm just too tired, and that I need to lie down for a minute instead. This room is always cooler than anywhere else in the house, and as the second dose of the day unlocks into my bloodstream everything becomes much calmer in my brain, and so much quieter. A paradoxical effect. That's what it's called: the paradoxical effect. And Ritalin is named after the wife of the man who discovered the paradoxical effect on the brains of hyperactive children. The wife's name was Rita. How funny to know her name, and not his. How funny that I'm carrying the King Tut book with me, as if I can't afford to misplace it again. My name is written on the inside cover in my own handwriting of the time, and when I turn the first few pages I can see my old room, and myself on the bed reading these pages in the sunlight of 1978. If this book had disappeared into the estate sale or been donated that moment would be gone, too, along with the rainbow-printed pillows, the yellow ruffled curtains, the long heavy draft pillow shaped like a snake that I made in 4-H sewing club and kept wedged against the crack under the door. Maybe nothing would trigger that memory again, and how many others like it are gone already? Or still in my brain, but inaccessible? Unreadable against the background radiation of a smoking barbecue grill and burnt teriyaki marinade, a wooden pepper mill grinding, the gnashing electric can opener biting into a blue can of yellow pineapple rings. Damp fresh beauty bark banked around azaleas in the yard, everything steaming in the sunshine while I'm in my bedroom looking through the Tut book Warren has just given me.

The rumble of ice in the cooler. Another can of Rainier beer being opened on the back patio under the wavy fiberglass patio cover. Adult voices. The sound of wind chimes and the ticking of the sprinkler. Jeff wasn't there that day, but I'd been out there anyway for a minute, earlier.

"Hey, tubby, how do you like that book?" Warren had said from his lawn chair, a big Bloody Mary in his hand, eyes hidden behind dark glasses. His lips were always a little purple; he had that kind of circulation. And not too much later, it would kill him.

"Hey," said Terry sharply, turning away from the barbecue to point the long metal tongs at his father. "Don't talk to her like that. Apologize to her."

"She knows I'm kidding. I brought her a present."

"Did you hear what I said?"

"Well, who's not tubby?" Warren said. "Everybody here is tubby—me, you, everybody!"

"I don't consider myself tubby," said Ursula.

I was already back inside the house, heading for my room through a tableau like a compressed actuarial table, an accordion-folded sheet of graph paper where only some of the columns are visible, moments that flicker, just one selection among all the possibilities. Into the kitchen, across the entryway, the feeling of the rest of the house, the split levels, partly underground, cool, but dark. Something always present. And from here, I'm not sure how that was my life. How, but also why? It somehow does not seem—correct. From here it feels like there was an error, some kind of cosmic miscalculation.

Some time later, my mother appeared.

"Honey," she said when she came in. "Don't listen to him, his tits are bigger than everyone else's put together."

Which was true. I hadn't realized that Jandine was tipsy at the time. I hadn't wondered what those afternoons were like for her, during the time Heather was keeping Jeff away, when Warren and Ursula were not pleased, when nobody was happy.

I wish she had been happier, and healthier, for longer. By the time we might have talked about what that life was like, it was too late.

Along with the Tut book I bring a handful of the kind of paperbacks the library used to display by the checkout counter in a wire rack. *The Wolfen*, *Coma*, *The Dead Zone*. Some of Erich von Däniken's speculative histories of paleocontact with extraterrestrials: *Chariots of the Gods?*, *Gods from Outer Space*, *The Gold of the Gods* . . . I had been so naïve about loving these books, and then so disappointed by them. In college I had learned about the painstaking reconstruction of an ancient protolanguage that must have evolved into Sanskrit, Greek, and Latin, a hypothetical ancestor leaving no record of itself except in traces that appear in every subsequent language in the Indo-European tree. A professor showed slides of the comparative work, begun in the nineteenth century. So many tables, so much careful notation and cross-referencing of languages, including dead ones, and so much analysis by so many scholars and linguists. The volume and span of it was fascinating. I wasn't aware that what I felt was only an intellectual fascination until the professor played us an audio recording of Schleicher's fable, a short, artificial text constructed from the fragments of reconstructed roots, using common terms and concepts that persisted in various forms in the later languages, pointing back to a vanished common origin. It wasn't real, in other words, the professor told us, but it was a valuable tool for tracing the distant past, still alive somewhere inside our speech and thought. The pronunciation in the recording was based on informed and careful conjecture. But the reverse-engineering of how we think it might have sounded will probably continue to change.

The story itself was very short: A horse and a sheep meet on a road, have words, part ways. Even though I knew it wasn't real, hearing it had a cascading effect in my brain anyway, involuntary, like tumblers set in motion. After class, I went to the library to look for more recordings, but they were all of the same fable, because that's all there was, at the time. I reserved a media carrel and headphones anyway, and I listened again to an anonymous voice reading the artificial fable. It was only thirty seconds long, and I listened to it again and again.

I did an independent study on it during my senior year, and during one of our meetings, my professor referred dismissively to notions put forward by some historians who wanted to push the notion that speakers of Proto-Indo-European had originally come from the Caucasus region. It took me a minute to realize he meant that white nationalists were floating a version of prehistory in which the roots of the world's largest language tree, and therefore all the daughter languages now spoken natally by more than 40 percent of people alive, were ancestrally . . . Caucasian. Including politically relevant languages that were just then starting to come up regularly in mainstream American news, languages like Kurdish, and Farsi, and eventually Pashto. So I saw, and of course I still see, that there is often a racialized subtext to Western daydreams about antiquity. But I don't think that's what pulls most people to those daydreams. Human curiosity about the deep past is hard-wired. As inescapably hard-wired as our attraction to shiny gold artifacts. Which is probably why von Däniken has sold so many copies—sixty million? Something like that?

Erich von Däniken is a charismatic writer, people often say, rather than a conscientious one, and I get it, I was charmed by his description of hours spent in the library of his school, directed there by his Jesuit teachers, and also by his epiphany that changing a handful of words in the Old Testament would explain everything about the ancient world. But it's also true that his first book, the bestseller that set the pattern for all his others, was rejected by publishers in Germany before being rewritten by a former propagandist and editor for the Nazi Party newspaper, who was then credited as the editor in the original edition. When I open this old copy of *Gods from Outer Space*, originally published as *Return to the Stars*, I see the author's name, and the translator's name, and although there's no editor listed, per se, between the contents and the foreword, there's a short entry titled About Erich von Däniken, signed William Roggersdorf, which is one of the pseudonyms used by Wilhelm Utermann, the propagandist. He's sometimes described as a best-selling Nazi author, but there's not much detail about him online, at least not in English. But his place of death is listed as the town of Roggersdorf, in Bavaria. His contribution to the book that popularized the belief that ancient civilizations could not have engineered their own achievements without help from extraterrestrials is significant, whether you think paleocontact is an inherently racist idea or not.

Anyway. What I took away from my visceral experience of hearing the artificial fable spoken in PIE was that words of power, as they might be used in incantations, have a real effect, regardless of whether they themselves are real.

The book has glyphs and carvings throughout, and a section of black-and-white photos, like the Temple of the Inscriptions at Palenque. The Gate of the Sun at Tiahuanaco. Small, unclear aerial shots from the Nazca plains, and other sites, on other continents, some unnamed, some punctuated with rhetorical questions. There's a non sequitur Venus of Willendorf. It all seems jumbled together, disordered, but familiar, and, paradoxically, I fall asleep.

Chapter Thirty-One

When I open my eyes the cold air blowing in the hallway smells like hamburgers. And pickles. Jeff is here. I find him sitting cross-legged on the living room floor, listening to coffee shop music on a TV satellite station and also watching TV. I thought I'd changed the locks since the last time he had a key? This is in fact why I installed the kind of dead bolt that you can rekey yourself. Provided you get around to doing so.

The sight of him watching one thing and listening to another at the same time makes me carsick enough to have to look away. Jasper is staring at him, crouched on a crumpled In-N-Out Burger bag on the floor. She looks up at me, then rises stiffly and trots to the kitchen, like a potbellied piglet, because it's past time for her dinner.

"Hey," says Jeff. He's getting a little potbelly himself, the beginnings of the kind that Terry and Warren both had. Tubby, maybe Warren would say. Jeff prefers not to think about his genetic risk factors. I don't blame him. After all, I don't want to know if Alzheimer's is coming for me. I don't think I do.

My face feels puffy. I'm not awake. How did we both get so old?

"Hi," I say, and try not to wrinkle my face. Hamburgers do not cause a pee smell in the air per se. And who knows what he smells when he lets himself in and stands in this living room.

I cleaned everything up before Jeff arrived, the best I could.

He says, "Everything okay?"

"Yes," I say. "You?"

"Fine," he says. "I thought you weren't home at first, but then I saw you asleep in my room."

"It's cooler on the east side of the house," I say, when I should have said, *It's my guest room, and it used to be Jandine's room. How is it yours?* I know I'm not direct enough, even in my thoughts. It's a problem of long standing.

"So," he says, giving up on stretching. His arms and legs are irritatingly tan. There's a white line at the edge of the back of his neck, meaning he's had a haircut. "I'm going to swim some laps tomorrow morning," he says. "Do you want to come? What time does the pool open in the morning?"

"It'll be too hot for me tomorrow," I say. I take the remote away, so that I can watch the early-evening news, recorded in case they mention the attack here. If he doesn't like it, he can go elsewhere to listen to the satellite music that I'm paying for. Using the Wi-Fi I also pay for. Why am I thinking like this? So small-minded and petty, and so cranky?

I hate recording the news—I miss the way that if you really wanted to see something, you had to make time for it in your life, hurrying home to watch the next episode of *The X-Files*, or *Twin Peaks*, because if you missed an episode back then, you might never get another chance. Not until boxed sets of VHS tapes. Can you imagine? And now there's no shared world anymore. Just a billion little fragments. Instead of my friends and me around a TV with black coffee and cherry pie on Thursday nights.

"No, thanks," I say.

"Oh, come on," he says. "Let's swim early, while it's still cool."

Quit living in the past, I think, and fast-forward until I see the Crime Stoppers logo.

"Did you record this?" he says. "Why don't you just look it up?"

"Recent trouble in Paradise," says the female anchor. "Residents of one east-valley neighborhood are on guard after an attempted burglary turned violent earlier this week."

The male anchor adds, "And residents of Paradise near the intersection of Pecos and Tropicana are being warned to stay on the lookout for a man accused of attempted breaking and entering in the early-morning hours."

Jeff says, "Is that near here or something?"

"That's us," I say. "That's the end of this row of houses."

"Huh," he says, resting his forearms on his knees. "No way."

I turn to look at him, and he must know what I'm going to say, because he looks only at the TV. But I have to say it anyway. "Jeff," I say. "This is Vegas. We have to keep the doors locked." I hate myself for using the plural; he is the one who needs to be better about this. Not me.

He says, "Well, of course. That's a no-brainer."

I say, "It's important."

He doesn't answer.

"Is the front door locked right now?" I ask.

"Right now I'm sitting here," he says. "Nobody is going to break in with me sitting right here."

The side of his face is flushing. Already I have somehow failed to make him understand. I shake my head. "Paloma told me to keep the doors and windows locked," I say, because it doesn't matter if he respects Paloma or not; anyone's voice carries more weight than mine. It sucks, but it's expedient.

"All right," he says. "I'm not stupid."

He is accustomed to living alone, just like I am. We are both too set in our ways.

I go into the kitchen. He's only here for the long weekend, I tell myself. And maybe it's a good time to have another person around. A male in the house. I can easily survive the anxiety that he'll cause for the next two days and sometime soon he'll meet a pretty new girl, and then he'll stay in L.A. instead of driving here to visit now and then. The new girlfriend won't like me—they never seem to—and we will get along fine again from a distance.

After he goes upstairs to bed I seethingly lock the front door and then spend an hour quietly hunting for the pool key, which I've misplaced, so that I can leave it out for him to find in the morning. I resist the urge to stick a Post-it note by the dead bolt, saying, *Please keep this door locked at all times.* I don't know why I'm the one who feels bad; now I'll have to wait until he forgets to lock the door, so that I can point out a real thing, and not just a hypothetical what-if, which he probably learned from his father to disregard after witnessing all the years of my mother's concerns left unaddressed, all those years of Terry saying, *Everything is fine, what on earth are you worrying about now? What now?* And of Jandine never pushing back.

But their kind of told you so only works as long as nothing truly bad happens.

I am on the couch with Jasper, trying to fix my split fingernails when he appears on the stairs in his pajamas a few hours later for a drink of water. On his way down, he stops, and says, "What are you doing?" Even though I think it's pretty obvious that I am trying to open a stubborn bottle of cruelty-free nail hardener with a vise grip and some Channellocks, while also watching a documentary about sci-fi special effects in pre-CGI movies.

On his way back upstairs, he stops again, and says, "Anyway, don't worry, I know it's important. I'll lock the doors."

"Great," I say. "Thanks."

I notice that on his feet are a pair of my slippers, formerly Jandine's slippers. He must have found them under the bed.

I say, "They didn't mention what the attack was. On the news. Aren't you curious?"

He's already partway up the stairs with his glass of water, wanting to go back to bed. "No," he says. "Why would I be curious?"

I say, "A neighbor got bitten."

"Bitten," he says. He's shaking his head.

"Why are you shaking your head?"

"Because I know what you're thinking about."

"If you know what I'm thinking about, then knock wood, will you?" I say. I want him to be a little more superstitious. Or to at least remember when he was.

"Mandy," he says.

"I just thought you should know."

He says, "Just for the sake of argument. Do you think locking a door would do any good, if this were in that realm?"

"It can't hurt," I say.

He starts trudging back up the stairs.

"Jeff," I say, "Wait. Are you listening? She bit her own hand. And she was scratched. Three deep scratches."

He doesn't wait, he goes up and closes the bedroom door behind him, and he gets back into the bed, and though I listen I don't hear him knocking the edge of the dresser with his knuckles, touching wood for luck, because he doesn't believe in anything anymore.

I wake up late for a Memorial Day barbecue at memory care—hamburgers, hot dogs, and for the vegetarians some potato salad with a dash of paprika. So strange to know the holiday parties continue there without us. Jeff has gone out by the time I come downstairs. The front door is locked; good for him, for now.

In the kitchen it's clear he's been to the grocery store by the wadded plastic bags and the full carton of milk standing out on the kitchen counter. It's embarrassing and a little fatiguing, and I don't know whether to leave it out or put it back, because if I do he'll drink it without remembering that he forgot to refrigerate it all this time. I know that if I tell him, he will only hear that I'm criticizing him, instead of hearing that I don't want him to get food poisoning with a side of diarrhea on the drive home. I've given up on reminding him why factory milk is bad for everyone, not just for the blind, elderly cows but also for everybody who will come to regret the overuse of antibiotics later, when the superbugs eventually come home to roost. I don't understand how a grown person can live this long without feeling any responsibility for anything.

I'll have to hide Jasper's little pints of organic whole milk in a paper lunch bag, folded shut, so that he won't help himself—which would be fine if I could trust him not to leave it out on the counter and put it back much later without my knowing.

After I fill Jasper's saucer I refold the lunch bag shut and I write, in black marker: *Caution: Veterinary Stool Softener.*

Why is this a thing at all?

Jeff eventually comes back to the house dressed in damp swim trunks and a T-shirt, his skin tight with chlorine and his hair standing up in all directions after a day under one of the shade umbrellas, drinking plastic bottle after plastic bottle of water to stay hydrated.

"I'm going out tonight," he says, dropping onto the couch, and I wince, wondering how wet his shorts are. "I made other plans, since I'm guessing you won't want to go out."

"Of course," I say. "Have a good time."

From my room I hear him getting ready to leave for the evening, whistling, trailing aftershave. When I come out after he's gone I glance through the half-open door of the hall bathroom and see my Tut book sitting open and face down on the back of the toilet, and I swear for a moment I think I'm actually going to have the cardiovascular event I fear when a quick bright light strobes behind my eyes. I must have left that book out in plain sight and now here it is, face down on the shitter. Infuriating. I take the book and put it away.

I will hunker down until he leaves on Monday. And in the meantime, because I can't trust him to lock up, I will sleep with the dead bolt flipped on my bedroom door and I won't let Jasper out until morning no matter how much she begs, for fear that Jeff might let her out onto the patio, and forget, or just not realize, and leave her stranded in the heat, without a bowl of water.

I'm rewatching the scene that popped into my mind, from the last movie Jeff and I saw together in a theater . . . the female head, sliding apart like the tumblers of a safe . . . Apparently the internet remembers that character as the Two Weeks lady, because that's what she repeats to the immigration officer on Mars: How long are you staying? *Two weeks.*

Are you bringing any produce to the planet? *Two weeks* . . . It's more uncanny to me now than it was at the time. That persistent strange smile she gives, and the strange look on Schwarzenegger's face inside when her head opens. I watch it a couple of times. Then I find the same scene online with commentary—recent commentary?—from Schwarzenegger, who's in his seventies by now, and Verhoeven, the director, in his eighties. I want to know how that practical effect was done. But I'm distracted by the fact that in the first ten seconds of the clip they refer to the Two Weeks lady as an "old lady," "a fat old lady," and "the fat lady," which is in fact how she's credited. Since I'm this far into the wormhole I check her age, and see that she and the director were the same age, both of them fifty-two years old, at the time.

"Bye," calls Jeff from downstairs. "I'm locking the door," he adds, like it's a special occasion.

Jeff is still asleep when I get up the next morning, shut Jasper into my room, put on sunscreen and a hat and head out quietly to go about my business. I know, obviously, that I need to be getting rid of what I have, not bringing more home with me from someone else's life . . . But there's an estate sale nearby with some items of interest in the sale notice. I can't explain what sends me there any better than that.

Run by family members or by professionals, estate sales let strangers in to see all the private little fixes to appliances and doorknobs and light switches. All the good-enough solutions you might not want others to see. But of course if this is your house, then you're already not here.

This sale is run by the family. A pretty, slender woman in her early fifties is wearily but efficiently overseeing the dismantling of a household established for decades in a late-1970s-built house, with yellowing fiberglass vanities and countertops. Cocoa shag in the living room under a faceted orange glass chandelier. Her husband is unobtrusively deferring to her about prices not yet marked, and he wanders the rooms with a roll of blue painters tape and a black marker, adding price tags and helping carry bulky items to the cars of the people taking them away.

I recognize the way all of this works. The combination of fatigue, grief, and forward movement in the woman's face.

"I'm doing this for my sister," she says. "Her husband died of a heart attack out of nowhere."

Her eyes flick over and rest on her own husband for a moment.

I want to say I'm sorry for their loss, and that I've done it, too, and it's hard to see everything going out the door but in some way it's also a relief, because it has to be done. But I don't have Jandine's knack of knowing how. Her husband points me to the garage where his brother-in-law's books, posters, magazines, and VHS tapes sit on card tables in orderly rows. I pick out a 1977 issue of *Treasure Search* (Clues to the Ancient Inca Signal Stone), as well as a 1976 issue of *Psychic World and the Occult* (Yul Brenner Talks About the Power of Psychic Healing), a 1975 issue of *True West* (Treasure & Mining Issue), and half a dozen issues of *Fate* magazine, which is what I truly came for.

In the biggest bedroom I see a beautiful ceramic lamp, crackle glazed in a deep, earthy yellow. I'm a sucker for crackle glaze and the woman sees me looking.

"Ten dollars," she says.

The bedroom still holds a bed with a headboard and matching dressers.

"Does that leave you without a light in the room?" I ask; a lot of older houses here don't have overhead fixtures, just a wall switch wired for one outlet in each room where you can hang a swag. You just have to figure out which is the hot-wired outlet, but they're usually upside down.

"We're not sleeping here anymore," she says. She pulls open the blinds and I remember the way we camped in Tacoma during and after the estate sale, with wrapped snacks and bottled water, any pretense of really living there already over and done with.

Up and down the hallway there are framed color photos of the now-vanished Dunes casino in all its past Trucolor glory.

"Did he work at the Dunes?" I ask. "Your brother-in-law?"

"He did," says the woman. "For a long time. There's a lot more memorabilia out front. My sister just can't—"

She shrugs.

"You can't keep everything," I say.

As I'm paying, her husband packs my magazines into a brown paper grocery bag.

"That's okay," I say, "I don't need a bag."

"Here," he says, reaching to the bookshelf in the living room. "I'm throwing in some books you might be interested in."

I'm about to demur when I remember that it's not about me; every little bit he can give away now helps lessen the load for later, when the estate sale ends.

Estate sales are my way of seeing into neighborhoods, of driving down all the streets you might never see otherwise and all the houses you'd never walk into, unless maybe they were for sale. Soon enough, most will be. So I'll watch the listings and later, sometime, when a house has been emptied and put on the market I'll have descriptions for something, to be used at some point: *mature landscaping, vintage cement sunbreak, lovely little blue pool, partial-shade patio, fruit-bearing fig tree, vintage Vegas, naturally cool. Original hand-painted tile. Period kitchen. Peaceful.* If need be, I can come back to take a photo of the outside myself. Because my boss says it's good if the photos are a little amateurish. Then people who signed up to feed their property-flipping daydreams don't feel they're being lied to, or condescended to, or marketed to overtly, the way they might if the photos looked professional.

When I get home I leave everything in the car so that Jeff won't ask, *What is that, how much did you pay for those, where will you put them, do you really think you need any more stuff?* But first I look through a few pages. In the issues of *Fate*, and others, even right away I recognize the contour lines of my own curiosity about the unseen world, and what might lie under or behind, or within. I find that I don't want to call them articles, even though I mean no disrespect; these are the stories that made me, after all. But it's hot. I can't stay in the car forever.

There is a small feeling of greasiness inside the lock of the back door, something not right when I put the key in and turn it.

It feels like penance. When he's here.

I find Jeff in the kitchen, making breakfast. He hands me a plate with an egg and toast the way I liked it when I was ten or twelve years old. I haven't been able to stomach hot heavy food during the day for a long time. I accept the plate and by this stage of his visits I can feel my shoulders and face start to relax at the prospect of getting my personal space back. I can sit outside under the UV cover, and drink my tea on the patio with him. I almost look forward to these last twenty minutes or so. I can't relax around him, but as long as I remember this fact, things can be okay until he goes.

About a year ago I finally hung Terry's wind chimes in a corner of the patio, which Jeff hasn't noticed even though they're three feet in length and hard to miss. But now he hears the old familiar sound, a soft hollow *clunk* and the musical shiver as the smaller chimes touch. It's startling, how deeply a forgotten sound can touch you.

"Hey," he says, captivated. "Are those my dad's?"

I don't have to answer because of course they're Terry's, and whenever the chimes touch, the world of the old house still exists. The aboveground pool in the backyard that Terry set up and maintained for us. The basketball hoop he put up, the azaleas and the rhododendrons. The birdbath. The beauty bark and the big rocks. All the wandering shaggy cats. We sit without speaking for a minute or two, and it's sad, it's so sad. Everything is gone and there's no good reason except the entropy that settled over the old house like a spell in a fairy tale.

"When I heard that sound just now I expected to hear my dad's voice, too," says Jeff. "Yelling at something."

"Or slamming the screen door."

"Yeah," says Jeff. A moment later, he says, "My dad should have oiled that door."

I almost answer. It would be the most normal thing in the world, to remind him that Terry left the back screen door loud on purpose because he wanted to hear it if anyone ever tried to get into the house while he was out working in the yard. Terry's attention to security; we both remember that. It could almost be a little bit funny. But underneath whatever we're talking about, Jeff hates that I remember anything he doesn't. Maybe because it means I spent more time there than he did. Which is of course true. So I say nothing, and things are fine, and pretty soon he takes his bag and goes out to his car in the front lot and drives away, back to his life in L.A.

Even years later I still can't stand the bland smell of easy deli sandwiches like the ones dropped off by the wives of Terry's friends during the estate sale. Or Crystal Light, or homemade oatmeal cookies. The clothes and shoes I wore as I cleared out cupboards and packed up closets had to be thrown out because they took on a pasty odor like the old toothpaste in the drawers in Terry's bathroom, which was not a place I ever expected to be; I'm not sure I'd ever entered that room, before he died, now that I think about it. Anyway. So many things had taken on a smell of basement carpet that flooded, dried out, and reflooded over the years. And of the shelters Terry had built in the backyard for the many abandoned neighborhood cats, rained on, dried out, faintly mildewed, marked with urine.

Jeff wouldn't weigh in about so many objects from the house. Like the chimes. He left it to me, and I took them down from their original hook behind the old house and packed them in Bubble Wrap and later shipped them here with everything else, and then I unpacked them and scrubbed away the mildew and sap from the years they hung under the fiberglass roof by the woodpile. I checked inside for spiders, and spider eggs. And eventually I got out the ladder and hung them here. I'm sure Jeff has no memory now of having stood on the uneven paving stones displaced by the roots of trees in the backyard after his father died, no memory of pointing to where they hung above the filthy insulated doghouses used by cats and raccoons, stuffed with ruined thermal beds and heating pads dangerously soaked with piss and rain, strung on a grid of aged outdoor extension cords. He doesn't remember saying, *Toss everything*. I had already shut off the breaker before touching anything after I found a heating pad in Terry's outdoor chair, tucked between the rain-soaked cushions. He could in theory have been electrocuted. But I know what Terry was thinking: He was looking at the old yard cats and providing warmth in the grim damp for their little light bones and his own lumbar trouble. Jeff does not remember that he pointed at Terry's AM/FM radio, the pewter ashtray full of cigar butts, the two barbecues—one gas, the other old-school with a bag of melting charcoal inside—and the rusty tongs and scrapers, the thermometer shaped like a pine cone and the plastic rain gauge we gave him for Father's Day ages ago. He does not remember saying, *There's nothing to salvage, call the junk people, get it over with*.

We had sold Terry's nineteen-foot Livingston fishing boat that afternoon. The scar from the place where it sat undisturbed for a decade was still fresh and dark in the moss, and so were the footmarks of the man who bought it and whose two big sons helped maneuver it to their truck and boat hitch out front. When one of the sons wondered under his breath how the boat ever got back there to begin with, I burst into the kind of laughter you eventually get grateful for, and I said, *If you think that's bad, there's a pool table downstairs we'll have to dismantle to get out of the house. Want to take it with you?*

The older man had chuckled, the way people do when they know what it's like, people who have gone through it all already for their own dead parents. The estate sales. Getting a house ready to sell. Emptying the rooms. The way sentimentality and blue book prices fall away like scales from your eyes, and you find yourself trying to hand off the biggest, bulkiest encumbrances to anyone who'll take them.

Good luck with that pool table, he said, as they pushed through the hedges that grew close-up to the side of the house, while Jeff stood with his arms folded, watching that man and his sons working together to fit the Livingston around the tight corner, working together as handily as if they did it every day.

Jeff had to leave before everything was finished. One of the last tasks I did at the house was to try to get the leaky hose off the spigot out back, which I couldn't do without fear of snapping the pipe, so I had to just leave it where it was, staining the cement with rust. The real estate agent promised to send someone to shut off the water and wrap the pipes, even though the plumbing was already shot; how much more damage could be done? There can always be more, apparently, but that was not our problem anymore. When I finally took down Terry's wind chimes on the last evening I thought I could hear smaller ones, somewhere farther back in the trees. I found them with the beam of one of Terry's heavy flashlights, glinting in the drooping evergreens, hung around a plastic squirrel feeder Terry had protected with an old umbrella. He'd nailed up a few old outdoor plastic thermometers, giveaways from his client agencies, mostly defunct. There were peanut shells and a corncob or two on the ground, and a churned area that might have been serving as a toilet for the outdoor cats. And then right there, just above eye level, I suddenly saw the flashlight beam hitting the web around one of those gigantic reddish-brown spiders, with long legs, like jointed pine needles. Yard spiders, all over the place. They were always between the branches, across the paths, waiting in the corners of windows and doorways. Spiders hanging motionless at eye level, hair level, mouth level, invisible until you might shift your focus and find one poised directly in front of your face.

The thermometers probably would have shattered if I tried to pry them loose. I left the old chimes disintegrating in the branches.

It's just stuff, I know that.

But it is also the material of life. Then, and therefore now.

PART FOUR

SOCRATES: One, two, three; but where, my dear Timaeus, is the fourth of those who were yesterday my guests and are to be my entertainers to-day?

TIMAEUS: He has been taken ill, Socrates; for he would not willingly have been absent from this gathering.

SOCRATES: Then, if he is not coming, you and the two others must supply his place.

PLATO, *Timaeus*
(TRANS. BENJAMIN JOWETT)

I had said unto them: Every living thing that groweth up out the ground shall be food for you; but of everything wherein is the breath of life, which is of blood and spirit, ye shall not eat. Whoso sheddeth blood, wherein is life, by himself inviteth his own blood and spirit to the spoil.

JOHN BALLOU NEWBROUGH, *Oahspe: A New Bible in the Words of Jehovih and His Angel Embassadors. A Sacred History of the Dominions of the Higher and Lower Heavens on the Earth for the Past Twenty Four Thousand Years*

And they replied, "We go on our hands, so that we may eat flesh, and we crawl along upon our hands, so that we may drink blood."

R. CAMPBELL THOMPSON, TRANSLATOR, *The Devils and Evil Spirits of Babylonia, Being Babylonian and Assyrian Incantations Against the Demons, Ghouls, Vampires, Hobgoblins, Ghosts, and Kindred Evil Spirits, Which Attack Mankind.*

Chapter Thirty-Two

My grad school orientation took place at the end of August, when the daytime temperature was consistently over a hundred degrees, but every indoor space on campus was air-conditioned and sometimes so cold that I learned to carry a cardigan for my bare arms and some socks for my sandaled feet. And then to take them off again before going back out into the sun. Stepping outdoors after dark was uncannily even hotter sometimes, when the collected heat of the day rose up from concrete surfaces. And there was concrete everywhere. It seemed I was always walking through parking lots, at dusk, through a low layer of heat as heavy as the water in a wading pool. It was not the life I had imagined, back when I set the gears in motion to bring me to this unfamiliar place.

But the longer I was here, the more weirdly euphoric I began to feel. I thought maybe it was some kind of metaphysical desert intoxication; later, I realized I was being bombarded with more UV rays than I'd ever experienced in my life. Was this what people meant, when talking about seasonal affective disorders? I'd never known what I was missing.

I stayed in that rental apartment for years, because I was happy with the granite countertops and new appliances, the rooms that were full of light. In retrospect it was identical to thousands of other Las Vegas rentals built around the same time—granite countertops, beige carpet, beige vertical blinds, easy neutral colors—but I appreciated it all. The second-floor balcony that was safely inaccessible from the ground. The huge garden bathtub. Maybe I didn't love the wall-to-wall carpet, but at least it had been new when I moved in. Anyway, everything was easy, I could lock the security door, set the air-conditioning, and sleep soundly in rooms where every corner was easily visible and accessible. My mind was clearer than it had ever been. I felt in tune with signals from out in the world that weren't creepy. Often I might be driving, and feel a small urge to turn, maybe take a left instead of a right, and then I would find myself in a new thrift store holding some particular item that I had only just been thinking about, often something vintage, just some everyday thing I remembered from the farm. Not, of course, the very thing itself, but another iteration. The shelves and racks seemed seeded with Easter eggs and treasures, dispersed for me to potentially find, if I could manage to keep the right depth of mental focus. Now I recognize from neurofeedback therapy that I was balancing the ratio between my beta and theta brainwaves, by luck or by chance. It was amazing, to experience what a dry climate can do to preserve things, and I didn't miss the pervasive smell of damp that I had never actually known I was smelling, my entire life, never having been away from it.

These weren't the kind of synchronicities to get a story out of, or submit to a paranormal podcast. Nothing was striking in a way that would have been meaningful to anybody else, and anyway such resonances always sound like a stretch if you try to articulate them. In junior high shop class, I had made a wooden pen stand for Terry, which then sat permanently on his desk, with an unused ballpoint upside down in the swiveling plastic pen trumpet. The wooden base was shaped like a cat and I had learned to use a jigsaw by cutting it out. In a thrift store here I found some other cat that some other kid, I assume it was a kid, had made, probably also a gift, and though most of the hardware was missing, I recognized the empty socket. I had wanted the pen to sit at a jaunty angle, hoping it would look like a tail, and though I thought I'd invented the pattern, somebody else must have had the same idea. And the empty brass socket looked so much like a cat's butthole that it had to be a cosmic joke, sitting there for me to find. I was twenty-seven years old, and it was the first time in my life that I could believe the unseen part of this world might have a sense of humor. No doubt it helped that I was reading Jung in a graduate seminar at the time.

The synchronicities tapered off after Terry died, probably

because I shut everything peripheral down when I went back to Tacoma, and closed myself off, by necessity. But it was great while it lasted.

I was aware of the ordinary background sounds in that busy apartment complex, but they didn't usually keep me awake. Neighbors slamming car doors and setting car alarms at all hours, coming and going in a twenty-four-hour city. In fact I liked knowing there were people around, and I felt safe in that apartment. Until one night after I'd been there a few years, when I woke because everything was quiet. Even the doves under my window were eerily silent. It wasn't light out yet, but the mirrored closet doors in my bedroom glinted with a little stray light from outside. Reflected in them I could see the silhouette of a man. Someone standing behind me, in the bedroom doorway, watching me.

My whole body went cold. I had one clear thought: Terry was right. He worried about me living here alone and wanted to buy me a gun. Now it was too late.

My hand flew to the bedside table, I turned on the lamp—but the hall was empty. I got out of bed fast, tangled in a sheet, feeling too light and halfway out of control as I ran to the front door but found it still bolted. I was alone in the apartment.

I looked in all the closets, behind furniture, under my bed, checking everywhere, double-checking everywhere—pulling away the shower curtain, and the drapes, checking under furniture, behind the clothes hanging in the closets. I even looked in the cupboard under the kitchen sink. I checked every window. I checked the front door again and again, and kept finding it bolted, as it was when I'd gone to bed.

My bone marrow was throbbing with adrenaline, and I was too afraid to go back to bed, too afraid of seeing something behind me in the mirrored closet doors again. I tried to sleep on the couch, but I kept noticing so many sounds, everywhere, inside and outside. Until finally I fell asleep, some time after it was light out. The next afternoon I woke with my phone still in my hand, ringing, ringing—the caller ID said *Mom & Terry*. But it was Jeff. Calling because Terry had had a heart attack during the night.

"How bad?" I said, with fumbling thoughts about booking a flight. Missing classes. Surface details.

Jeff said something I couldn't make out.

"Sorry, can you say that again?" I asked.

"Jandine found him this morning," he said, and there was a long pause, in which I heard my mother's voice echoing somewhere in the background and realized belatedly that of course he was there, at the house.

"He's gone," said Jeff. "He's dead."

Everything stopped. Went still.

Jeff said more things and I left for the airport dragging a half-empty carry-on without remembering to book a ticket before walking out the door. I didn't think to call a cab, either, I just parked in the long-term parking lot and headed for the Southwest counter with no idea how long I would actually be gone.

Jeff must have taken a similar journey, hours earlier. Jandine probably called him right away. But why didn't she call me after calling him? Why didn't she call me at all?

I hadn't eaten or changed clothes or washed my face and I boarded that plane in my pajamas like a sleepwalker, then buckled into my seat and curled up facing the window. While the plane was in the air I kept turning over the idea Jandine and Jeff hadn't called me right away. My mind stuck to that, in a way that it couldn't yet stick to the idea that Terry was gone. I kept closing my eyes and slipping a little, losing track for a few seconds at a time, long enough to forget and expect Terry to be there, pulled up outside baggage claim where he always picked us up. And then I would remember, repeatedly. I was in such a state of mind that it only hit me when we started the descent into Sea-Tac that maybe it was Terry I had seen in the hall the night before, as he was leaving this world.

Chapter Thirty-Three

The concrete driveway of Terry's house was buckled and cracked, the spruces on either side so overgrown that the shuttle driver lingered, backing up a little to check that I was all right where I stood on the front porch waiting to be let in. Even some of the other passengers watched. When I heard the locks inside being undone I waved, and the driver put the shuttle back in gear, and drove away slowly, as if expecting me to realize I had the wrong address.

When Jandine swung open the front door she looked as thin and dirty as an old broom handle, and so disconnected from the moment that at first she behaved as if nothing had happened. She smiled a little too brightly, and made some pleased motions of surprise to find me there before patting me into an odd hug. But when she stepped back and saw my face she composed her own to match.

Jeff was standing a few feet behind her, and when he looked up, swollen eyed, I knew it was true. I had hoped for some kind of a mistake. The way everyone always does.

I shut the heavy front door behind me and the chain lock swung, swung, swung against the wood, repeating an arc long scuffed into the varnish. Jandine stood waiting. Jeff still didn't speak. The quiet was unnerving and by the time the lock stopped swinging I had realized why: There was no TV on, no surround sound speakers blaring a ball game or a cop show at high volume. Terry's leather armchair was huge in the darkened living room, like a giant broken-in baseball glove, with the lamp beside it off and the living room in darkness.

The silence, the heavy drapes, the dim lighting, so much cocoa and burgundy carpet . . . my ears were already ringing. When the furnace kicked in and hot air rose from the sunken vents in the living room carpet, I found it hard to breathe.

By the next day I would know to step up, driving Jandine to the funeral home, filling out forms, making decisions she couldn't and guessing at what Terry would have wanted before handing over their credit cards to pay for arrangements as they were presented to us. *Sign here*, I told Jandine. *And initial here*. I tried to include Jeff in the decisions, but he would say, *Just do whatever Jandine thinks is best*. And Jandine would pause, hesitant to hurt anyone's feelings by making one selection over another if multiple choices were offered. So I would tick the boxes. And then track down and notify banks and retirement accounts and insurance companies and Social Security, ordering extra official copies of his death certificate for these purposes. As if in a dream, I would find myself writing his obituary and choosing a photo of him to send to the Sunday newspapers in Tacoma, Bremerton, Bellingham, Portland, the places where he had business contacts of long standing. And I would make an appointment with Jandine's primary care doctor. But that first night nothing was clear. I went through the open pocket door into the cluttered kitchen, found a bottle of red wine, and set about trying to uncork it with one of the gadgets from a drawer overflowing with cork stabbers, vacuum pumps, and an electric thing that made a grinding sound but didn't open the bottle.

"This is useless," I said, dropping it and digging through the drawers for a plain corkscrew. All the while ignoring a silence that I had been dreading most of my life. The pocket door to the dining room was open and from long habit I averted my eyes from the darkness under the dining room table, the folds of the voluminous drapes, and I kept searching until I finally found a corkscrew on the windowsill over the sink.

I kept my attention on Jeff as he told me what all he knew or surmised about when, where, and how Terry had died: during the night, upstairs, of a massive coronary event.

I kept turning the corkscrew into the neck of the bottle, and listening to Jeff, and looking down to where the rubber baffle over the garbage disposal should have been. But the folds of black rubber were old, cracked, torn away in places. I could see the grinders inside; they would be loud without the rubber baffle. Jeff kept talking, because when somebody dies you have to turn whatever you think you know over and over until you can hold it. He paused, and then either he started over again or it all caught up to me from a long distance.

I pulled out the cork. I inclined the bottle at him, but he shook his head. My mother smiled. I poured a glass for myself and then, with some hesitation, a small one for her. She took the glass from me and held it up, as if expecting a toast of some kind, now that we were all together. Her face was as calm as if we were discussing something that had happened somewhere else, to someone else. She was sympathetic, and didn't want to pry, but she knew that she was missing something.

"I don't know where to sleep tonight," Jeff said. "It looks like somebody has been sleeping in the guest room, but I can't tell because all the light bulbs are burned out. Their bed looks okay, but yours is totally buried in stuff. And maybe it would be good if she's not alone, because this—this is a real problem," he said, gesturing very slightly toward Jandine.

Jeff and I looked at each other then; we'd both known the house was getting more and more uncomfortable. That fact was why neither of us came to visit more often. But how did it get this neglected, and so overwhelmed with clutter? And when? Was it really so long since either of us had been here? I could see the time catching up now suddenly in both our minds.

Jandine cleared her throat and spoke.

"Well," she said. "It's always been the same arrangement. For you kids."

I turned back to him.

"You should have called me," I said, suddenly. "You should have told me about your dad right away, and also that something else was wrong as soon as you got here—I would have come to help right away—"

"I did call you," he snapped, "and by the way, I have no clue what's going on here."

"Well," said Jandine, choosing her words with great deliberation. I noticed, absurdly, that she wasn't wearing any makeup. That her hair seemed so dark, so straight. "You should both just crawl into bed and get some sleep and hope everything will look better in the morning."

Jeff gestured, helplessly. I couldn't look away, though I felt I should.

"I assume you'd rather not sleep in their bed? Or in the basement?" I asked, and he looked at me with such a stricken expression that I almost burst out laughing, or crying, or both. He shook his head.

"Have you been sleeping upstairs or downstairs?" I asked Jandine. She moved her glass of wine, as if to say, *Sometimes, maybe?* "You're going to sleep upstairs tonight, okay?" I said.

"Of course," she said.

"Will you be all right in the guest room?" I asked him.

He nodded, then turned and embraced Jandine quickly, and me, too, surprisingly, and then he went straight downstairs and shut the guest room door behind himself.

My mother and I were alone; it had been a while. She had such a bright, fragile smile.

"How are you doing?" I said, and waited, to see how she wanted things to be.

Her eyes were slightly bloodshot, her irises very green. After a moment she looked away, and then sighed. It didn't feel like a real sigh but I couldn't tell if we both knew this.

"Sometimes, it just is what it is," she said. "Sometimes all you can do is crawl into bed and get some sleep, and hope that everything will look better in the morning."

"Okay," I said. "Let's do that, then."

She set her untouched glass of wine on the counter, thanked me for coming, and went toward the stairs. I followed and saw her pause, looking down at my bag in the entryway.

"That's my bag," I said. And then, more gently, "You should go upstairs and crawl into bed. You should get some sleep."

She turned back, and touched my face.

"Thanks for coming, sweetheart," she said. "It means a lot."

She went up the stairs and the sounds underfoot were so familiar as she disappeared down the hall. The bedroom and bathroom doors were golden oak veneer over hollow cores, so light, rattling faintly in the frames as she passed. I heard her open the door to their bedroom, and now I can imagine her seeing the king bed and all the other heavy furniture, covered with ceramic ashtrays full of coins, unlabeled keys, and scattered cough drops. All the remote controls, receipts, electrical cords, and phone chargers. Ballpoint pens, batteries . . . all the many things that I would go through later, sorting, filing, shredding, throwing away. It wasn't until I heard Jandine close the bedroom door behind her that I felt fully alone, with my back to the front door and Terry's house spread out before me, and him somehow no longer there.

Terry had been found on the shag carpet of the floor between his side of the bed and their en suite bathroom, but it wasn't the idea of sleeping in the room where he died that stopped me from following her upstairs. I just didn't think I could handle it if she turned out the light and fell asleep, like on any other night.

I felt the wine. I hadn't eaten in a while. Terry, I thought suddenly; how did this happen?

I picked my way up the stairs between the piles of magazines and newspapers and some unopened UPS boxes and Costco-sized packs of tissues, noticing the way the brown carpet parted greasily at the edge of each stair. The overhead light was burned out in my old bedroom, but in the light from the hall I could see that the bed was buried under a pile of what looked like—I don't know, laundry, maybe. Clothes and bath towels, some Bubble Wrap, and a length of crumpled brown paper. It looked like there were rolling metal clothes racks on either side of the bed, new since I'd been there last, filled with hanging coats and other bulky garments that hid the dressers behind them. I could have tried to push the piles of laundry off the bed, but there wouldn't have been room on the floor. The only clear area was the path at my feet from the door to the bed.

I wanted to put a door between me and the rest of the house. I wanted that enough to briefly consider sleeping in the tub in the hall bathroom. But it was full of magazines, hair curlers, and shoeboxes full of empty shampoo bottles. I also thought about maybe looking for the keys to Terry's car and driving to a hotel somewhere nearby, but who knew where the keys might be, and I didn't want to even pass through the dim garage now, at night, under all the shadows cast by Terry's fishing gear, the spiky nets and poles, and the waders hanging from the ceiling. The car-wash mittens on hooks and coiled garden hoses. And his shrouded classic Buick, and my childhood anxiety that someone or something might be sitting in the front seat, concealed by the silky car cover. So the living room was the best option? I'd seen a throw blanket in Terry's chair.

The furnace kicked on again. Jasper emerged from behind the couch and leaned against my ankles in a soft halo of sleepy fur, blinking at the chair where Terry should have been. It was unbearable. I set my wineglass down by his collection of remote controls, lifted her, and sat down in his place. The leather was cold, and she promptly huddled on my lap like a warm heavy hen.

My brain skipped from surface to surface. We had to figure out what to do. And I kept thinking *we, we, we*, thoughts bouncing like the colored lights of a psychedelic screen saver, breaking apart, coalescing, never settling. I was smoothing Jasper's fur. Waiting for the furnace to stop and bracing myself to chalk any sound up to Jeff in the guest room or Jandine upstairs or any plausible normal reason to hear something in an occupied house.

I could not remember sleeping out in the open like this since the last time Jeff and I took our sleeping bags downstairs to watch TV, however many years ago. Decades, by now.

I pulled at the throw blanket and heard the skittering sound of a pill case. Terry's, obviously. Yesterday's compartment was empty. Today's was still full. I selected the bluest tablet and fished my phone out of my pocket to look up the number stamp: zolpidem tartrate.

Terry, I said silently. Can I have your Ambien?

No answer, of course. I swallowed it with the wine in my glass.

Certain kinds of healers and teachers, and deliverance ministers, and exorcists—those who recognize the horror of the abyss all around us and have the fortitude to confront it—seem to agree that drinking alcohol or using drugs weakens your defenses. But I was grateful to find Terry's blue pills in time to put myself under before the furnace stopped. I'd seen the look on Jeff's face when I asked him about sleeping down in the basement; I assumed he'd be awake all night, listening to the creaking in the vents and the brush of hedges against the aluminum siding, to the many small gnawing sounds a hoard will make as it settles down in darkness. I pulled the throw blanket over my head, and didn't open my eyes until I heard Jandine in the kitchen making coffee at dawn.

Chapter Thirty-Four

The next morning Jeff and I had a brief moment of accord when we agreed that obviously Jandine couldn't stay in the house on her own, not just in the long term, but for any length of time. Because I could stay for a while, that's how it had to be, for now. Jeff had to get back to L.A. for work but he promised he'd be back soon to help sort out the house.

In the meantime I wanted Jandine to see her doctor right away. She had sounded normal whenever I called, normal enough that I hoped she wasn't facing what we all feared. Maybe it was something temporary, reversible. Maybe the big bottles of supplements covering the kitchen counters were interacting with her prescriptions. When was the last time anyone checked her blood pressure? She didn't look like she'd been eating properly, either.

"Speaking of which, I'm going out to find something to eat," he said, pausing at the door to the garage.

"Maybe we should all go for breakfast?" I said.

"I need a break, frankly," he said, jingling Terry's keys in one hand. He put a hand to the dead bolt. "Can I get back in? Should I take the key?"

The question startled me. Did neither of us still have a key to the house at all? Probably not, I realized. But more than that I was surprised that he asked because that key never left that lock. Terry only turned it at night. Didn't Jeff remember that? Or maybe he'd never known? Never noticed?

"I think that's the only copy," I said. "So leave it, and just use the garage door opener in Terry's car."

Jandine appeared at the top of the stairs and for a moment her face lit up like she was glad to see us.

"I'll be back," said Jeff, leaving without looking back.

"Okay," said Jandine, turning away. Concealing, I thought, that she'd briefly forgotten the reason we'd come.

—

Jandine readily agreed to move, when we sat down with her later. Too readily, maybe. Had she understood what we meant? Yes, she understood about moving somewhere smaller and easier. She thanked us. She said she had a question. No, actually; it was a firm condition. She did not want anything in the house thrown away. Or donated, or recycled, or given away. At that point I remember wondering if she was fucking with us. Jeff sat back, ready to drop the subject until some other better time. But I couldn't bear the idea of dragging it all out. I'd been locking myself in a bathroom to cry my eyes out several times a day, and so had Jeff, I knew. It was gutting, to see now how long Terry had been covering for Jandine's decline, and trying to manage his own health and stress, without asking for help—of course not. He never would have.

Jeff found it hard to tell her a lie that big, but I didn't. I promised Jandine that if it was really what she wanted, we would find a way to keep it all.

We started the process of getting her out of the house right away, doing as much as we could before Jeff had to leave. He and I worked at clearing areas, loading six of Terry's favorite CDs at a time and letting them play on random while we shifted furniture, vacuumed, dusted, discarded. Jandine made piles of things she wanted to keep, but kept adding to the piles until everything was lost again under new piles. *Churning*; that's the term used in hoarding studies. Later, I would realize it wasn't really hoarding, though. Not exactly. More a combination of factors, including her executive functions being completely overwhelmed, when her cognitive trouble made everyday tasks that had always been a bit of a struggle into an impossible situation. She didn't want to throw anything out, but she didn't seem to actually care about any of it enough to want to hoard it. It was baffling, and terrible.

Also terrible were the grocery bags Jeff found in the guest

room full of family photos from the farm mixed with coupons and gas station receipts. They looked like trash, and it was lucky he'd bothered to check. I was so angry that I had to lock myself in the bathroom to sob again, this time because nothing seemed to mean anything to her. But then later, when she saw me sorting through the bags, it seemed instead like everything mattered to her, like every little thing was so important that she couldn't prioritize, and that's why everything was so mixed up. Was that any better? Maybe. But none of the options were good.

From the second night on, I slept in the big bedroom with her. There really wasn't anywhere else, and it was a relief to be upstairs, behind a closed door, even though right after I took another of Terry's blue pills I remembered the laundry chute in the closet. I had always felt that the bedrooms up here were safe, because they were separate, somehow. But would I still feel that way if someone were standing just below that little trapdoor, down in the dark laundry alcove?

Terry had sealed that chute, right?

Jandine was asleep and even if she hadn't been I wasn't sure she could answer if I asked, which meant I had to look now, before the blue pill hit.

I made myself get up out of bed and quietly open the closet, but I nearly shut it again because Terry's clothes were all hanging there in darkness that smelled of Old Spice aftershave. But I did it, I leaned in and swept my phone's weak flashlight around until I caught the gleam of brass wood screws around the hatch. I shut the closet door again, softly, so as not to wake Jandine, and turned around to slip back into bed.

She was sitting up, watching me.

"Jeez—you scared me," I said.

"Did you hear something?" she asked.

I wish I had hit pause then. I really wish I had stopped, and slowed down, in case this was a chance to really talk to her, because those opportunities would be so rare and so tenuous. But she looked so unsettled.

"No," I said, "I don't think so."

"Okay, that's good," she said, turning away again, and falling asleep. As on any other night.

In those first few days in the house I would catch myself moving between rooms in ways that were so habitual that they seemed involuntary, automatic, but so specifically tied to the house that I would not have remembered them at all if I hadn't been there again. Like the way my hand would lift on its own when I went from one room to another while my steps halted and I reached forward, always leaning over the door sills to turn on the overhead lights first. Only reaching back to turn a light off after I'd stepped out, always without looking back. It may have been the normal way of going from one room to another, but still, it was a shock to feel my hands and feet moving on their own, as if they remembered how to brace against being surprised. And that was another strange realization. It wasn't quite accurate to say that I didn't want to be surprised. The feeling of something in the house was not surprising: It was a constant, pretty much. I was avoiding being startled, because being startled makes you react involuntarily. I had worked so hard to avoid revealing to whatever was in the house that I knew it was there. I hadn't articulated this, even to myself, but in retrospect, I took it for granted that my safety depended on this.

"I have an idea," said Jeff. "Let's get some daylight in here."

I didn't want that. But Jandine answered before I could.

"Sure," she said, sounding enthusiastic. Chirpy, like a songbird trapped in a cave.

We wore masks and gloves while pulling yards of heavy fabric off the sharp old-fashioned drapery pins. We took down all the drapes, on all the floors, and the air everywhere in the house filled with dust. We also took down the rugs and tapestries from the walls and rolled them and taped them into contractor bags and piled them in the garage, to be dealt with later, leaving bright bare places on the walls where the paint colors were visible again, like they'd been years earlier.

"Wow," said Jandine, looking at the newly uncovered rectangle on the tall atrium wall. "That's an interesting choice."

Jeff didn't want to help clean the carpets; he wanted to pull down drapes. He didn't want to help set up the tall ladder to remove the cobwebby chandelier globes, run them through the dishwasher, and then put them back up again; he was so impatient to pry the bolts out of the kitchen fireplace doors that he stripped them, leaving sharp, chewed-up metal behind. I'm not saying he was wrong, necessarily, about doing any of those things. It was the order of it. It was the way grand acts caught his interest, but not the cleaning up afterward. When he disappeared while Jandine and I were washing the windows I felt like I had to go check, to see what he was up to. I found him examining the wood paneling of the den walls with a putty knife, prying at the corners, trying to pull it up. I didn't want to tell him what to do. But it was too ridiculous.

"That's a phase-two project," I said. "There are other things to do first."

"It will be good for resale," he said. "This is so dated."

"After you pull the panels off are you planning to fill the nail holes? And sand them down? Are you going to prep the walls and paint them after?" I asked.

"You don't have to always be such a know-it-all," he said.

That night he met up with some people from high school he hadn't seen in a while, going out to places that had changed so much since we'd lived here that I'm sure I would have barely recognized them.

I had offered to drive Jeff to the airport, but he declined. I went out for sandwiches and by the time I got back to the house he'd showered and packed and was ready to go, with his bags in the entryway. He accepted half a sandwich and hung around the front door with it in one hand, watching for the shuttle. He had his phone in the other hand, snapping pictures of random little details. Like the brass mail slot, blocked, all these years.

"Taking nostalgia pics?" I said.

"Hardly," he said. "Everything will have to be fixed before the house goes on the market." I looked to see if Jandine was listening. Because evening was coming, and who knew, she might not want to talk about selling the house. Or about leaving.

"If you're going to get estimates from a contractor it might help to have pictures," he said.

"I don't know if that needs a professional," I said, peering at it. What I really meant was stop polishing the brass on the *Titanic*. There are much bigger problems to fix here. But I didn't want him to feel like I was shutting him down. I needed him to come back, after all. And as for the mail slot, I'd never looked closely, or if I had, I didn't remember. "Is it actually sealed?"

He prodded lightly at the flap with his phone. "Maybe not," he said. "Maybe it's just stuck." He put his phone and sandwich down and pulled at the edges. Don't, I thought. Maybe don't do that just yet. But he got one of the corners loose and with a gummy sound he pried the flap up from where it had been sealed with double-sided tape, so long ago. He pulled the tape from one end, and it came off in a long, disgusting strip.

"What do you think," he said. "Twenty years? Twenty-five?"

"At least," I said.

He stuck the tape to the back of the door and looked into the dark interior of the mail slot.

"There's something stuck in there," he said. He didn't want to put his hand in, and neither did I.

"Is there mail in there?" asked Jandine.

"Probably," he said. He managed to get ahold of a corner of

whatever it was, and drew it out. Part of a Sunday paper. The Tacoma *News Tribune*. Sports and weather.

"Why do they put the paper in there?" said Jandine. "Who's going to think to check in there."

"It's been in there since 1980," he said, glancing, then dropping it into one of the boxes of paper to recycle that we'd left sitting around everywhere. Which reminded me about the bins; Terry kept them in the backyard and putting them out for the morning pickup meant unlocking a padlock on a gate before wheeling them out to the alley. Jeff had agreed to help, but we'd left it too late, because by the time I remembered it the shuttle was there to pick him up.

He texted later to let us know he was home. *I feel like shit*, he said. *Home safe, talk later.* No wonder he felt sick. So did we, from breathing the dust after pulling the curtains down. Jandine was restless, and went to bed early. I didn't like the bare windows downstairs, and followed soon after.

When I turned the bedside lamp off a faint phosphorescence materialized in the jumbled items on Terry's bureau; it turned out to be a glow-in-the-dark key chain from a local bank that had been closed for decades, in the shape of a number one, with a PO box and serial number stamped on the back. *If found, drop into any US mailbox.* They looked like the keys to Warren and Ursula's old house, which had been sold decades ago. The keys were a little dulled by use, but still looked functional. I was tempted to drop them into a mailbox. Just to give them a chance.

So many things were like this. Warren's eyeglasses. Ursula's manicure kit. I took a picture of them all together and sent it: Did Jeff remember the evenings she babysat us, while filing and painting her nails? Did he want the keys, the glasses, or the manicure set?

No thanks.

"What's that?" Jandine asked sharply, when she saw me adding Warren's glasses to a box of fragile items to be donated.

Before I could remind her of whose they'd been, she smiled, and said, "Oh, he was a funny man."

"He was?" I asked. This wasn't how I remembered Warren, particularly.

"Oh, sure," she said. "He was very funny."

It wasn't that I mistrusted her memories. She had much better recall of the distant past than she did of recent events.

"Maybe someone else can use them," I said.

"That's a nice idea," she said. "I hope so."

A moment later, she said again, and with the same tone of suspicion: "What's that?"

I showed her Ursula's manicure kit, but by then she seemed angry that I was holding it, even though she said she didn't want it.

"Just do whatever you're planning to do behind my back," she finally said.

Mortified, I set the manicure kit down where she could see it, thinking she might relent if she saw it still there. Still there, among tens of thousands of other things, almost all of which needed to go. But she was in a fractious mood the rest of the afternoon. By the time we heated frozen dinners in the microwave she was distant, and tired, and wouldn't make eye contact with me for more than a moment.

Tineke had suffered terrible mood swings two decades earlier, but what I had seen was less like anger and more like anxious despair, and pressure to find the children, the animals, the people she couldn't name, who were not safe, for reasons she wouldn't or couldn't explain. In those moments, she wouldn't look at anyone, either.

I tried not to think about what form the suffering might take for Jandine. Or for me, eventually.

I moved the red leatherette manicure kit into the donation box, assuming she would forget it, but when I reached for my shoes in the morning I found the kit just under the bed. Could she have really slipped out of the room while I was asleep and found this one object among so many? And then put it here?

More likely there were two red kits in the house, though that didn't explain why it was suddenly there. I paid better attention after that. I saw her take a stack of baking sheets out of a cupboard and then push them, one by one, out of sight underneath the refrigerator, and when she realized I was watching, she turned on me with all the anger anybody might have about feeling watched and then catching whoever was watching.

I must not have been as watchful as I thought, though, because a few days later I pulled open a drawer downstairs in the guest bathroom and found Warren's glasses staring up at me. When I lifted them, one of the lenses fell away from the frame. Maybe Jandine had tried to clean them, popping one loose with the effort—I could too easily imagine my mother standing in her socks and nightgown in that mildewed, brown-carpeted bathroom, working away at the glass and plastic that had been so much a part of Warren's big face. But the lenses seemed greasier, the hinges more sprung, and maybe these weren't the same pair? Who could say, for sure. I wrapped them in a bag and put them deep in the trash. And that evening, after Jandine went to bed, I moved all the boxes and bags and containers earmarked for *Garbage*, *Donation*, *Recycling*, *Shredding*, *To be kept for Jeff*, *To be kept for Mandy*, *To be packed for Jandine's new place*—I put them out of sight in the garage, in the empty space where the everyday Buick had been parked before we moved it out into the driveway to make room for a staging area as the house began, slowly, to empty.

To keep Jandine out of the garage, I would have to remove the deadbolt key and take it with me. I wasn't worried about her going through the piles out there, I was worried she might open the big overhead door and walk outside and disappear. Or leave the doors wide-open, all night. That much we'd learned, when it was Tineke.

Holding the key in my hand was physically a little sickening. I nearly stuck it right back into the lock. But I turned around and without lifting my eyes from the steps directly in front of me I went back upstairs and I attached that key to one of the sensor rings I had given Jandine for Christmas years earlier, still in the unopened packaging. I tested the remote so that I could click it and find the key, just in case. But I was still too anxious about losing the only copy, and the next day I put the key back into the garage door dead bolt and left it there until I could have more copies made or come up with a better solution.

Chapter Thirty-Five

I was grateful for the distraction of working on the dispatches for a few hours at the end of the day, alone in the kitchen. I'd hung temporary paper privacy shades on all the windows, but they didn't do much to disguise the darkness outside. As soon as the sun went down, Jandine would get ready for bed, following her bedtime routine.

I had just finished scraping together the next few days' worth of copy at my makeshift desk on the kitchen table. I glanced at the clock on the oven. It was 9:00 p.m., and in this pause I realized that I could hear something beyond the kitchen, something moving on the stairs. I froze, listening; I'd been expecting this. But no, this sounded lighter, quicker. It sounded alive. I went out expecting to see—what? Jandine, probably. I put a hand on the railing and leaned forward until I could see down into the den. She was unlocking the dead bolt on the door to the garage, and as I watched she turned the knob and hesitantly pulled the door open. It was so much darker in the garage; I felt the cold of the concrete floor, the single-paned windows. The gaps where the old concrete of the driveway was now too uneven for the overhead door to sit properly when closed.

"Terry?" she called into the dark garage.

"Mom," I said, softly, not wanting to startle her. I turned on the chandelier, which was so dim overhead that it barely made any difference.

She looked up at me, without closing the door. "Oh, honey, hi," she said. "I think Terry's out there smoking."

A lot went through my mind. Including the possibility that he really was out there, in some way, sitting in the darkness. But I knew he wasn't. And, anyway, he had only ever smoked in the backyard.

Jandine had shown me, a long time before, how to handle this, through the way she'd been with her own mother. Because Tineke had gone looking for her own dead, as well, in the stretch of years between familiar life and something else entirely. *There's no need to put her through it*, Jandine had said, when people who meant well had tried to put Tineke back into the present. Including Jake, who couldn't seem to believe that she could have forgotten that her parents had died. Her mother in her sleep, her father from congestive heart failure and pneumonia.

They're still asleep, Jandine had said to her mother. *Let them sleep in late today. Help me get some coffee ready?* And they would go to the kitchen area of the group home where my grandmother lived her last years, two miles from the farm. Where Jake had driven to see her every day. And then had driven himself home alone.

"Terry will come back inside when he's ready," I said. "But I'll keep you company in the meantime."

She shut the door and came up the stairs toward me, out of the shadows, her face luminous, uncertain, her hand moving along the iron railing until she reached me, then linked her arm with mine and pulled closer.

"I didn't know if you were still here or not," she said, though I am pretty sure she had forgotten I was in the house at all. I know now that it must have cost her a lot of energy to accept every moment so lightly, without stopping to entertain the millions of flickering doubts she must have constantly felt.

"Do you want to watch a cooking show on TV?" I asked.

"Always," she said. "Where do you want to sit?"

"Upstairs," I said. And we went up. I left the lights on in the kitchen, and my laptop open on the kitchen table, though it troubled my mind a little to leave everything just as though I might return at any moment. By the time we were in their bedroom she seemed to recalibrate, and she knew that Terry was not there, because she remembered that he was dead.

It was better to skew the days early, I thought. Settle down to watch whatever she wanted, and wait to take the blue pill until she fell asleep. But then somehow I fell asleep first, as she watched strangers baking cakes the size of Hula-Hoops.

It must have been very late when I heard her softly opening the bedroom door. I sat up just in time to see the door closing, and then I heard her moving around in the hallway, softly crinkling the brown paper grocery bags filled with old magazines to recycle. Then the creaking of the stairs. I didn't think she would try to go outside, but what would I do if she did? At that I got up a little quicker and quietly followed.

From the landing I could see the crown of her head as she went down to the den, her arms clasped around a bag, but she ignored the door to the garage. After she disappeared out of sight I heard the unmistakable sound of the basement door opening. Fuck. Holy *hell*. I should have been quicker to stop her before she made it that far.

The basement door was ajar, and she'd turned on the lights downstairs, thank god for that. I got there in time to see her open the door to Jeff's room and chuck the bag of papers in.

All the times she'd sent me down to the extra fridge for pickles, for pearl onions—had she ever been afraid of the basement?

I called out her name, so that she would know it was me. But she didn't respond, and maybe she couldn't quite hear me. The acoustics, maybe. So I followed her, I went down the steps, and near the bottom I felt one of those hardwired movements take over, briefly, those habitual gestures triggered in specific places in the house. Here, my left arm tucked itself in against my side before I got to the bottom step, as I had done countless times to avoid catching a sleeve or bracelet on the end of the curling iron handrail, a habit born from a moment of pure horror when a bangle on my wrist snagged the railing. I'd felt something catch, and I'd pulled my hand away so violently that I broke my little finger, and had to wear a brace for weeks. I hadn't been able to stop myself. I had looked down and seen that my bracelet was caught, but it hadn't mattered, the how of it hadn't mattered at all in that moment. I tried to let my arm hang normally now, but couldn't.

She turned, realizing I was there.

"What, are you following me now?" she said, annoyed.

"No," I said, but it came out wrong. Also, technically I *was* following her.

It's a terrible memory that I would love later, of the bright flashing edge of her half-concealed resentment.

"That was amazing," I said. "What you just did. You've been very brave for a long time."

She put her hands on her hips, her attitude softening.

"You can say that again," she said, almost lightly.

After that night I installed a small sliding bolt on the door to the garage, like the one Jake put on their back door for Tineke, when she started hearing a baby crying out in the yard at night. He'd put the bolt overhead, and because habit stays, meaning Jandine might remember that other door, I put this bolt in the shadows at ankle height, where I hoped it would never occur to her to look.

Chapter Thirty-Six

I knew about the Stone Tape Theory by then, of course, the idea that some residue from strong emotions like grief and fear can imprint on natural materials, like stone, similar to how sound and light are recorded on magnetic tape or film. For the duration of that stay, I convinced myself that this accounted for whatever had been wrong in the house, and also for why it now seemed so much weaker than before. Images can fade over time, I told myself. It's a workable theory. Deep down, that's not what I believed. But it was what I could live with.

I decided this after finding a book by John Keel in my old bedroom, one I hadn't taken seriously when I had to read it for an undergrad mythology class. This was partly because I didn't like the tone, which struck me as paranoid and negative, but also because the cryptid sightings he'd gone to West Virginia to investigate were of a tall humanoid with red eyes and leathery wings—too specific, I thought then, to be anything other than the product of Christian imagery lurking in the subconscious minds of the witnesses. But it wasn't the subject matter that got under my skin, now. It was that as he put attention and effort toward getting to the bottom of the sightings, the more some unknown "phenomenon"—as he referred to it—drew closer to him, undermining his life in eerie, almost cartoonish ways that sounded like bullshit to other people. No wonder he sounded so paranoid, and so miserable. He had never really gotten free of it.

I didn't want to end up like that. I didn't even want to reread the whole book. I kept my eyes down. I continued packing. I decided it was just some residual trace, because if it wasn't, then I didn't want to give it any attention or sustenance, but I'd think more on all that later, if I wanted to, after we were out of the house.

—

We'd been stacking some old, cracking-apart wicker lampshades in a box, along with window valances so faded by sunlight that it didn't seem right to donate them, and before I put the box out with the trash I asked her, as a formality, what she wanted to do with what we'd just removed. I didn't ask her this every time, about everything; sometimes asking about too many things overwhelmed her. Which was understandable. But every day I made a point to defer to her about something.

"What do *I* want to do with those things?"

"Do you want to keep them?" I said.

She looked into the box for a long moment.

"Not really," she said. "But I don't have a choice. You'll understand someday."

So I dragged the box to the garage without pressing her to tell me why she thought she needed those wicker dust catchers or the flouncy curtain things that she'd never liked. The days ended better without hounding her to explain feelings she couldn't. When I felt frustrated, I tried to remember to step away.

She went to bed early and I found her later just lying on her back, as if she didn't have the energy to even roll onto her side to face away from me. Though I kind of wished she would, to be honest. I was waiting until I was sure she was asleep before swallowing a blue pill and turning out the bedside lamp. I kept getting the feeling she was awake, but whenever I looked, her eyes were closed.

I think we were both half asleep when a faint hum carried through the vent the way it always did a few seconds ahead of a rush of hot flat air. But instead there was a horrible chaotic sound, echoing like something falling apart in the basement. In the furnace, specifically. I sat up straight, fully awake.

Jandine said, sleepily, "That doesn't sound right."

"I guess I'll check it out in the morning," I said. Because no way was I going downstairs now. And if I'd been there alone, I would have waited, even despite a battering sound like that. Or because of a sound like that. But she was already up and at the door so I followed and watched as she pressed the off button on the thermostat in the entryway. It took a moment to catch up, but the warm air was rattling away to nothing by the time we were back upstairs in the bedroom.

I found the number of an HVAC company on a refrigerator magnet next to others from their dentist, optician, and veterinarian. Terry's name was in their system and they sent a technician that afternoon, upbeat and professional.

I wished the workroom was more presentable. I kept wanting to apologize for everything, including the old litter boxes that used to be kept down there and the dusty feeling that now seemed permanent.

"Not at all," he said. "Let's just see what we've got." He was checking his clipboard. "It's been a while since the last tune-up?"

"Oh, I couldn't even begin to tell you when that might have been!" said Jandine.

He made a note.

I wanted to open the outside door in the workroom for some air, but hadn't yet found the keys to the double-sided dead bolt. I did try to turn the shop lights on, but the bulbs were burned out.

"So," he said, setting down his tool kit. "I'll take a look and then make sure there's no damage, nothing dangerous going on. You were hearing some loud noises?"

"In the middle of the night," said Jandine.

"It's good you turned it off," he said. "Better safe than sorry, and that's not me being an alarmist. That's just the truth."

He was removing the vented metal cover as he spoke, easing it away. "Okay," he said. "Well, first, you really do need to change your filters twice a year. Once they're full of dust and pet dander and whatever other kinds of particulates you might have, they're going to obstruct the airflow. And bad airflow is a real strain on an old unit like this one."

He set the cover aside, gritty where it rested against the cement floor.

"Any time there's a strain, parts are going to deteriorate faster."

He turned to look up at me.

"Is this a family house?" he asked. "Your parents live here?"

"Yes," I said. "But things are kind of up in the air at the moment," I added, because Jandine was there. He nodded. He smiled at Jandine. He tapped the top edge of the furnace with a penlight.

"If the airflow is impeded, then everything has to work harder," he said. "Things wear out faster. And when they wear out, they're unsafe."

"This is all so interesting," said Jandine.

And this got a little chuckle out of him, though he didn't look away from what he was doing.

"You must see a lot. . . ." she said, but trailed off, not sure what he might see a lot of, and probably also not finding the mostly innocent innuendos that used to come to her so easily.

"So these are your burners," he said, pointing out a horizontal line of four round dark holes about the diameter of silver dollars. Each the mouth of a tunnel into darkness.

"I could pull these burners out and put a camera in to look for cracks," he said. He ran his light over all four burners in turn, dipping a little ways into each. "But I'm not going to touch this manifold yet, because—you heard a clattering? That could be a crack. A crack of any kind is dangerous. We need to know about that, and there's an easy way to check."

We were looking over his shoulder at the beam of light playing over the metal.

"Have you ever seen inside this furnace before?" I asked Jandine.

"I didn't even know this was down here," she said.

You see how easy it might be, to assume she was fine? If you didn't know she'd lived in the house for thirty years?

He was speaking with the cadence of an unfolding process and I realized the slow play of light wasn't for him, but for us. I wondered if he ever taught or took on apprentices.

"I'm going to leave your heating system off but I'll turn on the blower," he said, clicking off the light and slipping it into his shirt pocket. "You'll hear it in a moment."

That word, *your*, changes everything, doesn't it? Elsewhere, under other circumstances, I would have been paying attention to the thing itself. But now it wasn't a thing in its own right, it was a dangerous part of the house, and we needed to be careful with it.

He opened his kit, still without looking back up at us. "You're probably thinking, Why is this guy giving us the blow-by-blow tour," he said. He picked up and extended a telescoping wand like the antenna of a transistor radio. "But I want you to see this."

"What are those?" I asked impulsively.

"These?" he said. "These are just grabbers. All-purpose grabbers." He depressed a button and a tiny claw moved at the far end, half barnacle frond, half arcade crane pinching at stuffed animals inside a glass box. He touched the end to a stray washer on the floor by his foot, and it stuck. "Magic," he said. He pulled the washer off the grabbers and set it aside. "A lit match is enough to tell us if there's a crack," he said.

There was a box of kitchen matches in his kit and he struck one, and we watched it flare, subside, and then burn in a steady, normal way. Like a proper match.

I looked over at Jandine's face. She was staring at the little flame.

"You won't see any flickering unless there's something wrong inside," he said, talking to Jandine now. "There's a blower under here, and if there are any cracks in your heat exchanger then that air can get to the flame. And we don't want that." He took the match with the claw end of the grabbers and reached into the first burner hole, much farther than I would have expected. The match lit up the interior of the tunnel with golden light, like a birthday candle around a dark corner.

"This looks okay," he said. He moved the match to the second burner tunnel. It felt so peculiar to watch. An old metal hole. The valiant little piece of wood carrying the bright little flame. I shifted my position to see better.

"This one looks good, too," he said, and carefully withdrew the match.

"I have a silly question," I said. My mouth felt dry.

"It's safe," he said, "if that's your question. And it's not a silly one. The air intake for your blowers is nowhere near your gas line. And you'd know, if there was a gas leak. You'd smell it." He held the second match a moment, until it was steady. "You have a pilot light down here somewhere," he said, "so there's already an open flame in the room, for what it's worth."

Seeing the yellow flame brought to the burner tunnel felt like watching somebody approaching a horizontal well. The gold light flickered a little, and then before it had even fully entered the cylinder it blew out abruptly in a current of air that we couldn't feel. There was no odor of smoke after.

Jandine and I were both staring. I thought I might be sick.

"That's the one," he said. "I'll show you how it looks when it's lit."

I wasn't prepared for the sight of all the burners on. One hole started to glow first, then the next, all four heating up in a line. I heard gas rushing, and the metal of the burners turned from red to bright yellow.

"We'll give it another minute," he said. "You'll hear the blower in a second. This looks fine right now," he said. "But wait until the blower kicks in."

Each of the metal burners changed again, from yellow heat to something pinker, and then all four burners went blue and the blower kicked in.

"Okay, so you can hear that," he said, over the rush of air trapped inside all that cast iron. "Watch the burner that put out the match."

Three of the burners were tidily directing a contained swell of blue flame backward, away from us, down into the furnace. The other was trying to do that, but a brighter tongue of yellow flame kept breaking free and lolling outward, sprawling and disorderly, before disappearing back into the burner hole, and then reappearing and raggedly repeating.

"See," he said, "that's not good. I don't even need to do a visual inspection. I'm going to shut this off now, and I'll do a carbon monoxide test, but I recommend you take a look at your warranty to find out whether your heat exchanger is covered. A lot of furnaces have lifetime warranties on the heat exchangers, or fifteen years, twenty years, somewhere in that range. Take a look through any paperwork you have and find that out. But you cannot run this furnace again until it's been fully repaired."

Maybe he saw me glance at Jandine; I was thinking there was no way that she would remember to leave the heat off. It would mean breaking the long-set pattern of checking that the front door was locked, adjusting the thermostat, and then turning the lights off, one by one, before going up the stairs to bed.

He unplugged the igniter. He closed the gas valve, shut the gas supply off at the wall, and then, for good measure, he flipped the breaker switch in the fuse box.

"Whether it's us or whether it's somebody else who services this, you need to get it repaired right away. So, the first step is to find your paperwork. Depending on what your plans are, you might just want to look at replacing the whole thing. Or, just the heat returner. But those are your choices. Replace that part, or replace the whole thing. You probably can't sell the house in this condition, and you really can't live with it like this, either." And then, with that uplift in the voice that signals the end of an appointment, he said, "Okay then? No questions for me? Let me fill out my part and then I'm going to leave you a copy of the inspection. And as soon as you find that warranty, you go ahead and give us a call back. Or at least call someone else to do it. My other clipboard's in the truck, I'll just be a minute with that."

When he brought the invoice back, we stood on the porch while he finished making a last notation. I noticed he was left-handed. "I understand," he said, "that a lot of people feel more comfortable with a second opinion, and that's fine. But don't run that furnace. Whatever you decide to do, don't run that furnace. You need to get that seen to, ASAP. Can you initial here for me, in three places?"

He'd added at the bottom:

furnace has been disabled.

customer has been told furnace is not safe to operate.

Athanor heat & air is not liable if customer turns furnace on.

"You said this was a family house?"

"Yes," I said. And I felt sorrow about opening it up to the world. "They weren't well," I said. "Maintenance kind of fell off."

"It happens a lot," he said. "Especially with older people. Getting it checked once, twice a year, that's the kind of thing that falls off the radar. But this," he said, lifting the paperwork. "You can't," he said again.

"I won't," I said. "I don't want us to wake up dead next time."

"Nobody ever does," he said, and tore off my copy. The goldenrod carbon.

"I doubt I'll find that warranty," I said.

"I hear that a lot, too," he said. "Take a look, though. Take the serial number and call the company. The labor won't be covered, but the part may well be."

Jandine appeared in the front door, behind the screen.

"Can I get you a beer?" she called out.

"No, ma'am," he said, "I'm just leaving, but thank you."

"Your loss!" she said.

"Your mom's a sweet lady," he said. He was choosing his words. "This probably would not have ended well," he said, finally. "It's lucky they didn't die in their sleep."

After he left, I called Jeff; I think I just wanted him to know with me how precariously they'd been living. But I made the mistake of bursting into tears when repeating the last part of what the technician said.

"And?" said Jeff. "Why are you upset now? Are you saying it's not safe to stay there?"

"No," I said. I was confused by his reaction. "No, it's all shut off."

"What do you want me to do about it from here?" he said.

"Nothing," I said, and I could hear the false lift in my own voice. The tone of never mind. "Just keeping you in the loop. That's all."

"Thanks," he said. "But, you know, you can email me, too." He said a few words to someone, half muffled. "You can always email me if you need anything, okay? And I'll talk to you later."

Chapter Thirty-Seven

I hung back from calling Jeff, after that. I'd been texting him pictures of stray old things as I came across them, things I thought he might find funny, or terrible, or nostalgic, or all of the above, like the stray props from an old magic kit from Warren, including the large hollow plastic man-size thumb in an unflattering shade of Caucasian that called enough attention to itself that any sleight of hand with it was impossible; the funny part was that in retrospect, we'd missed such a good opportunity to use the obviously false finger to direct attention away from any real magic being done by the other hand. But we didn't think of that, at the time. And Jeff had been so disenchanted that he threw the hollow thumb across the room. Anyway, instead of sending pictures I started a new box of liminal items in the garage, things he might like to see, if not to keep. Nothing that couldn't wait until he came for the estate sale.

"Why did they have multiples of everything?" he'd asked, while we were setting up the sale tables in the garage and driveway. The question was a reminder of how long I'd been there already, asking myself some of the same questions he was only now remarking as he examined a pile of little ratchet multi-tools as if he had only just become aware of the possibilities of such a cool problem solver. Terry had several, all identical, and I kept one for myself.

"Do you think I can take this with me in a carry-on?"

I shrugged; I thought probably not, since a couple of the attachments were bladelike, but hesitated to say so, because Jeff had said it himself, more than once; I was a know-it-all. But, he did ask. And it might be confiscated at the security checkpoint, and if it were me, I'd be upset about that. Upset if it ended up in a garbage can. Maybe he could turn it in as a lost item, if he couldn't take it on the plane, since lost and found items would probably get donated after a period of time and then at least somebody would get to use it? But I knew he wasn't asking for such what-ifs, from me.

"I don't know," I said.

He made a noncommittal noise and put it back down on one of the sale tables.

It took both of us to shift some of Warren's old office-computer components, found under a tarp in a far corner of the garage. One had a last fax in the tray, on thermal paper that had faded and was unreadable.

"Maybe my dad thought they'd be valuable someday," said Jeff.

"Or he forgot about them," I said.

During the sale people would whistle and tap these heavy beige things with their shoes, like kicking tires, marveling at how bulky electronics used to be. We put out Warren's portable phone, built into a brown vinyl briefcase like a prop from an old spy movie, and someone took it off our hands along with a couple of battered Polaroid cameras Terry would take on fishing trips.

In between making change for strangers, I showed Jeff the stacks of pictures of Terry holding salmon up by the gills, taken by his fishing buddies, old fraternity brothers, other sales reps, one or two of his cousins. Also the ones of Mount St. Helens erupting; we'd all watched it from the front porch, over the field across the street, snapping Polaroids of the ash plume on the horizon. Those pictures looked so distant, and so small. Much less terrifying than my memory of carrying masks to school in case the volcano buried us in razor-sharp dust.

"Get rid of them," he said. "If you want pictures of what happened, you can look online."

"And these?" I said, about the fishing-trip photos.

He glanced through them again.

"I don't know," he said, and handed them back.

After we'd pulled the tables into the garage and stowed everything to be set up again in the morning, I dropped onto my back in the grass of the side yard; Terry would have died all over again if he could have seen the state of the sod. But even though it looked dry and brown, the earth below was damp in the creeping Northwest way that makes your clothes prickle against your skin.

Jandine sat in a lawn chair, wearing a sun visor.

"It's so nice out here," she said.

Jeff brought out two cold beers.

I shared mine with Jandine; I was apprehensive about seeing her drink alcohol until we knew what was wrong, but still, it was thoughtless.

He was oblivious and preoccupied by the pile of electronics on the curb.

"Collectible?" he said. "Maybe somebody wants them for scrap?"

I didn't disabuse him of the notion.

He put a *Free* sign on the pile. After another beer he replaced it with a sign that said *Scrap Parts and Metal Ect $25*. I pointed out that he'd misspelled *et cetera*, and this seemed funny enough to him at the time that he added: *Cash Onely*, and then went into the house to get ready to meet up with the friends who still lived in town. I don't know why it surprised me that he had plans again, but it did.

"I might be staying over with someone tonight," he said. "So don't worry if you don't see me later."

Later, before turning in, I made a quick trip down to make sure I hadn't locked Jeff out by turning the key out of habit. But it was missing. Something tightened in my chest and a few things ran through my head. Could someone have taken it during the sale? Possibly, I guess?

Jeff, though. Jeff must have taken it. Right?

I texted him: *Did you take the dead bolt key?*

He didn't answer—normally he was glued to his phone, but not now?

Hey, did you take the key from the dead bolt here?

I waited, didn't hear back, and then I called him and he didn't answer, so I called him again and when he picked up I could hear the sounds of a bar in the background. A brewpub, was my guess.

"Hi," he said. "Everything okay?"

"Did you see my texts?"

"Texts? No," he said, and held the phone away to read them.

"Do you have the key?" I said.

"Hold on, I'm checking," he said. "Yes, I have it."

"It's not on a key ring—is it just loose in your pocket?"

"Yeah," he said, "it's in my pocket, it's fine. I'll put it back in the morning. Force of habit, I guess I just grabbed it on the way out."

"It's a good thing you didn't lock it behind you," I said, "or we wouldn't be able to open it."

"You could just go around if you need to," he said. "You could open it from the other side."

"It's a two-sided lock!" I said, though that was somewhat beside the exact point of the moment. "Are you coming back?"

"I'll be back in the morning," he said.

"Can you please bring the key back tonight?" I said; I realized I sounded more upset than the situation probably called for, given the fact that there were also sliding bolts to rely on, now that I knew he wouldn't need to get in—but still, if he'd been that upset about something, I think I would have cared.

"I'll bring it back tomorrow," he said.

"Please put it on Terry's key ring for tonight," I said. "Please don't lose it."

"Like I'm going to lose it," he said. "And even if I did, it's not the end of the world."

"What time will you be back?"

He sighed.

"Jeez, Mandy. I don't know yet, okay?"

"We're starting early," I said. "The sale."

"Then I'll be back early," he said.

I hesitated over the word *then*. As if he was only just learning that we needed him there?

Did we, though? Need him there? Was that his point?

"I'll see you," he said, "I've got to go."

And he hung up on me.

He got back the next day a little after we were already underway, and he put the key back without being asked. But he spent the next hour in the guest bathroom off the den, taking a long shower, and that's the problem, really. He was technically present, but without being present. He was handling it however he was handling it, whether I saw him handling it or not. But he wasn't acknowledging Jandine's situation—as if he didn't have to. As if everything that had yet to be sorted out no longer concerned him. He left on the shuttle before the last of the sale was even cleared from the driveway, with only his carry-on bag, ignoring the empty suitcases I'd left out for him to fill with whatever he wanted to take back with him. The box of liminal items I'd put out for him was untouched, including that awful hollow thumb from the magic-trick kit. I'd wanted to show it to him. *Magic is everywhere, all the time*, he'd said back then, practicing the act, working through the book of instructions, still fiddling with the silk scarf, the bright fake coins. Until he abruptly lost interest in such things. Or at least he lost interest in showing them to me. I don't know why it took me such a long time to understand that he just doesn't like me. He probably never did. Under other circumstances it might have been easier to keep drifting out of touch, the way you might do with friends whose lives continue moving forward even though your own doesn't. In the natural way of things. But the time around a death is holy. Not unlike the way I've heard other people describe the time around the birth of a new baby. Right after Terry died, I felt something like that, and assumed that Jeff and Jandine and I were in the same place, somehow, when we weren't.

Chapter Thirty-Eight

I waited to pack Jandine's personal items until the house was nearly done, and then did a little at a time, while she was in another part of the house. When I opened the cedar chest at the foot of the bed I found my own baby book inside, with the first few pages filled out in Tineke's handwriting. A few entries were written in a shaky but recognizable version of Jandine's. But most of the pages were empty. Evidence of the concussion she'd suffered, in the car accident. Evidence of the low tide of my mother's life during the first years of mine, the expanse of flat grayness between her and the rest of the world. I imagined it like the packed smooth sand of the Oregon coast; I knew they'd been there for their honeymoon. One of very few details I knew about my parents' life together.

Why was she in the car? Where were they both going that evening after he got home from work? And how did I not know something like that, and who could I even ask so long after the fact? County records? Newspapers? It looked like she'd kept copies of most of what I could have hoped to find on my own, if I wanted to try, and from them I couldn't tell much.

There was something more, though: a pair of albums, one covered in coral pink satin, the other in blue and turquoise, each with gold script in cursive across the front: *Photographs*. They must have been in the bottom of her cedar chest all along and I had never seen them before. Photos of a modest wedding ceremony at the courthouse. My mother: a different person. I recognized her, obviously—but from what I could see of her face, posture, demeanor, she was also not the same person at all. Her hand on my father's shoulder, his arm around her waist.

His shoulder, his arm. His face. His smiling face.

Pictures of them with Tineke and Jake and then with Mrs. Field and Mr. Field—the Vanderveldens, I should say. One of everyone together in front of a car I didn't recognize, taken by some obliging stranger.

My father looked like his parents in that odd alchemical way in which two people who don't look alike can have a child that somehow resembles both. But before I had a chance to start looking for traces of my own face I heard Jandine in the hall, so I closed the albums gently, and I put them safely on a high shelf in Terry's closet, pushed back to where she would never ordinarily look so that neither would be swept back into the Sargasso Sea of the house.

Eventually it was obvious that the room was being emptied, of course. When she pulled open a drawer in Terry's bathroom and found nothing inside, I felt real satisfaction at the sight. But she did not.

"Where's the rest?" she said, in a weirdly conversational tone. But she was speaking through gritted teeth, which was disconcerting. It was a little like the stiff smile of a ventriloquist who wants you to remember that it's an act, in order to imply the dummy doesn't know it's an act, or that someone doesn't, or something like that.

"What's wrong?" I said.

She looked at me deliberately, pointedly, the way she had when I was little and about to say something loudly inappropriate. It was a look that specifically said: *Others can hear you.*

"Just stop it," she said. "Please."

I felt such a pang—not guilt. More like shame, that I was so busy tearing things out that I could forget that she would not always remember what was happening.

"Please," she said again.

She looked at the bedroom door, then back, with such guardedness—unfamiliar, but at the same time this had somehow always been the way.

"Is that Jeff?" she said. "Is he back already?"

I felt sweaty, suddenly, and my neck and hairline went cold, like a window had just been opened wide somewhere. Then my fragile mother pulled open the bedroom door and slipped out like she expected me to try to stop her. She waited for me at the end of the hall, where the atrium opened to the ceiling above our heads and all the house lay below us in partial darkness, illuminated here and there by surge protectors and power switches now that so much of the furniture had been sold.

She leaned out over the iron railing, looking down to Terry's office in the den two floors below, to the circle of light by the door to the garage where I'd plugged in a small night-light.

"Jeff?" she said.

But then she turned her attention in the other direction, to the darkened living room, and after a moment she went down to the entryway.

"Mom," I said.

She was reaching for the intercom. Almost forgotten, after all this time.

"Oh, no," I said. "Come on, don't do that."

She turned the tiny corrugated brown knob and I heard the system click on everywhere, sending a faint buzz of static through the house. She turned the dial slowly, scrolling through the denser static of stations too indistinct to pick up. She was on the AM band, and it sounded horrendous, echoing against the walls.

I wanted to go back to the bedroom and hide.

Only residual impressions, I reminded myself. There's nothing here but echoes.

She continued rotating the dial, all the way to the end, then back. She was half turned away, but I could see the tight smile, her gritted teeth and false cheer. I hadn't seen this side of her in so long, and then only rarely.

"We're almost done here," she said. Her weight was on one foot, coquettish, girlish—her feet were bare, and I hated to see that. The dirty floor. The horrible greasy carpet of the stairs.

Bits of distant human voices popped and died away downstairs through the speakers on other floors, as if those speakers were in better condition than the one closer to us, but she didn't stop long enough to pick up anything but broken sounds.

"Mom," I said. "Please, come back upstairs."

She seemed poised to go into the kitchen, out of sight.

"Jandine," I said.

Instead of looking at me on the landing above she looked down the stairs, toward the darkness of the den. My heart began to pound, painfully. There was nothing down there, I thought. But just please don't acknowledge it, either way.

She cocked her head, like posing a question.

"Goddamn it," I said, "who are you looking at?"

I knew it was a mistake as soon as I said it.

In the crackling static from the intercom I heard the faint tones of the crowd-pleasing reminder of a game in progress; six tones from an organ, the cheery "Charge" tune that I'd learned a long time ago meant I was looking in the right direction. Meaning, the wrong direction.

With one finger she pressed the square black button labeled *Talk*. She leaned forward, as if to speak directly into the intercom, but said nothing. I could hear the empty echoing of that open line down the guest room hall off the den, and downstairs in the basement, and the hair on my arms stood up. I thought I was going to—I don't know, piss myself? Have a heart attack?

She released the button, and waited.

There was a change in the static, something I would only recognize years later in the office of a cardiologist as the sound of my own blood moving under the pressure of a Doppler ultrasound, or something similar. The stream of a pulse, magnified, and the intercom speaker in the basement, flaring, the way it did whenever someone down there touched the volume knob.

She pulled her hand back and turned, and suddenly she

was glad to see me waiting on the landing. Without turning off the intercom she came hesitantly up the stairs, reaching to find my hand, and I pulled her along the hall with me. I'd never been afraid that something might come upstairs. I still believed nothing would, but I felt the acute need to get inside, close the door behind us, and build up the layers of blankets and pillows and anything else at hand that would help muffle the sound of the intercom and anything else.

"I shouldn't have done that," she said, with the bedroom door closed, now that she was with me again and not against me. I could still hear the static; maybe it was because the house was nearly empty? That must have helped the sound carry even farther.

"We can talk about it tomorrow," I said.

She was huddled in the bed with her back against the headboard. She watched as I shot the bolt on the bedroom door.

"Put the chair under the knob, too," she said.

"I will," I said. Even though the chair was already gone.

"Make a pile," she said. "Put things in the way. That's what you have to do."

"Okay," I said. Her cedar chest was heavy, but it had brass casters. I could probably push it far enough to block the door, but she shook her head.

"Nothing obvious," she said.

I opened Terry's closet, and dragged out the box of everything important, or possibly important, that I'd been saving for Jeff, none of which he'd taken back to L.A. with him. Inside were a couple of his childhood stuffed animals, and a baby blanket that wasn't mine, and I assumed must be his, and a box of Warren's business cards from the appliance shop, and a beautiful camel hair coat that had belonged to Ursula, and more. Terry's softball mitt and the glove he'd worn while golfing. A heavy gift box from a department store I'd never heard of, embossed with a pattern like alligator, full of black-and-white studio portraits and baby pictures and high school yearbook photos of people I didn't recognize, some with lips and cheeks touched faintly with pink by someone at a long-ago photography studio, back when it must have looked normal. Things I still believed Jeff should be the one to make decisions about. I pulled the box out and left it in front of the door, so that we could at least try to sleep.

Chapter Thirty-Nine

Because he hadn't replied to my texts or sent his flight info, I finally had to call Jeff the week before the empty shipping crate would be delivered to the driveway. He called me back on the house phone and said, abruptly, "Yeah, hi. What's up?"

That already felt a little weird. Like when the person you're talking to is occupied with looking at a computer screen at the same time.

"Just checking in," I said. "About details for this weekend."

"Sure," he said. "You have movers coming, right?"

I was gripping the phone in the kitchen, looking out of the window at the place in the backyard where Terry's smoking chair had been.

"Yes," I said. "The movers come in three days."

"Great," he said. "Then it sounds like you won't need me there, too."

"But you—I thought you wanted to be here."

"You think I want to be there?" he said. He gave a half laugh that sounded like a slow shake of the head. It might have come across as rueful, in person. But it made me wonder whether the half laugh was for someone there in the room with him.

"You're almost done," he said. "Mission accomplished. You'll be out of the house soon and then you can finally stop giving yourself the creeps."

I waited a moment. Then I said, "What about your room."

"There's nothing down there for me," he said. "But if I'm wrong then you have my permission to throw away anything of mine that you find. You don't have to keep anything for me."

He was typing something on a keyboard. Only half present, even for this.

Even for this? Was I wrong to think this was important?

I was looking out at the backyard through the curtainless windows, and I couldn't pretend I wasn't upset. But I didn't have anything to say. So I put the phone down on the kitchen table, without another word. Maybe at some point he noticed the line was empty, but either way, he must have eventually hung up.

I found the key to the workroom's outside door in the back of one of Terry's drawers and we opened it finally, to let in some daylight and fresh air. Better late than never. Terry's tools were gone, either sold in the estate sale or already packed to go to Las Vegas, and the workroom was mostly empty, except for the last bits and pieces at the end of emptying an enormous, densely packed house in a cold damp climate inhabited for over three decades by a couple whose own respective parents had lived through the Depression and trained them never to throw anything away. And in the end, none of them ever had to.

I shone a flashlight under the workbenches and into every drawer, every corner, including the one that had been occupied by the extra refrigerator, recently picked up during an energy-smart campaign in exchange for a small credit to the surprisingly high electric bill. I wanted to apologize to all the scraps of wood and bent nails that would now go into the garbage. And also to the newly discovered half-empty cans of mineral spirits and spray paint and WD-40 that I bundled into a contractor's bag and labeled *Hazardous*. Anything not marked for the movers to load would be thrown out by someone else, and the Realtor said not to bother cleaning, because regardless of what we did or didn't get to, at the end they'd still have to hire someone to go through and clean the whole house. They were so nice about it. As if they deal with houses like Terry's all the time.

Jandine kept me company, wandering in, wandering out, and when the workroom was done we moved on to Jeff's room, which I'd left until last. When the door swung open I was tempted to close it again and go upstairs and pretend I hadn't seen anything. Because when I opened that door I found not only the bag of papers I'd seen Jandine throw in, but solid layers of older and dustier papers in an accumulation so dense and so high that most of the rear wall was obscured.

"What the fuck?" I said.

"I know," Jandine said. "How do you think I feel?"

From just a cursory look I could see masses of old insurance and bank statements, postcard reminders about dental and medical appointments, car-registration renewal notices. Some had once needed attention, but some should never have been kept, the kind of flyers and coupons meant to linger for a week or two, then disappear. At the edge, near my feet, I saw a pile of tissue paper flowers, but when I nudged them with my foot I realized I was looking at an overflowing pile of used and possibly crapped-on holiday wrapping paper.

"Are you kidding me?" I said.

"It was the cats," she said helplessly, with a small, suppressed laugh of mortification so close to crying that I couldn't gauge whether it was a relatively healthy outlet of emotions, or something so alien that I couldn't handle it just then.

I started to say—but what does it matter what I might have said? The time for whatever I might have said had already come and gone, maybe years earlier, without my noticing. It wouldn't have helped either of us, and I'm glad I stopped myself.

But as I kept staring into the pile, I remembered what Jeff had said on the phone, and I realized he might well have looked into the room, seen this abomination, and flown home already knowing he wouldn't be back. I was not happy about that. I was frankly pretty pissed off.

But maybe it was also possible he hadn't gone into his old room at all. Because each time he showed up, he seemed to care less. Genuinely somehow less and less.

I thought I could prioritize, maybe set aside the most important-looking piles to be dealt with later . . . but when I tried to find a good place to start, there were no discernable piles to work with. Just a solid, waist-high accumulation. The paper wasn't stacked, but interleaved together, and the effort it took to separate and shift enough to even get a look inside had me sweating. I just wanted to know if it was all paper. Like taking a core sample.

Jandine and I resorted to shoveling armloads into big contractor bags, just to get it out of the way. Some of the ephemera that turned up was Jandine's, some Terry's, and a little was Jeff's. Some of it was mine, though I hadn't been the one to dump it down here. There were a few books mixed in, and some magazines, but most of it was mail, much of it unopened. Utility bills and bank statements. Explanations of insurance benefits. We didn't realize we'd made the first bag too heavy, so then we had to transfer half of the contents into another bag just to drag it out to the rec room. The more layers I pulled apart, the crazier I felt. We'll never be done, I thought. We'll never be done with this. I swallowed a sob, and turned away from Jandine, so that she wouldn't see the despair I felt when I realized that as we were ruffling up the compacted papers, their volume kept increasing.

I lifted another armload of papers and dropped them abruptly when I felt a damp patch, but when I checked, using the damp meter, they were as dry as anything else. Near that spot, though, I saw the corner of a buried cardboard box protruding, and I decided to take it as an indication: If anything inside that box suggested we should keep going, then we would stay for the extra days it would take to find out what else was underneath.

But getting into that one box meant not just removing the papers piled on top, but also clearing enough room on every side so that papers from nearby wouldn't just slip down and rebury it. I found myself thinking about the stories I'd heard of people drowning in silos of grain. The paper had a little of that quality, the potential for so many individual pieces thrown together to become something else. Something like quicksand. Once there was enough cleared space to maneuver, I pulled open a top flap and saw that the box was filled with more old papers. I pulled up all the flaps and shone my flashlight over the crinkly pale surfaces that had at one point gotten flooded somehow, or at least wet enough to make the ink run, but then long since dried so that now they were hard to separate and nothing I saw was legible. I slit the cardboard corners vertically with the box knife, knowing I should have worn gloves, but not wanting to stop to find any, because when I glanced up at the window shaft there was still a little time before the sun went down. Maybe just enough to get a look inside before Jandine began to get restless.

Peeling back the cardboard revealed a cube of compacted papier-mâché, as if pressed into a square mold and left to dry for a decade. In places it was stained with capillary-blue bank statements and old yellow report cards, pink carbon copies and lavender mimeographed homework assignments. It was too heavy to move. According to the damp meter it was dry, but the sides gave off that chemical warmth you feel around a pile of forgotten sawdust or grass clippings. And that slightly fermented, faintly turpentine smell of rotting wood.

I heard a rustling behind me; Jandine was sitting on the floor, flipping through some of the books that had emerged. I felt the cold cement underfoot, underneath the shag carpet, and a slight current of air. It sounds like such a small thing, I know. But there hadn't been any airflow down there for a long time.

Jandine looked up at me and said, "This is one of my books from college."

"We can bring it with us," I said.

"Oh?" she said. "I doubt I'll ever need it again."

Long ago she had written inside the front cover that the book was for her sophomore philosophy class, at Western, a small paperback edition of Descartes that had been heavily annotated in the margins in her neat handwriting. There were some splashy round marks, like ink spots, some with a faint line or two radiating out asymmetrically. This caught my eye, and held it.

"Are those your notes?" I said. "Were you using a fountain pen?"

"I don't think so," she said, rubbing her finger over the spots.

I picked up another old paperback and rifled through: It had plenty of spots, too. Blue-black, mostly, but a few were the color of old blood, like the meat spots you sometimes find in a hen's egg. It didn't look or smell like mold, or I wouldn't have touched it.

"Are these yours?" said Jandine, about another dozen familiar paperbacks, some from secondhand bookstores, some from Ritchie, some from independent studies I'd done in college. They all had spots, in clusters and occasionally in rows. I flipped all the way through several but I could have saved myself the trouble; they all had spots that were inky, dark, dry, and seemed non-biological. But who would have made the marks? We found no pens in the pile. I doubt anybody bigger than a mouse could have discovered just the books among all those recipes Jandine had printed from websites or torn out of magazines, and all the catalogs, and all the catalog order forms, and all the packing slips that had arrived in boxes of things they'd ordered.

I kept flipping through one of my independent study textbooks: *Visions, Apparitions, Alien Visitors: A Comparative Study of the Entity Enigma*. I stopped when I realized I was seeing stars and tick marks and underlinings done by me, with the inky blue ballpoint pens I'd favored at the time. Before roller balls were a thing.

> There are other continuous situations, such as that of the lonely child, who creates an imaginary companion for herself. What is the immediate occasion that causes the entity to appear?

"Mandy," said Jandine.

The induced-dream hypothesis, of which we noted several variants, requires that the percipient shall be in an appropriate state to receive it. Hence, no doubt, the preponderance of sightings that occur when the percipient is in a relaxed, passive or dissociated state.

"Amanda!" she said. And even though she never called me that, I looked up expecting to see her with another book she'd found and wanted to show me, and saw instead that she was sitting motionlessly with her back against the wall, looking at the door to the closet, which was now more visible, but still blocked shut by the papers around the dense cube, some of which were already starting to slide back toward filling in the area we'd cleared.

"It looks like it's getting dark," she said, and she was right, the daylight in the recessed well of the window was nearly gone. But she wasn't looking at the window, or at me; she was looking at the closet door.

"Mom," I said. "What are you looking at?"

She placed a finger over her lips.

"Please don't do that," I said. "Not right now."

She looked at me then and pointed at the door. "I remember *this* book," she said, in the bright, strange tone that meant she was talking about the door, I think, and not the book in her hand. "Don't you remember it, too?"

"Is there something there?" I said. "Something you want to tell me about?"

She said, "I saw something moving in between the pages."

I wish I could report that I was the brave girl in the bedtime story or the lucid dreamer who finally confronts the unseen monster. I wish I had opened that closet door and found nothing there.

Fucking hell: What a miserable place this had been.

I picked up the books we'd been looking through and motioned for Jandine to get up and join me. She did, and we stepped out of the room quietly, without turning off the overhead light. I had to relock the workroom door before we could go back upstairs, which I did, with all the fumbling hurry I could manage without dropping the keys or the books, and all the time the wall that the workroom shared with Jeff's room felt permeable, temporary. The way barriers do, when you think you're being watched, or eavesdropped on. I held out my hand again and Jandine and I went up the stairs. At the top, out of force of habit, I flipped the light off as we passed but she reached back down to turn it on before closing the door behind us.

She said, "It's a little easier when you know there's a light on."

Right then, I made the decision to leave early, as easily as snapping a sugar cookie in half. The movers could close up any boxes we left half-filled and add them to the load going to Las Vegas. For Jeff's room, I hired a professional document-destruction company to come and collect the contents. Anything truly irreplaceable would fit into the car. I'd already made sure the insurance and roadside-assistance policies were up to date and that the car was in good order. We would throw away the clothes we'd been wearing to clear the house. The movers could get rid of the mattress and box spring and anything else not earmarked to follow in the moving pod, but by then, we'd be gone.

Chapter Forty

I waited to pack the photo albums until just before leaving, so that there would be no chance of losing them in the shuffle. On the last night, after she was asleep, after everything we were taking with us in the car was packed and ready, I reached up to the closet shelf and found it empty. She hadn't even known I'd hidden the albums, yet she still somehow found them. It was uncanny how canny she could sometimes be. Had always been.

With most of the boxes already taped shut thoroughly, it would have been real a job for her to get one open, add the albums, and then seal it up again well enough to look untouched. There was a bit of furniture left, but not a lot in which to conceal something that size. I got up early and at dawn I checked every place upstairs that I could think of, every box not yet sealed, I went from room to room, checking every closet, every shelf, cupboard and kitchen drawer. I checked the freezer, the oven, any place that might be big enough. Even places that weren't big enough. I looked for edges where the carpet might have been pulled up and shone a flashlight in all the corners of the garage. Under the bushes in the yard. Inside the garbage cans outside. Even behind that fucking furnace, and I also looked as best as I could in Jeff's room, and I added a request to the document company, that if anything like them turned up . . . but if that's where they were, I knew I wouldn't see them again.

At the last minute I did try to draw her out. But asking Jandine a direct question when you really needed a direct answer was like trying to pull a fishhook out of your own face; you'd have to remove any barbs first and then pull gently and counterintuitively, without tensing up. Because the more you needed to know, the less she would say.

"Well, we have absolutely everything now," I said. We were sipping bottled coffee drinks at the kitchen table and unwrapping protein bars in the morning. "Every single thing in the house is ready to go. There's nothing hidden away anywhere. Isn't that great? There's nothing left hidden anywhere in the house. What do you think of that?"

I looked up to find her watching me; she clearly knew there was something up.

"I'm so glad," she said.

"If you think there's anything here that you don't want to leave behind forever, now's the time to go get it."

"I can't think of anything," she said. "What a load off my mind! I can never thank you enough for everything you've done. I appreciate it. I really appreciate everything."

For a searing moment I was so angry, for every reason. Including that being mad would absorb the hurt.

But that's not the way I wanted to leave the house.

They'll turn up, I thought. They have to be somewhere. Unless I imagined them; I knew I hadn't, obviously, but it was one of those acceptable shortcuts of thought that serve well enough as a placeholder, to get over a certain kind of moment without thinking too deeply until you're on the other side.

When everything was done I locked the front door behind us and we walked to the grassy field across the street. We took in as much of the house as we could see behind the two enormous blue spruce trees and the beautifully green, now-unruly hedges.

"Have you ever looked at the house from here before?" I asked.

"No," she said. "It somehow never occurred to me."

It was still so early in the morning that the sky was the color of nacre under moving water.

And thirty years passes, just like that.

"It's like a house in a fairy tale," Jandine said. "From here, anyway."

The Electra was waiting in the driveway with our overnight bags and some valuables and essential paperwork in the trunk. It was a crazy plan, to drive the Electra all the way to Las Vegas. But Terry's everyday Buick had already been sold. Getting a flight with Jandine and Jasper and Terry's ashes somehow seemed even more hectic, and we weren't in a rush. Jasper was secure in the back seat, in a huge carrier held in place by the seat belt, and I'd made reservations for rooms along the way at places that accepted pets. Beside the carrier sat the heavy, compact box that cradled the urn full of Terry's ashes. That was it. We'd done as much as we were able to, and if the house wasn't empty, it would be soon.

The engine started easily. In the morning light it sounded velvety, reliable, the way it must have sounded when Terry drove to classic-car shows on sunny weekend mornings. He'd washed it, and waxed it, and he'd taken good care of the engine for a long time. He was long gone, I knew. But leaving in the Electra felt like a chance to cast off the mooring lines on his behalf, too, and we drove away with the windows down, listening to AM radio. The timing was good, not too hot for the drive, and not too cold. Jandine tied a pretty scarf over her hair, and in a few days we would arrive in the brightly lit meadows of Las Vegas.

PART FIVE

It is said by physicists that most animals live about five times as long as is required for them to mature. Applying this rule to man he ought to live to be at least one hundred and five years old. That he does not live to this age is because he does not understand the laws of life and the real nature of disease. He knows nothing about controlling the atoms which compose his body nor how to use the Cosmic forces with which he is constantly surrounded for the purpose of revivifying his physical body.

RICHARD INGALESE, *The History and Power of Mind*

This is the undisclosed mystery, which none of the prophets dared divulge in words; but they revealed it solely to the initiated. They called it the brain stone in their symbolic writings, the non-stone stone, the unknown thing that is known to all, the despised thing that is most precious, the thing given and not given by God . . . it is the only one, in our work, that rules matter.

ZOSIMUS OF PANOPOLIS, *Collection des Anciens Alchimistes Grecs, Vol. 2: Comprenant, Les Œuvres de Zosime: Texte Grec et Traduction Française, Avec Variantes, Notes et Commentaires* (TRANS. CHARLES-ÉMILE RUELLE)

Chapter Forty-One

It's hot even under the air-conditioning. Jasper is restless, all night, but I don't have the heart to shift her away, because her kidneys are going, and she has arthritis, and I know she's uncomfortable. In the morning I find her curled up in the laundry basket. The vet told me that kidney failure and anemia go together for elderly cats, and now that I look, Jasper's gums are stone white; I should have known. Her vet will keep her overnight to flush her system with more than the subcutaneous fluids she gets every three days at home, plus a shot of erythropoietin that will in four weeks charm new red blood cells from her marrow. Plus a vitamin B_{12} injection, for appetite, because to paraphrase the vet: *If kitty won't eat, kitty can't get well*. And a new diet of high-calorie canned food, as well.

While waiting for the written estimate in the exam room at the animal hospital I get a text from Jeff, floating the idea of coming back this weekend.

WTF—why?

Gotta catch up with a friend who'll be in town.

Nobody likes leaving a veterinary clinic with empty hands, and people in the waiting room shrink back, instinctively, when you leave without an animal. Because everyone who loves an animal knows from the first that their lives are so much shorter than ours.

Jasper comes home in the morning with a purple compression dressing on one leg, which can come off any time. Under it there's a shaved spot, with a slack little catheter hole in her velvety skin. All's well again for a while. But while I'm still looking at it, that little hole in her skin droops open and blood starts running copiously down her leg and streaming over her foot onto the kitchen floor, onto my clothes, everywhere. I pinch the hole shut and pick her up with one arm to find my phone. The speed of the blood is shocking but on the phone the vet tech says it's all right, it happens, just put the bandage back on for a while longer. I rewrap her leg. The bleeding stops. Jasper is already purring.

My back is hurting and I need to lie down with—is it heat or ice? I don't know if it's a new strain or the chronic thing so I do one and then the other, alternating as I lie on the couch with Jasper, whose fur still smells of iron.

"You know, Mandy," says Jeff, not looking at me, just looking down at the floor, at the bloody spots I thought I'd wiped up but apparently hadn't. "I don't like to come in here and sound like I'm judging you, or telling you how to live."

"Oh good," I say, from the couch.

"But," he says, lifting his palms as if trying to spare me an awful truth. "This floor is disgusting."

I sigh, and get up, creakily. The bummer here is not that he's wrong, necessarily, it's more that I wonder what it might be like if he could just wipe it up himself. If he were someone who would do that, after seeing me on the couch with the ice pack and seeing Jasper sleeping with the bright-purple compression bandage.

Jeff is shaking his head.

"It's blood," he says. "That's obviously blood on the floor."

Actually, forget about me for the moment: Jasper was Terry's last little cat and he loved her.

I say, "Blood on the floor, and yet you haven't asked if Jasper is all right. Or if I'm all right."

"Are you all right?" he says. "Don't you think that's alarming for me to walk in and find?"

Sometimes I can almost see him trying out different approaches, slightly turning a dial, then turning it a little more, looking for—looking for some way to get a reaction? Is that it?

". . . And don't you find this embarrassing at all? I mean, for crying out loud."

This was one of my mother's habitual phrases—*for crying out loud*—and hearing it from Jeff startles me: Where did that come from, after all this time? I've never heard him say that before. But it takes me back to an afternoon before Heather tried to stop the visitations, when Terry had been busy edging flower beds in the front and side yards before topping them off with cedar beauty bark. The kind with a damp, oily, almost petrochemical odor. That smell of a hardware store in springtime, of heavy rectangular plastic bags in the sun, humidly outgassing through the vent holes.

My mother and Jeff and I had been out doing whatever one did then on a Saturday afternoon with a couple of kids tagging along, including ice cream cones at the Kmart ice cream counter. Jeff got licorice, which he didn't even like, because it left a dramatic green-black line around his lips that my mother looked at in the rearview mirror. We were helping unload groceries at home when we saw crimson blotches of blood across the driveway—big ones, close together, in a wavering line. We followed the blood trail up the steps, through the unlocked front door, across the slate entryway, and over the yellow linoleum to the kitchen sink. Jeff was whimpering. I don't know what I thought. My mother held us back with one hand and peered into the sink, at blood-soaked paper towels like bright carnations and an open box of bandages on the counter. Then she was out the back door, the screen banging behind her with an aluminum clash.

"Terry!" she called.

"What," he said, from somewhere out back.

By then Jeff was crying and I took his hand and pulled him along with me. We found the two adults standing by a pile of sod scraps out back. She was holding Terry's hand, examining his fingers, one of which was wrapped in a wad of gauze so saturated with blood that it fell heavily into the grass when she touched it. I didn't see the actual injury then, but he'd cut the tip of his middle finger nearly off.

Later that night my mother would take Polaroids of Terry flipping off the camera with a real bandage, looking a few beers worse for wear. But in the yard Jeff threw his arms around

Terry's waist, saying, *Please go to emergency, please go to emergency*, over and over, until Terry rubbed his hair and told him to quit crying, buddy, everything was fine. My mother gathered Jeff up to go back inside, but had to pause first to let him throw up in the rhododendron bushes by the back door.

Terry did go to the hospital finally but lost the end of that finger anyway, because he'd waited too long to get stitches. He didn't seem to care and when he got back he made Jeff go out with the garden hose to spray tarry vomit out of the bushes in the twilight of the evening, while he gathered up his tools and binned the cut sod.

"Hello?" says Jeff. "Why aren't you listening to me?"

I have the Simple Green out and I'm cleaning up the blood; I look down and realize that you can't just clean part of a floor. One clean spot makes the rest look filthy by comparison.

I'm sure I have a steam mop, somewhere. Part of Jandine's cache of small appliances.

"Here," he says, grumpily. "I can help."

"It's done," I say. But how often does he do that? Offering to help only after some task is already done?

"Suit yourself," he says. He opens the refrigerator. I'm putting the cleaning things away when he says, "There's no people food in here." He still sounds grumpy. "It's just cat food and wine and vegan corn dogs. And fiber."

"That's for Jasper," I say. "But I read somewhere that it can slow down sugar absorption and prevent fatty liver in humans."

He pauses, for effect, and says, "Maybe this is a stupid question, but why not just cut back on the midnight candy?"

I say, "I don't want to cut back on midnight candy."

"Well okay," he says. "Can't argue with that, I guess."

He looks into the hanging wire basket, at some empty paper towel rolls. He's about to toss them until I say, "Those are for hair balls."

"Hair balls," he says, looking at the one in his hand.

"Yes," I say. "When Jasper—"

"I know what a hair ball is," he says, and I think, Yes, but have you ever cleaned up a hair ball in your life?

Instead, I say, "Those tubes are the right size to sort of scoop—"

"I don't need a visual," he says. "God, Mandy. The way you live."

I'm moving slowly, careful of my back, and he doesn't notice. All he does is poke the basket until it swings. "Toilet paper rolls in the kitchen. At eye level!"

I say, "They're paper towel rolls. Cut in half. Reduce, then reuse."

"It's not funny," he says. "It's not normal to plan your life around cat vomit."

I'm going back to the couch. "Are hair balls technically vomit?" I say, over my shoulder.

His cheeks are starting to color slightly. "Do you know how this looks to somebody who doesn't know you?"

"People who don't know me don't hang out in my kitchen."

He doesn't answer. And then a sick feeling comes, and I turn back to him. "Or would you rather let a stranger find a hair ball on the floor? Would that make a better impression?"

"Neither," he says. "Honestly, neither makes a good impression."

He lives in a breezy apartment on a street that smells like gardenias and freshly brewed espresso, and his tolerances are different from mine, and so are his priorities. But we both remember how repulsive it is to step on a cold wet lump of thrown-up hair in bare feet.

"You can hide those under the sink," I say, "if it hurts you to look at them. But if I see a fresh hair ball on the floor today I'm leaving it for you to pick up."

"Don't be childish," he says, "I'm just trying to talk to you."

But nonetheless he puts the cardboard rolls under the sink, because he doesn't want to be any more embarrassed than necessary in front of a hypothetical stranger, someone he just might happen to invite over while he's here. Even if I ask him not to. I can't believe I somehow didn't realize that he's been coming to see somebody he's dating, or hoping to date. How could I have assumed otherwise.

He's up early the next morning, shifting around in the downstairs closet and cursing while dislodging a pool noodle from under a box of spare laminate floorboards, kept in case I ever need to replace a section of the floor. Like, if a fish tank leaks and causes water damage. Just for example.

How did I forget to factor in the pretties? Those individual young women who turn up daily at the pool across the lawn from my front door, young women doing whatever young women do when they are biding their time in Vegas. Jeff is already talking to one of them, with a bright-orange pool noodle under one arm and my bright-blue beach towel over his shoulder as he pulls a chaise longue closer to hers under one of the shade umbrellas.

They seem so unencumbered, those girls. But I guess at some point it would have seemed reasonable to me, too, lying out by the pool, after your day shift or before your evening shift at whatever job fits your needs and your temperament at the moment. Waiting tables or serving cocktails in any of thousands of places to go out after dark in Vegas.

Chapter Forty-Two

Her name is Belén and she has been right there the whole time, right outside reading a book under a sun umbrella by the pool. The girl from the Bain de Soleil ad; she's the friend in town he wanted to see—not someone passing through, as he'd implied. He mentions her as he leaves through the front door that evening and walks along the path in the warm, dry dusk, checking his phone. He planned to pick her up at her place, but she comes out to meet him before he gets very far. I'm still at my desk, and I can see them walking to the parking lot. She swings a small handbag and reaches up to tuck her long, loose, sun-streaked hair behind her ear, glancing around a little.

On such a lovely evening—a comfortable ninety degrees—I feel a pang of envy. She's wearing a green cotton sundress, and her arms are bare and glowing. It looks like a dress chosen for a dinner date with a new guy, which of course it is. He opens the car door for her and she slips into the passenger seat. It is not her evening plans I envy, not her youth or her beauty. It's that she'll enjoy whatever restaurant Jeff picked after looking at menus online all afternoon despite the crushing knowledge that whatever arrives on her plate is already dead. And maybe also that it probably won't seem pointless to her to go for a stroll later in her pretty silver sandals somewhere outside, by fountains, probably just to people watch.

TK is over by the pool, emptying the ashtray can. I drop the blinds back in place. I guess what happens next officially, regarding him: nothing. Because if Paloma's friend, the woman I still haven't met, technically caused her own injuries—bit her own hand, if that's what happened . . . I don't know anything for sure . . . but if so, then he won't technically have been responsible, and this will be conclusive enough but also confusing enough to distract from the question of why he was there in her patio at all. All of which makes me uneasy. It's not simple, and really I don't like the way we say that someone who isn't well *isn't themself* . . . though I've also seen things done and said, potentially by anyone with a degenerative brain condition or a brain injury or brain dysfunction, that the person would not have done before. I'm comfortable assuming that Tineke did not actually believe I was some unknown person from Canada whom she fell out with decades before I was born. Unless in some way I am—but of course only in the way that everyone is everyone, the further in and down you go. Anyway. The more I try to explain what I mean, the more the meaning scatters. But there was a day a long time ago when Tineke told me that she hated me. I don't believe it. But I can't unhear it. Sometimes things sit in proximity without being related in the ways we assume, but also, it's weird and creepy, and I'm certainly not saying that he's in the same situation of someone with a serious—but what do I know? That brains are not simple? All I really know is that this is a gross understatement.

The next day Jeff's good mood is so obvious, so expansive, so audible, and so obnoxious that it fills the house and I can't concentrate. I understand that most people wouldn't lose a perfectly good day just because he putters around smiling and saying nice things to the cat. But I know he's only hanging around because he wants to talk about her, and I can't bring myself to indulge him. Partly because he's exhausting me, and partly because I expect him to start scanning again shortly to find whatever mean little thing will get a reaction. It will take me a day or two to recover after he goes home. So I don't look up and I don't make eye contact, and eventually when he goes downstairs I softly close the office door and try to get down to work.

I don't think I can ever go back to spending my days around other people. I'm too much like the French lady in the woods on *Lost*, hiding on the island, setting booby traps, hearing voices in the rustling leaves. To paraphrase: I've lived alone for too long.

By afternoon Jeff's feelings are hurt and he goes out of his way to let me know without saying so. "Eleven," he says, knocking on the office door and opening it; he's sweating, partly because he can't take the heat, even when the air conditioner is blowing, and partly because he's mad. "I just found eleven lamp cords still in the boxes they came in, stuffed into a drawer. Do you honestly think you're going to use them?"

There's no good outcome to engaging.

I look up, and say, "Sorry, what?"

He goes away. Once more I close my office door, but Jasper begs to be let in, then begs to be let out, and the sound in both directions sets my teeth on edge. It's not Jasper's fault.

There are flecks of gold in the seascape hanging over my desk, which used to hang over Terry's desk at the old house, and flecks of gold in the shade on a lamp made from driftwood found at Ocean Shores, made by the wife of one of Terry's fishing buddies. I rewired it last year with one of the replacement cords Jeff is complaining about. I have had plans for a while now to rewire a beautiful brass lamp that once belonged to Ursula; I couldn't bear to see it sold for two bucks at the estate sale, so I kept it aside for Jeff, even though the cord is so brittle it's a wonder Terry and my mother didn't burn the house to the ground with this and all their other forms of . . . of what? Carelessness? Exhaustion?

If Jeff doesn't care about keeping things, why do I care about holding on to them until he might? Why would I rewire something else first, to get the hang of it before doing Ursula's lamp? I don't know, and I think that's why it feels like it's my fault that I'm miserable around him. Why it feels like even my good impulses are wrong.

Because I'd rather stay in my office even though it's Saturday I cobble together a draft of an extra dispatch, trying to get ahead, and then I look at the MLS, then try to blow off excessive energy of the unproductive kind by poking around online, scrolling among corded solar panels to make a circulating fountain for the solitary native bees that like the hanging baskets of flowers in my patio, trying to break the habit of pausing over ads in the margins for things that I used to shop for that would have been good for Jandine. Soft pants with pockets and elastic waistbands, easy pop-over shirts that wash well and aren't sheer and won't cling. Everything faded in the hard hot water of the laundry at memory care, but I couldn't bear to see her looking neglected or unloved and I replaced her clothes regularly. Bright colors. Pinks, purples. Pretty florals, because that's what she'd always liked.

Even long before I knew about the ADHD my own closet was filled with beige, gray, tan, one of many ways of turning down the volume and lessening the visual noise around me, to manage my environment without knowing what I was doing or why. I have spent so much energy, so much time, groping toward solutions that in retrospect I didn't have to reinvent alone.

But now Jeff's there in the doorway and I nearly spill my cup of tea.

"Is this what you do all day?" he says, leaning far enough into the room to see my screen.

"What?"

"Shopping," he says.

"I'm not shopping," I say. "And no. I'm working."

"Right," he says.

I'm aware that I sound defensive and it makes me mad.

"I don't care what you do, I'm just making an observation," he says, going into the guest room and kicking off his flip-flops, which hit the wall. Because he needs attention?

Does it count as attention, if there's no reaction? I mean, if I'm in another room noticing, without visibly reacting, does he still get some kind of residual benefit? If not, why bother?

He appears in the doorway again and says, "How can you even think straight in such a messy room?"

I'm not saying it doesn't affect me. But I don't think it's just about me.

"That reminds me," I say. "Did you hang the guest parking tag on your rearview mirror?"

"Yes, I know to do that," he says. I'd say it's fifty-fifty, whether he bothered with it or not.

"Okay, good," I say. "I wouldn't want your window to get stickered."

He starts the water in the tub and the sound of it is so annoying, the pipes, the water moving, the way he bangs things around and lets the water run and run, to let it warm up, even though it takes no time at all and even though we're in a desert and also he lives in California and how can he not know about conserving water?

Apparently, there were even more prosthetic heads in *Total Recall* than I realized, like when the villain's head is crushed, and when the huge tracker is pulled out through Schwarzenegger's nostril. When the prophet and his conjoined twin appear together on-screen they're both puppets being controlled from off-screen. And Schwarzenegger's head inside the mask of the Two Weeks lady was a prosthetic, too. How many heads did I miss? All of them, probably, because I had my eyes covered a lot. The movie may have been released in 1990, but it's got an eighties sensibility, and for me there was too much going on. Everything so bright, flashy, discordant, and distracting.

I hear the shower stop so I put the computer to sleep and go quietly into my room and shut the door, because that's the way of it, now. Jeff's presence might spark memories, but that doesn't mean he shares them, or, more to the point, that I want to invite him to shit on them.

Everything takes so much energy. I think I just need to lie down for a few minutes.

He goes downstairs to watch TV. He turns the volume up, so loud. On purpose, probably.

I put in my earbuds and follow one of the guided visualizations I've started collecting, at the suggestion of the doc. The placid mountain lake. The hike through a peaceful forest. Usually outdoor imagery, because anything in or around houses or buildings or even crystal caves seems to include being slowly and deliberately led down a set of steps. Which doesn't work for me. The very thought of a stranger's voice leading me down one step, then another, then another—it stresses me out. Obviously because of the basement in the Tacoma house, but also all the sketchy comedy magic shows Jandine and I saw for free when she first moved here. Locals could get last-minute tickets then, because empty seats in the audience look bad in front of full-price ticket holders. We saw music, sometimes, and magic shows that asked for volunteers willing to be hypnotized. I certainly wouldn't let Jandine volunteer, and I didn't even want her listening to the induction part, neither the dramatically paced counting down, to put people under, nor the counting back up to bring them out of a trance. Especially not after watching half a dozen hypnotized volunteers agree to audition for an adult movie, using a beer bottle as a prop—obviously that's fine, totally fine, if the volunteers are into it. But that's what I wasn't sure about. I know everybody says you can't be led to do anything under hypnosis you wouldn't otherwise do, and afterward everybody on that stage seemed to think the whole thing was hilarious *because* it was embarrassing. But they were told under hypnosis that they would feel great about it, weren't they?

"Are those people supposed to be doing that?" Jandine had asked me, and I burst out laughing. Because, how do you answer that?

Among the guided visualizations I find a place to sit on a rock and watch waves on a beach, and maybe later I'll have the fortitude to listen to whatever Jeff wants to say about this new pretty girl he likes so much that he can't hold his enthusiasm in without doing damage to his innards; maybe I can listen without reflexively hating him a little for moving so much more lightly through this life than I could ever imagine, and also for never noticing that I'm not doing well at all.

When I open my eyes, a few minutes before the alarm goes off, I can't hear anything. Then abruptly I hear the white noise of the world again, like an infinity of grain falling into a silo. I don't hear the TV, and I think Jeff must have gone out.

But when I open the door he's standing in the hallway holding a cardboard box. I wonder how long he's been waiting there, to let me see him in the act of carrying it downstairs. Such a baby.

"Okay," I say, following him down. "What's in that box?"

He says, "Shit that should be donated, and if you don't believe me you should go through it in the garage before the Goodwill truck comes."

"You called Goodwill to arrange a donation pickup?" I ask, momentarily impressed that he took the initiative.

"I plan to," he says.

The first thing I see inside the box is a white faux-fur bonnet of Jandine's that I once chose to wear under a Betsy Ross costume she made for me in fifth grade, like a pre–Alexander McQueen bustle hump. In the photos from that day the sun is in my face and I'm wearing cinnamon-frost-colored lipstick, holding a version of the American flag she stitched as part of my history project. The women on the list of historical figures to choose from had all played supporting parts, and the only detail I've retained about Ross is that it was her idea to give the stars five points, instead of six. Mostly, I remember that, for Jandine, anything could be presented with a little extra glamour.

I look up from the box, and I say, "This isn't even your stuff. What's wrong with you?"

"What's wrong with me is that I can't keep helping you," he says. "I've done everything I can, and it's just enabling you."

I am distantly aware that if I had allowed him to vent hearts and flowers about the girl, he might not be doing this so early.

"You," he says, and he gestures at everything around us. "You and your everything. Your unsustainable life. I'm out of ideas."

"What ideas," I say, even though he doesn't want to talk, he just wants to say dramatic things.

He says, "One of these days, there will be nobody who cares. You'll have nobody at all. You'll be buried alone in stuff. Do you see that?"

A little voice somewhere inside reacts with an *oh thank god* at the thought of being left in peace. But he's not finished.

"You're going to be a crazy old cat lady who dies alone in a crummy condo."

I have one cat, obviously. His dad's cat. But I don't say that.

"This is a town house," I say. "It's not a condo, and it's not crummy."

Jeff shakes his head. Shakes it and shakes it. "You're too much," he says. He looks at the kitchen shelves. "What's this?" he says. "Two dead light bulbs in a cardboard box?"

I say, "I take those to the CFL-recycling bin at the hardware store."

He says, "Do you honestly think the hardware store won't just throw them away in their dumpster when nobody's looking?" He goes to the garbage can, pushes the lever with his foot, and drops the bulbs in, container and all. He says, "You'll never take them to be recycled anyway, so what's the point? How often do you even go to the hardware store?"

You see? He barely knows me.

I'll wait until he leaves, until he drives back to L.A. And next time I'll tell him that he can't stay here. At least not for a while.

"I assume those are rhetorical questions," I say. "But there's real mercury in those bulbs and it sounds like you just broke one."

He says, "I assume a lot of things, too. Like, I assume you're done with these?" He lifts a stack of flyers I've collected at real estate open houses. "Let's see. This one is, what . . ." He rifles through. "This one is two months old, and this one is three months old. How could these possibly be relevant to anything?"

I catch myself, or I catch the minnows in my mind trying to find a branch in a stream that offers a possibility, even a distant possibility, that this might actually be his clumsy way of wanting to support me, somehow. Which wouldn't make it right. But it would be something.

"Are you making this place into a pigsty on purpose?" he says. "Are you leaving all this clutter so that I won't come to visit?"

"No," I say. Though I appreciate it as a viable strategy.

"Could have fooled me," he says, and stamps on the foot pedal of the kitchen trash, again. The flyers fan out of his hands, falling over broken glass. Over mercury.

The air is thickening a little as he's talking. Part of my brain is listening, and observing him . . . but with detachment. Like the moment you know you're in strange territory, in a certain kind of movie, when a character seems to slip loose from the script, and look around differently, moving at a slightly different speed. Seeing something other than the set. And he doesn't realize. Because he's falling into his pattern.

I think I could probably look away, and he wouldn't notice, and I might see this house mapped out strangely, maybe something structural, or just the electricity or the plumbing or the airflow, or maybe I would see all the outlines of living things that have come and gone, like the way science teachers used to tell us that if everything else here suddenly disappeared except all the entwined earthworms in the soil of this planet, they would retain the shape of the Earth, floating in space. Though they could never answer how long this would last, or what would happen to the worms. Maybe I'll see the version of the room that includes only elements made from the fibers of trees and plants, just cotton, flax, linen, the shadowy outlines of standing forests and rustling fields before they were rendered into pillows and woven rugs and the wood of the furniture. Or the animals, whose skin would become shoe leather. Whose bones would be rendered into the glue holding the pages of all the books in place, and all the other everyday substances most of us don't realize have come from a slaughterhouse.

If Jeff looked at me with a slow turn of the head, if he was present but not able to break from the script—what would I do? Would I meet him in that strange other plane? But he doesn't, of course, and he doesn't stop talking, he just keeps following his path until time clicks back into normal gear and obscures whatever other possibility might have been briefly here. Until he's looking at me and waiting.

"Why won't you even try?" he says, maybe repeating a question. "Why can't you at least try to be happy?"

But it's not a question, and he turns away and leaves through the living room, out through the front door, pointedly without locking it behind him.

Underneath Jandine's faux-fur bonnet in the box he's dropped carelessly onto the kitchen table there's a coiled Jerry Garcia tie, an old birthday present I'd given Terry, and which he wore to my college graduation along with a yellow ribbon and an Operation Desert Storm tiepin. He and Jandine and Jeff sat with other families on folded chairs in the red-brick quad while the Redstone drum band performed the processional. John Taylor Gatto gave the commencement speech, having just published his first book, *Dumbing Us Down: The Hidden Curriculum of Compulsory Schooling*. From a clearing in the trees rose the smoke of a bonfire being kindled for an all-night meadow party later and the brewing of mushroom tea. One of my housemates was on her way to Santa Cruz for grad school in ocean sciences and the other had an internship lined up to work in sustainable forestry, both of which impressed Terry. When we all went out for dinner, Terry paid, brushing off the protests and thanks of the other parents. During dinner Jeff had disappeared for a while, off to play Hacky Sack with friendly strangers in the parking lot and he'd come back with stoned red eyes and wearing a puka-shell necklace. The necklace floated around the house for years and during the move I'd put it with other things for Jeff to make decisions about, and eventually I put it away with Terry's tie. Maybe Jeff had recognized it and maybe it set him off, but a scrap of explanation like that, something I might pull together to excuse what I couldn't understand about him, was only good enough in these last few years when everything had felt like triage, all my attention going to Jandine, and it was easier to make excuses for Jeff than to admit even to myself how much he drains me, and that I have always felt responsible for the way he treats me.

Chapter Forty-Three

He returns in a couple of hours, bringing Belén with him. They've come to watch a movie—he hopes that's okay, he says. But it's not a real hope, of course, and he knows that I would have liked a little advance notice, a chance to tidy up first. He knows it embarrasses me to let strangers in. I'm a little shocked by how much I hate him for wanting to make me uncomfortable in my own house, by how childish everything has to be. But that's not a good reason to make her feel unwelcome.

She's young. She moves deliberately, carefully, stepping over the threshold as if carrying something fragile in the little fabric backpack on her back, both hands holding the straps steady against the shoulders of a soft and much-laundered Hanes pocket T-shirt.

"Hello," she says, "we've almost met, I think. Across the way. Right?"

"At the pool, yes," I say. "Hello. Come in."

She neatly and automatically steps out of her canvas sneakers when she enters the house and her bare feet appear to be immaculate, which I find disconcerting. This is an impossible city to keep your feet clean in during the summer. The heat-vaporized asphalt is grimy, getting into sandals, into little summer shoes. Into mine, anyway.

"You don't have to take your shoes off here," I say. "I mean, please do if you want to, of course, but the floors—there's a cat. The floors aren't delicate." I sound compulsively uncomfortable, I know, because I am.

"Yeah, better not to go barefoot in here," says Jeff, dryly.

Something in the whole dynamic already doesn't seem quite right.

Her eyes meet mine, but her attention seems to be sliding past me, to the stairs behind me. Or maybe I'm just aware of what the exposed boards look like, streaked with primer, dotted with glinting nails, one with an empty knothole. I removed the old carpet that was here when I moved in, and I washed and sanded and primed the stairs myself, but years later I still somehow haven't painted them. The primer looks filthy. But it's so easy to stop seeing what you pass by every day, until you see someone else looking at it.

"Looks like you're doing the work yourself," she says; it's a question, I think. I nod.

I realize that she is still standing there in her bare feet, waiting to be invited farther into the house. The air-conditioning is blowing. The front door stands open behind them. "Come in," I say again. "I have extra socks, if you want to put some on."

Why did I say that? That's weird.

She's still taking things in, still processing.

"Thanks," she says. "I believe I will borrow a pair, if you don't mind."

"Plenty of extra around here," says Jeff. "Plenty of everything."

He's actually going to make this into the kind of encounter in which a stranger must pretend not to notice the unpleasantness under the surface between people who know each other well. But she pivots away from that path.

"What's wrong with the socks?" she says.

This takes him slightly by surprise.

"Nothing, probably," he says. "Mandy just has too much stuff."

"I do," I say. "There's a lot being stored here." And I'm thinking to myself, Isn't it odd that as soon as she steps inside we're showing her everything?

"I'll be right back," I say, relieved to get up the stairs and away from them. I have a full pack of Terry's Goldtoes from Costco in the closet, never worn. I hesitate because giving her a new pair seems awkward, but older socks probably aren't better. The new ones haven't been washed yet and there might be manufacturing chemicals on them. They're the best option, though. If I could toss them down from the landing, without having to join them, I would. I'd toss the whole package to them. But I take the pair down and hand them to her, where she still stands patiently beside the door.

When she leans down to put them on her hair swings forward, hiding her face. It's dark underneath, and I catch the odor of herbal shampoo. No salon highlights; all that gold is just from sunlight.

"Keep them," I say, heading back upstairs before Belén can look up at me again with that cool, uninflected gaze.

She and Jeff watch TV in the living room until pretty late and then I hear him step out the front door when she leaves, to walk her home—audibly locking the door behind him—but then he's back again so quickly that I'm still in the kitchen. I had hoped to get Jasper's food and bedtime broth and be back upstairs in my room with my door shut by the time he returned.

"She must live nearby," I say. "I mean, that was so quick."

"Yeah," he says, looking down at his phone. "She's staying with a relative here and she won't let me anywhere near."

"Hmm," I say.

"She said she'll text when she's home safe."

Given what happened here, and given that I showed him the freaking Crime Stoppers announcement, I think it's shabby not to insist on at least seeing that she's at the door safely. Whether she wanted him to or not. Maybe. I don't know.

"*Home safe*," he reads. "I don't know what the deal is," he says, and shrugs.

"Maybe she's married," I say.

I can see by his face that this hadn't occurred to him.

"I don't think that's it."

"You're probably right," I say. "She'd be sneakier if she was married."

He looks up from his phone, looks hard at me.

"None of my business," I say, palms up. But as I'm saying it, I realize it is my business because he'll be bringing her here, and probably expecting to invite her here overnight; he doesn't like to be alone. He's never liked to spend time by himself.

Belén herself is actually unobjectionable. And even if her stillness and her indirect watchfulness make me uncomfortable, that's mostly because I'm falling apart, which has nothing to do with her. In fact, something about her reminds me a little of my friends and me in the nineties. Probably the droopy Levi's and the Hanes pocket T-shirts. And the long smooth hair.

In the kitchen the next afternoon, she appears at my elbow just as I'm making a cup of tea and I nearly jump out of my skin. She accepts one when I offer.

"There's milk in the fridge," I say. "I recommend the oat milk."

She opens the door, lifts Jasper's little bag of milk, reads the label, and then laughs. It's a low chuckle. Jeff is out in the living room.

"That's for the cat," I say.

"I see that," she says, and puts the bag precisely back in its place.

Her fingernails are trimmed and neat, her fingers small and slender. Her silky hair falls as if freshly trimmed.

"Were you a military kid?" I ask.

She looks over at me, studies my face for a beat too long.

"Why do you ask?"

I say, "You're effortlessly tidy."

"That's funny," she says. "No, I wasn't a military kid."

Suddenly I feel really old. I'm about to excuse myself, when she says, "Jeff says you taught at the university here. He said you were studying—what was it?"

"Oh," I say, embarrassed even now by my poor planning back then. "I didn't end up doing what I'd originally planned."

And what was it, anyway, that I originally planned?

She nods, and waits, as if I'm supposed to say something more. Then finally she leaves me alone in the kitchen.

I am right there again making tea in the kitchen the next morning when I hear the floorboards creaking in the hall upstairs, and the bathroom door opening and closing, and I realize she must have stayed over. I feel a pang of disgust.

After she's gone, and as he gets his things together to load his car, I almost start relaxing. I'm on the computer when he leans into the room, I assume to say goodbye. But instead, he says, "Hey, is that one of Ursula's scarves?"

"Yes," I say. I'm wearing it to hold my hair back as I work at my desk. It's one of those Vera Neumann silk prints. Pink and pale orange.

"You took that?" he asks. "From the house?"

"It was in the pile of leftovers after the estate sale. It felt too weird to give it to the Goodwill."

This unsettles him, I can tell. He shifts, goes quiet. What is he thinking?

"Can I have it?" he says.

Of course. But I'm curious.

"Why now?" I ask.

"What do you mean, why?" He seems genuinely confused by the question. "It was Ursula's, that's why."

"But you didn't want it. After the estate sale I even sent you photos of things and offered to save anything you thought you might want to keep."

"Yes, you did. You sent pictures of the frippery," he said, repeating the word that Warren had always used. "I gave that scarf to her. My mom took me to Peoples department store and let me pick it out. I couldn't decide between pink or blue. I went with this one."

My head is itching now under the pretty bit of silk, which I don't wear very often, because I can't get it out of my mind that the silkworms are boiled alive to harvest their silk. But keeping it folded away someplace unworn sometimes seems even more pointless. So it's a relief to give it back to him, and I reach to untie the knot.

"You said to donate everything to charity," I remind him.

"There was too much stuff. I couldn't make any decisions," he says. As if I don't know all about it.

I hold the scarf out to him.

He says, "Sorry. I didn't mean you had to take it off right now."

Oh, the assumptions he makes. Of course I don't have to do anything. But maybe that's part of the misunderstanding here.

He steps into the office for it, then goes back to the doorway. And although this could be told as a pleasant moment in which he realizes that he's glad to have it, instead he turns back to look at me like it's something I took, instead of something I kept.

I will nonetheless offer him a bottle of water for the drive, because I know he doesn't keep emergency water in his car. He'll tell me not to worry so much, and he'll look pointedly at the bottle, and he'll say, *So much for reducing and recycling, I guess.* Which isn't much of a zinger, really, except as a reflexive twitch in a habitual direction that simply isn't nice.

But by this stage in a visit from him . . . it's strange. I almost appreciate how sour he is, and not only because of how much better I'm going to feel when he leaves. I'll give him every opportunity to be better. I'll ask if he has everything, and he won't dignify the question with a response beyond a certain exasperated frown I'm well familiar with.

"I just don't want you to forget anything," I'll say.

But the relief after he's gone is not actually a positive feeling. It's just the absence of discomfort. It doesn't last long. I'm out in the garage stuffing the guest bedding into the washing machine when I start to feel the bulk of everything pressing in again, and the weight of how behind I am in my own life. The pressure is almost like a physical compression, a squeezing in my chest. It's too hot to walk around the block, but I need to be doing something, so I pull a random box out to the patio and open it to get rid of everything like a sea cucumber in a moment of stress, just voiding its own intestines. Because offloading whatever you have control over is better than doing nothing sometimes.

Inside the box, though, I find challenges, like a navy blue—singlet? Vintage men's swimsuit? It's got some structural elements made of stretchy nylon gone too stiff and crumbly for a vintage shop to want. I have to let it go to a landfill. And with it, the old trapped light inside, from the summer days when someone wore it in the water. There's also a mason jar of buttons, which may seem easy to donate, but only until I take a cursory look and find a safety-deposit box key pushed down among the buttons. I also find three gold dental crowns, warm to the touch. I can't deal with them at the moment and I put everything back into the jar, and the key, too, and leave the jar aside to be dealt with another day when I have the energy to sort through every individual item, which isn't going to happen today, not when I don't know whose teeth these are or what the proper thing to do with them might be. Or where that safety-deposit box key might fit. I suppose I could add the teeth to the container of Jandine's jewelry when it turns up. It was supposed to come with us in the Buick. But on the day we left, that container was too heavy to lift. I'd sealed it already with so many layers of strapping tape that it would have taken time, to find a box knife, to cut the tape open, then time to find other strong-enough boxes and repack everything, and get the strapping tape and reseal everything. By then I just wanted to get us out. But I didn't want to leave that way, in a last-minute panic. I wanted it to somehow be better than that.

"Jandine," I'd said. "What do you think, what would you like to do? Should we repack this container and take it with us in the car? Or should we just go, and leave this container for the movers to pack up and they can deliver it with everything else?"

She had looked at the container for a long moment, then crouched down and tried to shift it, experimentally, by the handles.

"It's so heavy," she said. "I don't know. What do you think?"

I realized the time for asking her to make decisions had ended. That it wasn't really a courtesy in this case. It was just pressure. And if she didn't remember what all was inside, then it wouldn't cause her any anxiety, would it?

"It's so heavy," she said again. "If there are movers coming, then I don't mind leaving it for them, if you don't mind."

She always had the most practical insight. I hadn't appreciated that in time. Now I wanted her to tell me which choice to make, knowing it would probably never be like that again. Not in this life, anyway.

"Everything important will catch up, right?" she said. "It'll follow us?"

I was aware of all the blank time ahead, with the container sitting in the empty house, and the various people who would come and go, the loading, the transit time, the real possibility of not seeing it again, even if only by accident or misadventure, the way things sometimes just go astray, not stolen, just lost along the way.

"You could add a label saying it's something nobody else would want. Something heavy. Like firewood?"

Maybe she was thinking of the woodpile in Bellingham. Where I'd once nearly broken my own nose looking for baby mice I could hear in a nest among the neatly stacked pine splits. I'm not sure anyone would pack up and pay to move firewood to another state, but she was right. On every side of the container, in black marker I'd written *Fragile—Ceramic Tiles*.

But then I wasn't sure; it wouldn't feel like tiles to anyone who might shift it, but I'd written it already. So I added *& Grout Mix* . . . but would anyone pay to have movers transport grout mix? I was overthinking it. Which was making me antsy . . . and so I added: *Custom Tint Match*. Which was the best reason I could think of to stay attached to something that otherwise might seem easily replaceable . . . even though it wasn't logical if the nonexistent grout was going to a different house, where it presumably wouldn't match anything . . . but in such moments of course it's not about the logic, it's about figuring out how to allay your own concerns and fears and anxieties, so that's what we went with.

Anyway: Also in the box are two long-sleeved floral nightgowns that I don't recognize, from a world before everyone knew not to smoke in bed, apparently, since one lace collar has a scorch mark. Whose are these? Jandine had never smoked. I wish I hadn't opened the box. Maybe the nightgowns are like DNA cross contamination in a forensics lab. Under them are a few short white elastic suspenders attached to nothing, which I assume must be for—men's dress socks? But the shape seems off and would they be white? No, they would not, which makes me realize they can only have been meant to keep old-fashioned sanitary pads inside your underpants and then I flick one away involuntarily. Why the *fuck* would anyone keep them this long? And incidentally why manufacture them in bright white? Talk about setting everybody up to fail.

Their elastic is cracking apart in the heat, too.

Sepia would have been a better universal color. More practical.

Net discards for the day: the blue—let's call it a singlet, the nightgowns, the menstrual (?) items. All folded up in a brown paper bag and placed in the trash like a time capsule. I don't deal with the buttons. And I can't make myself get rid of a cookie tin full of carbon receipts from a furniture store whose name is slightly familiar. The receipts are too carefully folded to throw away, and the edges are too dark, this evidence of something older than acid-free paper. I have no idea where the other items came from but these receipts must be for the living room furniture my grandparents bought on credit and paid off in weekly installments, decades ago. Receipts they kept, for some reason. Am I really supposed to throw these away as if they never meant anything, just because they may not mean the same thing now?

Apparently yes, and I'm the only one left to do it.

See how the days go? And this is with Adderall.

I put the can of receipts with some of Jandine's papers in my closet where I keep all the important papers I either can't figure out what to do with or can't bear to keep looking at. All the paperwork that mattered most. Her medical records, her financial documents, and her official death certificate, which I'll keep, of course, even though I'll probably never actually need to show it again to anyone.

Chapter Forty-Four

The formative horror movies I watched or caught glimpses of as a kid did not pander to a child's sensibilities, and between that and living on the farm I know the sound of buzzing flies is a bad sign. Especially the loud, juicy, berserking *Amityville Horror*–type flies that cue feelings of dread even before you realize what you're hearing—which might be another one of nature's ways of protecting you, since you cannot unsee whatever those flies are signifying. Something hidden. Something in the tall grass on the side of the road. Or concealed just off the path through the trees in the undeveloped lot you've been told not to cut through on your way home from school. If you're close enough to understand what you're hearing, you're probably close enough to catch the smell of horror in the next few steps, if you don't turn back. In my mind every Pacific Northwest child of the 1970s knows that whatever draws the flies might be there for a long time, and you might always be a little careful in those places even long after you forget the details. Even after the trees are long gone, and the road has been widened, you might be driving past some evening when you're back in town for some reason and you might still feel a stir of unease you don't recall the reason for.

I hear the flies as soon as I open the patio door, and I stand there anyway, listening, with a little jar of sugar water in my hand for the hummingbird feeder. Then I shut the door, and brace myself to go out and see what's wrong. I put on long sleeves and gloves, thinking there might be something dead in my patio, and I hope not. But if so, then I hope nobody put it there.

The good news, I guess I'd have to call it good news, is that I screwed up a DIY self-wicking planter box, and didn't realize the growing medium and the roots of the poor raspberry plants were trapped and rotting in stagnant water, in the summer heat of an accidentally airless plastic box. With no sign that anything was wrong inside, until this day of sudden flies. Maybe the overflow hole I'd cut with a box knife is blocked. I press the side of the plastic tote, and in response, thick, gravy-colored liquid purls out of the hole. The moment it hits the air it's so putrid that I assume I'm dealing with the worst of it. Until a cloud of mosquitoes emerges from inside the planter. It's a box of hell. Baking in the sun for weeks, right here, and I somehow didn't know. The fetid runoff quickly fills the shallow plastic tray under the planter, and I reach for anything shallow enough to get under the overflow hole, but everything fills faster than I know what to do with—this is why I need a utility sink out here. There's no drain in the cement to get rid of what looks and smells and even slops around like diarrhea.

The flies are red-eyed, with pale stripes. One pelts me in the arm and bounces off like a raisin. A mosquito lands on the bare skin above my rubber glove and I can't stand it, I know it's my mistake to fix, and the sooner the better, but fuck me, I'm want to run back into the house. I swipe the mosquito off and now that some of the weight has leaked out of the planter box I can at least get the side with the drainhole wedged high enough to stop the flow for the moment. I can feel some peat-like slurry inside my gloves, and the weird feel of it against my skin is triggering my gag reflex. It's just from plants, I remind myself—but that's not true actually; this is a bacterial stink, like what comes after nicking an abscess to drain it. I'm sorry about this, I think, to the raspberry plants. I've got to figure out where to dump it all. The mosquitos are already skimming over the trembling surface of the bilgewater in all the plant saucers I somehow managed to fill without spilling too much down into the cracks in the cement underfoot.

The first floor guest bathroom gets used mostly for water changes and sterilizing aquarium equipment so I leave the door shut, to keep Jasper from touching her little nose to any bucket full of bleach water I might forget in there. I've got to slowly flush this accident down the toilet in batches. But first I need to wash my hands and arms. And of course the doorknob won't turn. I assume it's because my gloves are filthy and slippery, but fuck this motherfucker of a thing, this fucking doorknob—I wipe a glove on my pant leg and the doorknob still won't turn. Maybe I hit the privacy lock by accident last night dragging out a five-gallon bucket of clean dechlorinated water. So I get a thin screwdriver from a kitchen drawer and I stick it into the center of the knob to release the privacy lock. But it won't unlock. So I start removing the two extra-long screws on either side of the knob, which is tiresome. It takes a while. And as I'm unscrewing those bastard screws I realize that I feel a little . . . nervous, maybe. Though that might be too strong a word for something only just flickering around my attention like a shadow around a bare bulb, something you notice while you're too busy to notice, because you're doing something besides looking for shadows. But I don't think I feel the ordinary emptiness that should be there on the other side of the bathroom door.

It's not that I think something or somebody is hiding in there. It's more like a feeling you might get if you found yourself at a small gathering, among fewer people than you thought would be there, without being able to remember whether you assumed there would be more people, or whether someone told you that deliberately. There's a bathroom down the hall, away from where the people are—friends of a friend, not people you know well—a long hall in a surprisingly big house, and the bathroom a little disconcertingly far. It's like being given directions to the washrooms in a bar in a city where you're a visitor, at some funny, liminal hour, like nine o'clock at night, nine thirty, ten o'clock, in what you thought was a bar but which you now realize after following the directions is also a music venue? One that doesn't seem to be open yet. The lights aren't bright, and nobody is around, not in this part of the building, where the walls are painted black and there are old flyers stapled everywhere, and stickers stuck to the paint, layers and layers of them, and a sour smell of years of beer coming from somewhere, and by the time you find the bathroom, you don't want to go in. It's partly the unknown beyond the door, and partly everything. Not unlike the weird feeling at the gathering at the house of a friend of a friend with only a few people around, as you walk down the long hallway, past a few other doors, some closed, some ajar. By the time you get to either bathroom—always the last door, you can't miss it—you might admit to a slight feeling that it's possible, not likely, but possible that someone could be inside the bathroom, even if nobody answers your knock. Waiting? No, not really. But something. Something . . . off. It's not that I'm unfamiliar with that feeling of being on guard, there's nothing unfamiliar about that; it's just that I don't usually have that feeling here. Not in my own house.

I don't hear anything. Of course not. I remove the knob on my side of the door and pull out the first two-inch screw, then the other; the interior doorknob falls loudly onto the tile bathroom floor in the dark on the other side of the door. The inner mechanism is still in place and through the square little hole vacated by the spindle of the knob, I see darkness on the other side, and a gleam from the mirror over the sink, now that I've let in a little light.

The mechanism still won't turn. I have to crack it apart with a screwdriver, before the bolt will pop free of the strike plate in the door frame. I hesitate again; if somebody is in fact standing silently inside the dark bathroom, then they've been there this whole time, listening as I take the knob apart, then watching the light from the living room filter in through the hole where the knob should be.

My gut impulse is to leave. To step away long enough to give an intruder the opportunity to leave by the front door when I'm not looking. It's crazy, I realize. But this is the feeling, the old feeling that I remember. Every day, doing this kind of bargaining with some potential but palpable horror. If I don't look into the living room, or down into the den, if I always look away, if I don't push my luck. If I never open the drapes. If I don't pay attention to the floor under the hanging clothing when I open a closet. If I don't look past the open door to the refrigerator, never check under the car cover in the garage, if I stay upstairs at night, and if I don't open this door now then I won't have to know if it's real. It's so easy, still, to slip back into the habit.

I push the door open—of course I do. This is my house. I pay the bills and I make the rules and I open the door and I turn on the light, to dispel the feeling of a concealed presence. The room, of course, is empty. I wash my hands, find some new rubber gloves, spray myself with lavender oil and eucalyptus oil and peppermint oil, anything to repel mosquitoes, and then I retrieve and pour out the containers and flush the sulfur away, but the stink lingers in the house for hours. For days. I can't tell how long it lingers, because I never really do stop imagining it faintly everywhere.

Chapter Forty-Five

Out in the world there are so many decorations, coming and going in the supermarkets and garden centers. First Mother's Day, then Father's Day, and now the Fourth of July. Each a milestone in a first year without Jandine.

Jeff's here again, though. He texted when he was already halfway to Vegas. So upbeat, so casual—*Hey I'm in Barstow, do you have a barbecue? Is my dad's in the garage? Want help looking?*

He's been told already so many times that the HOA rules forbid barbecuing under patio covers and also that I don't have a barbecue. Including last summer, when he brought a bunch of bratwurst into my house and then left them behind, until I figured out what was rotting in one of the produce drawers.

It's July, so it's hot, with an afternoon high of 108 degrees, but then long after dark the night turns eerie and windy and the air smells like damp; midnight rainstorms here are cataclysmic, but usually over by dawn. Under my bedroom window I hear Terry's wind chimes as wind tumbles around the patio, trapped between the stone walls. As the wind picks up they get so loud that I muffle them with a kitchen towel, while the fascia overhead creaks and the sun fabric tries to billow away from the nails. Somewhere a neighbor's smaller wind chimes are jangling. When I go back inside I consider leaving the patio door open a while to let the wind stir the interior of the house for a minute. But I don't like the depressing look of the back patio, the plants that have begun to look fried by the sun, and the odor of now-damp cardboard recycling that I'll have to just throw away so I close the door, lock up, and turn off the kitchen light. Then on impulse instead of going back to bed I open the front door to stand under the small overhang that protects the little cement square of my front doorstep, because when it rains here the hedges outside smell beautiful. Like rosemary, but also creosote, dry soil, and sage.

There's nobody around. Behind the weather I hear a few sporadic, flat-sounding fireworks in the distance.

The grass is bright and green in the wet, and as the rain falls the whole lawn looks to be crawling in a hundred places at once. Runoff from the spout on my roof abruptly starts to pour continuously with the kind of rain that causes flash floods here, pooling in low places hidden in plain sight until they fill with water too deep to walk or drive through. The wind picks up and lightning sparkles in the sky beyond the other town houses. No thunder. Just the feeling of waiting for it. Every year, someone drowns in the valley during flash floods. Some years, more than one.

In my peripheral vision something tumbles out from behind the corner of the house, making me jump, but it's just a paper grocery bag filled with wind and rolling like a tumbleweed. When the breeze dies back it settles in the grass, rocking.

A heavy-bodied bug lifts up from the grass and weaves over my shrubs to tap against my front window before it drops out of sight. Then another does the same thing. I shut off the porch light, and another rises, hovers unsteadily over the grass, but then drops right back down in place. I go out into the weather, crouching down close for a look, but I'm only quick enough to see the faint gleam of a hard golden shell sinking in the grass, while rain falls down one side of my neck like a cool external pulse.

From here I can see the glowing green rectangle of the swimming pool through the palms, and a shape in the water. The pool closes at night and nobody should be swimming now anyway, not with lightning in the sky. For a second I think I must be imagining it, among the moving branches, the rushing sounds in the air. But it's TK, floating on his back with his arms and legs wide, his face turned up to the sky.

By now the runoff rainwater sounds like a spigot turned on full and forgotten.

I refuse to go over there and check on him. For every reason.

At least he's wearing clothes. Shorts and a T-shirt.

I could wake up Paloma.

But what is he doing? He must know about the security cameras . . . unless he's the one in charge of the security cameras now? If he were floating face down I would call 911. But he's face up and I think he's got something under him, some recreational flotation device. The sprinklers kick in, as they do every night around midnight, rain or no rain. A few more golden beetles trundle up into the air, hover in the uncommonly damp heat, and dreamily float back to their beds in the roots of the grass.

A minute later I am tapping on Jeff's door, in case TK is in real trouble over there.

It occurs to me that there's no icon on the crime map for natural death or accident.

On the other side of the door I hear the sound of the bed frame shifting and a footstep, and I realize too late I could have taken a photo, as proof of something odd. If we look again and there's nobody in the pool, Jeff will never believe me. But what kind of a creep takes a photo like that.

Then Belén cracks open the door.

"I'm sorry to wake you," I say, and hesitate; what am I asking for, exactly?

"Is everything all right?" she says, opening the door. The bedside lamp is on, but Jeff appears deeply asleep and totally oblivious. And to my surprise Jasper is there, too, unembarrassed to be caught curled up on Belén's folded cardigan at the foot of the bed next to a couple of books from the shelves downstairs. One of them face down. She must have been reading it.

"I thought I saw something—someone—floating in the pool. You can probably see better from this window. I just want to know if I'm overreacting."

"Floating?" she says. "Swimming?"

"I'm not sure," I say. "No. Not like swimming."

Belén is already back at the window, kneeling on the bed beside Jeff's head on the other pillow, reaching her slim hand through the blinds and silently sliding the window open. Damp air blows into the room, and she steadies the horizontal slats against the breeze as she looks out.

The rain is already tapering rapidly away, and suddenly it's quiet. Until someone sets off another firecracker somewhere in the distance, and I jump at the sharp report. Belén doesn't react. Another goes off, and then there's the sound of running, some older kids, laughing from a different direction. It is a Friday night, after all. But it's like those sounds are coming from a parallel night that doesn't overlap with this one.

Little shits, I think.

"The firecracker woke him up," says Belén, and I look to Jeff, before I realize she's still looking out the window.

Jeff hasn't moved. It's a little weird. He's breathing, though, I can see that much.

"He's getting out of the water," says Belén. And then, like a spell breaking, Jeff does roll over, and I am surprised that I feel relieved.

"Are you okay?" I ask him.

"Is there a dead guy floating in the pool?" he asks, without opening his eyes.

"He's putting on his shoes," narrates Belén, still at the window.

"Okay," Jeff says, and is asleep again.

"Okay," I say, "thanks—thanks, Belén. I'm sorry to wake you."

"Glad you did," she says, without leaving her place at the window.

And I quietly close the guest room door and take myself away to the other room, where a contrite Jasper is already waiting for me on the big bed, her little paws sinking into the memory foam mattress.

Later I hear steps on the stairs and the sound of the front door being unlocked. When nobody comes back up I go down, as well, and find Belén standing more or less where I had been an hour before, with the porch light off. Her arms are crossed and she's gazing toward the pool, which now looks empty.

"Anything strange?" I say, and she shakes her head.

The paper bag moves slightly in the breeze.

Another firecracker goes off somewhere, with a long fizzling hiss.

Belén nods across the grass. "He lives just across, right?"

The windows of TK's and Stacia's town houses are dark, and Loretta's, and so is every other window in their row of houses across the lawn from this one.

"A light went on for a minute upstairs in the house on the end. But I didn't see him go in," she says.

I say, "I think he comes and goes from the garage."

She nods. And it's her interest in what may or may not be going on across the way that makes me glad for once that I'm not alone in the house.

Chapter Forty-Six

The next morning Loretta, Stacia's older sister, is found standing barefoot on the path outside of her town house by two women on their way to the pool. She's wearing a pale pretty nightgown, and when she sees them coming she points to the swimming pool gate. Later, Paloma tells me that her fingers are so bloody that the women misunderstand, thinking she must be sending them to find someone she had tried to help but couldn't.

I hear the voices and look out in time to see Paloma already halfway across the grass to the small group of women. I open the front door to blazing early sun. But I hesitate before stepping out. Stacia's already there, after all. And Paloma. I want to help somehow, of course, but I also want to allow them the scrap of privacy I can by staying here. I hope the beetles are deep under the lawn by now.

Stacia is trying to take Loretta back into her town house. One of the women is on her phone. I don't see TK anywhere, and then I realize with a start that Belén is right behind me, looking out over my shoulder. Her shoes are already on and her little backpack is in place across her shoulders. She takes my upper arm firmly, and gives me a light push.

She says, "Mandy, you're good in a crisis, why don't you go over there and make sure they don't call Metro. The lady probably just needs a few stitches."

I'm watching the activity. But I'm not part of it.

"Go," she says. "People appreciate being told what to do."

I should tell someone that we saw him last night. But it sounds like nothing.

Belén pushes me forward. "She probably just had a small accident and tried to find Stacia next door and got disoriented. That's all," Belén says. "If so, there's no need for anyone to panic. And if so, then you need to make sure they don't call the police." She lightly pushes me again, so that she can get past, and then she's rounding the corner on those silent little shoes, turning away from the activity across the way. I become aware of the sound of Stacia's voice, rising and falling like a dry sob over the lawn, and I'm afraid TK will appear. And afraid I'll see Loretta's face with an expression as drained and empty as TK's when he was lying on the floor of my kitchen.

But I take the path and do what Belén told me to.

"Loretta," I say. "Loretta, are you all right?"

She turns toward me.

"I was in my kitchen," she says.

"Loretta, did you hurt yourself?" I ask.

"I hurt my hand and I was trying to find you," she says, to Stacia, who gently looks under the bloody paper towel she's been holding around Loretta's fingers.

Paloma says, "If she needs stitches, I can drive you there." She looks at me.

"Antibiotics, maybe?" I say.

"Right," says Paloma. "I'll bring the car around."

The other women are starting to drift away.

"Thank you," calls Stacia, as they go.

Loretta is patting Stacia's arm, not the other way around.

"Do you want a change of clothes, maybe?" I ask Loretta, because otherwise she'll be stuck in the bloody nightgown all day. "I can wait here if you want to grab something for her," I say to Stacia. But she hesitates.

"Or tell me what to get and where, if that's better," I say.

"Upstairs," says Stacia, "main bedroom, bottom dresser drawer. You'll see tops and bottoms."

I go to Loretta's front door and find it locked. I gesture at Stacia.

"Did you come out the back?" she asks Loretta.

"I came out the back," says Loretta. "There was someone . . ."

I go around and find her garage door open, and as I step onto the patio I shut the garage door behind me, and the kitchen door, locking up, and upstairs I grab a pink velour tracksuit and a T-shirt, a bralette, a pair of sneakers and everything else, including a purse on the dresser, in case she needs her ID, her Medicare card. At the top of the stairs, though, I realize I've done the idiotic thing that everybody knows not to do—I went into a house that I'm not sure is empty, and then I went upstairs. And now I'm standing at the top of a set of stairs that matches the ones in my own home, and I can't seem to move. *There was someone* . . .

The bedroom at the end of this hall must be the mirror image of the one where Jeff is still asleep. And maybe TK is in there. Or maybe he's downstairs. Or he might be anywhere I didn't look. So then I'm quick down the stairs and out the front door.

"Should I lock the knob?" I ask, before I pull Loretta's front door shut behind me. "You have keys?"

"Yes," she says, "thanks, we've all got keys."

Stacia and Loretta get into the back seat of Paloma's car and I pass the clothes and purse and shoes to them.

"Lock my door, too, could you?" asks Stacia, and I nod and shut the car door.

About a week after we had picked up Jandine's new glasses, and after deciding to use the distance lenses for every day, she misjudged one of the shallow steps on the footpath during one of our walks around the complex. It happened roughly where Loretta had been standing. Jandine misstepped and went down, but so slowly that I didn't realize what was happening. Then it was too late to help, and I heard the sickeningly dull thump of her skull connecting with the edge of one of the steps. Horrified, I helped her sit up as gently as possible. She stared back at me. For a split second I was so grateful, because she didn't look hurt, even though she was clearly stunned. But then an oval split appeared in the skin of her forehead. It opened wide, and blood began to pour down her face while I fumbled to unlock my phone through the blood on my hands as I tried to stop the bleeding. My hands were shaking badly. In the moment before the bleeding started, I'd seen bone.

By the time the EMTs arrived she was answering questions from behind the cardigan I had pressed to her forehead. But she did not look good. When they lifted her into the ambulance I found her new glasses lying in the grass, both lenses gory. I hadn't understood until I saw through them that the optometrist had given her glasses with progressive lenses. One set for distance, and another for close-up, but nonetheless progressive lenses in both pairs. She must have felt so dizzy, and yet she had tried to keep wearing them. In retrospect, she'd been a little hesitant. But she hadn't complained.

I still have that pair of glasses, still bloody, still wrapped in a paper bag like a forensic sample, because for a long time I wanted to do some kind of right thing with them—maybe present them while filing an official complaint about the eye doctor who wouldn't listen. Or maybe go back and show him and then stab that motherfucker in the face with them. I was so angry. I could have killed him. But I was too busy for that because Jandine needed fourteen stitches and three follow-up CAT scans in between rechecks with a neurologist. First for the concussion, and then for postconcussion complications.

I can't say he hasn't crossed my mind, in these last few months. There have been moments, I will admit, when I've wondered whether I could recognize him in a parking lot, if for example he happened to step out in front of my car some evening. I've even wondered, idly, whether a concussion of his own might reframe a few things for him.

Later, Jeff just wants to talk about Belén.

He seems excited. But I can muster no response and I'd like to put earplugs into my ears to block him out, because now that I've woken the memory of it, I can't block out the sound of Jandine's skull hitting the step. It took me so long to stop hearing it, and for years I couldn't walk past that part of the path without hearing it again inside my own skull, a loop of memory.

". . . Really different than anyone else I know," he's saying.

"Jeff," I say. "You realize that something terrible happened here today?"

"Of course," he says, his face closing in on itself as if I've told him he doesn't deserve to be happy. He goes quiet. For a while.

Why can't it be more normal than this?

"Listen," he says. "I tried to get her to come to L.A."

"That's a great idea," I say quickly.

"But she needs to be here for family reasons," he says.

And isn't that how this works? When Jeff is ready, some young woman will stroll into his field of vision, shining in the filtered light of his readiness. And that's what makes the world turn.

"Long-distance relationships are hard," I say, trying not to sound too obvious. "But if she joins you there, that would be perfect."

"Well," he says. "She won't come to L.A."

"Why not? She can get back in a hurry if her family needs her."

"Mandy," he says, putting the milk carton down on the counter and turning to look at me. "I'm thinking about quitting my job and coming to Vegas."

"No," I say. "You can't."

He crosses his arms and leans back against the counter. "The timing sucks. I wish I could explain it—so many women would shut the door in my face if I said I might be out of work for a while. But she doesn't care." He looks puzzled, but happy. The fucker; I feel like shaking him. I open my mouth but I can't find any right thing to say. Some engine inside me has stalled, and now I'm internally hissing in the silence, waiting for a generator to kick in and help explain what I'm hearing.

"This is going to be good," he says.

"No it's not," I say.

But he goes on. “My being here will be good for you, too. You’ve had to deal with too much on your own. I’m going to help you get organized. You deserve some help. Seeing how Belén is planning around her family . . . it’s eye-opening.”

Eye-opening.

He says, “I’m sorry that I didn’t understand how much pressure you’ve been under, between the stuff from the old house, and Jandine’s illness, and . . . whatever else you’re dealing with. But I want to help.”

I’m casting back, thinking about yesterday, trying to figure out where this is coming from—he seemed pretty out of it last night and he still looks weirdly relaxed. Maybe he took something he’s not used to? An Ambien, or some other sleeping pill? Possibly something he got from Belén, I guess that’s possible. Or something from my medicine cabinet. I resist the urge to snap my fingers in front of his face.

I say, “Jeff. You can’t just put your whole life on hold. Not for somebody you just met.”

I think I’m paraphrasing something he said to me after Terry died. Not when we were deciding that I would stay in Tacoma and he would come back to help, but later, when he said he couldn’t.

“Mandy,” he says, “can I ask you something?”

“You have a life there,” I say. “You said it yourself. You can’t leave.”

“I want to ask you something serious,” he says.

“No,” I say. “I think we should keep talking about ways to help convince your girlfriend to move in with you instead.”

He says, “Didn’t you tell me when the old house went on the market there was an issue with the furnace?”

“Yes,” I say. “Jandine had to pay to replace the furnace completely before selling the house. Why?”

“So the furnace was unsafe?” he says. “Was it unsafe because of carbon monoxide?”

Now I feel awkward, because the truth of the matter is that Terry and Jandine might have easily died in their sleep at any time, and he or I could have, too, when we were there. Terry was in charge of keeping details like that in order. I'm not blaming him. But there's no good way to talk about this to Jeff without him assuming that I am.

Jeff says, "Did they check for carbon monoxide in the house? Did they use a meter?"

I say, "Why do you care now?"

He says, "Do you know the symptoms of carbon monoxide poisoning?"

He's going to explain this to me? Now? After the fact?

"Jeff," I say, "I told you about that stuff ages ago."

"Told me about what?" he says, irritated; I have spoiled some big reveal.

I say, "I assume you're alluding to the way carbon monoxide leaks make places feel haunted. Which I told you about a long time ago, after I heard about the house inspection."

He's frowning. "No," he says, "I'm not talking about that bullshit. I'm talking about the fact that carbon monoxide poisoning causes brain damage and heart disease."

"I know it can," I say. "I know that."

"And neurological issues," he says.

"I know," I say again. I have tried to look into this myself, believe me, to see if there's a link between carbon monoxide exposure and dementia. I either don't find much or I don't have the patience to go about it in a more systematic way.

He says, "I don't want you to take this the wrong way. I really don't. But maybe you should consider finding out what kind of effect it may have had."

It takes a moment for this to sink in.

"Wait, are you talking about me?" I say.

He has the good grace to blush, those two spots of warmth on his face.

"Listen," he says, "I'm really not trying to be a dick when I say this. But look at all three of you. Maybe it wouldn't hurt to at least find out. Ask a doctor who might know about these things."

For years I had a recurring dream that I was a crane fly trapped and bumping against a ceiling, trying to say something, anything, but I could never squeeze any words out. I feel the same way now. I'm trying to say, *You want to be with that girl, and she won't leave Las Vegas, so don't pretend this is anything else.*

There was a time, a long stretch of time, when I wanted a real offer of help from him, because I thought he was the only living soul who could help, and who should help, and who should be part of the transition and the closure. The sorting out of the past. But I don't believe him now. Because this is what always happens, in some variant, again and again. He seems real, and I forget that with the inevitability of an Aesop fable he will be awful, because that's what he does, and I will do what I always do, which is to curl away in shock in a way that even I find pathetic. There's always a script nudging me back in the expected direction. It seems so obvious that I almost want to say to Jeff, *Do you feel that?* But I can't—because of course that's in the script, too. Me trying to describe it, and him calling bullshit.

"Mandy," he says. "I know you don't like to ask for help. Now you don't have to."

"You can't stay here," I say.

He shakes his head. I leave the kitchen, going for the stairs.

"I can see now how much strain you've been under," he calls out after me.

How do I keep forgetting? That his disdain for me is always there? That his presence is disruptive and harmful? I've often imagined it passively, like an old forgotten fishing net he drags along behind him filled with rusty tin cans, bits of Styrofoam and fiberglass and other dangerous junk he may not even be aware of. But he must by now see the effect it has on others. On me, at least.

I don't see any point in talking to him again. And so I stay in my room until after he leaves in the morning to drive himself back to L.A.

Chapter Forty-Seven

I feel haggard as I do the dishes, as I scoop the cat box, and as I open the upstairs windows despite the heat that spills in through the gap. I leave them open just enough to burn a bowl of sage and cedar and see the smoke being pulled out of the house.

I told myself I would always try to make Jeff welcome. I don't know how to do that without feeling shitty myself, and I thought this was nobody's fault, just a by-product of the circumstances. But now I'm starting to think making me feel shitty is what makes him feel welcome. It's a terrible thought. When I hear a text come in I know it's from him before I look.

Hey Belén left earrings can she pick them up?

This wrecks my head; whenever I hear from him by text it's as if everything is normal. Maybe it's his way of pretending that we get along. I know he doesn't exactly like me. But is it also true that I don't like him? How long have I held myself away from admitting this?

I find the earrings on the windowsill in the guest room, a pretty little pair of copper infinity hoops. I also find the bed stripped. His towels and sheets are sitting in the dryer, clean and ready to be folded. I'm quite sure it wasn't him who did this.

That's fine, I reply.

She doesn't ring the bell, just knocks, lightly, and stands looking down at her phone, which gives me a brief moment to look at her when I first open the door; she's wearing another faded pocket T-shirt, a different pair of slouchy pants, and the same clean little canvas shoes on bare feet. I don't get it. I just can't see a match between her and Jeff. She looks up, and then she smiles, and the sequence is a little disconcerting; it seems purposeful, as if she's just given me the moment in which to look at her, and be disarmed. Like that moment at the swimming pool, turning her back, revealing her scar.

When I drop the earrings into her palm she puts them on immediately, still standing in the doorway, and her relief at having them back is such that I then can't hurry her out. Her hair is held up by two small dark sticks, and now, against the earrings, I can see they're coppery, too.

"Thanks," she says. "I'd be terrified of losing these."

"Sentimental value?" I ask, and then I regret saying anything at all, in case it sounds like I don't think they're nice earrings. They're perfectly nice earrings.

She says, "They were my mom's."

There are a few fine lines around her eyes and they crinkle in a smile that suggests her mother is no longer living.

"Well," I say, shifting back a little, ready to swing the door shut. Ready to say goodbye.

"Is there any news about Loretta?" she says, in a tone like she knows she's putting a foot in the door to hold it open.

"No," I say. "I mean, not that I've heard."

She's looking past me, toward the bowl of charcoal still smoldering on the coffee table. It must be obvious that I'm clearing out the residue of Jeff's presence, or at least trying to get the smell of him out. Which I guess is essentially the same thing.

"All things in moderation," she says, nodding at the incense burner. "You know what they say."

"What do they say?"

"About the unclean spirit who goes out and comes back to find that the house has been swept thoroughly, so then it goes out to bring back seven more to fill the place up again. Sometimes clearing things out just creates space for more trouble."

"Right," I say. "Like the hygiene hypothesis. Keeping things too sterile kills the good bacteria. Then the bad bacteria can move in. Or like overusing antibiotics."

"All things in moderation," she says again. "And about

Loretta. What do you think happened? Do you think she did the damage to herself?"

"What?" I say.

"Oh," she says, "Jeff told me."

"Told you what?"

"About that scar. On his hand."

He has a scar? I'd never noticed.

"Your friend is over there a lot," she says. "At Loretta's house."

"He's not really my friend," I say. "And she's his aunt. And they live in the same row. So, yes, he would be over there a lot."

"He seems a little different lately."

Her line of questioning is intrusive, and I feel myself retracting, taking another half step back. Most people would take the hint, wouldn't they?

"What happened to your friend?" she asks. "Your friend. What happened?"

"He hit his head," I say.

"He hit his head," she repeats. "He hit his head, and then what?"

Why does she keep asking?

"That's all I know," I say.

"Oh," she says. "I thought Jeff told me you thought there was something off about him, after he hit his head."

I say, "I'm pretty sure Jeff and I didn't talk about him at all."

"That's funny, I got the impression from Jeff that maybe you thought he was dangerous."

And then I wonder what I'm doing, not telling another woman to be careful, whether or not I understand what I'm worried about. A gut feeling is enough to go on, I know that, and when I realize what I'm doing, the tension falls away, like the way fatigue can suddenly catch up with you before you realize you're tired.

"It seems like bad things happen around him," I say. "Whether he's actually doing anything or not . . ."

I'm not sure how to even say this. But she waits.

"Two older women," I say. "They have similar injuries, self-inflicted. The first woman, he couldn't have actually injured. But it sounds like he was in her patio, outside, when it happened. His aunt has a similar injury, but I don't know if he was around or not when it happened. Why would they both do the same thing to themselves?"

"You're suggesting each of them—bit themselves," she says. "Just to clarify, that's what you're saying? In his presence, on different occasions, in different locations, two women did that."

"I know how it sounds," I say.

"How do you think it sounds?" she says.

And I start to say, *Once I met a woman standing in line at a thrift store who told me there was an angel attached to the stub of blue candle in her basket . . .*

"It doesn't sound like that," she says, interrupting me. "What else do the two women have in common?"

I let out a breath I didn't realize I was holding, and realize that the door is drifting slowly closed again, as if I'm trying to keep what she's implying out of my house.

"Where did he hit his head? It was here, wasn't it?" she says, with just a faint note of impatience.

She gestures, in the general direction of the kitchen. She hasn't actually asked to come inside. But now I feel conspicuously rude. It's very hot out there. What's wrong with me?

I step aside, and as I invite her in she is already heel-toeing her shoes off and I'm closing the front door behind her. I'm glad I just finished cleaning the kitchen, and suddenly I have a flashing remembrance of Tineke being upset by my toothbrush on the edge of the bathroom sink at the farm when I'd come back to visit. She had been embarrassed, and I didn't understand. *Put your brush in the cupboard, it's not a new clean sink here, not like at your mama's house.* But I remember how often she scoured that sink with Comet powder, shaken out of a green foil can, left to stand a minute and then scrubbed away. Always working on something but always self-conscious about something she hadn't quite finished. My heart nearly buckles at the memory. Because she did so much. And because I also feel an almost visceral shame for everything that's always falling apart.

"He was helping put in a new sink."

"That sink?" she says, gesturing at the kitchen.

"It's just the same kitchen sink you've seen," I say. "It's just a sink."

Belén rests a hand on the tile counter. "Cast iron?"

"Yes. I bought it at the resale shop. Surplus." I hesitated; he'd been there, right? When I bought it? And when it was installed, of course.

"Something happened," she says, looking at my face. "But you don't know what?"

"I don't know what happened," I reluctantly agree.

Chapter Forty-Eight

I'm putting the kettle on, trying to remember when I first felt anything strange. About TK, I mean. Was it as long ago as the first time he spoke to Jandine, at the surplus store, with his unfunny, outdated shtick about how women drivers do this and women shoppers do that? I hand Belén a cup of chamomile tea. She nods, listening. She's noncommittal, sometimes looking at me, sometimes looking around the room. Her eyes fall on the guppy hospital tank, at the water inside, cloudy and sulfurous with powdered medication. Abruptly her attention shifts away and she's asking about a few things, like the floors, the baseboards, the stairs. And she asks about the windows; did I know what type of glass they were made of? Was there any kind of gas sealed in between the panes?

This throws me off. Because nobody cares—really, nobody cares about the details of someone else's DIY projects. Not unless they're planning a similar project and want to avoid any really obvious ways of fucking things up, in which case it's a lot simpler to just refer to the many hours of YouTube videos of other people removing baseboards and pulling up flooring and painting and refinishing cabinets and every other kind of renovation you can imagine. I have the disappointing feeling again that she's purposely leading me to talk about impressions and gut reactions, unverifiable feelings that are easy to discount and undermine, and that even if she's not inherently mean-spirited she'll nonetheless be on the phone shortly to repeat whatever I might say to Jeff. Though somehow that doesn't quite seem right, either.

"What's your friend like?" she asks again.

"What are you asking?" I say. "What is it you want to know about?"

"Just whatever strikes you," she says. "Like what you see him doing with his time. Does he have hobbies."

"Hobbies?" I say. "He's always picking up cigarette butts and dog shit. As far as I know, those are his hobbies."

She quietly sips her tea.

"Those are his hobbies," she says, finally. "As far as you know."

I don't know if she's agreeing or being skeptical.

"Those are his hobbies," she says. "Cigarette butts and dog shit."

Saying it that way sounds wrong and uncharitable. I should rephrase that.

"Sorry," she says. "Can you tell me again about the day you met him?"

So I tell her about that day, at the surplus store, and as I do I recall something like a look in his eyes and a tone in his voice that was easy to ignore at the time, especially because I didn't want to engage with him. But in retrospect I would not have been surprised to learn later that something bad was happening, like that the surplus shop was being robbed and nobody else knew, and he was talking nonstop in the moment as a distraction to preserve the surface of the afternoon so that nobody would be hurt.

"So it seemed like a pretty normal interaction," she says. "But it wasn't normal."

"Too normal, maybe," I say.

"And he kept talking so that nobody would be hurt. And now bad things are happening around him, whether he's responsible or not."

I don't know why it's so chilling when she says it like that.

"Something like that," I say.

She sets her mug on the counter, and says, "What steps are you taking to keep him out of your house now?"

"Are you kidding?" I say.

She waits for me to give a better answer.

"Security here isn't ideal at the moment," I say. "I had replacement windows and a new patio door installed, and the vinyl frames were too wide to reinstall the iron bars that were here when I moved in."

I realize I still haven't given her a direct answer.

"I should take additional steps," I say. And then, without meaning to, I say, "I meant to get some estimates. But it's been a hard year."

I'm looking at the patio door, which has tempered glass and a highly rated multipoint locking mechanism. I added a sensor that goes off like an alarm if the door is opened, as long as I remember to switch it on. But now that my anxiety is stirring, it all seems so flimsy.

"Relax," she says. "It's okay. Iron bars are a good way to keep bad energy out, but they're not the only way. You could try running water. That's quick and simple, but it should work."

Bad energy? So maybe she's fucking with me after all. What she says is true, though, isn't it. About running water.

"Evil won't cross running water," I say. I don't know if I'm asking, or agreeing.

"A lot of things won't," she says. "Do you know where the pipes are, under your house?"

"No. Should I?"

"That other neighbor, the first lady," she says. "Where does she live?"

Is it me, or does she keep shifting direction, again and again?

"At the other end of this row of town houses."

"So she lives in a house like this one?"

"Yes. It would have the same floor plan, since it's an end unit. But laid out the other way."

"She lives in a house like this one, at the other end of this row, and it's a mirror image of yours?"

"Yes," I say. It's true, but not completely accurate. "Maybe," I say. "It depends on where you put the mirror. The layout would be the same, but everything on the right in her house would be on the left side here. So I guess it's a left-to-right mirror image of mine."

"And where does Loretta live?"

"She lives . . ." I stop. I'm trying to describe the differences, in words. "Loretta lives across the grass in an end unit. All the end units have the same floor plan. So Loretta's place is a front-to-back mirror image of the first lady's house."

"To clarify, then, Loretta's house has the same layout as your house, but it's a back-to-front as well as a left-to-right mirror image of your house."

"Yes," I say.

"Interesting," she says.

"What are you suggesting?"

"I'm not suggesting anything," she says. "I'm just looking for patterns."

"You think there are patterns here?"

"Sure," she says. "There are patterns everywhere, all the time."

I can't put my finger on why comparing the placement of the houses reminds of a feeling I used to get sometimes in the evenings during the first year or two that Jandine was living in memory care, when I would go over there to watch TV with her. To set her hair in hot rollers. And afterward she would walk me to the door of her residence, and she would watch as I stepped out into the darkened grounds, where big band music played softly from speakers hidden in the rockery. She would watch me walk away, waving from behind the glass doors if I looked back. I worried that she wouldn't go back inside. Worried that she would keep standing there, looking out, and that she might forget I'd been there and start to think she was waiting for someone. For me or someone else, and then nobody would come. It's such a vivid memory of the grounds at night, the plants, the music playing quietly to an empty courtyard. I would round the corner of another building and wait a moment and then look back, but Jandine would still be there, outlined in the glass door. Waving again, as if she knew I'd do this. Sometimes I would call memory care from the parking lot, asking the switchboard to transfer me to her residence, and I would ask to speak to her, so that one of the aides could call her to the phone, a good reason to step away from the door and stop looking out into the evening. She would pick up the common phone in the living room, and say, *Hello?* I would tell her I was just calling to say good night. As if I hadn't just been there. And she would thank me for calling. Tell me that she loved me. *I hope we can visit*, she used to say. Or, *I hope to see you sometime soon*. I felt strange sidestepping the fact that I had just seen her, but I didn't know if referring to the fact that I'd just walked out the door behind her would be even more disorienting. Then I stopped worrying about it, since having the right elements, even in a jumbled order, still seemed to make sense to her.

Belén has pulled the copper sticks from her hair and holds them lightly as she paces across the living room, then back over the same area. It's like she's looking for the back of an earring or a contact lens in the days when everything wasn't quite so disposable. Before I used to find Jeff's used contact lenses everywhere, sometimes long after he's gone. Small wrinkled disks, almost invisible, discarded on the coffee table next to the TV remote control.

The flashing copper rods move independently, like two bright creatures scanning the room with interest. One of them turns lightly in her hand, panning in my direction; I can almost feel it clocking me.

"Here," she says, touching a spot on the floor with her toes. "You've got water coming in from the garage, under the patio, right along here."

"How do you know?" I don't know why I even ask when clearly she's dowsing.

"It's just obvious," she says. "Copper has high conductivity."

What I'm really asking is whether she's using the copper sticks like a flashlight in a darkened room, or like a planchette on a talking board.

"There's water, or there's not," she says. "It's like passing your hand above a burner to see if the stove is hot." She steps back, letting gravity bring the rods down and apart. When she steps forward the rods come back together, audibly crossing. She turns in another direction and they slip apart again.

"So," she says, "you have a narrow strip of the floor here where it looks like he'll be able to walk without crossing over running water under the house." She steps back and contemplates the route he might take through the garage, through the patio, and over the sill of the patio door to the kitchen. "He has to stay in the southern half of the house. That means he can't make use of your front door, not unless the water to the whole house is turned off in the alley."

She walks slowly through the living room again, to the stairs by the front door, and on the third step the rods touch. "He also can't go up the stairs," she says. "Even if the water is shut off, your floating staircase is made of iron."

"Are you sure about all of that?" I say.

"I'm pretty sure," she says. She comes back down the steps. She walks toward the fifty-five-gallon tank and the rods lean together. "There must be something underground here," she says. "The tanks are big, but they aren't running water."

I say, "The tanks are cycled. Does that matter?"

"Don't know," she says. "I don't know anything about aquariums."

In a cycled tank, nitrifying bacteria consume the waste chemicals and clean the water, which is reoxygenated by the airstones. So it's naturally filtered and circulating water. Wouldn't that count?

"Beats me," she says.

I'm concerned by her lack of concern. Also, by her lack of interest.

"How do you know the rods aren't just pointing to where *you* think there's running water?"

She says, "Even if that's all the rods are doing, in my experience, that still tells us where he'll walk and where he won't, if he's allowed to enter the house. I can't explain it any better than that."

That day in the kitchen only the water supply to the sink was off. He wouldn't open the back door for himself; when that door is closed, the door handle is right on the line where she says there's water underfoot.

"He can pass through the door, just not directly over the pipes," she says. "If you watch him come in, you'll probably notice him leaning a little to one side, to avoid it."

I'm sure this seems basic to her. But I'm not at all sure about any of it.

"Anywhere you don't want him," she says, "you can easily use the water to block him. If you want to figure out if he's averse to the tank, you could test for that. I don't know how you would, because he'd need to step over it. But that's an interesting question."

"This is too much," I say, and I don't just mean this, right now, with the water. I mean all of it. All this casual talk about directing evil safely through the house. And the surprising realization that I am skeptical of her and not the other way around.

"I don't make the rules," she says. "But I think the placement of your door handle means he won't want to open that door on his own. If you'd like a little extra peace of mind, you might try leaving your hose in front of your door and leaving it on a little. Just let the water trickle into your plants."

She's being awfully specific about unproven things.

"Okay, listen," she says. "At the end of the day, whether or not he's actually dangerous to you, are you uncomfortable with the possibility of him turning up here uninvited?"

"Yes," I say.

"Then just use the garden hose. If it works, then you'll feel better. It won't matter why it works, or how. Do you have an old phone or an old camera you don't care about? Maybe I can take the infrared filter out. Then you can use it to see into dark corners."

I bring her the one I used for taking pictures of his blood on the kitchen floor.

"It's not in service," I say.

"Do you have anything older?" she says, looking it over. "Anything easier to take apart? Maybe a digital camera you don't use?"

I bring out the box where I've been putting old electronics as I find them, including a couple of nice digital cameras that Terry bought and probably never used. They aren't that old, really. But the possibility that they're already obsolete, or obsolete enough to dismantle, is unexpectedly painful. She looks through the box, and when she takes out an older camera that I don't recognize, I'm relieved.

"How about this one?" she says. It's an old Canon PowerShot. I've never seen it before. It might be Jeff's for all I know.

"Go ahead," I say.

"Are you sure?" she says.

"Yes," I say, "it's fine." Do I even want to be able to see in the dark? I'm not sure why she's doing this, or whether the idea of someone hanging around in the dark will make me feel more secure, or less.

"This camera is probably fifteen years old by now," she says.

"It's fine," I say. "Just make sure the memory card is empty."

"It's dead," she says. And for a moment, I almost forget that fifteen years ago, you couldn't plug every single thing in and expect it to power up again shortly.

"Do you have any AA batteries?"

I find the batteries.

"Perfect," she says. "Do you have any painter's tape? Or masking tape?"

I find a roll of blue painter's tape in the kitchen drawer. She tears off a long piece, loops with the tacky side out, and presses it down onto the tabletop in a line. She asks for more things, and I retrieve them all. Paper towels. Some rubbing alcohol. A razor blade. A set of Terry's small precision screwdrivers from the kitchen drawer. As she disassembles the camera on a paper towel, she carefully places each screw onto the masking tape in a rough map of where each came from, both to avoid losing any and to remember where to put them all back. Why does she know how to do this? Getting the camera casing open takes a while. Detaching one end of the membrane cable—that's what she calls it—takes a while, and so does prying up the sensor. She carefully moves layered parts aside, without detaching them, and then she turns the camera over and gives it a gentle shake. What falls out onto the paper towel is a small square that looks like a cover slip for a microscope slide. Thin, transparent, easy to lose track of.

"There it is," she says.

"Why do I need this camera again?"

"I'll show you," she says. But first she begins working in reverse. I watch the meticulous steps of replacing, reattaching, reassembling. Of returning each of the tiny screws to their places. When she's done, I'm surprised to find the process has taken just under an hour, but I can't say whether it felt like more or less time had gone by.

She stands, and stretches, after bending over the small close work.

"What should I do with this?" I ask, holding the little square of glass in my palm.

"The filter? I don't think there's much you can do with it, now."

Seen from one angle, the little square is clear. From another it appears greenish, and from a third, almost topaz. It's beautiful, and looks like it should be kept somewhere safe, even if it will never be used again.

"What's it made out of?"

"Glass, probably. Excuse me a moment," she says. "I have to check in with someone."

She steps out of the room to make a brief phone call. Not so far that I can't hear her, though. For a moment I have the weird impression there isn't anyone on the other end, as if she's talking to herself, or maybe talking to me, obliquely.

"Yes," she says. And then: "In the same complex." She listens, and then says, "No, stay there. I'll be there soon."

I say, "Was that Jeff?" even though I know it wasn't.

She says, "That was my late godmother's husband."

It crosses my mind to ask how that's not her godfather, but of course it's different. Just like Heather is not my stepmother, but the mother of my stepbrother, though that's just a polite convention now. Does anyone ever say, *That's my ex-stepsibling?* I've meant to look that up before and I always forget.

She reaches into her backpack and removes a little black tube from a zippered pocket. I think it's a lipstick at first.

"You'll need to use something like this when looking through the camera," she says. "It's an infrared illuminator. Use it like a flashlight."

I'm slightly confused about the logistics of doing this simultaneously.

"Without the filter, the camera will let you see in the dark, but it won't provide any illumination. So you need this, as a source of infrared illumination, okay?" She briefly demonstrates, looking at the screen of the camera, while pointing the illuminator at whatever she sees on the screen. Then she hands the camera and flashlight to me, without making sure I know what I'm doing. Which I guess I appreciate.

"I wish I didn't have to ask this," she says. "But I need a favor, and I don't know very many people here."

"What is it?" I say.

She seems different now, somehow, a little tired but also more settled, reaching confidently into her fabric backpack to draw out a cheap little AM/FM radio. It's like she's making herself comfortable. The radio emits a faint white noise when she turns it on, and then she's slowly pacing the living room floor again, as with the copper dowsing rods, now with her head bowed over the little percussive radio in her hands, which sounds always like she's about to stumble onto a clear station that never materializes.

"What are you doing?" I ask, suddenly wary. It's that scanning sound. I don't like it.

"I'm just kind of looking for garbage," she says. "Pollution."

It's almost as if she's been waiting for something like this? Not just to get into the house, but also to check inside the house? Maybe even since I saw her sitting by the pool, glancing up over an open book. It's unlikely, but it's possible. It's disturbing. Maybe it's also slightly reassuring. But that, too, is disturbing. And then, with an offhand delivery that's somehow slightly too casual, she says, "Would it help any if you didn't have to deal with Jeff for a while? If he's stressing you out I can ask him to hang back. That's something practical that I can do to help."

All afternoon my blood pressure has been a little more, and a little more, all afternoon a presence everywhere—and it's been a long afternoon, hasn't it? Now there's a pause, and then a long second later my heart beats again normally. Just a stress flutter. That's what beta-blockers are for. But what's the right response when a person you don't know well enough to trust offers you, as a favor, something you want, but are ashamed to admit? Because I would love it if Jeff weren't coming around. And yet I feel too conflicted to say this out loud.

"Pollution like what?"

"Like anything. But it's hard to say, because you have all of this over here," she says, with a gesture to the TV, the modem.

She pulls the antenna out as she wanders farther afield in the house, pacing slowly in her bare feet, returning the antenna again with the series of snicks that a telescoping tube of thin metal makes. All I can hear is the static, punctuated sometimes with a burr or a whine that rises and falls away as she walks. At which I feel again the old habit of bracing myself.

"Mostly I'm checking for EMF," she says, without looking up. "Do you know how?"

"I've seen it done," I say. "On TV. But I've never done it."

"FM encodes info using frequency modulation. That's why you don't hear a lot of distortion, which is why that's where the music is." I've noticed she tends to talk like this: FM does this, or FM does that. AM does it differently.

"AM does it differently," she says. "AM uses amplitude,

which is why the signal breaks up when you move around with an AM radio, and almost by accident it can let us know about types of interference we can't see. FM doesn't tell you. But AM will."

She pushes the antenna back down again. "That's not doing anything. I just like the sound it makes," she says. "For AM there's a rod antenna inside to do the work."

She still hasn't looked up from the radio, even though she's not turning the dial, and I'm fairly sure there's nothing to see there, nothing related to the rise and fall inside the static that she's following.

"If you ever need to do this, just find some empty static," she says.

The sound of it is really getting under my skin.

"Turn the dial and leave it where it can't pick up any stations. In the static you'll hear the change when you get close to something."

"Doesn't that sound bother you?" I say. I'm trying not to grit my teeth.

"The empty static doesn't bother me," she says.

Her face looks peaceful, as she moves slowly along, hesitating near the tanks. But it sounds like hell, to me. I wonder, though, does that mean AM will tell you if something is moving toward you, if you and the radio are standing still?

"Wireless, however, I don't like," she says, still pacing. "It's not the wireless itself. It's all the processing. I can hear the chip in your microwave. The display on the front of your fridge. Different patterns out of different equipment. There's lot of radio hissing under the surface. It can sound pretty nasty," she says. "But cable is the worst. Cable leaks like fuck, and you can hear voices in it."

"You can hear voices in—cable?" I say. I don't exactly know what she means.

"It'll wreck your head," she says. "You should get rid of it."

"I don't have cable," I say.

"You do," she says.

She's on the move again.

"But I'm particularly sensitive," she says. "Because I'm not used to being around all of this."

Sensitive to it, but yet she goes around looking for the noise.

"It's no problem," she says. "I'll ask Jeff to hang back. Family can be a lot. Speaking of which—the favor I was going to ask."

She's not looking at me.

"Would it be all right if I bring my godmother's husband here for a little while? You won't need to do anything special for him," she says. "I'm trying to work out all the details on his behalf. There's so much to do, to make sure he gets what he needs. But I worry about leaving him home alone at the moment."

I remember, of course, Jeff did tell me she was caring for a family member. It's possible I had not entirely believed it at the time.

"I think it's best not have them both here at the same time," she says. "Him and Jeff, I mean."

"Okay," I say. "Sure." Interesting that she doesn't want Jeff to meet him. But it's true that I'm a reasonably trustworthy option to ask to look after a person who isn't well.

"Great. Thanks," she says, swiftly. "Listen, he's under a doctor's care for something that's a little hard to describe. But it's not dementia," she says.

"Oh?" I say.

"It's . . . It might seem that way," she says. "He's completely aware of what's going on with his health. It's a deficiency, a pretty rare one to treat, and that's what I'm helping him sort out. He's got a specialist lined up."

I'd like to acknowledge what she's doing. Stepping up to help this man. But there's something distant in the way she describes him and now she's already out on the patio, draping a garden hose across the welcome mat of the back door, adjusting the attached watering wand so that a tiny trickle escapes continuously into the planter box of basil, parsley, and catnip.

She texts me her phone number and reminds me to change the battery on the old camera. Before she leaves I find the chalk line reel in the kitchen junk drawer and ask her to show me again where the waterlines are, and to hold the hook end of the string while I stretch it and then snap a straight chalk line in the relevant places. After she leaves I finally have my space back. Except that now I have that feeling of being too alert to every little sound. I used to wonder why Terry spent so much time moving hoses around the lawns when he could have had underground sprinklers installed instead. It would have made his life a lot easier. But maybe he was moving the hoses around by instinct, without knowing why it quelled this kind of feeling.

To prevent Jasper smudging the chalk lines, I put a line of clear packing tape over each.

The old camera is lying on the counter. I guess I should try it out, now that it's getting dark. Do a trial run, in case I ever find myself in the position of needing to look into a dark room or dark patio or garage—Jesus Christ. What am I even thinking?

But I do it. I go out to the security door between my patio and my garage, and with one hand I shine the infrared illuminator in through the bars, like an invisible flashlight, and I see nothing, of course. When I hold up the camera, and turn it on, the contents of the garage leap onto it's screen with a weird colorless clarity that is also somehow purplish and flat. I see the bumper of my car, looming, and my tool bench with shelves full of things squeezed in along the wall with the washer and dryer. I can't see the Buick from here, on the other side of my car, but I know it's there, under the cover. I don't know why I keep the cover on it, unless it's because Terry always did.

There's an adjustable focus to the illuminator, so that you can train the invisible spotlight onto something closer to you or farther from you—I wonder why she has something like this. And carries it with her, to boot? It's probably manufactured for hunters who are out at night, hunting in the dark. I turn it off and go back inside quickly, because it's impossible to look through the camera like that without already expecting to see movement.

My phone shivers, and it also gives a faint chime, though the ringer is still off. Did she change that? I don't think she handled my phone, did she?

His name is Sam, she texts. *I forgot to say the illuminator is faintly visible if seen head-on so just remember they'll know you're looking. We'll come tomorrow evening.*

Who will know where I'm looking?? I reply.

Whoever you're looking for in the dark.

Chapter Forty-Nine

I wake up with an itch that tells me it's time for a 20 percent water change in the tanks.

In the fifty-five-gallon tank downstairs I see a cory flashing; they give a quick little flick against the sand like that when irritated, like they're trying to scratch themselves. But of course they can't get away from the water chemistry. And even though the nitrifying cycle efficiently turns ammonia into nitrite, and nitrite into nitrate, and the nitrate at the end of the cycle is much less toxic, it's nonetheless still toxic. The fish live with it the way you'd be able to live in a space colony on a poisonous planet among chain-smokers whose lush plant biofilters clean the air efficiently but perhaps also give off a stink of brimstone. You'd be fine, with regular maintenance. But no matter how much you might want to open a window on occasion, you can't.

Water changes work out well here because the patio plants love nitrate-rich tank water. Which is why any kid with an interest in colonizing Mars should be given a starter aquarium and shown how to cultivate a healthy bacterial cycle within the transparent confines of a closed system full of fragile living creatures.

I'll be wearing elbow-high aquarium gloves until my hands heal, but I still clean my hands well in the kitchen sink to avoid traces of soap, or Neosporin, or sunscreen, or anything else. When I open the blinds over the sink I see TK's face across the patio, and it startles me. He's in the shady stillness of the fly corner, wearing mirrored sunglasses, and I don't know if he can see me at the window or not. I was told these windows would be somewhat opaque during daylight hours. But of course I've never tried to look in at myself from the patio.

He's here, I text Belén, feeling mildly panicked. *He's standing in my patio.*

He won't want to step over the hose, she replies.

Why now? I ask. *He wasn't doing this before.*

She doesn't reply. I swallow some pills, switch on the kettle, make a cup of tea, and check through the window again in time to see a fly swing wide of the vortex and pelt him in the neck. It bounces back to the others, and he doesn't react. I unlock the patio door and open it a couple of inches, but he doesn't seem to notice that, either. I wish it had a chain lock, even if locks are fallible. The hose is still in place. Isn't a hose just a different kind of lock, though? I.e., fallible?

I say, "Excuse me."

"Good morning," he says, turning his head.

"What are you doing?"

"I'm here to help out."

"With what?"

"To help with a few things around the house."

He doesn't sound quite right. I close the door and lock it, but a few minutes later I can't help myself and I open it again, and though he must hear me at the door he doesn't react.

"I don't need any help today. You should go home."

He says, "I'm already here, so we may as well get cracking."

His speech sounds like words cut from a newspaper and arranged into a note. I look down at my hand, holding my tea; the wounds don't look great. My nails are peeling, and half of them seem to be broken.

He says, "You've had your hands full for a long time."

There's a lump in my throat. Which I swallow.

He's looking past me into the house, I think. I turn to see what he's staring at. It must be the barometer from the farm, which I keep even though it doesn't work very well here. All those little coils inside are poised and ready, but now, for example, the golden arrow sits over the word *Rain*.

I look back at him and he's a little closer to the doorway where I'm standing.

"Mandy?" he says.

He sounds suddenly like himself.

"I think there's something in your hair," he says.

He waits, one hand tentatively lifted. I'm closer to the threshold than I realized, closer to the waterline.

"What's in my hair?" I can't keep my voice from rising, because it would have to be a wasp, wouldn't it?

"There's an app," he says. "An app? Do you want me to try to identify—"

"Just look and tell me," I say.

His hand is still in the air, as he's assessing. "*Hymenoptera?*"

The word seems unfamiliar to him. "*Polistes* . . ." he says. "*Polistes aurifer?* I think it's a paper wasp?"

I feel it now where the sun meets my hair. A small gyroscope, temporarily motionless. One of my legs is shaking slightly from the effort to hold still while expecting that horizontal zigzag movement wasps make in the air, so often seen from the corner of the eye.

I say, "Don't hurt . . ."

His hand blocks the light. I turn my face away, focusing instead on the barometer on the wall, which was visible from the gravel driveway of my grandparents' house, through the window in between the red-and-purple fuchsias in hanging cedar baskets that are still, somewhere, creaking softly, and still suspended from the eaves.

But the window is too low, and too close, and too much like my own kitchen window where I never would have seen the blood clot hanging on the wall or heard it ticking in an odd three-quarter profile view. I close my eyes, and open my eyes, and remember that it was a blue clock hanging on the wall. Not a blood clot. Ridiculous.

The vibration lifts away from my skull and in the palm of TK's hand sits a golden paper wasp, as perfect and still as a cipher. I'm afraid of how delicate it is, how motionless, but I feel a rush of gratitude. Because it wasn't one of the thread-waisted ones with nothing but a long needle-thin segment, the petiole connecting thorax to abdomen—the idea of that impossibly delicate and terrifying filament getting tangled in my hair . . . My fear of being stung, but also my fear of accidentally severing that thread, of cutting off the swollen gaster of the lower half of the body by accident . . .

The wings flicker. Then the paper wasp is gone, away into the air.

I step backward and close the door in TK's face, lock it, and go upstairs to sit on a step between the small landing and the upstairs hallway. From here I can't see any of the windows. It's a small place in the house that cannot be observed from outside, and I put my head between my knees and wait until I'm able to get up.

And then I will get up forthwith and I will act as if this is a normal day, and when I look out again half an hour later, from the bedroom window, down through the sun fabric, I'll see that TK is no longer on the patio.

There is no one else to tell, so I text Belén again.

He's gone. I hesitate, and then I add: *You asked about languages, he said some words in Latin—but it was an animal name.*

Will be there 8pm. And then: *What Latin?*

I have to search for the spelling.

Polistes aurifer? A golden paper wasp.

LOL, she replies, *I'll ask.*

Ask whom? Ask Sam? I wait for her reply.

Your friend is probably just fucking with you, she says. *I would ignore.*

Belén taps the front door at eight, and when I open she steps aside to present Sam. He's wearing, of all things, a Tilley Endurables hat, which is funny to me now because I wanted a hat like that so much, back when I hoped or expected to have a robust life out in the world, under the sun, with one foot planted in the ancient world and the other in a present very different from this one. I guess I do live under the sun now, but I've forgotten ever wanting anything as simply as I once wanted that hat.

As he shakes my hand his eyes move over mine, or between them, trying to see both of my pupils at the same time,

I think? He takes the hat off and his hair is dark and graying with a few surprising curls, and a neat salt-and-pepper mustache and beard. I recognize his checked shirt and khaki pants from ads for traveling clothes of an expensive type that sometimes appear in the dispatches, marketed to people of retirement age who dream of traveling the world with nothing but a carry-on, some cash in a concealed-wallet belt, and clothing that will wash easily in hotel sinks and dry overnight. He also carries a walking stick. Blackthorn, by the look of it.

"Come in," I say, and step aside.

"I'm a geologist," he says, looking around the room. "From Canada."

"All right then," I say. "Nice to meet you."

"Sam has a few questions for you," Belén says to me, with the air of someone dropping someone off somewhere. He looks at her, and frowns.

"You have questions for me?" I say to Sam, surprised.

I had expected him to be medically fragile, but his eyes are bright, and his hair and his fingernails are glossy and clean, and so are his eyebrows and eyelashes, all of which I'm paying attention to now in order to avoid acknowledging the way she stands behind him where he can't see the way she's watching him, with her face set in an expression so neutral that it almost looks like a mask.

It takes me a little while to see that he's thinner than the impression his clothes make. That his kneecaps stand out through the lightweight technical fabric of his pants when he crosses one leg over the other as he sits down at the table in the living room.

Belén checks that the curtains are firmly closed.

Sam would not care for something to drink. But I feel compelled to keep asking. A mug of tea? A glass of water, at least?

"No," he says. "But I thank you for your hospitality. And for your kindness."

That's a curious thing to say; it somehow makes me feel as though I'm not being kind at all. I mean, as if I should make an effort to be kinder. He rests both elbows on the table, and brings his fingertips together into a steeple.

"Belén told me about your mother's illness," he says. "It sounds like you took great care in helping her. I'm very sorry for your loss."

The lump in the throat.

"Thank you," I say.

"I know what it means to be the caregiver."

"I'm sorry," I say. Because what else can I say.

He gets up from his chair. "I'm tired, and I don't have questions for you tonight."

"Oh, right," says Belén, to me. "I assume it's all right if Sam sleeps in your guest room?"

"What the fuck?" I say, downstairs, after we've shown Sam to the guest bed. "You didn't mention he'd be staying here overnight."

He coughs upstairs, with the sound of pre-OSHA times.

"I'm sorry to be so abrupt," she says, gathering her bag, her shoes. "Like I said, he's sick. But he's very interested in hearing about your friend. His late wife, Hadley, knew a lot about this kind of thing. And he's motivated to figure out what's happening to your friend."

"This kind of thing?" I say. "Remind me, what kind of thing is this?"

Belén says, "I'll really appreciate it if you can just let him stay here, and keep him company sometimes. The best thing you can do is listen when he wants to talk about Hadley. Maybe he'll remember something useful. All right?"

What can I say.

"If you want to ask him anything, just ask in the mornings."

Mornings? Plural?

"He's clearheaded in the mornings," she said. "And if he wants to talk, you should listen."

I say, "But I have to work."

"He might say something more important than you realize."

I say, "Important how? About what?"

She smiles. That's the way it is, with distant people. Once you think you see them present, even briefly, they can trick you so easily.

"Just listen for anything that feels a little off."

"A little off?" I say.

"Can you live without putting the chain on the door?"

I'm looking at the door behind her, then at her.

"Yes," she says. "Sorry. I have Jeff's key. Listen, though. Your friend won't try to get into your house, and if it makes you feel better about going to bed without putting the chain on, you can always lock yourself in your bedroom. Sam will be okay and I'll be back soon."

That she's leaving Sam here is—I guess?—reassuring. But I feel less reassured when she asks me to disconnect the Wi-Fi.

She says, "You should text a coworker in the morning to let them know your internet is down and that it's going to be spotty for a couple of days. Say it will probably be back by afternoon. And we'll talk tomorrow before that."

There's a shift in the house as she unplugs the router. Like some background noise suddenly stopping. In that feeling of quiet, it seems for a moment as though I ought to check in with Jeff, somehow, but it's just a vestigial feeling, and a contrary one, since I did after all agree to this arrangement with Belén in order to keep him away.

PART SIX

It is admitted, by all investigators, that fraud runs through much of the phenomena, but it is equally true that there is a residuum wherein neither conscious nor unconscious fraud exists and this becomes more and more evident as the accumulation of evidence multiplies.

RICHARD AND ISABELLA INGALESE, *Fragments of Truth*

SOCRATES: Do you need me to tell you what I mean by this, Ion?

ION: Lord, yes, I do, Socrates. I love to hear you wise men talk.

PLATO, *Ion*
(TRANS. PAUL WOODRUFF)

Chapter Fifty

To my surprise, which is code for annoyance, Belén taps at my door the next morning, and then continues tapping until I'm awake, before asking me to come downstairs to hear from Sam. "This is the best chance," she says. The sun is up, at least.

It's ride-to-the-airport early. Jasper, nonplussed, doesn't move from her crinkle blanket at the foot of the bed.

"Black tea with oat milk, right?" Belén holds out a stoneware mug, the one I habitually use. Am I prepared to drink whatever she's handing me? I think not. But that's paranoid. Right? But then again, am I prepared to decide anything before I'm awake?

"Sorry," she says. "But he'd like a chance to speak with you before . . ."

"It's fine," I say, putting my feet down on the floor. "I just need a minute."

"I know it's early," she says.

"It's fine," I say, again. I'm waiting for her to leave before I stand, just in case my ear is fucked, just in case I'm dizzy without knowing it yet. She hesitates, like she thinks I might go back to bed and fall asleep, but then sets the mug of tea down on the dresser before she shuts the door. I pour the contents down the sink in the en suite bathroom, exasperated with myself, but still, I don't feel good about drinking it.

Sam is seated at one corner of the dining room table in the living room, wearing the same clothing, in the same posture, but now the cuffs of his shirt are turned up and I can see a bracelet of prayer beads around one wrist. I reach for the chair across from him, but Belén appears from the kitchen, motioning for me to sit beside him, at the head of the table, and I do. I wish I hadn't, though. The window it faces is a bit bright. It doesn't help that my morning pills haven't kicked in yet. I could get up, I could make more tea, the caffeine would help, but now that I'm sitting here, like this, it seems too much effort to get up again.

I can barely look at Sam, I realize. Because of the stakes involved in believing what Belén says, i.e., that whatever is happening or will happen to him is *not dementia*. I won't ask, of course. But I do wonder, about a deficiency that causes symptoms that might appear to be dementia, but can be reversed when the deficiency is corrected. What might that be? I remember hoping for something like that, for Jandine. Praying for it.

"Mandy," Sam says, politely. I hear one of his joints crack faintly, as he leans forward. "I'm glad to have this opportunity to thank you, in advance, for bearing with me. And for bearing with the chaos." The beads around his wrist are dark red, meditative looking, and he puts that hand out for mine. A handshake, I assume, but then he doesn't let go. It's a surprisingly warm greeting. But awkward, and kind of uncomfortable.

"Muscle weakness," he says, "I have muscle weakness, and I tire easily, and I lose my train of thought. You might also hear changes in my voice sometimes—but is this all right for now? You can hear me all right?"

He's gazing at me, still holding my hand clasped in his. I hear a tapping sound, and realize it's my own foot, tapping the floor, under the table. Tapping on its own.

"Yes," I say.

"That's great," he says, in a pleasant, soft voice. "I'm glad, if I've been speaking in a way that you can hear."

Of course I can hear him. What's he talking about, I wonder?—but before I even finish that thought he lets go of my hand abruptly, dropping it with more force than necessary. I don't think he was trying to hurt me. But for a moment I'm speechless with surprise.

"I hope you can forgive me, Mandy," he says.

I already don't like him. But I also realize he's waiting on critical treatment, and it must be hard on him. On both of them.

And I remember how it felt to wait, helpless, while Jandine's medications were in limbo. Watching the effects on her.

Where is Belén, I wonder?

"Can we start over, Mandy?"

"Sure," I say.

He opens his hands, like he's showing me that they're empty. "Your friend is dealing with one hell of a strange situation, and he needs to get help, as soon possible."

I hear Belén, now, moving in the kitchen.

"Belén," he says, without breaking eye contact with me. "Can you come back at three o'clock this afternoon?" he says.

"I'm not leaving yet," she says, and I hear her filling the kettle.

He's still looking at me.

"Your friend is having surgery soon, isn't he? In the next four or five days, is that right?"

"Yes," I say, though I'm not sure it's true.

I will never forgive what Medicare did to Jandine, when they stopped refilling her medication without notifying me. I'm still carrying around all of the rage I had to swallow, in order to sound reasonable, in order appear calm enough that the people on the other end of the phone line would want to help.

Sam is watching me.

I hear the kettle in the kitchen, warming.

Medicare wouldn't tell me what was happening at first, even though I was the legal contact person, had been for years. Then they said the medication was too expensive, she would have to try something less expensive, and if—they really meant when—it didn't work they would resume covering the patch her doctor had prescribed. But she was already taking the only drug approved by the FDA to protect cognition; what did they want her to take instead? *We mailed you a table of alternate medications*, they said. I asked them to talk me through this: they were forcing her to take drugs for other conditions? Because they were cheaper? Where had they sent these warning notices? The person I spoke to couldn't tell from the records. I felt an icy calm, layered over a homicidal intensity.

I forgot to take my blood pressure medication last night.

I realize this only when I feel my pulse pounding inside my skull.

Sam is looking at me expectantly. But then maybe I'm rusty at reading people. Because I am tired of people. I couldn't remove Jandine's physical address from her Medicare file or the rest of her prescriptions wouldn't be delivered. The staff at memory care knew to save correspondence for me, especially anything official. Until the new management started switching up the assignments, shuffling staff members around, to keep them from forming bonds with the residents or the families. There were new faces, all the time, a higher staff turnover, and then I would sometimes find mail crumpled into her dresser drawers and coat pockets. Even when those letters were important. Even after those abrupt medication swings had been the beginning of the end.

"Mandy?" Sam says.

"What's going on here?" I say.

"Good question," he says. "That's a fantastic question."

I wait. I feel slightly lightheaded. I didn't ask a rhetorical question. Did I?

He's looking at me calmly, and somehow I can so easily see him getting off a plane somewhere, arriving at a private airfield on the outskirts of a city into which he'll shortly disappear, wearing a tan coat and carrying a locked briefcase into the concealed privacy of a certain kind of spy movie circa 1979. As if nothing can hurt him.

"A fantastic question deserves a fantastic answer," he says. "Wouldn't you agree?"

"What are you talking about?" I say.

He's lightly snapping the beads of his bracelet.

"Mandy," he says. "Can I just call it a demon?"

"We're not calling it that," Belén says, from the kitchen. "Remember?"

The booming of my heart in my temples tells me I'm being treated like an idiot, and yet I think I'm being answered with unusual frankness. And what is my life, that I can't tell the difference.

"What are you talking about?" I say again.

"Belén and I are familiar with the problem your friend is dealing with at the moment," he says. "Belén and I, together with my late wife, Hadley."

Am I missing something?

"My late wife," he says. "Hadley, my late wife, was researching a variation on this phenomenon, and now Belén and I are hoping to complete the work on Hadley's behalf."

"Phenomenon?" I ask.

"The phenomenon that you've been treating like a demon," he says.

"I've never said anything like that," I say.

"But," he says, "obviously . . ."

I can't tell if the hesitation in his words is happening with him, or with me.

"Obviously we can call it something else," he says. "We can call it whatever you want." He leans forward. "What sounds right to you? Shall we call it a particle? Can we do that?"

"A particle of what?" I feel like I'm repeating myself, even when I'm not.

"It's not really a particle *of* anything," he says. "It's more like a particle *in* something."

The rhythm of his speech bothers me. But I also might be getting used to it.

"It's windy," observes Belén, leaning in the kitchen doorway. I look to the window in front of me. And it's true. The mesquite bush outside is moving, moving. The mesquite bush outside is a moving shadow on the surface of the glass.

"Yes," says Sam. "It's been windy for three days in a row. Have you noticed?"

"Yes," I say. "I noticed."

Then he smiles. For the first time?

I wait. He waits.

He glances at Belén. Behind her, in the kitchen, I can hear the kettle, just about to boil.

"Forgive me, if I've been a little scattered this morning," he says, softly, leaning back. I can feel myself squinting. I think I kind of get what he's doing, though I also can't quite put my finger on it.

He's watching me. "We can have a conversation, can't we?"

"Sure," I say.

"I'm glad," he says.

If they expect to collect information, they should be talking to TK. Not me.

"Mandy, you also have an interest in this—did we decide what to call it?"

He waits.

I say, "I thought it was a particle."

"Thank you," he says. "That's right, then, a particle."

Belén sets down a mug of tea for me.

"Black tea," she says. "With oat milk. Right?"

I look at the mug. The opaque surface of it, and the reflection. I don't think I can drink it. But we did this already, didn't we?

"There's nothing wrong with it," she says.

So I pick it up.

"Mandy, you have history with the particle," says Sam. "Belén spoke to your brother. She's filled me in, about the ways in which your early life was blighted."

I start to object. Or maybe I don't. Maybe it was blighted. I know it was.

I look at her, and she looks totally normal. "Jeff talked to you about the Tacoma house?" I ask her. "What did he say?"

Sam says, "We're going to make your friend as comfortable as possible. I know this looks like bad luck, for him. But you can help steer this to a good outcome. You, more than anyone."

I don't know what to say.

"Take a little time to think it over," he says.

"Think what over?" I ask.

He looks at me over the top of his glasses. Has he been wearing glasses, all this time?

"I understand your mother was sick."

"Yes," I say. "She was."

"I also know what it means, to be the caretaker," he says.

He said that already. Didn't he?

"I know there are things your mother experienced that you'll never tell anyone, for privacy's sake. For dignity's sake. She was the only other person who really knew how difficult the last few years have been—but, at the same time, I'm sure you hope she didn't know. Not fully. But that leaves you even more alone. Do you know what I mean?"

This is slightly too much for me. Like putting pressure directly on a trigger point. Nauseatingly painful. Until the knot spasms and the muscle gives up, and then the pain is gone, temporarily. But I'm not going to participate in that with him.

"You won't always feel this way," he says. "I just want you to know that I sympathize."

"Obviously you need the Wi-Fi," says Belén, smoothly breaking in. "I'll turn it back on now, but Sam would very much appreciate it if you could turn it off, whenever possible."

"Time without the extra cognitive noise helps me," he says. "It helps me regroup, and rest. And I'm sorry, but I need to do that now, so that we can talk again later. But first, Mandy, will you tell me if I've gone too far? Did I say too much, before?"

I don't intend to answer, but then, for some reason, I say, "No. It's fine."

"I hope you know that you can answer with real candor. I wouldn't want to offend anyone as kind as you."

I've just realized that Jasper hasn't come downstairs for her breakfast.

"Okay," I say. "Please make yourself comfortable—there's not much in the kitchen, but help yourself to whatever you want." Belén is watching me, but I just want to get back upstairs.

Jasper's fine, though, and sitting wide-awake at the foot of the bed. So I pick her up and take her into the office, to get the day started. Even though our daily routine has already been broken.

From my seat at the desk I can't tell whether Sam, in the guest room, has been asleep for the last two hours; I keep thinking that I can hear something. The door stays closed. Maybe he's waiting for me to step away, so I go downstairs to give him a moment to get himself together in privacy. Use the bathroom. Whatever. I turn off the Wi-Fi, too.

He comes downstairs right away, and takes a seat in the filtered sunlight, his clothes looking so unwrinkled that I picture him laid out on top of the bed without moving and without sleeping. Then again, they're travel clothes. They're supposed to look right, all the time.

"Can we talk?" he says.

"Go right ahead," I say.

"You encountered something, a long time ago? I'd like to know more about that."

I know how this goes; even people who generally aren't interested in other people will sometimes belatedly ask a question or two as a gesture at equilibrium, whether they know it consciously or not.

"There's not much to tell, I'm afraid," I say.

Fucking Jeff. Talking about things to other people that he refuses to speak about with me.

"Would you like some lunch?" I say.

"It's wonderfully kind of you to offer," he says, in a way that is somehow a refusal.

"It's no trouble," I say.

"It's been a while since I needed three meals a day," he says. "But thank you for everything."

"You're welcome," I say.

He smiles.

"I wanted to ask you something. It should only take five more minutes of your time," he says. "If that's all right?"

"That's fine," I say. "What's the question?"

"The question is, are *you* willing to tell me what you encountered in the house where you lived with your parents?"

That sounds like maybe Jeff did not in fact talk about it?

"Whenever you're ready," he says.

But without there having been much escalation, or resolution, there's no story. So there's not much I can tell him that could ever convey how it felt.

"But it sounds like your brain was doing it's best to warn you, in whatever way it could, about something humans aren't wired to perceive."

"That's one possibility," I say.

"Would you say it was familiar?" he says.

"No," I say.

"Unfamiliar?" he says.

"No," I say. "I wouldn't say it was unfamiliar, either."

"What did you hear?"

"I don't know," I say.

"And what did you feel?"

"I don't know," I say.

He's rubbing his hands lightly, like he's waiting for a better answer.

"This happened at a different house," I say. "But my foot went through a rotten floor, once. I couldn't see into the cellar under me, but I thought I felt a hand touch my ankle, and then a second hand cupping the back of my heel. Like the way a sales clerk in an old-fashioned department store might reach to slip a shoe off your foot."

"You were, what, how old? Six? Seven? Were you eight years old? Nine at the time?"

I'm shaking my head.

"Can we say, for the sake of example, that you were ten years old?"

"Sure," I say, because now, I don't know if I remember exactly how old I was.

"And would you say that cellar smelled like bacon?" he says.

"No," I say. "What? Bacon? No."

"Was there an odor of charred meat in general?"

"No."

"Was there any smell at all?"

That's kind of a ridiculous question, isn't it?

"I mean any unexpected smell," he says.

"A few weeks after that my grandparents cleared out the cellar, and they found a jar that wasn't meant to be opened. And it broke. I was exposed to that, but it didn't smell like bacon. It stank like rotten blood and fermented urine."

I don't think I have to actually say it was a witch bottle. I think that's obvious. For a moment, I feel the pressure of nausea, rising in my throat.

"And you're sure it wasn't meaty," he says.

This guy. I shake my head. And then I sit up a little straighter, to get ready to find a way to politely excuse myself. But I'm surprised to find that I'm sweating, and I don't feel too well.

"And you're sure there was nothing else?"

I don't particularly care to mention it to him, but once, when I'd come home during the winter break of my first year of college, there had been something else. After going out with friends, I'd come home late, to find the house quiet. Jandine and Terry had already gone to bed and I assumed Jeff was probably asleep. But as soon as I started up the stairs, I heard him calling me. And I went downstairs.

"You would not have gone downstairs ordinarily?" says Sam.

"Fuck no," I say. "Wait—was I talking out loud?"

"You heard him calling. But it wasn't Jeff, I assume," says Sam.

"I think I knew it wasn't Jeff as soon as I opened the basement door," I say. "But I went down there anyway. In case he needed something, I guess. It was hard to know what I heard.

The sound was always distorted. Sometimes the air even looked sort of hazy."

"Smoke," says Sam. He's rolling his beads between his fingers.

"No, not like smoke."

I'm not sure where I'm going with this.

"There was an album turning on the stereo, and the needle kept hissing in the last groove. It was an automatic turntable, and it should have stopped on its own. But I could hear it turning."

"Was the record player in the far corner of the room?"

"The farthest corner of that room," I say. And actually, it's true.

I close my eyes; I can almost feel the carpet underfoot, and the pressure of stepping into the narrow space between the dry bar and the wall of shelves that strained under the weight of stereo equipment, and dusty glass bottles of peach schnapps, triple sec, and vermouth that had been left behind for years after guests had stopped coming to the house. The mirrored bar signs, glinting, with the chance of reflections behind me that I didn't want to look at. We'd learned to avoid getting glimpses of anything in them.

"You were cornered," he says.

It must be obvious that I didn't mean to talk about this. That I feel sick, now, at the memory of walking through that long room. That basement, under Terry's house.

"Mandy, I hope you already know this. But you've done a lot of work here to make your house feel safe," he says. "You've done good things."

"Thank you," I say. A default response.

He says, "I doubt anything unwelcome is going to slip in here without you knowing."

"Thank you," I say again. And then: "I've wondered, many times, whether I brought something from that old house with me when we moved. Something that attached itself to me. Something that had been trapped in the cellar."

"Yes," he says, "It sounds that way."

"But if it was trapped inside the jar, until it broke," I say, "then how could whatever it was have pulled off my boot?"

"Well, Mandy," he says, "if it was trapped, then it probably didn't pull your boot off. That's not a very satisfying explanation, I realize."

"It doesn't make sense," I say. "Even if there was something bad under that house, it doesn't make sense."

He says, "I think that's just the nature of the phenomenon. Like water, pooling to the path of least resistance, it does what the moment dictates."

"I have to go," I say, because it's not a good enough explanation. "I have things to do."

"That's fine," he says. "I'll wait here."

He's still on the couch an hour later, when I go downstairs to see what he's doing, since I haven't heard a sound.

"Do you want me to turn the TV on for you?" I ask.

Instead of answering, he points to a framed photo on the bookshelves, and says, abruptly, "Is that your mother?"

"Yes," I say.

"There's a family resemblance."

"Thanks," I say.

He's fiddling with the beads around his wrist again.

"Sometimes you can pick out family traits after only seeing one or two people together. Especially the really striking family traits . . ."

Sometimes, I get the impression he's talking only for the sake of talking.

"For example," he says, and points across the room, at something, or at the window.

I feel compelled to turn my head to look.

"With a hi-fi version . . . maybe some people inherit an ability to hear things differently."

Is it worth stopping to figure out what he means? Probably not. He looks around the room, glancing at the windows, at the dark TV screen, the slate-topped coffee table, then at the fish tanks, and then at the bookshelves. Then back at me. And now I'm sitting at the far end of the couch.

He says, "Hadley was a paleobotanist, did I tell you so already? She trained as a geologist. But in the end, she worked mostly with amoebas."

I wonder if he lives alone now. And if he's been lonely. I also wonder if he's a compulsive talker that I'm somehow now saddled with. Belén is nowhere in sight.

"I see fossils on your bookshelves. She collected a great many fossils."

I don't mind coming down here to check on him. At the same time, I'm not a retired geologist with ample afternoon conversational time on my hands. But I have a question—I'm kicking myself—but still, I just have to ask: "Amoebas aren't plants, are they?"

His face smooths itself out quickly.

"You've obviously been to Pahrump," he says, abruptly.

"Pahrump, Nevada? No. Why?"

"There's a shale deposit there, with billions and billions of vase-shaped microfossils. Foraminifera, specifically—those were the creatures Hadley was working on."

He is exhausting. And so repetitive.

"That was part of Hadley's work," he says again. "Foraminifera."

"I'm not familiar with that," I say.

He gestures at my bookshelves. "You are. Almost all the ancient monuments in your picture books are built from blocks of sedimentary stone comprised of billions and billions of foraminifera. The Giza plateau was underwater, and the forams lived and died above it. For a very long time. A very long time ago."

"How does an amoeba leave a fossil?" I ask. Not disbelieving. Merely asking.

"Good question," he says. "They wouldn't, strictly speaking." He snaps his beads lightly against his wrist. "Let's say they're similar to amoebas," he says. "But also like plankton. They're like a few different things. Chimeric, maybe. And Hadley was interested in them because . . ."

He takes a moment.

Is he just making this shit up as he goes?

"All right," he says. "I have an answer for you. Some early forams extracted minerals from seawater to make their own shells. A bit like your fingernails," he says, "if they were made of stone."

I look down at my hands, involuntarily.

"But other forams didn't, instead they just collected whatever little bits and pieces of materials they could, and they became the agglutinated foraminifera," he said. "That's the term. Agglutinated foraminifera. Because they built their own protective structures out of found materials."

Like caddis flies, I think; I love caddis flies. Several lived in one of the tanks a couple of years ago, after half a dozen arrived in a batch of aquarium plants. I noticed a tiny green pulse, at the bottom of the white bucket where I rinse new plants, something moving in the debris. Goldie had arrived the same way, when he was smaller than a grain of rice, so I got out my magnifier, and saw a tiny green inchworm, pulling together a little structure to hide inside. What a calamity, for the creature. Trying to save itself by doing what it always does. But unluckily this time in the bottom of a bucket, about to be tossed into the plants, or dumped down the toilet. Once I knew what to look for I found the others and put them into a cory tank, where they stayed for months, before eventually turning into silvery-brown winged insects, waiting under the canopy in the mornings, and I took them outside, one by one. The last stayed much longer than the others. He floated busily around in the tank for a year, collecting and eating soft broken bits of plant material, always standing vertical in a tiny woven basket, like a translucent Baron·Munchausen. Until one morning I found him, silvery brown, with wings. I took the new baron to the patio, set him in the leaves, and watched until he flew away, too.

On Etsy you can buy jewelry made from the cast-off casings of caddis flies who build with small stones. But the ones here built with green plants, and left nothing behind when they went.

"Agglutinated foraminifera," Sam repeats, calling me back.

Jesus Christ, I think. He is relentless.

"They made *tests*, I should say. That's the term. Not shells. Some creatures can secrete their own shells, but others have to assemble their own tests."

"Are you sure I can't get you some toast?" I say. "Before I go back upstairs in a moment?"

He lifts a few fingers. "Can you stay another moment?" he says. "I was hoping to describe the forams to you."

I sit back.

"Their tests—their shells—their defensive structures—do you understand?"

He looks like he's really asking, not just making sure I haven't drifted away.

"These are very interesting creatures. Their defensive structures were perforated with many little holes, through which they would extend filaments, like tiny whiskers."

"So, that would be an amoeba with a shell and whiskers?" I say.

"Yes. A tiny single-celled creature with a flexible cell wall, living in a stone house with a hundred windows. Extruding filaments of itself out through the windows, to grope around in every direction in search of food."

He gives me a moment in which to imagine. He seems to want me to—do what? To agree with him, somehow? But I can't, I'm still back with the tiny baron, who lived in the tank, such a long time ago now, and I feel very unsettled. It would be so easy for whatever he's trying to describe to have consumed the baron, long before he flew from the patio, so easy that it still feels almost possible now.

"In fact, if you were a foram, you could send a thread of yourself all the way into the kitchen from here to fetch anything you wanted. You could probably even reach up the stairs."

I'm repulsed. But then I'm instantly sorry when his demeanor seems to just fold up, like he's suddenly too exhausted by the effort of trying to make conversation with me when it's clear I want to leave. He gestures to the cushion on the couch, which is printed with a dandelion-puffball pattern. One of those mid-century skeletonized flower heads in silhouette.

"I'm sorry," he says. "I don't mean to go on and on. But they look like that, like a dandelion clock. It just reminded me."

Dandelion clock? Where have I heard that phrase before? In some novel for children, I think, some engrossing English story set in a big lonely house, among solitary children who meet in the shadowy corridors and explore the house and grounds by candlelight, together.

"Or their descendants do, anyway," he says. "Their living descendants look like that. There's a catalog of them being compiled somewhere in Puget Sound."

"Are you sure I can't get you anything?" I ask. "Before I get back to work?"

"No, thank you," he says. "Belén will bring me something, later."

"Don't forget to drink more water while you're here than you would in Canada."

"I'm not from Canada," he says. "I misspoke, earlier. We lived in . . . California. . . ." he says.

Maybe he hesitates when he's figuring out how much to say. Or how much I'll believe. He's a little all over the place, I think, but so it goes, and so am I, and who isn't.

Before I go back upstairs I find the water bottle I ordered for Jandine, with the hours of the day marked in ounces and a built-in straw. We learn to drink from the rim of a cup early, as babies, without realizing we can unlearn it again someday.

Anyway. The bottle was supposed to be a way to keep

Jandine from getting dehydrated. Sam won't take it from my hand, so I leave it on the coffee table.

He says, "I remembered what it was that I wanted to tell you: the experiments we were talking about? Looking for dark particles? Those collisions aren't as rare as you think."

"I don't think that was me," I say.

"No? I'm sorry," he says, and he's quiet a moment. "I was talking about Hadley's work, wasn't I? She was interested in those experiments."

"I thought you said she was interested in botany. And geology."

"And dark matter," he says. "It's quite difficult to boil Hadley's work down into a simple description. Hadley was . . . She was atheoretical."

I'm standing, waiting, poised to go. He knows full well that he's keeping me here, detaining me. I think he must know that.

"I'm going to need to turn the Wi-Fi back on now."

"Imagine the peace," he says.

"Without the Wi-Fi, you mean?"

"The peace of the world in the Precambrian era, when every living cell got what it needed from seawater or by using photosynthesis."

We weren't talking about the Precambrian era—were we? I guess we were. When I'd first met Jeff, he said he wanted to show me a prehistoric toy. I was imagining hot lava and meteorites full of space parasites. He showed me a lacing card for threading a shoelace in and out of prepunched holes around a cartoon stegosaurus. It was the shittiest toy I had ever seen. I should have just let him enjoy it. But I had hated the simplicity of it. The babyishness.

"Peaceful," I say. "That's funny, I would have thought early life was short and brutal."

For some reason, I really want Sam to retract what he just said about early life being peaceful. I don't know why. Except that it makes me feel angry.

He says, "No. That's a heresy."

I cross the room, to restore the Wi-Fi.

"But you have to admit, it's strange," he says suddenly.

"What's strange?" I say.

"Cannibalism," he says, leaning forward.

I know he's trying to keep the Wi-Fi off as long as possible, trying to keep me listening, and it makes me sad. Maybe I can at least work offline for a while. Then I catch myself: Why am I assuming that he really does feel the Wi-Fi? He's not from Canada, after all.

"Photosynthesis worked," he says. "It worked so well that its by-products changed the chemistry of the world. And then any cells that couldn't continue photosynthesizing in the new chemistry had to find some other way to survive. But why did they eat each other?"

Children ask this question, don't they. Like Babe, the piglet, in the movie. And the answer is just the answer: Everybody's baby has to eat, which sometimes means eating somebody else's baby. Even the farmer. And all the farmer's babies. But for a moment I feel the chill of what it really means to know this truth about the world. It's this chill you have to put away somewhere, in order to function.

"Please," he says. "Try to imagine. One living cell eating another, in a world where this had never happened before."

I cannot.

"It would be . . ." he starts to say.

I'll wait, and let him finish this last part, and then I'll go up.

"You and I are both breathing normally," he says. "How many normal breaths have you or I taken, since the moment you invited me into your home? Maybe fifteen thousand breaths each? What if one of us realized we could inhale the other, right now. It's unimaginable. But does that make it impossible?"

"Well," I say. "That's quite an unpleasant image, and I really do need to turn the wireless back on."

"I understand," he says. He sits back. "I'll wait for you here."

—

Upstairs, back at my desk, I almost don't know what to look up first.

Some of the vase-shaped microfossils online do indeed look like tiny vases, some of them perfectly round, with stems, like you might find stacked at IKEA. But the ones that constructed their own shells—tests—whatever—are rougher, and in scanning electron microscope images the individual grains of silt mortared together are still clearly visible. Just as the forams built them, six hundred million years ago. One observer describes a kind of foram alive today in the Antarctic, big enough to see with the eye, maybe with a magnifier, one that, if I'm reading this right, seems to select neutral-colored grains of uniform size and color, and one larger red capstone. It's the red stones that really stay with me. But then I can't find anything more about them.

I refuse to ask Sam about this.

I don't really want to go back down there.

I'm not even all the way down the stairs when he says, "I have a story to tell you." He opens his hands, wordlessly. So I turn off the router. It occurs to me that he's seen me doing this, and that he could turn it off himself. If he chose to.

"Egg family," he says. "It's the story of the egg family."

"What did you say?"

"It's the story of the family Eggerellidae. They're a large family of forams who built their own tests. Like little masons."

"Why did you say it like that?" I ask.

"Like what?"

"Like it's a children's story."

"Ah," he says. "That's funny. Hadley thought forams would be good in a children's picture book. A tide of ravenous little hermits, floating in their fortresses of stone and bone, casting hungry fingers out in every direction."

"That's nice," I say. "You called it Egg Family—why did you say it like that?"

"I didn't name them. Eggerelloidea is a superfamily."

"Hmm," I say.

He says, "Would you like to hear about the family tree? The phylum? That's Foraminifera. And the class is Globothalamea."

"Okay," I say.

"Textulariana," he says. "Textulariida. Textulariina. That's the subclass, order, and suborder."

"Okay," I say, again. Because it's getting tiresome now.

"Superfamily Eggerelloidea," he says. "Then Family Eggerellidae. Subfamily Eggerellinae. And then genus *Eggerella*."

I don't know why it upset me. Unless it was because of the way Jeff upset me when he tried to claim the Mushroom Family. A long time ago.

"They look like the Venus of Willendorf," says Sam. "Many do."

This almost makes me pause, but there is zero sex in his face. Zero. And I can pretty much picture what he means.

"Billions of forams contributed to the monoliths of the ancient world," he says. "All the places on your bookshelves, not just the pyramids and the Great Sphinx, but Göbekli Tepe, Karahan Tepe, the other monolithic compounds in Asia Minor. And Ġgantija, and Ħagar Qim, on Malta. All the famous places, and plenty we don't know about. So imagine," he says, "certain materials, certain shapes, certain proportions—"

I was following, or I thought I was, but I am not.

"Okay, Mandy," he says. "I'm trying to convey that the sandstone humanity has been quarrying and building with for thousands of years is made out of the tests of microscopic forams . . ."

I wait. No sense in adding pressure to the pressure already there.

I don't know where this sudden feeling of calm and patience is coming from.

"There must have been moments when everything aligned."

"Aligned?" I say. "Aligned with what?"

"Hadley believed that some forams built tests that either

allowed something passing through to get stuck in them, or allowed them to catch something passing through, and either way, something that wasn't supposed to interact with them got hung up in this world. Ordinarily these particles pass right through the earth. Ordinarily, there's no contact. But Hadley believed that some of those particles were trapped here, probably by the members of Family Eggerellidae."

He's got one of his arms out, as if to persuade me to be silent, or persuade me not to move; his face looks like he's been working all night to set up a series of small mirrors and now we're on the verge of the moment when the sun will flood through an opening overhead, and all the pieces he's assembled will light up simultaneously. The way some people say the interior chambers deep inside some of the ancient structures he's describing must have been lit.

"Those forams," he says. "Those forams must have constructed billions of physical spaces until one or more of them found the sacred geometry capable of catching and holding the impossible. Something from the nonluminous universe. A flash of true darkness."

I am sitting on the couch again. And suddenly this has been a really long day already.

"Mandy," he says, "now that you understand what I'm saying, can I have another moment, please?"

"All right," I say.

"What do you assume is behind that flash of darkness?"

"Absence of light," I say.

"But we live in a universe that is predicated on light," he says. "One way or another, every living thing on Earth is filled with sunlight."

He rests his elbows on his knees, fingers together, again in a steeple, and it seems to help him focus. He's pressing hard enough that his fingertips are pale.

"There was no way physical life here could have defended itself. Not against the hunger of the void on the other side.

Everything alive on Earth had evolved to live in constant contact with seawater," he says. "And to feed on light. They had everything, and they had it all without conflict. When they didn't, they died. But they weren't deliberately slain."

I still don't know why this makes me so angry, so stubborn.

"Think about it," he says. "No hunger, and no accumulation of waste. No threat from another creature. Just balance. One individual life might end, but not because something else took that life. Do you see what I mean? We were the ocean. We had flexible bodies, bodies like water. Under the right circumstances, we would have lived forever."

I'm really starting to wonder where Belén is now.

"But evolution depends on pressure," I say. "Maybe the pressure of hunger was inevitable. And it was necessary for the brains to develop."

"I'm not talking about hunger," he says.

"You said hunger," I say. "I'm pretty sure you specifically said hunger."

"I meant fear," he says. "Don't you know?" he says. "Fear is the reason behind everything. Fear, and gravity. Between them, they explain everything. Fear and gravity are the reason you have a beginning and end. They're the reason you have a mouth, and an anus."

I say, "Well. That's a theory I have not heard before."

A sound from behind startles me—it's Belén. I didn't hear her come in.

"Don't let me interrupt," she says. "Really. But sunset happens at seven forty and your friend will turn up some time after that."

She opens her bag. She's looking at Sam, hard, as she takes things out and arrange them on the dining room table. A withered apple, two sunken navel oranges, and a stalk of rainbow chard from my container garden. It looks like a recipe for a gut ache. "These are for you," she says, pushing them toward him on the table, one at a time, counting them down.

"Five, four, three, two. I must have lost one. Are we good? Mandy, are you good?"

"I think so," I say. I look to the window, where the shadow of the mesquite bush has fallen away already. It must be later than I realized. But as I am thinking this, the exhaustion of the afternoon catches up with me, all at once.

She stifles a yawn, and as she starts to climb the stairs she says, over her shoulder, not quite an afterthought but definitely not a question, "Since your bed is huge, I'll just crash on the side you don't use. Hope that's okay." And then she disappears up the stairs.

For fuck's sake: My room is a mess. That's just not fair. Who does that?

"I'll turn in for a while, as well," Sam says. "Especially if you're going to turn on the . . ."

He gestures at the modem and router. But he doesn't stand.

"Mandy," he says. "Do you know anything about . . ."

He's not looking up at me. He's looking up.

"Do you know much about music?" he says, finally.

"No," I say, flatly. Because I just don't think I can embark on another leg of his storytelling right now. But he doesn't notice.

"Me, neither," he says. Which is almost certainly a lie; I expect he's got something to say about any subject. But he lifts a finger, and I realize he's not just staring at nothing, but listening to a faint sound. Like music? It is music, I realize. From my room? Belén, listening to something on her phone? Setting an alarm, maybe.

"Hear that?" he says. But she's turned it down, or off.

"That's germanium," he says. "You'll recognize it."

Parts of his face look a little violet from one angle, a little greenish from another. I start to ask about the germanium, but he's already climbing the stairs on his own.

He's given me a headache.

I restore the Wi-Fi and go upstairs, as well, to my office.

The bedroom doors at either end of the hall are shut, the occupants seemingly already asleep. What's wrong with me? With them? Is she looking through my things?

Jasper is also asleep, in her bed under Terry's desk.

My eyes are burning too much to go back to my computer. What else is there to do, except unroll a yoga mat, and take a short nap myself.

Chapter Fifty-One

Later I hear Belén pacing slowly in the hall, talking to Jeff on the phone, telling him again that she has family . . . family in town . . . family responsibilities. . . . She sounds normal about breaking some kind of tentative weekend plans, except that she's doing it where I'll overhear.

Belén ends her call and goes down the stairs to the kitchen.

How many days of this did I agree to?

She's at the counter, scooping pieces of cut watermelon, cantaloupe, and honeydew out of a plastic clamshell container, half filled with a wash of pinkish-greenish water.

"May I?" she says, as she's taking down a bowl.

"Is that fruit okay?" I ask. Because it looks more than a little mealy.

"This is the way he wants it," she says, before taking a spoon from the drawer.

A spoon? That hardly seems like the easiest utensil to use.

As if she's reading my mind, she says, "He declines to use a fork. So it's going to take him a while to eat this, and it's best if you don't go up there for a while."

"Like, for how long?"

"Until he's gone," she says.

"Are you serious?"

"Listen," she says, and we both fall silent. "Do you hear that?"

It's too faint to know if I'm actually hearing something through the vent in the kitchen ceiling. Possibly it's the sound of him, repeating something.

"He prays for hours," she says. "And it's going to increase. I'll take this up to him now," she says, glancing at the clock; it's two minutes before the hour. "He'll take a meal like this alone, once a day, and I'll wait at the other end of the hall, in case he needs anything. Both doors will be closed for the duration. I don't want to get into it right now, but for the sake of simplicity, don't come up unless you absolutely have to. I mean, you can, of course, nobody's going to stop you, but don't give him any reason to think that you're trying to figure out what he's doing."

I find this shocking.

"Now, excuse me," she says, and instinctively I step out of the way, and then up the stairs she goes. And downstairs is where I stay. And though I don't want to eavesdrop, I hear the murmur of voices: hers, strangely unfamiliar, maybe just formal, then his. And surprisingly it's an exchange; I might mistake it for a distant conversation, except for the formal feeling. I think it's the cadence that makes it seem so impersonal.

I must have drifted off, in the armchair. When I'm suddenly awake again, after what felt like just a quick moment, I find that TK is there, sitting in the armchair. He has a day or two of silver stubble, and apparently he's just been sitting there, waiting for me to wake up.

What's that phrase? Hell is other people?

"Mandy," he says, "the lock on your back door isn't working. I wish I'd known, I'd have brought over a better one for you, before now." He sounds so normal, but I wonder how he got into the house over the hose, because when I last looked it was still in place as a barrier across the back door, but maybe we're already at the point where any rules that have been puzzled out so far begin to fall apart. Surely this can't be anything like that stage in a horror movie? Not already?

"Thanks," I say. "Can you help me haul some window bars?"

"Sure," he says, a little mechanically. "If you can find any. Waiting times are long. Materials are scarce, I've been hearing. A lot of iron is already depleted, and getting harder to come by. But, Mandy? Can you hear something?"

I hear the refrigerator and the tank filters and airstones, but that's about all except for the light bulb at the far end of the room, hissing faintly, and another somewhere behind me.

Their collective sound seems to be gathering across the ceiling like smoke. But odorless, invisible.

"What is that?" I ask.

"I have no idea," he says.

The bulb in the lamp beside me whines like a mosquito. Maybe it's always been this way. Two dogs on different patios outside are fretting as a helicopter makes a lazy circle overhead in the distance, and then a third dog starts to fret, as well, as if they've also always been doing this, and now they always will be.

"Mandy," he says. "I came by to tell you that I think something's wrong. Are you getting that feeling, too?"

The light bulb in the lamp beside me makes the splitting sound of a bug zapper and I hope for a thread of smoke to intervene, the way blowing out a candle always changes everything. But nothing happens except that the front door rattles on its hinges when some heavy vehicle passes back and forth on a street outside in the process of hauling something nearby that sounds like a hundred big plastic cooler bottles of water, destined for after-hours deliveries to quiet offices, while Sam lies unmoving upstairs and TK sits across from me, with his head turned slightly, listening for the source of his uneasiness without realizing that it's anchored inside his head.

This is nothing I can explain to him. Or to myself, actually.

He leans back. Leans away. And I feel . . . better? A little better.

"I think I need to go, but only if you're all right," he says. He glances around, uneasily. At the ceiling, then behind him, at the darkened kitchen.

"I'm okay," I say. But it's hard to say anything. It's like trying to wake up from a dream. So much effort just to move a little.

He's moving toward the kitchen. "I'm sorry," he says. "I have to go. I'm tying up loose ends at home, before I have the . . ."

He gestures upward, maybe at his head.

"I'll check back tomorrow. Unless you need anything?"

"I'm all right," I say again. To make him leave. Please, I hope he leaves, and that when he goes this abrasiveness—I hope it goes with him. He gets up and I can't turn my head but I hear him go out through the back door. And shortly after that I hear Sam coming cautiously down the stairs. He presses three fingers to the inside of my wrist, and I want to shake him away, even though I know he's just taking my pulse, because the cool even pressure makes me want to scream, but screaming would cost far too much effort.

"I can't risk letting him see me until we know for sure he's alone," says Sam.

I don't care what Sam wants. The wave of everything intruding on me is receding, a little, but the patio door is ajar and I can still hear too much from the world out there. Sam goes to the kitchen to close it, dragging his feet. He looks worse now than he did when he went upstairs a few hours ago. I don't see how these changes can be temporary, whatever Belén says.

"Did he sound like himself?"

"Yes," I say.

I can't watch Sam talking, because he's different than he was, or maybe I'm seeing him differently now, and either way his face is like a piece of leather speaking, and I lose track of what's being said. Belén appears a few minutes later. Sam keeps talking. I'd like to get up to get away from him. I need a lemon and some salt because my electrolytes are off-balance.

"You don't look well," she says.

"Feed Jasper," I say. I know there are other things that should be done, but that's all I can think of. "Please make sure she has water."

Belén takes Sam back up the stairs, and I hear her filling Jasper's food dish, topping off the water fountain. It's still warm outside, but the air-conditioning will keep it down to seventy-nine at night, and before she disappears she gives me the throw blanket from the couch. Sometime later, after she's gone, I hear Jasper crunching in the kitchen, a skittering sound before she daintily climbs into my lap, since Jasper is a mind reader, after all.

Chapter Fifty-Two

I wake up on the couch too early the next morning with Sam already sitting at the far end, over by the dandelion-print cushion, watching as the ramp timers slowly increase the tank lights. It's dawn outside, too, by the time he turns to look at me. I'm surprised he got that close to my feet, while I was sleeping, and I didn't notice.

Some movement in his face reminds me to be a little more careful.

"How much do you know about particle physics?" he says. "And quantum physics and quantum mechanics, et cetera?" he says.

I say, "I need to wake up before you ask me anything further."

He lifts both hands, more acknowledgment than apology.

He says, "My apologies."

He lifts the cushion.

"I ask because this looks like a neutrino," he says. "Or like an artist's rendering, since they're obviously too small and too fast for us to see."

"Okay," I say, sitting up; what else can one possibly say?

"What's your interest in the solar neutrino?"

"None," I say. "That's a dandelion, as far as I know."

He looks at the pillow.

"It's a dandelion clock," I say. "You told me that."

I'm feeling around my pockets for the pill case I've started keeping with me, after realizing that their presence would throw me off to the point of forgetting my own schedule. Or that anything I might need could easily be tampered with, or hidden from me.

He says, "*In ille tempore . . .*"

I resist.

"*In ille tempore*," he says again. "It means *in another time.*

Long ago. Particles," he says. "Old particles are relevant to what we'll be talking about today."

"Can you hold that thought," I say; I wonder what he was like, before he got sick. I think he was probably the kind of husband of one of your friends whom you only realize you never quite liked after they split up. Suddenly I remember the woman who lived in the bedroom, down the hall from Jandine, at memory care, for a long time. The woman who told me she had another dementia, not Alzheimer's disease, not frontotemporal, but something else, and I didn't ask what. She told me what it was like, for her. *I can't answer questions anymore*, she said, *even when I know the answers. I can't make decisions anymore, even when I know what I would choose.* I don't know if she had memory trouble, or not. She showed me photos in a photo album, and she knew who the people in the photos were. She pointed to herself, her husband, her adult children. Her affect was entirely flat when I met her, and it remained flat. Whatever is happening for Sam is not the same as what that woman was dealing with, but she's on my mind now. Of all the other residents who came and went, over the years, she was the only one who had been there before Jandine moved in who was still there on the day we moved to a different area. To hospice, essentially. I always meant to say goodbye to her. By the time Jandine was gone, and I was able, I was a stranger to the new staff at the reception area out front, who had no reason to let me into the memory-care area. I wasn't on her list of visitors, after all. I hope it didn't matter to her. It seems uncharitable to assume that. But I hope so.

"If we're talking about a spore," he says, "then it's one we can't perceive, and vice versa, because it can't perceive us."

What were we talking about?

"I'm going to the bathroom," I say.

I close the door, and lock it.

"Spores are microscopic," I hear him saying; it sounds like

he's standing pretty damn close to the bathroom door now. "Can you hear me?" he says.

"Yes," I say.

"A spore can drift," he says. "But when it lands, it puts down roots."

I'm thinking of the pollen. And whatever else gets in.

I wash my hands, and I come back out, and I'm skeptical, and I'm also mildly confused.

He's right there. No sense of personal space.

"Hadley," he says. "I was telling you about Hadley."

I will admit it; hearing him invoke the name of Hadley makes me suddenly feel like my shoes are half a size too small. Or maybe it just makes me aware now that I slept without taking them off, as one might do on an overnight flight, and that I was commensurately uncomfortable all night long.

"Fossils. One-celled organisms." He gestures at some books he's taken from the shelves and piled on the coffee table. "Easy to find, when you know where to look . . ."

I'm a sucker for a glossy coffee-table book full of mystery. But I need a buffer zone of time in order to wake up first.

"I looked through all three of those books for photos of forams this morning. And now the look on your face is proof I've bored you already," he says, gently. "But you're still listening."

"Yes," I say.

He smiles, faintly. "So, Mandy, like we did before, let's talk about things as if they're true. Is that all right with you?"

"Sure," I say.

His voice sounds fainter now, farther away. Maybe this is what he warned me about, the first morning, when he said I might notice the changes happening. Whenever that was. Yesterday?

"As you can imagine, the vegetarians had to float close enough to the surface of the ocean to harvest chemicals made by sunlight."

"The vegetarians?" I say.

"The photosynthesizers, I mean. They needed some sunlight, but not too much. They had to stay deep enough in the water to survive the ultraviolet light."

"Yes," I say. "Some aquarium filters come with UV sterilizers. The bulb inside the filter kills off parasites and algae."

"Thank you," he says, "that's interesting. But I'd like us to stay on topic. The spore we were just talking about would be completely immune to ultraviolet light."

He waits in the living room while I fill Jasper's food dish, top off her water fountain, and get the tea things ready. As soon as he hears me lift the loudly boiling kettle away from its base, he appears in the doorway.

"Can we go back a little?" he says. "You see how a spore could get hung up inside a test, trapped inside, with a creature, and the creature might not even know. Neither would know. But the other living creatures nearby, they would know, and they would fear it."

"It's a spore now?" I say. "Or still a particle?"

He doesn't answer.

"Okay," I say. "I guess it's both."

"Thank you," he says, "that sounds right. And spores put out roots. That's what they do. And what do roots do?"

"They collect nutrients?" I say.

"That's right," he says. "And this would have put new pressure on the old system here, if each spore was rooted here but collecting something for the other side. For the dark side. And if each spore was trapped inside a cell that was in the water, then each of the spores must have had access to everything else that was alive in the water at the same time."

A shadow moves outside, just something, just nothing, and I flinch like a rabbit under a sky that might be filled with birds. Or branches. But to live, you must assume the shadows are always at least potentially birds, never merely branches. I can't remember a time before learning what Riddley Walker means, in the novel, when he says: "Why is Punch crookit?

Why wil he all ways kil the babby if he can? Parbly I wont never know its jus on me to think on it."

Again I suddenly do not like him. Sam.

"There are alternate models of life," says Sam, mildly. He's not arguing. He's doing something else. "Like mushrooms and mycelium," he says. "You've heard stories about gentle mushroom colonies. Receiving without taking anything away from other living creatures."

Maybe it's just the Adderall kicking in, but if anything had happened differently, we would not be us. Generally I mean.

I start to say, "Yes, but if we were mushroom people . . ."

I'm being slightly more sarcastic than necessary but suddenly I am struck dumb. Because of the Mushroom Family.

What's really happening?

His hand is resting casually on the fabric pillow. Why did I ever think that it looked like a dandelion? When it's clearly a spore print? Like the kind advertised by mail in the back of certain earthy but also spacey magazines in order to propagate hallucinogenic mushrooms? Nothing illegal to it, then, because there were no mushrooms involved. Only the potential of a mushroom, somewhere in the future, and the potential wasn't illegal.

Sam is speaking deliberately, and so slowly.

"I think you already know that there's one here now. By pure accident, there's a spore lodged inside your friend's skull. And now—especially at night, when the sky is quiet—others can feel the roots extending outward, and hear them moving. Even if it's just for a moment, that's long enough to make other people panic. And when they panic, most people will just give it what it wants. And what it wants is the light stored inside living flesh."

He gives me a moment to take this in.

"That's a lot," I say. "It really sounds like a bunch of bullshit."

"Mandy, it's physics," he says. "Don't assume it's even really a spore and don't hate the messenger and don't assume

I tell this kind of gloomy saturnine story very often, because I don't."

"All right," I say, because it's getting easier to let it all roll off, as if he's not even talking to me, half the time.

"You understand," he says. "It's old, and slow, but it's big. A relic. From some part of the universe we can't perceive."

"The ghost of a rare dark matter particle," I say.

"Mandy, what's wrong with you?" he says. "It's not a ghost. And it's not rare, I've already told you. Tens of millions are passing through you every moment that you're outside."

"In sunlight," I say.

"No," he says, "no, they're older than the sun—they pass through at night, mostly at night."

"Like a ghost does," I say again.

He's staring at me. "I thought you were a good listener," he says. "I still think you could be a good listener."

I don't want to be a listener; it's like I'm trying to catch my own attention and remind myself that I don't want that, whatever it means, whatever he means by that.

"Do you want to hear this or not?" he says.

I both do and don't; the problem with saying yes is that you can't change your mind later. Whereas if you don't listen, you might still have the chance to make a different decision, later. But this is too complicated to try to explain.

"Yes," I say.

"By indirect detection we know that they're big enough and slow enough to interfere with biological life. Big enough and slow enough to tamper with individual cells. This is true. They can interact and they do cause cell mutations."

"Oh," I say. Because this is starting to sound a bit more legitimate.

But Belén is back. She stops in the kitchen to refill a water bottle from the filter dispenser in the door of the fridge, and then she's with us, but only for a moment.

Help me out, I want to say. But not in front of him.

"Sorry," she says—maybe to me? And then she disappears

upstairs, into my room, and I hear the door shut. Sam goes upstairs, as well, almost automatically, to the guest room, and shuts the door.

These broken up days. Their routine. The way they never seem to eat anything, which makes it easy for me to forget to eat until it's too late to care and then I feel awful. I start things, but I don't finish. Speaking of which: laundry. Forgotten again in the machine.

When I go out to the garage to add soap and run another cycle there's something different, somehow a little different, about the area where I've piled boxes that are small and heavy, obviously books; they seem slightly disarranged? Maybe that's a sign to just open them and put them right onto a bookshelf in the house. I need something to look forward to, I guess. A dopamine hit of some kind. Because I'm not drinking while these people are in the house, because it doesn't seem wise.

And then in no time at all I've carried half a dozen small dense boxes of books into the living room, one by one. I'm doing this instead of anything else. I wish I'd known to pack everything into smaller boxes, because they're so much easier to face. But just when I'm settling down to open one, and almost looking forward to it, Sam appears on the stairs.

"Mandy, what do you have there?" he asks.

There's no reprieve from him.

"Don't let me interrupt you," he says.

Is it late afternoon? I don't know how long I was out in the garage. I should probably go put the clean laundry in the dryer now, otherwise I'll forget later. I may have already forgotten, and let it go too long again. Because of the heat. The damp in the washer drum.

"Just books from when I was younger."

I don't want to open any of the boxes in front of him, these boxes that I'm sure hold bits and pieces of my misunderstandings about the world picked up from tatty magazines and shallow coffee-table books. My occult library of ridiculous daydreams and my ignorance of the limitations of my executive functions. Realities that I wouldn't understand for decades, a much bigger ADHD parable, but at the moment, I can't quite get to it, even in my own head.

"Some people like to say that books don't matter. That only the information inside matters."

I realize he's waiting for me to say something.

I wonder whether, in another life, I might have found poker interesting. For the way people represent their cards. But maybe that's only a notion held by nonplayers. It's probably just a trope.

"I like books," I say. "Physical books."

"I've got nothing against reading on a screen," he says. "I've now been able to read scans of books I can't find physical copies of. But still. Holding the book as you read. That's a different experience. Touching the pages."

His face is softer. But it's gross, somehow, to think of him touching pages.

I wish he would go back upstairs.

He says, "Your life's work should have been something more esoteric than the work you're doing now."

In another life . . . But there's not another life. There's just this one.

"Did Belén tell you?" he says.

"Tell me what?"

I must look honestly confused.

"No," she says suddenly, from somewhere, and I jump a little: She's on the couch. "I didn't."

"No? I'm sure Mandy would be interested. I know she would be."

"You'll have to ask Mandy herself, then," she says.

To me, he says, "Hadley and I gathered a collection of rare books, on esoteric topics. Some are rare and some are priceless, and some are common, but they're all valuable, all of them. I'd like to invite you to visit. I'd like to invite you to our library after all of this concludes."

He seems to mean it.

But suddenly I am like the housekeeper in *The Turn of the Screw*, who looks away when the well-educated but bad-at-reading-the-room governess asks her to read the letter that arrives from the school of one of the children they're looking after. The housekeeper who looks down, and says, "Such things are not for me." She says it because she can't read, and I say it because I'm pretty sure that such things are, indeed, not for me. Ciphers, and charts, and languages I never learned. My brain is too old now, too inflexible to learn all the things I wanted to. And I'm just become so awkward around people.

But after all my mournful thoughts about the alternate lives I might have had, an invitation like this arrives, and I don't accept?

Do I actually want to visit his secluded compound, in some unspecified location?

No, obviously not. I have Jasper, and the fish. There's nobody I trust to house-sit and look after them. No, for a hundred reasons.

Would Belén be there, too?

"It's true," says Belén. "When you rest your eyes on those pages, on the vellum . . . on parchment . . ." She's looking at me now; why is she here, doing this, again? Doing what? I'm confused, a little. "You know what's interesting?" she says. "I couldn't read any of those pages written in Latin or Greek or Arabic, and the ones in English were so cramped I couldn't make them out, either, but I kept looking anyway. And I got to know certain pages by their individual scars from when the animals whose skins you'll be reading were still alive. That's normal—that's the way old books are, old European books especially, full of little insect bites, little scrapes where the animal might have scratched an itch against a tree or something, out in a pasture, on a sunny day. It's hard to believe now, but my favorite page had a cut that wouldn't stay closed. I'm sure it would have healed, if the skin had still been on the animal and the animal had still been alive, but it wasn't, and so at some point some careful scribe two hundred years ago stitched it up with tiny flat sutures. It looked like lace. I thought it was only a decoration."

"I guess that's probably common," I say. "For old pages."

"I wouldn't say common. Definitely not as common as the follicles—Sam's best books have hair follicles everywhere. Those visible follicles are inescapable."

She knows this is making my skin crawl.

And by hesitating, I have offended him.

"Thank you," I say, to him, belatedly. "Maybe after everything falls into place here—"

"Also," she says, interrupting me. "Some pages have visible capillaries."

"You don't know anything," he says to her. "I didn't show you anything important."

She crosses her arms. But instead of continuing she takes a breath and uncrosses her arms, like she's not going to finish whatever she started to say.

"I'm listening," I say.

But she shakes her head.

"You'll find whatever you'll find," she says. "I shouldn't try to stop you. But—can I tell you? Can I just tell you?"

She sounds tired, all of a sudden. It's got nothing to do with me, or whether I'll ever see that library. This sounds like sadness catching up with her.

"Sure," I say. "Tell me."

"The library has a smell that is borderline unpleasant. And the windows don't open."

That's not what I expected her to say.

"Because of the air quality, you might be a little distracted, so you might not notice right away when your attention starts being pulled toward something on the periphery. At first, I would just get the feeling I'd accidentally skipped a page. Or that maybe there was something at the edge of the reading table, a flash from one of the windows or a reflection from the skylight. Once, I thought it was a scratch on my reading glasses that moved with me when I turned my head to look."

Sam exhales, loudly. But doesn't say anything.

"Sometimes it felt like a gold thread in a tapestry across a room, a gold thread that you can only see from an angle," she says. "Barely there. Easy to forget. But you still end up rereading a paragraph or a page, looking for something you missed, and then before you know it you're following one of those threads up from the page, into the air, because you can feel that it's attached to something important. But if you try to understand what you're following, or where it's going, you lose track of it."

She's cupping one of her hands, as if holding something invisible in her empty palm.

"That's how it feels to brush up against something beyond your own mind. Something you can't approach as if it's part of the ordinary world."

Now Sam is listening, too.

"Sam and Hadley have to monitor ambient conditions in the room to protect the books, so there's no extra time to spend being indirect. There's too much foundational information to get through first, to much to memorize about the material world before you give any serious thought to the kind of energy you can't see."

"I've seen it," says Sam. But she's not talking to him. She's looking at me.

"It's easy to accept, in principle, that correspondences exist between this world and other realities," she says. "But feeling them? That's entirely different."

Her hand opens like she's acknowledging a weight heavier than air.

"Mandy," she says. "Do you know what the *Picatrix* is?"

"Yes," I say. "A little." I don't tell her that I tried to read translations of it a long time ago, one from the Latin version and one from the Arabic. But I couldn't finish either. There were so many procedural descriptions that I found too painful to read.

She's still standing that way, as if holding something I can't see in her hand.

"*Wasps love rose water,*" she says. "*Wasps love and seek rose water and are attracted to the odor of the herb called thyme.*"

It's as if a bell has been rung. And we are listening for a response.

What comes to me is an aquamarine sky and the coral roses near the rain barrel, growing in some years alongside amaranth and chicory. The air is velvet and overblown. It's the sunlight of a nearly endless summer. But with a deep cold weight on a wide arc, swinging overhead.

Suddenly she presses the heels of her hands against her eyes.

Sam clears his throat.

I close my eyes for a moment, willing him not to speak.

She uncovers her eyes. They look red, and I don't want her to cry, not if she doesn't want to cry here. In front of him, I mean.

"It was such a beautiful moment," she says. "I was twelve, when I read that. But the very next sentence was a reminder that eating chickpeas increases the volume of a man's sperm."

Sam is looking down at the box I've just opened. It looks like he is not impressed by the books he can see, namely an old library-discard paperback copy of *Invasion of the Body Snatchers*. He turns and goes back upstairs without another word to either of us.

In the box, underneath *Invasion of the Body Snatchers*, I see another copy. No, actually, it's the early version published before the movie, before either movie, when it had been simply *The Body Snatchers*. I'd forgotten that I had both, or that there had even been more than one. And again, isn't it funny, that you don't remember something until you're reminded and then you know it has always been with you. On the first page of *Invasion*,

I read: "For me it began around six o'clock, a Thursday evening, October 20, 1976 . . ."

There's also a paperback of Shirley Jackson's *We Have Always Lived in the Castle*, with Merricat looking through a hole in a fence post. And the Edith Hamilton book of Greek mythology, with an illustration of Pandora opening a box that looks a bit like the Ark of the Covenant in *Raiders*. I didn't know that Pandora had a jar, originally, or that this detail had been lost in translation, somehow, until my second year of college, when I was reading classics. It seemed an especially egregious mistranslation, indeed, after my Canadian roommate, who was in the same seminar group, pointed out that *box* was slang for *vagina*, at least north of the border. I remember thinking it might have made a good band name: *Pandora's Box, Indeed*.

Belén, on the couch, asks to look at whatever I'm looking at. I hand her some paperbacks, and she reads for a while, in silence.

And then I'm opening my eyes without having closed them.

"I need to sit down," I say.

"Mandy," TK says, "You're already sitting. Are you sure you're all right?"

I look down at myself and he's right, my body is in the chair, and it looks like I've been reading from an assorted handful of the old paperbacks plus a book about lucid dreaming, published the year I graduated from high school. And Belén's not here.

He says, "Do you have a minute? I just want to flesh out an idea for you."

In his mouth that idea is horrible: To flesh out a thought is to stock it with meat and bone, and everything else. I don't look down because I can feel that my hand is fumbling for a light switch somewhere down a long hallway, and it feels horrible.

He says, "What are you doing? Here," he says, "there's a lamp beside you. Did you want to turn it on? Or off?"

"I'll wait," I say, because if I move I'll throw up.

"Okay," he says. "I'll wait with you."

He turns up the volume—or gives me the flashlight? If he looks at whatever I look at, somehow that illuminates it to the exclusion of whatever's around it. This time I think I'm prepared, but then I'm confronted by the stink of everything—the dead skin on the surface of my own face is enough even without the necrotic odor of spent air, from everybody's lungs. I want away from this. The lamp smells like molten sand pouring and a bead of metal spinning out into a wire more than a mile long. I see him through dust motes suspended in the air, through sediment kicked up along the banks of a river, and I really have no choice but to inhale a normal breath, and then see the agitation of countless particles streaming toward me. That's just the cost of doing business.

"I don't think either of us is in great shape," I hear him say.

I'm distracted by the hum of the wiring in the walls and the creaking of the beams of my house behind the plaster. Plaster that minutely adjusts in a squeak that goes on, in a way that's unexpectedly greasy sounding.

He says, "What are you trying to do with that light?"

My arm is still too long, like I'm operating it by means of a loosely attached rope and pulley. I swing my hand out toward the lamp like a crane and fumble for the switch. The bulb turns on, with a snapping sound, and the light scalds my skin. People used to say you couldn't turn a light on or off in a dream. I figured it was worth trying.

I can't turn my head, but Pinky, my lovely golden-pink crowntail betta, is hanging at the smudgy glass of his five-gallon rimless tank, watching. When he sees my face he paddles his plumy fins, churning water suddenly thick with dissolved stone. Pinky's magnificent cells refract a different color with every movement, through faint tendrils of ammonia slipping out from his gills and dispersing. But it's his face—it's his face I can't look away from, not as long as Pinky is looking at me, in the way that I can feel, even if I can't turn my head to look.

TK stands up and Pinky retreats under his waterweeds.

"I'm sorry you're feeling sick, too," TK says. He moves my chair, the armchair in my living room, like a chair in a dentist's office, where there was a park outside, with swings, but they were empty every time you watched from the window whenever you sat with trays of fluoride—that vomitous cold clinging gel against your teeth—about which Jandine says, *There's always a speed trap right there, at that stop sign*—she clicks the turn signal—the keys swing, a metallic jangle against the steering column—

"I'm sorry to ask . . . One or two things I wanted to run past you . . . I don't think I can talk here—I think I must be allergic to something in your house. . . . No offense intended . . ."

I feel so battened down by gravity that I can't protest as he extends the footrest and tips the headrest back. And when he steps away, Jasper slips forward from somewhere, and sits near my dangling hand, in a posture of waiting this out with me. And Pinky, too, though I can't see him, Pinky floats at the glass, waiting it out with me.

I feel the pulse inside each of the plants, and there's an itch, a small itch on the side of a ceramic pot—the golden beetle, adjusting itself in a long sleep, a dream among the roots.

He says, "I'll look in again tomorrow. I think it's better to check in during the day."

All I can do is lift a few fingers.

He says, "It's just in case . . . anything happens . . . in case anything happens to me . . ."

He moves away, and it feels as if the glamour, the spell, whatever is happening is wearing thin enough for me to suspect a flaw that I can't quite work out. There must be other flaws I can't put a finger on, too, but I have other problems now, because I know I'm lying on my back, with my hands at my sides, but it feels like I'm lying face down, prone, and all I can think is that this must be an early moment of what the uncertainty was like for Jandine. Back when everything seemed the way it always had, except for ripples like this, moments of catching a glimpse of the gap between you, yourself, and the brain you've always believed you were, moments when the evidence of your senses can't be right. He lets go of my forearm—somehow I hadn't even felt him holding that arm, but as soon as he lets go I feel angry at myself for not keeping track of the arm that is still mine.

"You're a morning person, aren't you?" he says, and he waits.

"Sure," I say: I am not a morning person. I say it more to escape this moment than to see the next, in which I might throw up right now. In which I hear a greasy clicking sound somewhere inside my neck, my vertebrae, a moment in which my grandmother turns away from the sink—she is wearing a cotton apron, with a few drops of garnet splashed over her heart from cooking boysenberries. I know because I mixed the granulated white sugar into the bowl of them a little while ago, but what is new to me is that—behind the window there's a sound like the wind moving—and behind the smooth cool glass of the window over the sink where water moves I hear the filters, and there's a glow of evening inside my tanks. Outside, the flutter underfoot of a hundred years of gravel pouring out into a driveway is the substrate under the cories, and the world is revealed as contiguous, and continuous, so much so that I'm back in the living room, and TK has left again, through the back patio, as before.

Sam comes downstairs and asks if I'm all right. When I don't answer he pulls the blanket from the couch over me. Then, somewhat awkwardly, he lifts Jasper from the floor and puts her down on my lap before going to lock the back door. He turns down the lights, and goes back upstairs, leaving me with my thoughts, and with Jasper and with Pinky.

Chapter Fifty-Three

In the morning I feel more hungover than I have in a long time, even though I had nothing to drink. Sam is sitting at the far end of the couch, looking at the big tank, and soon Belén brings a mug of what must be some kind of instant powdered-mushroom drink that she says is for me, that I have to decline, with a hard swallow, because the mushrooms have that mushroom smell.

"It's your own tea," she says, "but okay."

She hands me a can of cola, a glass of ice.

She says, "He'll be predictable."

I'm about to ask how they know anything—but then again I feel that prickle of warning, a reminder to be a little careful.

She's right, TK is there on the patio a little later that morning, much the way he was the day before, standing in the same place. Which is to say, the fly corner.

"The garage door isn't even open," I say. "How did he get into the patio?"

"He must have come over the wall," says Sam.

I say, "Come on. You don't think he could climb that wall."

I see them exchange a look.

"You let him in," I say. "Didn't you."

"He might have some other way in through your garage," says Belén.

"That's ridiculous. Someone would have seen him," I say.

"He could have come over the wall before the sun was up," says Sam. "Or maybe he's been standing there all night."

"You don't actually know, do you? The running water didn't even keep him out of the house last night."

"That's my doing," says Belén. "I left the hose off, but only because we were watching," she adds, as if this will make me feel better. "Your couch is behind the waterlines that run under the living room, so you were fine, since I didn't turn off the water to the house."

"I wasn't on the couch," I say. "How would that work? If there's no tap turned on, the water isn't actually running, any more than the water sitting in the hose—right?"

She shrugs.

"I only know that it works," she says. "I don't know the how or the why of it."

Abruptly, Sam says, "There's one question I have to ask. What did you call the presence in your parents' house?"

"We didn't talk about it," I say.

"Mandy, it's just the three of us here," he says. "It's safe to repeat whatever name you had for it."

"It wasn't me," I say. "Jeff called it Ivy."

"Jeff," he says. "Ivy."

"Does it need to have a name?" I say.

"No," says Belén.

"Why did Jeff call it Ivy?"

I'm embarrassed now.

"We had a Ouija board. Jeff asked its name. Something answered, or seemed to answer, with the letter I, then the letter V. So, Ivy."

"I," Sam says. "Five. I, five."

"I-5?" I ask. "The interstate?"

"Maybe you heard from five voices combined."

"Or four," I say. "Roman numeral four."

"Yes," says Sam. "All of the above, and more."

From the office I can hear Sam going downstairs, then back upstairs, and downstairs again, and he repeats this enough times that I wonder if he's racking up steps on a pedometer I haven't noticed, until I go down to the kitchen, and he follows me, and I realize he's been getting his energy together to come talk to me. I brace myself to hear about the library again. And then I wonder whether the kind of low-challenge task that worked sometimes for Jandine might help him settle. So I take a seat at the dining table and as he starts talking I dump out a jar of colored glass pebbles, the kind you can buy in mesh bags at the dollar store, or in aquarium-safe versions at your local fish store. Jandine and I moved these glass pieces around like we were doing a puzzle, with no actual image in mind. Sorting them just to keep her brain engaged, and keep her hands moving. And mine.

"Your stepbrother has a scar?" he says. "On his thumb? Like the ladies here with injuries to their hands."

"Apparently," I say.

"There are Paleolithic paintings on the walls of caves over grottoes filled with the bones of animals. You've seen cave paintings of animals, I'm sure. Have you seen the hands, as well?"

I say, "In photos."

"Look it up," he says. "Look up Paleolithic hands with missing fingers."

He looks down at the spill of color across the pale tablecloth, and begins sorting out the green ones, and the gold ones.

The light from the window makes the glass pebbles beautiful, and the shadows they cast on the tablecloth are full of color.

"They're stenciled, not painted," he says. "Many are missing all or part of a finger, or fingers. Western scholars think these are frostbite injuries or ritual amputations. But Western scholars don't know everything," he says.

I'm sorting colored glass now, too.

"An Incan skull discovered in Peru," he says, "in the late nineteenth century, with a hole in it—that's not unusual, of course, people have survived trepanation for thousands of years. But the skull from Cusco had a square hole, with signs of healing. It blew science's mind. A round hole is easy to assume is a ritual to let evil spirits out. But a square hole? That's clearly a surgical procedure. Yet the academics who gathered in

New York and Paris at the time couldn't believe an indigenous culture was performing neurosurgery five hundred years ago."

He looks up from the glass pebbles.

"What do *you* think?"

In an archaeology class, one of my undergrad professors showed a slide of a ceramic pitcher decorated with red starbursts and floating human figures and asked us what it was. We speculated about purpose, context, symbolism. We made religio-astronomical guesses, said it looked Greek and had probably held wine. Then the professor made a movement in the air of pouring from an invisible pitcher, tilting forward and back, forward and back. Nobody knew for sure, he said, but it was probably made to amuse a child. The figures looked like acrobats that jumped when the pitcher tilted. I don't think it was even Greek. Minoan, maybe? His point was that not everything from the ancient world is an object of cultic significance.

Sam returns to sorting the colors.

"I suppose we hold up fingers when we're counting," he says. "Different cultures might use different fingers by convention, but it's a common impulse. Or it could be some form of sign language. Or both. Like the sign of an exchange."

I watch as he keeps separating out pebbles by color, dropping them into the plain white bowls I've set out, also from the dollar store, which I used to fill, with Jandine, like this. At this table.

"Has anyone lost a finger?" he asks. "To your knowledge?"

Good question. Jeff did not. Paloma's friend did not?

Loretta . . . did not. I'd have heard.

Terry's finger?

"How much of a finger?" I ask.

He shakes his head, like I'm asking the wrong question.

"There's something we're missing," he says. "Something we don't understand."

"No shit," I say.

He's probably just trying to set me a task like in the cookie experiments: Give people an unsolvable math problem to see how long they'll keep trying. And then do it again, to see how long people will keep trying if they know there's a cookie in the room. In other words, distraction shortens the length of time people are willing to keep banging their heads against the exam table. And I have to wonder how many exams I've failed by not just calling time, and taking the cookie.

Anyway; it's not the first time I've had the feeling he's only winding me up.

He says, "You should ask the first lady who was injured here if anything has changed about her beliefs. Or, on second thought, you should ask your friend next door to find out."

"Why?" I say.

"Hadley thought a person's beliefs become untethered in proximity to the particle. For the record, it happens in ways they're not aware of, if the offer is accepted."

"I'm not sure I understand," I say.

"Just get your friend next door to ask whether she believes in the paranormal now. I think you'll find that she does not. Or says that she does not."

I don't know what happened at the house while we were wandering the aisles at Kmart under the floating retail music and the flickering fluorescent lights on the day we found Terry's blood spattered across the driveway. Maybe Terry had done . . . whatever it is that Sam's describing? Is he describing something? It's a ludicrous thought. Isn't it?

I'm tired. And I haven't eaten in a while.

"I don't remember why I brought it up," he says. "But I think . . . I think I meant . . ."

But then he shakes his head, like the thought has gone.

"If it's important, it will come back to me," he says.

When I hear Sinatra over the wall, I catch up with Paloma in the alley.

"Paloma," I say, "would you ask your friend something?"

She knows whom I mean. "She won't talk about the biting thing. She just point-blank will not."

"That's okay," I say, "it's something else. Will you ask her . . ." And here I realize I have not put enough thought into how or what to ask. How to phrase it. "Will you ask her if she thinks she could have seen something paranormal?"

I know I sound apologetic and weird. And here Paloma herself is looking at me like I'm a little bit weirdly and apologetically blue-candle-ish.

"You mean, like, was it a ghost?" Paloma says.

My impulse is to cringe, until I realize she only looks puzzled, and not dismissive.

"Sure, yes. A ghost or . . . yes, a ghost, maybe."

"Well, I know she used to watch some of those shows about mediums," she says. "She likes the ones that communicate messages from departed loved ones. If we go stand out front, we'll see her with her little dog. She goes by at five thirty these days. She wants to get back inside well before dusk. Poor thing. And I would, too."

I say, "Would you just ask her, is she going to watch the new series on Netflix about mediums?"

"Which series?" says Paloma.

"I don't think it matters. Just ask?"

"Okay, sweet pea," she says. "I'll let you know."

I find myself sitting on the couch. Alone and waiting. How long has it been since I just sat and did nothing? For a moment my head clears, and I wonder, suddenly, and again, why I'm allowing any of this.

I hear a text come in from Paloma: *I said are you watching the psychics on TV tonight? She said she never did believe any of that bullshit.*

I try to take advantage of a quiet moment to slip upstairs for access to my own things, mainly for a shower and a change of clothes, but I stop on the landing when I hear Belén helping Sam, in the upstairs bathroom. I can't hear what he's saying, or what she's saying, just the quiet murmur of voices. Possibly one of the exchanges I've been trying hard not to overhear. But I'll admit, I'm curious. Until I hear the door open and the sound of a pair of nitrile gloves being tossed into the wastebasket, and then she says, to him, "All right. Can you stand up, please?"

It could be lots of things; Jandine had prescription diclofenac gel applied to her knees twice a day for arthritis by the med techs in memory care, who wore new gloves each time to avoid absorbing it through their own skin. I go, quietly, back down to the living room.

Sam appears downstairs for a while, to tell me things. He grasps my forearm and looks into my face, trying again to see both of my eyes at once. He says, "One or two things to remember—try to always keep three feet or more of physical distance. Try to avoid unbroken eye contact for more than a moment."

I don't want to repeat the night before. So, I'm listening.

"If I've learned anything at all, it's that they'll drain you before you realize what's happening."

Belén is transferring cut honeydew into the bowl again.

I don't seem to have my own life. I seem to just watch other people.

"I want you to know," she says, while she moves the pieces. She's using spoons. It's an awkward process. "The library is probably worth seeing. But I want you to know that he thinks you're a good listener. So ask yourself how much more listening you're up for."

I'm tired. I don't think I can listen to much more. But once he starts, I'm too exhausted to get up and leave. It doesn't make sense, even to me, but the path of least resistance seems like the only path, in those moments. From here, though, I don't understand how traveling to California could ever seem like the path of least resistance. But there are moments when it already does.

“They were always into some slightly weird shit.” she says.

“Like, occult weird shit?”

“I’d say unconventionally religious. But this is different. He’s gotten further into it, since Hadley’s been gone.”

“Further into *what*?”

“I don’t know where to begin,” she says.

I hope whatever I’m imagining is worse than whatever she’s talking about. That’s how it goes, when you’re left to fill in the blanks for yourself.

“I thought you’d want to factor that in, if you’re seriously considering a visit to the library.”

“Factor *what* in?” I say, exasperated.

“I’m sure he’s already talking to you about it.”

She closes up the clamshell, puts it back into a bag, puts the bag back into a produce drawer.

“Talking about religion? He hasn’t been.”

“Obliquely I’m sure he has been,” she says. “Under the right circumstances, he can be pretty evangelical.”

“Is it a cult?” I ask.

She says, “Cults are in the eye of the beholder. That would sound like I’m talking down, and I don’t mean it that way.”

She’s holding the big bowl of soft, almost rotten fruit. She sighs, looking down at it.

“He was really lost when Hadley died,” she says. “He’s always been a seeker, you know? Always curious, always looking for something. But he got so restless, after she died, and it was hard to talk to him. Hard to keep in touch, even. Now it’s been a couple of years since I’ve gone to visit him, and I didn’t realize he was doing this new . . . religious practice. I mean, based in a religious tradition. As far as he’s concerned, he and the people he’s with are followers of a real religion, one almost persecuted out of existence. But personally I think it’s pretty obvious he’s making it up as he goes.”

“Which religion was it based in?”

“I don’t even want to say,” she says. “I’m embarrassed for him.”

“Did you grow up in the same . . . church?”

“No,” she says. “It wasn’t like this. At all.”

“So, hold on a second. You don’t like whatever Sam is into, and they’re evangelical, but you’re leaving me here alone with him all day and you’re also asking me to listen to him?”

She smiles suddenly.

“That’s funny,” she says. “No, I’m not facilitating for him. I’m trying to get all his ducks in a row. And on top of that, his way of doing things at the moment requires that whoever gets his meals for him doesn’t hang around nearby, if that makes sense.”

“No,” I say, “that does not make sense.”

“It’s part of the practice,” she says. “He needs someone to—” She gestures. “To prep his meals in a certain way. And then to leave him alone. I’m only doing this because he’s sick and I know it’s important to him, right now, especially.”

She’s leaning against the counter, holding the bowl and the spoon, watching the clock on the stove.

“I brought all the paperwork he was going to need for this procedure, this infusion he’s waiting on. It’s a long story—anyway, he did something with all of it. All his records. Even the money. It’s going to be expensive, but he and Hadley kept a lot of cash at their house, and it seemed simpler at the time to just bring enough, rather than try to get into their accounts. And I swear, I don’t know how, but he made it disappear. I don’t own a lot of stuff. But he hid it somewhere, and I just hope he didn’t manage to throw it away. It might be here, for all I know. I don’t think he had it on him. But I don’t know.”

“What does it look like?” I say. “I’ll keep an eye out for it.”

She sighs. “It’s just a regular manila envelope,” she says, and my heart sinks, because there are so many of those around. I probably have dozens, in drawers and boxes, in the filing cabinet in my bedroom closet.

“Anything written on it?” I ask.

“No,” she says. “Just plain. It’s sealed, at least.”

She’s shaking her head, still watching the clock.

"I don't mind doing all of this in the short term. But the clock is ticking, you know?"

She empties her face of expression before she takes the bowl upstairs to him, and a moment later I hear the faintest rise and fall of voices coming from the guest room. Hers, then his, then hers, and then his again, for a long time, and I sympathize.

Chapter Fifty-Four

This pace of doing nothing is relentless. The birds outside in the trees are relentless, and I don't think it's morning already, but TK is here, again, standing with his back to the stone wall of the patio, and I'm so bleary after looking closely through the bucket of tank water that I forgot about and left under the table, a bucket of water I apparently didn't dump into the plants after whenever the last water change was. I briefly consider dousing TK in the face with it. But who has the energy for such a show. Also, it would only hurt TK. Not hurt. You know what I mean. When I pick up the hose with the watering wand attached he moves slightly away. I don't know what I expect—that he'll suddenly reveal that he's healthier than he should be, by scaling the stone wall and disappearing? Or that the water from the hose will burn him, the way silver burns a vampire or a crucifix burns a demon? That's just Hollywood.

That's Hollywood. That's Hollywood? It's been a long time, but that was another show on TV I watched with my grandparents. There was a tiny little person caught in a spider's web at the end of a movie I never saw. The tiny person with a white powdery face, tightly wrapped in spider silk, crying out in a high, peeping voice, "Kill me! Kill me!" at a person passing by who could pick up a rock, and who must decide whether to do it or not because the spider is already on the way toward the little person.

What are we watching! said Tineke, but that was the seventies. You could glance up and anything at all might be happening, there on TV.

Maybe it was a scene from *The Fly*? From the black-and-white original?

TK's face doesn't seem real, maybe it's the mirrored glasses and how long he goes without moving, like time-lapse videos of a person standing in a corner while the busy world keeps going, all around. This busy world here is the stirring of the green plants, and the coming and going of the native bees, and of course the flies, twirling in their cone in the shadowy area behind him. He moves a little to avoid the full sun, I notice. But he lingers just beyond the slats of sunlight.

There was an afterlife meditation I used to sometimes follow, in which you imagine that you're sitting in a populated place where life is moving all around, and then, you imagine the same place on a similar day years from now, fifty or a hundred years in the future. It's a way of taking yourself out of the equation, which takes the pressure off. Whatever happens in this place will just happen, and will neither affect you nor will be affected by you, down the road. You see the bustle and the life, the movement and the play of energy, and because it's the future you're able to observe it without attachment, or agenda. Without need. Or pressure. Doing that meditation was like slipping into a cool side avenue that I had almost known was there, but hadn't recognized. But it was a dangerous state of mind to slip into while looking out the windows of my house, at the lawn here, at the paths, the mailboxes, toward the swimming pool and cement pool deck behind its chain-link fence where various of my neighbors, most of them strangers, come and go. Walking dogs, fetching mail, all the things that people do outside in the daylight hours.

The metal of the watering wand is cold in my hands and I wonder suddenly if it was only ever the structure that mattered, whether whatever had been in Terry's house was prevented from coming upstairs merely by the shape of the cast-iron plumbing in the house, or of the iron banisters on the stairs, or both, and the way water and iron must have crossed? And all that time I had subconsciously believed it was some other kind of rule with a specific and important meaning. Like that it couldn't get upstairs because Jandine refused to hear it, or because Terry didn't believe it was there? I had assumed they could protect us, just by being there.

But then, I had heard it on the stairs, hadn't I? Had I?

TK shifts, a little, following the edge of the dappled spot of sun in his corner protected from the breeze. A corner where the patio walls meet, framed by tomato plants and squash vine.

There have to be rules, or the matter of the world would fly apart, wouldn't it? Whatever is going to happen, or if nothing happens, either way will hurt TK, who of course has problems of his own. Jandine used to say that it was easier to be mad than to be sad. But I would rather feel sorry for a sick neighbor who's dealing with trouble in his brain than to have to figure out how to react to a neighbor who crawls into the patios and garages of women who live alone in end units—including mine. Including mine, no matter how distant everything feels.

But imagine being a person who would never . . . and then somehow realizing that you're the person doing it anyway. But doing what?

I drop the wand across the threshold of the kitchen door and go inside, locking the door behind me, as if the act of locking it will prolong the safety of my house. But then I nearly jump out of my skin because Sam is sitting in one of the kitchen chairs.

"What's different today?" I say. "Something seems different . . ."

Sam is sitting with his hat on his knee.

"Are you going somewhere?" I ask him, and he turns to look at me with an expression that suggests maybe he didn't fully hear the question.

"Me?" he says.

He's been telling me, for days, that when a particle accidentally makes contact here, it might get hung up in some corner of a shoe or a demon bowl or a witch bottle or a skull or a calcification or something here, maybe anything made out of minerals as long as it's in the right wrong configuration, a certain shape in a certain circumstance that such a particle can't navigate out of again, yet it continues feeding back to it's collective . . . Isn't that what he said? The whole time, every story has been about this. About a momentary alignment with a structure, a cave, a jar, a crystal, a shell, a basin, a bottle.

My hand goes to the electric kettle almost automatically, the carafe is glass, and there's a chalky-white buildup of minerals inside, visible around the bottom, which occasionally thickens into a ring and has to be detached and thrown out in pieces. Now it's thicker than I would've thought it should be, like a ring of whitening ice around the edges of a birdbath in winter.

"Can I just tell you . . ." says Sam, seated at the table behind me.

Don't I know already that these are connected? Him talking? And something in this world rushing to try to block him out with an accumulation of minerals? For all I know, that's what's happening inside my head at the same time. I lift the carafe and I hear it, the ring of buildup lifts and settles and makes a small sound, too small to hear, but almost a chime against the glass. And then he puts a hand up, as if to stop me.

"Mandy, just once, can you try to follow the thread of what I'm saying before you vanish into your own thoughts? At least wait to see if I've got something important to tell you."

I already can't remember the details from last time—yesterday?

It's like I keep waking up during the weirder sleep stories available for adults. You might wake up for some unrecognizable small moment, without later being able to remember what it was. Those moments in the night.

"I knew someone . . ." he says, and the sentence hangs in the air.

"I don't believe you," I say.

"I saw someone familiar at Circus Circus."

I say, "When were you at Circus Circus?"

He's just telling me a story. If you can call it that.

“He was retired but prior to that he’d worked a per diem gig at major casinos here. I knew him many years ago. An old lodge brother.”

“Is that right?” I say. “What’s his name?”

He pauses. “John,” he says. “It was my friend John.”

I open my mouth but maybe I have less to say than I thought I did.

“He had anger issues and ego issues that cost him a job and he wanted it back. He moved to Nevada expecting he’d get a chance to work at . . . the top of the Luxor,” he says. “The Luxor, here. He just showed up, hoping for the best. He thought he could just walk into doing exactly what he wanted to do.”

I nod, without knowing why. Except to agree that yes, the Luxor is a real casino here. Beyond that, I have to treat it all like fiction.

“Please, sit,” says Sam. Then I pull out a chair and sit. Aware that there are other things I need to do, of course, but all of that feels like another life entirely.

“My friend John believed that his migraines could be helped by exposure to the xenon lights at the top of the pyramid,” says Sam.

“That’s ridiculous,” I say.

“He wasn’t allowed up there to find out.”

“Those lights are so bright that people used to say they were visible from space,” I say.

“They were,” says Sam. “They used to be. Luxor was visible. And then it came to an end. That’s what he told me.”

I glance outside; TK is still there, just standing, like a statue in the plants, unable to hear us through the doors and windows. It strikes me as funny that he probably looks more like a work of marble statuary from the past than the white unpainted versions do.

“Mandy,” says Sam. “The person I’m describing was on his way from Circus Circus to the Luxor to look for something protective, he didn’t know exactly what, but he thought it would be hidden in plain sight. Probably an eye of some kind. A representation of an eye." He passes a hand in front of his face. "I just lost my train of thought," he says.

"You were telling me about a friend of yours, somebody you met at Circus Circus."

He looks at me like I'm completely wrong.

"Someone you met who had a terrible headache," I say. "Someone who thought he would be cured by bright lights."

It takes him a moment, and then he continues.

"That was more than a decade ago. He struck up a conversation with me, he traveled a lot for work, and so did I at the time, and we were both sitting at a bar counter somewhere, and he was ordering dinner."

This might not even be the same story.

"He worked on a project of the Ibis hotel chain to embed sensors in the mattresses so that sleep data could be turned into a work of art. To let a sleeper see a representation of their own sleep experience afterward. He'd done it somewhere, a prototype, or preview, and years later he wanted to do it again, to compare . . . but there was no program. I didn't follow everything he said, but that didn't matter. Do you know what I mean, Mandy?"

"I think so," I say.

"Good," says Sam, "because he was telling me at least two or three stories simultaneously, before I realized it was happening. Which is why I was going to tell you that it's not like a lighthouse. It's like a beacon. Those might look the same but they are not the same. Did I tell you this already? Did we already talk about things that look alike that could actually be opposites, and vice versa, among other possibilities?"

"I'm not sure," I say. "Maybe you could remind me."

"Alexandria had a library," he says. "Everyone knows that."

"Of course," I say.

"Alexandria had a lighthouse," he says. "Everybody knows that, too."

"Yes," I say.

“And did you know that Alexandria had knowledge of human anatomy? More than anywhere else in the ancient world.”

“No,” I say.

“Three versions of the same impulse,” he says.

“Are they, though?” I say.

“Ptolemy V banned the export of papyrus to Pergamon,” he says. “He assumed that if they didn’t have scrolls, they couldn’t copy manuscripts and wouldn’t compete with the library in Alexandria.”

There are parenthetical associations floating like ash above a bonfire, in the room. They come and go. Everything used to be something else. Or a lot of other things. Or he knew somebody who knew something about something else entirely, in a way that was not explicitly connected. But in a way that can be made to seem obvious.

“It backfired,” said Sam. “They turned to lambskin instead. In Pergamon, parchment as a writing material was invented, refined, and perfected.”

I am starting to feel the protoplasm of my mind, of my brain emerging from my skull, reaching out in diaphanous waves, touching the brains of others. In some non-local place. Where we might meet. Is that all he wanted, just to get that idea into my head?

“Can I tell you this part,” he says. “Before you go off thinking about something else?”

“Sure,” I say.

“Instead of going to Luxor, my friend John said he might find work in a decommissioned gold mine, but he’d have to find a place where this research is being done, like Australia, on the other side of the planet. But either way, xenon gas is heavy, and cold, and inert, no matter where you put it. So it makes as much sense to look for it here as there. It makes as much sense to look for it down under as it does to look for it here, above the Luxor. Do you know what I mean?”

“That it makes as much sense to look below as to look above? Sure.”

Maybe I should give TK the water bottle marked with the hours of the day, since Sam has never even touched it. Because the hours are passing. Marked or unremarked.

"People down there in the old gold mines are watching for a flash of light. Which would mean a particle that we cannot measure has touched something here as it passed. Does that make sense?" he asks.

Whether it does or not, I nod.

"My friend John didn't realize there's a closer facility," he says. "Because that's not public knowledge."

"How often does it happen?" I ask. "That flash of light? Who's got that kind of money, to chase a rare particle that won't be there even if they find it?"

"It's not rare," he says. "It's everywhere." He holds up one hand. "It's everybody's problem. They're all around us, all the time. It's not contact we're looking for. Just the aftermath of contact. The afterimage. The echo."

"And the Luxor casino is involved?"

"I did not say that. You intuited that."

I wait, but maybe it's gone, whatever the thought was. His, or mine. Belén says that the changes in him are temporary. If that's true . . . I'm not proud of this. But if that's true, I think I probably hate him. Because why should he be healed? Why him?

He says, "There's nowhere deep enough in Las Vegas to shield the xenon. From interference. From the interference of cosmic rays. In fact, up in the air, under a thin atmosphere . . . you can imagine. It changes the experiment."

I can't help myself. None of this is funny. And yet.

He sits with continued dignity. And is pissed off, I'll bet, because I'm not quite laughing.

"He told me that every pyramid needs an eye and two sphinxes," he says.

Is that a metaphor? Is that why it sounds vaguely dirty?

"The pyramid here has no eye and only a single sphinx."

"But it's not really a pyramid," I say.

"It's the third-largest pyramid on Earth," he says.

Then he blinks, and his eyes waver, and he looks down. And I wonder if the fragile skin of his eyelids is already thin enough to see right through, if he wanted to. Watchful even when his eyes are closed. Because whatever works works.

TK comes back that night, following the pattern. I'm resigned, but this is night three, isn't it? Which will surely be the last time, because things come in threes, so let's get it over with. Something to celebrate. Take it where you can. But has it really been three days, three nights?

They wanted to interview him? Sam has a satchel and a notebook; I thought he was waiting to take notes to add to Hadley's files, but he hasn't, not that I've seen. Neither has Belén, who's around, somewhere, waiting for a phone call from the surgeon who'll be in town for TK's surgery. Or, as they keep referring to it, for the operation.

I remind myself to remember to ask TK about this. About his surgery, which doesn't come up in conversation with him. Only in conversations about him.

TK hangs back, just inside the doorway to the kitchen, in shadow.

"Mandy?" he says. "Is everything all right here?"

What can I say?

He says, "I don't mean to be impolite, but I don't think I can join you there."

Behind him in shadow, my grandmother turns away from the sink—cotton apron, boysenberries and the cascade berries I'd forgotten about. I can't do the math. She's beautiful, ten years older than I am, maybe—maybe more, probably more—but it's so hard to tell how old people used to be. She turns to speak to someone behind me. "I know I'm right," she says. But she's smiling, and not until this moment do I realize that all my life I had the slight assumption that somehow she was probably less than happy. But all's well. She tucks a curl behind her ear. A curl? Her hair has a natural wave—did I know this? I thought I remembered the smell of home permanents. At the table.

She turns back to us—us? She sets down two white CorningWare coffee cups and saucers. A goldenrod border of squares and a design of tiny flowers. Both geometric and floral.

"There's your coffee milk, pet," she says to me. And then my mother reaches for the other cup, full of black coffee.

Jandine is sitting next to me on a beige vinyl kitchen chair, wearing a long-sleeved shirt with a round neckline. Very thin horizontal stripes of green and blue. Of gold, brown, and ruby red. She pours some sugar and takes a sip—she looks at me over the room of her cup, I mean, the rim, the rim of the cup. I hope she'll know that I'm here, now, too, I hope she'll recognize that this is not only a moment already scripted. She's almost like a teenager. But then she always looked twenty-something at thirtysomething.

Around her neck there's a thin gold chain with a floating heart pendant and a bird in flight, carved from shell. Mother-of-pearl. She blinks, and her eyelids are a shimmering pale blue.

"Mandy?" she says to me. "What's up?"

I don't care about anything else.

My grandfather passes through the kitchen and for a moment he and my grandmother link hands before I hear his boots on the steps, the swing of the door behind him.

What year is it? How can I ask this out loud? My hands, both of them, lift the cup up to my lips and I take a drink that I'm not ready for and I nearly choke instead of swallowing—or anyway I expect to choke, but I don't. The coffee milk has a syrupy taste even though it's just a single spoonful of what they're having, darkening the bottom of a cup of hot milk.

I want to look at Jandine. But I don't get to turn my own head.

I know this is the glamour of a June morning and that her hair is shiny like a Breck Girl's and soft like apple pectin after being rinsed with a bottle of flat beer the night before. I want to say everything to her. But of course I can't. She props her chin on her fist. She sees me looking at her and reaches over, rubs my cheek with her thumb.

"Anyway," says my grandmother. "I don't know why the place feels so bad."

"No," Jandine says, "no, I agree with you." She takes a sip and says, under her breath, "I wouldn't mind burning it down altogether."

"Well, something's not right," says my grandmother. "And it needs to be tidied up, especially if this one is looking for places to get into," she says, and she's talking about me, of course, and I want to say, *I won't get into anything, believe me.* But she's talking about something I did in fact already get into. Or that I already will. There's a corkboard above the brown phone behind me in the living room, and maybe I can turn and get a look at the *Sunset* magazine calendar, or the Sons of Norway calendar, or the Grange hall calendar, or the March of Dimes, and surely any one of those would tell me something. But I can't quite turn and look.

"Are you all right, chick?" My grandmother puts one hand on top of my head. I nod and take another sip. Her hands are cracked and they snag my hair just a little, as she moves away.

It occurs to me that what I'm fighting when I try to turn my head is only me—only the young version of me who sat in that chair on that day. So I stop trying to fight the movements of that body. Of my body.

A bag of fabric remnants. A crystal vase to catch sunbeams. The waffle iron and the chrome toaster, both cold. The sound of the pump inside the portable dishwasher on wheels that Tineke has to bring closer and connect to the sink with rubber hoses and clips every time. Out the window, I hear the riding lawn mower start up.

The grass tractor, he called it. My grandfather.

Smell of cut grass at the back of your soft palate as you breathe.

All of this is something about—I hear the pipes shudder,

the sound of the old washing machine drawing cold water, and a moment later Belén comes in from the patio pulling the long green length of the garden hose over the floor. The bird mister is still attached, still sending out a fine mist that somebody will need to mop up off my laminate flooring, whether it's rated as waterproof or not. TK moves ahead of her the way anyone would if you surprised them from behind with a hissing garden mister. She encourages him into the guest bathroom. As he gets closer I can't move my head without a vertiginous feeling, but I hear her arranging the hose and opening the front door. She leaves the door on the chain, open just enough to poke the end of the mister out into the bed of lantana by the door. It's too small an opening for Jasper to slip out through. Even as thin as she is these days. So that's something I won't have to worry about, if I'm passing out the way I expect to.

They're moving around my house as if I'm not here, she and Sam. The door keeps opening and closing. Sam's got an armful of papers from the recycling bin, all the flyers, coupon circulars, newspapers of the past week and he arranges these across the doorway of the bathroom without crossing the opening. Belén toggles the knob on the watering wand, and says, "Okay, water's off." And she stands back and watches. And Sam retreats to the dark kitchen, watching from a distance.

TK crouches to gather the pages.

"Here," he says, "you dropped . . ."

But once the papers are in his hand the print catches his attention, and he's staring without reading, and something about the tilt of his head makes me dizzy. I should close my eyes. Belén steps forward and closes the door to the bathroom again, slowly. He does not look up, and that's a terrible relief.

TK doesn't seem to want to leave the downstairs bathroom. The guest bathroom. The powder room, I believe it's called, technically. I watch as she opens the back door and the garage door before opening the powder room door, and TK doesn't look back at us as he goes; she lets him out like she's letting an unfamiliar animal out, making the route she wants him to take appear to be the only option.

Now the minutes he was in the bathroom feel like—like a bull's-eye. A puncture wound in the middle of a bruise? I'm not sure which part to worry about most.

I'm going to sleep down here tonight. In the chair. Again.

"He'll come tomorrow during the day, the way he has been. But instead of waiting on the patio, let's make it easy for him to go right back in here automatically," she says. "Don't worry, I'll tell you this again tomorrow. Since you're feeling unwell, too."

And then she leads Sam up the stairs, and I hear her putting him to bed, assisting him, and the house suddenly is quiet, and I fall asleep, or something.

Chapter Fifty-Five

I don't sleep much and I get up in the small hours to do a few things—minor tasks that seem important. Actually I don't know what I've been doing. Routine things. I realize I'm awake for the day when Sam and Belén drift down the stairs, into the kitchen, even though they don't care about breakfast. I've still never even seen Sam eat. I've only seen the rinsed clamshell containers of what she brings him. The bowls of cut fruit that he must eat alone. The dish is always put away clean in the cupboard, as if he never used it. He just looks at me with disgust, if I try to offer him anything.

He's in a good mood now, though.

"Mandy," he says. "I remembered what I wanted to ask you. Did you know that Russian cosmonauts found plankton on the outer surface of the International Space Station?"

"No," I say. "That doesn't ring a bell."

"Did you know the tail of a comet carries a powerful smell of urine?" he says.

"Somebody told you that comets stink like urine?"

"The tail does," he says. "I think that's fairly common knowledge. The vapor smells of urine, burnt matches, and rotten eggs."

What happened to the interviewing, the research? What would I think of so much vagueness coupled with such peculiar specificity under other circumstances? But of course there are no other circumstances. Just these. I have the kitchen towel in my hands and I realize I'm clutching it hard, so I shake it out a little, return it. Belén takes a cushion from the couch and leaves it in the middle of the small tile floor of the powder room, then looks up at the fixture of five globe light bulbs over the mirror, the standard vanity lights of seemingly all Vegas powder rooms.

"We're just waiting on your friend now."

"Why can he go in there?" I ask. "There's plumbing."

"Watch, when he gets here," she says. "You'll see that even if the door is wide-open, he'll squeeze all the way over to one side as he steps over the threshold. But once he's in that bathroom, he'll be fine. There's not much underfoot, except right by the toilet."

"What about the toilet?" I ask. "I hate to be indelicate, but can he use the toilet?"

"This is good," Sam says, from the other room, but it almost sounds like a question.

"All good," she agrees.

"Can you call *my* doctor now?"

He watches as Belén takes out a flip phone I've never seen before and dials a number, not saved in her contacts but entered digit by digit from memory. When someone answers she says a few words, and holds the phone out to Sam. I see his face; I remember moments like this for Jandine, too. Daily things becoming suddenly less automatic, habitual movements that don't feel quite right. Sam listens and then closes the phone with a snap and hands it back to Belén, who looks like she isn't sure whether he hung up in mid-call or not.

"Good," he says.

Somehow it's still early and I go upstairs to send something from my folder of recycled evergreen content, get a few things done, a few emails answered, maybe, to readers. I'm a mess. But nobody seems to notice that I'm less than halfway present. Just look at how easily I could just vanish, but for the copy I send. I feed Jasper and open the blinds in the office, so that she can watch the hummingbirds in the silk tree, but she sleeps, and I can't focus, so I go back down to wait in the kitchen. Belén has left the garage door half open, and we watch that horizontal slit of light, seen through the sunlit patio at the far end of the dark garage, beyond the long passenger side of my car.

Sam has things to say and I listen.

Until a shadow blocks the light in the garage and then Sam

is suddenly gone, back upstairs, even before TK stoops to get under the garage door. He follows the cramped corridor available to him through the garage, across the patio, to the back door, which Belén opens.

"Good morning," he says to her. And to me, "Good morning, Mandy. Would you mind—could I possibly use your bathroom?"

"Of course," I say. "Of course."

He goes in and closes the door behind him. Perhaps just the habit of politeness.

Belén sits down on the floor cross-legged just outside the bathroom with a thick stack of old soft playing cards. Here's the research, I guess, in the form of stacks that she shuffles, and shuffles. She says, "I'm going to ask him some questions that may sound pointless. But please don't weigh in, for now. Just give him room to think." Some of the cards in the stack she's shuffling are face up, some face down, all mixed together, from decks of all different colors. She shuffles again, and nods at me to open the door. But I don't want to. Because he's in the bathroom and it seems like a breach of etiquette.

She sighs, reaches up, turns the knob, and pushes, and he's sitting on the floor as if waiting for her to put two cards down on the floor, right at the doorway. Which she does.

Sitting like that—it can't be easy on his knees.

"Care to pick a card?" she says.

He's as agreeable as if she's offered to show him a magic trick. He leans forward, and considers. One card is a five of diamonds, and the other is face down, showing the red logo of a defunct casino.

"Well, now," he says. "I really don't know the rules."

"Just pick one," she says. "That's all."

She sweeps them aside and puts down two more cards in the same places. Two of clubs face up, the other card face down and unknown.

She watches him while he looks at the cards.

"Either," he says. "They both seem fine to me."

I have no idea what they're doing. I assume he doesn't, either, and that he's just being polite. She did say it would seem pointless, but there must be rules. Maybe figuring them out is the point?

She sweeps the cards aside, and puts down two more.

I can't seem to think in any way that isn't a question. So I wait. And the cards have a sound like . . . I don't know what. They sound softer than new cards would. They sound like a lot of days, a lot of nights. She lays out two more cards and asks him again to pick one.

"Don't allow yourself time to decide," she says, as if they haven't already done this many times. "Just pick one. Pick either."

But he doesn't seem to have the gut-level reaction that lets you choose between even two things you're indifferent about. Maybe this is the test? He watches the shuffle, watches each time she deals two cards, and sometimes he hesitates, as if he's listening through a hidden earpiece and expecting to be fed a response. Hearing nothing, evidently? He never picks a card, and the time he spends suspended between the options seems to wear him down. For Belén it seems to be just another meditative repetitive action requiring only a certain kind of attention. Like knitting, walking, gardening, handling beads, a low-stakes habitual motion. But it doesn't relax him, it just lowers him into moments of torpor that get a little longer and a little longer. Belén keeps a running tally of how long the moments of torpor seem to last, until eventually she puts the cards away, and flops down onto the couch, putting her bare feet up on the coffee table, while he remains in a pose of quietude.

I feel worn down, too, from watching. It reminded me of Jandine, taking the memory tests. Being asked what day of the week it was. What year. She had given me a desperate look. *Help me*, she'd said, in a low voice, as if the doctor couldn't hear. And I had to look away.

When I hear a text come in, I expect it to be from Jeff. But it's from Paloma:

Saw TK around your garage a while ago, she texts. *Is everything all right?*

Thanks yes, everything fine! I reply.

I put the phone down and look up to see Sam hovering on the landing, leaning down the stairs like he has something to say.

"I need one of you to shut that door," he says, when he catches my eye. He gestures in the direction of the bathroom.

I want to rest my head in my hands.

Belén is absently scrolling on her phone.

TK is leaning back against the sink cabinet, and I'm overwhelmed by seeing him there—it's unforgivable, to leave him on the floor like this, especially with his stiff knees. I don't understand this. I have to call Stacia.

"Belén!" says Sam.

Belén looks up again, and then says, to me, "I'm doing three things at the same time, can you please do that for him?"

Her voice drags, in places, like a slow cassette tape, stretching out in the angle of the afternoon light filtering in through the blinds. I can't even call it a hesitation. I don't know what it is.

Belén looks through a few cards, and holds one up to me, as if it means something.

"Five of clubs?" I say.

"Card tests are a classic, simple method," Sam says, coming down the steps. "It's eventually going to get easier for him. That's something to celebrate, Mandy, isn't it?"

My hand is resting on the door. His voice. A distortion, maybe. A little dip, maybe, in speech sometimes. Then his voice rises back up to normal as if it had been nothing.

Belén says, "I shouldn't be on my phone, I know." She sets it down, and smiles at me. "Don't be frightened," she says.

You can't say that, without making the other person uneasy.

I close the door, softly, so as not to wake TK.

"The astrophysicists call it dark power."

Will he ever stop talking, I wonder? Ever?

"Your family felt it, too."

My pulse quickens at the sudden change in his voice. I don't want to listen. Why do I? I can't seem to think through my own thoughts.

"Your parents," he says. "That's why they accumulated so much. They had some gift of discernment, but no information. So they must have done whatever seemed best in some way, to insulate against this, for themselves and for you."

"Not in a healthy way," I say.

"If they hadn't done what they managed to do, you might well be dead by now. If you'd spent more time in that house, you'd be in worse shape than you are now."

My eyes fill with tears.

"They were working by instinct," he says. "They bought themselves some time. And they must have done what they could, to keep you away from it."

Just like that, he makes the shameful into something almost holy.

"How do you know," I say. "You're just guessing."

"It's obvious," he says. "Let me tell you a few more things."

And of course I'm listening.

"Your friend has a pineocytoma," Sam says.

Does he seem more calculated today? The Wi-Fi is off, but it can't be that simple, can it?

"He has a tumor of the pineal gland and he's probably having headaches, and insomnia, and other problems you haven't heard him complain about. Like short-term memory problems, and balance problems. It looks like he's having small seizures, absent seizures. He would have needed an operation whether we found him or not."

"You found him?"

"No, I only meant the surgeon he found on his own is someone I've known a long time. You might say your friend's operation will be done by my friend, but the fact is, he reached out to my friend on his own."

Should I call Stacia now?

"Mandy," he says. "Truth, reality, and fact overlap, and you can't force them apart. I'm sorry if I've made you feel that I'm improperly involved in this. The truth is, I barely know the basics, and Belén knows even less."

He's watching me. The way he drags out the words keeps pulling at the edges of my attention. The little falter in his voice sometimes.

"If everything goes right, the operation should take about eight hours. It's a grueling proposition. I know that, because Hadley told me so."

He pauses, watching me.

"You don't want to do anything to heighten the risk for him, do you?" he says.

He's slurring his words, slightly.

"No," I say.

"Good," he says. "Just keep in mind that he's lucky to be having a keyhole operation, instead of the standard approach. He'll only have a small opening in the back of the skull. His headache should disappear immediately."

"That's good," I agree.

"Your friend has a pineal cystoma, as I told you," he says.

"Pineocytoma," Belén corrects.

"A pineal cytoma," he continues. "Mandy, as I'm sure you know, the pineal gland develops calcifications. You've probably heard all about people trying to crack the calcifications open on their own, to have a visionary experience. They don't realize that without that buffer, they're going to see things our ancestors actively blocked out. Those were hard lessons for the species. It was hard work, evolutionarily. We take it for granted, but only because almost everybody develops those calcifications around the pineal gland today. Without them it would be hard to live a normal modern life."

"Do you have them?" I ask.

"Almost everybody has them, and almost nobody has the opportunity to see them," says Sam. "In children those calcifications start out smooth, until various layers of phosphorus and calcium bunch up, into rough, crescent-shaped ridges. Adult calcifications are bulky, like little pine cones. That's where the name comes from. Pineal. They may be ugly, but those layers protect us like a pine cone protects the future trees it carries inside."

Belén is looking at her phone. Sam pauses, waiting until she puts it away.

"And yet some people still have calcifications that remain smooth. We don't know why. We don't know how many, because there's ordinarily no reason to check. But it's probably rare."

You know how it is when someone tells your fortune or publishes a broad-spectrum horoscope. You can't help but look for yourself in it. You can't help but look for details that seem to make sense of your own confusing experience of an individual life. I wonder what my own pineal gland looks like.

"And some theorists suggest that the development of those cell walls was the origin of individual experience," he says. "Of subjectivity."

"Sam," says Belén. "You're talking about calcifications."

"Yes," he says. He seems to recalibrate. "Mandy, as you know, some theorists have suggested that the calcifications might protect something more precious than we know. Sometimes those layers have a crystalline center. And to find a crystal in the case of someone with smooth calcifications . . . What you find in the center of a crystal like that is very rare indeed."

I don't know why. But this doesn't sound like bullshit to me somehow. Though it probably should, I realize.

"You can't see into a crystal that small, not even with an

acoustic microscope," he says. "But just imagine what you might be able to see, if you could."

I can't imagine what an acoustic microscope does.

"You can't cut into a crystal that small. You have to polish away the surface of those rough, hairy calcifications in tiny increments, to reveal whether there's a crystal inside it or not. You reveal the crystal in cross section—and of course by doing that you breach it. And if you're not careful when you breach the crystal, you lose whatever was trapped inside."

I intend to ask what he means by trapped inside. But instead, I say, "Hairy?"

Belén laughs a little, but puts a hand to her face to half conceal this.

"It's not funny," I say.

"It's really not funny," Sam says.

"No," she agrees. "It's lucky. A crystal like that is usually only recovered during an autopsy. The odds of the variables coming together are slim. And in this case," she says, "everybody wins. And your friend gets to walk away alive."

Sam is frowning at her. But it's the most honest answer I've gotten yet, even if—holy shit. Who are these people? It's like I'm briefly surfacing after being endlessly distracted to remember again that I have no idea why they're here. For a moment I'm sure she'll laugh again, and then she does, just a little. Just a smile, slightly in motion.

"It's almost pure coincidence," she says. "I was here for something else entirely, trying to connect with family I haven't seen in a long time, and I happened to notice your friend's symptoms at the pool. Which are very typical, by the way. He suddenly wouldn't walk normally, and it looked to me like he didn't want to step over running water in pipes under the pool deck. All the dogs around here seem to hate him now. He's the one who's been collecting their excrement, which is classic—"

"Wait," I say.

"You know about the dog shit. You said so yourself."

“The dung collecting really does have historical significance,” says Sam.

“That’s not fair,” I say. “He does a lot of work around here.”

She says, “He’ll be back to picking up the dog shit in a matter of weeks.”

“It’s come to be an essential part of the American social contract,” Sam says.

“How . . .” I start to ask, but I stop myself. Didn’t they tell me all of this was related? To Terry’s house? I thought—I don’t remember what I was thinking.

She says, “You want to know what it is?”

“I want to know why it happened to him,” I say.

“It’s not a parasite,” says Sam. “Just to clarify. It’s not a parasite, per se. Belén and I don’t agree. Which is fine,” he adds, holding up a hand. “But I would appreciate the courtesy of being allowed to finish speaking.”

She sighs, a little. Like a teenager. Or something.

I feel—stupid. That would be the word. And confused.

“You want to know why it happened,” Belén says. She has her arms crossed and she’s looking at me. “They pass through everything, all the time, and it usually doesn’t matter if they pass right through us, because we can’t interact. They’re not real in our experience. Until occasionally they somehow appear here, and get stuck. That’s the kind of accident this is. There is no reason. It just happens.”

I think Sam did tell me this. The other day.

“Children can adapt. Older brains can’t.” She’s staring at me. “Your parents seem to have isolated it in their house, somehow, and insulated it. But it took them years. He doesn’t have that kind of time, because he’s older.”

“What will happen to him? If it doesn’t get removed.”

Sam clears his throat, and says, “It must be removed. That’s not negotiable. But to answer your question, it’s like a small fly that occasionally feeds on the human brain, but only for a split second at a time before leaving. He’s got this one stuck inside, and it’s going to consume everything.”

"That's how you imagine it?" I say. "A brain fly?"

Sam says, "Well, obviously rough calcifications would make it a lot easier for a fly to climb in and out. Think about a pitcher plant. If your friend's calcifications are smooth, you can imagine how easily this fly just keeps slipping back into the gland."

"That's horrible," I say.

I can suddenly remember every trap I've set out for fruit flies, like wine in a bottle with a paper cone in the neck, easy to get into, hard to get out of, so that they drown in what they wanted most; I used wine hoping it might be painless. But I'm also thinking about Pandora's jar, all the witch bottles of the world, and the smooth ceramic demon traps that the ancients figured out and buried at the corners of homes in ancient Mesopotamia. And maybe the porcelain sides of my cast-iron sink. And the old bathtub in Mrs. Field's front yard, taken out of the house that sat above a cellar full of glass jars. I'm not saying it makes sense. Only that pieces keep getting thrown down together like dice, rolling into variations of a pattern.

"I can offer a metaphor that's a little less biological," says Sam.

"Please," I say.

"Think of it like a radio signal in the ether that can only be picked up by one receiver at a time. And now it's trapped in the receiver inside your friend's head."

"That's nicer," I say.

"Taking the crystal out intact means a signal trapped inside will be removed, too. And it will be perfectly preserved, until we can open it safely."

"Why on earth would you want to open a signal like that?" I say.

They both pause, strangely lit and arranged, like in a photo printed decades ago. She won't answer, I know. She'll leave it to him. She'll try to stay distant.

"For the research," he says, finally. "For the research, of course."

Chapter Fifty-Six

TK is at the back door before dawn. He looks bad. But enough like himself not to draw the attention of the world yet? I can't tell.

"May I?" he says. "Your bathroom? I'm sorry to be indelicate, but it's urgent."

He goes in and half collapses onto the couch cushion on the floor, as if it's a relief, and it occurs to me that maybe there's something protective in the iron in the walls of that room, in the old plumbing? Not protecting us from him, but vice versa?

"Mandy," she says. "We really are collecting information. Stay if you want to. But don't participate, all right?"

She asks for his glasses, and sets them aside, to see if he'll still scan the pages she sets down before him. She gives him smaller print, ever smaller, until she's checking my shelves for books with the smallest print available, to see at what point he'll stop reading.

"Do you have an old dictionary?" she says.

I won't give her my *Dictionary of Indo-European Roots*.

"Good morning again, Mandy," says TK. "It's okay."

She sees my face, and says, "His vision is just fine, if that makes you feel better. Probably better than ever before. And, look—all the doors are open and he's still here. Doesn't that suggest he wants to be here?"

She's talking about him as if he can't hear her.

I look to him.

"No complaints here," he says. "Though sitting like this is a good reminder that I never did refinish those chairs in my garage. Remember those?"

He's smiling, but there's also a look of suppressed panic in his eyes.

"I remember," I say.

Belén is leafing through a binder from Sam's heavy satchel.

She stops at a fresh page of grid paper, uncaps a black pen, and writes something down. I can see that the corners of the binder pucker a little.

"What?" she says, feeling me watching.

"Nothing," I say. "Is that binder made of leather?"

"This?" she says, looking down. "I'm sure it is. This is Sam's daily book, his cookbook, so they call it. Full of helpful hints and timely observations." She sounds dismissive as she writes without looking up again. "Your friend usually needs reading glasses," she says. "But now he doesn't. If you notice anything else different like that, please tell me."

"You mean like if he can suddenly see through walls?" I say.

"He can't see through walls," she says. "But he can see through an open door."

"He could see me around the corner, you're saying?"

"Sometimes," says Belén. "Sometimes it seems that way."

"Even though he's looking through the same eyes as yesterday," I say.

"It's not the eyes," says Belén. She makes a gesture in the air. "It's the cloud computing," she says. "Or whatever you want to call it."

I think back on the times I saw Belén, watchful, looking out from behind her book at the pool. Just observing. Is it strange that she hasn't mentioned Jeff at all?

Belén hands TK the next few pages from the recycling bin. He's polite as he straightens them into a neat stack, reading one page of the free paper, front and back, then another. When he's done, he hands the stack back to her. She hands him another stack, with some of what he's already read. How do I always end up with this much recycling? It's like it just slips in.

"Here, I'll trade you," he says. "I've already read this." He's handing pages back to her as if they're sharing a Sunday newspaper, and again he sounds so much like TK that it feels like they're doing a skit of some kind, but not a funny one.

"How do you know you've already read those pages?"

"Because I've read them," he says.

She's wearing him out, pulling his attention thin.

I am so tired that I can almost feel individual synapses firing in my head, one, then the next. One thought at a time. How long has it been since I had a drink? And where's Jasper?

Did I take my pills this morning? I didn't, I think.

"How long have you been here?" I say.

"Let me think . . ." she says, but somehow doesn't answer. She's looking through a book from the bookshelf. "This print is pretty small . . ." she says, and holds it up: *Amulets and Talismans*, by Sir E. A. Wallis Budge. The pages are falling out of the binding now and the dark spots on the pages have faded a little in the desert heat, away from the humidity and shade of the Tacoma house, but they're still everywhere. They look to me now like thoughts that tried to take root on the page. But where did the pigment come from? Maybe the spots drew ink away from the words through paper fibers, and condensed it. I wouldn't be surprised to find some pages entirely blank, someday.

"See if he can read this," she says, and hands it to me.

He takes the book and pages through politely.

When the doorbell rings I jump; Belén moves past me, opens the door.

"Oh, hi," she says, cheerfully, and steps out, closing it behind.

"Paloma," TK says, "that'll be Paloma checking in." But his eyes are on the stack of binders of *Man, Myth & Magic* issues, which have been left out. Maybe Belén flipped through them, looking for small print. I place my hand on the one on top. He shakes his head, faintly, almost imperceptibly. I touch the next. He doesn't nod, but continues to look at it. I flip it open: it's the first issue, the page numbers begin with two, and the pull quotes are welcoming, introductory. But that smell, of pages closed in a dark box, will never dissipate.

Never before has the full range of this fascinating subject been assembled in a single work of reference—all the facets of man's experience of the supernatural seen together as a whole.

Books always fall open to the pages visited most, or visited longest, but would binders? Probably not. They'd probably fall open between individual issues? Or maybe habit makes us pick a page, once familiar, long forgotten. Maybe we remember sequences, like the way songs play silently in your mind alongside other songs, following the memory of tracks on vinyl, or cassette, A-sides and B-sides completing themselves now when you hear one song alone. I close the binder, set the spine on the floor, and let it fall open at a place that seems random to me, or as close as possible to random, before setting it down and sliding it half over the sill.

I keep expecting him to have to lean down to see it better, but he doesn't.

The print is upside down, for me, which is a little dizzying, but I can see there's an inky-looking little starburst at the bottom of the page. I turn the book around to look at the starburst; it marks the entry for Magic:

> Magicians revel in what is secret, obscure, concealed and mysterious. This is one of the reasons for the obscurity of so much occult writing. If you are cherishing a great secret, it spoils it if you tell it to other people. But it also spoils it if you do not reveal at least a little bit of it, hence the occultist's love of hints, allusions, symbols and veiled language.

All the other divinatory tools—the talking boards, obviously, and in another way the cards, the rods, the pendulums, the runes and bones and stones and coins, you have to touch them actively and do something particular. But books, you just open them. The lines you find on any page are there already, whether you look or not, and it's passive. Isn't it? Present whether you look or not? I flip through pages randomly—as randomly as anyone who once believed in bibliomancy can, which is to say everything that flashes by both does and does not speak. The same way everything can be true and not true at the same time.

> Behind magic, and at the roots of mythology and magic, is a kind of thinking which is not random and which has its own curious logic, but it is not rationalist logic. It works through analogies, allegories, symbols—which means making connections between things which outwardly and rationally are not connected: the doll and the enemy, the tar barrels and the sun. It looks to man's deep inner wells of inspiration, imagination, insight, instinct as well as the supreme paths to truth.

I push the binder over the sill, and he fans through the pages, slowly, one issue at a time. When Belén doesn't return I follow and find her out front, chatting with Paloma.

"Oh, hi," says Paloma, "hi, Mandy. I saw TK around earlier and just wanted to make sure everything's okay."

Belén is smiling.

"Anyway," says Paloma, "It's almost wine o'clock, so I've got to go. See you."

"How do you do that?" I ask. "How did you charm Paloma so easily?"

Back indoors, she says it's easy enough; most people don't admit the ways in which they've missed being noticed, even to themselves. And when you find one of those ways, they'll respond. They can't help but respond. But you have to find something real.

"What's something you know for certain you're not strong in?"

TK is sitting on the powder room floor, listening politely, and she's still talking as if he's not even here.

"Tell me what you're not good at," she says, again.

"Organizational skills," I say, promptly. Because it's obvious and not a secret.

"Really?" she says, and pauses, considering.

"It's a weak point," I say, looking over to him. To include him in this conversation.

"That's just not what I expected you to say. Because I've seen the way you have the animal supplies set up so that you can solve problems with whatever you have on hand. When you found eggs about to hatch in your big tank, I saw you move them to a bowl and make a sponge filter out of a new foam hair curler from the dollar store, so they wouldn't be sucked into a stronger filter. You can open any drawer and find a way to fix a problem for the little ones in a heartbeat. Just like you found supplies for modifying that camera."

"Okay, that's enough," I say. "I get it." There's that recurring lump in my throat.

TK is looking at her now, as if he's looking away from me, to spare me the scrutiny.

"Jeff doesn't see why you have half a dozen paint-strainer bags hung on a nail in the garage. But I saw you put one over a caterpillar hanging out in the open."

Now I'm confused. "When did you see me do that?"

"Why did you do that?"

"Because whatever creature emerges will have to hang for a couple of hours before it can fly," I say. "A bird would have gotten it before it had a chance."

She says, "I wouldn't know to do that."

"Okay," I say, "thanks, I understand."

"People always know when they're being lied to," she says.

I don't feel necessarily like I'm being lied to, but I understand what she's doing. And I don't want it.

"It's not simple," she says.

"Stop manipulating me," I say. "I get the principle and I'm sorry I asked." But she's relentless.

"Those mesh paint strainers," she is saying, "hanging on that nail? A person might walk past them, over and over, and never recognize the presence of their purpose. Because you don't let other people see that you're doing everything so deliberately."

That's not true. About acting deliberately. It's just impulse. But I do know that I'll go to my grave without anyone else knowing what I have or haven't done with my time, because I myself didn't find out what I might be capable of. But magically here I am, half listening, half elsewhere and even though I know she's doing what she said she does to cultivate, convince, influence, and manipulate people while making them happy while it happens, I don't feel happy. I feel unsettled. There are moments when she is an unexpectedly real interlocutor, like Dick Hallorann in *The Shining* or Agent Smith in *The Matrix*. A stranger who acknowledges a distortion in the normal moment, while the soundtrack of the rest of the world continues unbroken.

By this moment, if I can remember to remember it, I will understand that she is manipulating me when it happens again as it surely will.

She then says, casually, offhandedly, "Did he say anything more about their place in California?"

At first I think she means Jeff.

"Sam? He hasn't mentioned it again," I say.

She glances upward, as if to remind us both that Sam is still in the house.

"He thinks he can trust you. But trust me when I say that the books are a burden that he needs to saddle somebody with." She seems a little angry. "You don't deserve that."

"It shouldn't be hard to find places for them," I say, "if they're that valuable."

"Sam wants the library kept intact and he wants somebody to make a life there. Among the books, in the trees." She smiles, sort of. "It's like an inheritance with a curse attached. But they don't have any other family. Just me, thrust upon them in their retirement."

"I'm sorry," I say. "It's none of my business."

"Be glad it's not your business," she says. "It's not my business, either."

"He should donate them to an archive," I say.

She rejects this before I finish the sentence.

"Personally I don't care whether books of magic are metaphorical or not," she says. "Because you can bet that somebody somewhere in history was willing to try anything, to get what they wanted, good or bad. I may not believe that those preparations necessarily objectively work, but it doesn't matter what I think. People have tried and they'll keep trying. And you can't unsee what's been written. Not once it's in your brain."

"Then why don't you just say yes and then, someday, in the future . . ."

"Torch them?"

"Lock them away, is what I meant."

She shrugs.

"I'll show you someday. See what you think then."

TK is looking down. Maybe embarrassed, or maybe in a moment of that stasis he's been in and out of, all day. And I'm also embarrassed.

"Mandy," she says. "Do you understand that I'm sparing you the details of what people have done to animals in Sam's books?"

Those are things that stay in the mind and memory. Like the scientist whose name and actual work I've forgotten, but whose cruelty and carelessness with the lives of the horses who made his great breakthrough possible stuck in my memory like a piece of broken glass for such a long time. I wish I hadn't just remembered it. Now it's stuck there, again.

I look to TK; he's shielding his face with one hand, shielding his eyes from the light, though it's not particularly bright in here. Or he's rubbing his forehead like he's tired, very tired.

"Are you okay?" I ask him.

He looks up, slowly.

"He's okay," she says.

"I didn't ask you," I say, "I asked him."

"He's okay—do you want to see for yourself? Go ahead, pick out one or two or three books for him. See if his interest revives your memories of parts you'd forgotten."

I've done something she doesn't have patience for, but I don't know what.

"Are you . . . all right?" I ask her. But it's hard to get the words out.

She's switching gears, abruptly. She's distant.

"Just pick something basic, something that's eventually going to get donated to charity. You won't see this kind of uncanniness very often. Not up close."

I look at him.

He says, "I'll take you up on that. A book or two would help pass the time."

I find a bag of books I've been planning to donate, and pick out one about fabric crafts, one about whittling, and a recipe book for canapés, crudités and food garnishes. I'm about to add a faded little yellow paperback copy of something, glancing at it first, but I stop, because among the line drawings on the back, there's one that could almost have been a sketch of Jandine. A woman with her hair loose, parted in the center, wearing a cowl-necked top under a feminine blazer.

Anyway. I set it aside, and maybe I'll glance through it later, before I part with it.

"Open them," says Belén. "Random is fine, face down, then give him a minute or two."

She waits only a minute or two, and then she opens the bathroom door wide so that I can see him. He's sitting in the same place, seemingly unmoved since last time, the books laid out in the way I left them.

"Thanks for the loan," he says. "I was interested to learn that Old Jumbo isn't all that difficult to carve."

Belén retreats to the far side of the sofa, where TK can't see her, and I resist the urge to turn and look at her, but in my peripheral vision I can see that she's sitting with her arms crossed.

"You can do a lot with a pocketknife," says TK.

I say, "Who's Old Jumbo?"

"Old Jumbo!" he says. "The elephant. I got a kick out of that stuck-up family of cats, as well." He's looking at me as if we're discussing a book we've previously agreed to read and talk about. "That angle, though? Their snooty heads? That's tricky."

"All right," I say. He's talking about projects in the books, all right, even though he couldn't have possibly looked through the pages that quickly.

"But Mandy . . . Don't look at the instructions for carving the girl's mother. That seems a little . . . unnecessary. It's an uncalled-for detail."

"You can just slide them back to me," I say.

He doesn't know that we're not just talking.

He picks up the cookbook. "I got a kick out of the Food Decorator tool descriptions in this one. We had one of those to get the segments out of cut grapefruit every morning." He hands over the book. "It seems like an awful lot of fancy language, though, just to say that if you push a wedge-shaped blade into a vegetable and pull it back out you can make a V shape. Don't you think?"

"Maybe so," I say.

He hands over the sewing book, the whittling book.

"Mandy, are you committed to making these projects?" he says.

"Nobody's making these projects, anymore," I say.

"I think you may be wrong about that," he says. "People like to whittle. People like to carve. It says so, right here in the book. And their number is legion."

Chapter Fifty-Seven

"I wanted you to witness it directly," she says. "It's different, when you hear it."

"He was directly quoting an old book about whittling," I say. "And he told me step by step how to make a frog-shaped garnish from an egg."

"A work done with frog albumin?" says Sam, who has rejoined us.

"No," I say. "A frog-shaped party garnish carved out of a hard-boiled egg."

Belén is laughing, but I'm not sure it's a nice laugh.

"I don't know why it's funny," she says. "But it doesn't matter what you supply. It works with whatever you provide."

"It wasn't funny," I say, "it was creepy. He said so many people like to whittle and carve with knives that their number is legion. I looked in the book—it actually uses that word. But, come on. There's a hundred other pages he didn't quote. He just picked one that sounds like it's about demons—how? How could he know what's on the pages of books he didn't even open?"

"That's what I mean," says Belén. "I wanted you to see the way it distills and distorts whatever comes to hand. The energy and the vocabulary always come from someone or something nearby. That's part of why it seems so uncanny."

The way she says this makes me look over at Sam; he's sitting at the table, with his back to my bookshelf. He clears his throat.

"That's why flood narratives are everywhere," he says. "They propagated because they were already encoded everywhere."

I look back at her. She doesn't nod, but it's as if she does.

"It's true," he says. "Flood narratives are recorded everywhere."

I'm getting the uncomfortable feeling of a prickling in my thumbs.

"Mandy, you know information can be recorded in natural materials."

"The stone tape theory," I say.

"Can you imagine being trapped in a blinding dimension that you don't recognize, trapped inside some filamentous living substance? Floating in a sea that also seems to be alive? That's the nightmare of the first flood story," he says. "It's written everywhere."

And I notice that the blue candle keeps burning in the room with us, the way it's been burning this whole time.

"Skeptical?" he says, suddenly. "Look over there—you believe in vinyl records, don't you? That's information stored in waveforms. That's all anything is. Why are some forms good enough for you, but other forms aren't?"

Belén is watching him.

"You'll listen to them but not to what I've been collecting on your behalf for days," he says. "Listen. That's all you have to do. Just listen. Because belief is the default. You can't escape that."

His pupils aren't moving, and yet they're pinwheeling.

"Look down," he says. "Let it all add up. Everything's right on hand, isn't it?"

I look down, at my hand, resting on the table.

"Is that a joke?" I say. "Is that a pun?"

"What's a finger?" he says.

I'm not going to answer.

"A digit," he says. "A digit. Get it? And what's a bite?"

It's like watching an android in an old movie, struggling against the damage in their wiring. Like Ash, in the movie *Alien*, which I shouldn't have watched as a kid but I did and look at me now: Because I did, I can now see that he's losing control of himself in a way he can't fix on his own.

"What's a bite?" he says. "Do you see what I mean?"

"Where's Belén?" I say suddenly; did she step out when I wasn't looking?

I have a sinking feeling, long overdue, like realizing belatedly that you're already unwell with a fever, and yet somehow you didn't notice.

Sam says, "Where's Hadley?"

A bead of sweat slips down from his hairline, and it wouldn't be sinister if I wasn't just thinking about the character of Ash, the way a small bump to his head shows that he bleeds something that isn't blood. From there it was only a short step to him losing control and the crew having to subdue him by knocking his head loose, permanently.

Did Belén actually leave? Is this that moment in a horror story when you realize the person you *almost* trusted is stepping aside to let something else get to you? Isn't that what Ash did, come to think of it?

No; I can hear that she's on the phone, somewhere.

I don't want to be alone with him, I don't want to be harangued, or manipulated, or whatever. Behind him, through the doorway of the kitchen, I can see the Lazarus shelf of glass jars, the roots in water and the green leaves. All the cuttings from supermarket vegetables that I can't bear to throw away if there's a chance they'll grow new roots. And some do.

"In the lap," says Sam.

"Whose lap?"

"In the lapse. The lapis. In the lapis lazuli. I'm going to write down everything," he says. "I'm going to keep a record of what you're saying."

"All right," I say.

He tears a sheet of paper from his notebook and makes notations.

Belén is in the doorway of the kitchen with a phone in her hand, and she's staring at him.

It's dawning on me that I've known the whole time that there's a Kobayashi story running along in the background—it might be *The Usual Suspects* kind, like the story in the movie, thrown together from plausible details hidden in plain sight and served up on Kobayashi stoneware. But maybe not; it could be something like the Starfleet academy Kobayashi

Maru simulation, the exam in which your decisions will always result in lives being lost, but it's the way in which you fail that matters most. It's what you do with the hand you're dealt. Because it's what you do in the moment of greatest pressure, under imperfect, messy circumstances, that reveals more than you consciously know about yourself.

Or both. I suppose it could be both, and more. I believe there is a comet, by the same name. But you may have to go looking for it.

He tosses the paper and the pen onto the table.

"Keep that," he says. "We'll need that." It's not clear if he's talking to her or to me but when I look at the page I see that it's unintelligible, like wavy lines a child might have imitated before learning cursive back when cursive was compulsory; I wonder whether he knows this but keeps up the pretense, or whether he really thought he was writing.

"Tomorrow," she says, to me, I think.

"What happens tomorrow?" someone says, wearily.

I turn, and I'm horrified to see that TK is still there, still sitting on the bathroom floor; where did I think he'd gone?

"Good question," says Belén. "Sam?"

He's gazing at TK, as if he doesn't hear her. So then I'm also gazing at TK, who suddenly reaches up to his forehead, as if reaching to resettle the brim of a cap he wears outside in the sun, sometimes, to shade his face. But he's not wearing it, and I see now that the place he's been touching, seen only out of the corner of my eye for days, is now a bloodless abrasion, like a skinned knee or elbow.

"Sam?" she says. "What's the plan for tomorrow?"

I can't look at the center of the lesion. The clear liquid center of it.

I say, to her, "Do you see the spot on his forehead?"

Belén comes to the threshold and leans down to look.

"He's getting down to the dura," she says.

"How do we stop it?" I say.

"You can't," says Sam. "And you shouldn't try."

Belén seems angry.

I say, "Is that something I was supposed to be watching out for? Because nobody told me to watch out for that. What other unexpected thing should I be on the lookout for?"

Except that it's not unexpected, is it? The slow but regular progress of a hole being bored in a skull? An accidental case of trepanning. But now I really am afraid to look.

"Before you ask," she says, "it won't help to tie his hands."

"I would never suggest that," I say.

"Well, what do you want, then?" she snaps. "Do you want this to stop?"

She leans down to address him directly. "Try to resist that urge. This is almost over."

There are moments when TK looks at us as if he's wondering who here might actually be real, and this is one of them. And also moments when I can hear something unfolding and fanning out above and behind me, and when I look back into the kitchen I can see through the window over the sink that perched on the roof of my garage there are a dozen cats in silhouette, staring down, eyes shining like moonstones.

All the boy barn cats are called Tommy, I remember now. And then some of the cats flick their ears. And Midnight, the female cats had been called Midnight, and that's twenty years of cats, I think, but surely they're not all here at once? The ones who lived and died in different years, who lived and died in the same place, together, but serially? And must have been related, some of them, at least, down through the years?

I feel the impulse to call Jeff, because this is a game, clearly, and it's drawing to a close and he's probably still on my old list of designated lifelines, people to call for help with an answer in some final round of a hypothetical challenge. But it's a different Jeff I'm thinking of. A different adult Jeff, in some other future that might have had roots, back where we used to be.

Belén says, but only to Sam, "Doesn't that prove to you that he can feel it? He knows there's something wrong."

"One blade of grass," Sam says, his voice faint. "Moving in a breeze."

I feel the words in the air, a pressure, a vibration that doesn't quite reach me intact. Not this late in the day. Not with the shadows this long already and with TK's eyes already closing.

"We need to rest," Sam says. His hand hovers, reaching for my arm, and I will myself not to flinch, which is practically the same as flinching; by looking at the tendons in his hand I don't have to look at his face and I give him my forearm and I steady him, and then TK's feet start moving, restless, and I see his hand go up, to briefly touch his own forehead again. Like he's impulsively reaching to make the sign of the cross, but stopping short. I don't know if he's Catholic. I don't even know if he's religious or not.

"He won't be awake for long," says Belén.

I assume she means TK but maybe Sam, as well. Maybe I haven't seen them up close, maybe I haven't been looking, but his irises seem swollen, like individual cords of muscle. I'm not sure how clearly he can see me.

It's unbearable.

"It's all right," says Belén. "It's still all right."

She's talking to—I guess maybe all of us?—in the way you speak to someone in trouble. Reassurance mattering more than the truth.

Sam seems lighter, and smaller. For me it's like a nightmare flashing past, speeding up. He lifts a hand, as if to touch something in the empty air, and says, "Did you know that every microwave oven is a broadcast unit registered with the FCC?"

"No," I say.

"That's how it works," he says. "The more familiar something is, the less you know about it."

Belén lifts Sam's grip from my arm, and goes with him, up the stairs, to start getting ready for bed.

I sit down, eye to eye with TK.

"What do you want to do?" I ask him.

“I want to tie up loose ends at home,” he says. “I keep starting. But then I lose track. I start projects, and don’t finish them, and then the next thing I know I’m on to something else. Nothing ever seems to get done. I don’t know how to prepare myself. I mean . . . what am I supposed to do? I don’t know how to think about this. But it’s like I’m trying too hard to figure out what it is that I feel like I’m forgetting to do.”

In the quiet, I realize that I’ve been hearing something in the background. A flicking sound at the screen security door, since morning. The wind, I guess, but also the kind of sound that, under other circumstances, you’d recognize as something trying to get your attention.

“I might have an idea,” I say. “A way to switch gears.”

“I’m listening,” he says.

“Let’s talk about something else,” I say. “It might take the pressure off. Like trying to remember something. You stop trying, and then you remember.”

“I’m listening,” he says again. But he sounds so defeated.

I bring a stack of books from the shelves in the living room.

“Can I have one, too?” he says.

“Sure,” I say. “Which one?”

“Any one,” he says. “It doesn’t matter.”

I slide him one of the books given to me at the estate sale, and I take up one of my Budge books. There are notes in the margins that I must have made a long time ago, when I was a different person, asking different questions.

What will happen to all of these, eventually?

I’m scanning for question marks.

“Okay,” I say. “Just see what you think. This book is a collection of different texts that have been published together as *The Egyptian Book of the Dead*. Some are older, some less old, and they don’t necessarily fit together, and here’s a question. In one, it’s written that if a person knows a certain text during life, and then after death they have it inscribed on their coffin, they’ll be able to cross through the underworld and find their home again there, in the field of reeds. And then, in the field of reeds, they'll live with the gods for eternity."

My copy of Budge's compilation of the texts lies open without complaint. TK's eyes rest on the page. I slide the book over the threshold.

"But other texts say that after death, a person who dies goes to the *Duat*, where Anubis will weigh their heart against a feather, and if they've done no wrong while they were alive then the scales will balance and they'll be granted passage into the field of reeds, and in the field of reeds, they get to live again in the afterlife. But if the heart is heavier than the feather, then the eater of souls will consume it. And then . . . nothing."

He says, "So you have to work on getting the balance right."

"But what does that mean,? What do you do, when the rules contradict each other?"

"It means you have to work with a good level," he says.

I say, "What if the scales don't balance, but the dead person knew the text and had it written on their own coffin? Which rule do you think is more important? Knowing the text, or doing the right things?"

He doesn't answer. Nobody ever answers.

"The text or the heart?" I ask.

"I'm thinking," he says.

"Don't think!" I say. "What's your gut answer?"

He says, "It's never going to come out perfect. But a spirit level is good enough, otherwise go and get yourself a laser level. Do you have one? It's essential, if you're working on a floor. Or thinking about working on a floor."

I've lost track of the point of this. Of what I was asking, and why. Because now I'm interested in the floor.

"What do you mean, working on the floor?" I say.

"Self-leveling compound," he says. "Let gravity do the work."

I hear a door close, upstairs.

"We're nearly done," he says. "You'd better take this back."

I stop and listen for Belén, moving around upstairs.

"Mandy," he says. "Are you listening to me? We're almost done."

He's holding out the book. On the cover, there's a stone head, or a brick head, two of them, actually. The one in the foreground has a small rectangular doorway built into its throat. *An Experiment in Time*, by J. W. Dunne.

I hear Belen on the stairs, then she's with us, dropping down to where we're sitting, near the floor.

"How do you feel?" she asks him.

He looks clammy, I see now, and he doesn't answer.

"TK?" she says.

Suddenly he turns and vomits into the toilet.

I'm not sure what to do, or I'm not sure whom to call. Stacia? When did I become so indecisive? I mean, on behalf of others? I should have noticed he wasn't looking too good. Instead of going on, about questions that sound meaningful.

Belén brings the water bottle, takes the top off, hands it to him.

This is terrible.

"How do you feel?" she asks him.

"I have a splitting headache," he says, sitting back against the wall.

He reaches over to close the toilet seat, reaches for the handle.

Has he even been eating anything?

When Jandine—the hematoma—she was sick to her stomach. As with a concussion. That was how we knew something was wrong, more wrong than we already knew.

I suddenly want more than anything to go out into the blinding heat coming up from the pavement, now that it's dark outside, now that everything feels like the surface of a pond with an underground source, a rolling tension underfoot pressing upward without breaking through. Like the sky under which Jandine used to sit on the picnic table, her feet on the bench, her hands at rest between her knees, looking up at the clouds, years before I was born. Watching the trees, with that dreamy look to her face under the pastel sky like water the moment before it boils. I must have seen a photo of her like that, somewhere.

Belén is helping him to his feet. She's young, and strong enough to shoulder any task like this. As I used to be. She tears open a new bandage and lays it over the wound in his forehead, then presses the tumbler of water into his hand.

"Drink slowly," she says. "Make sure you keep drinking, but stop at midnight. You can't have anything after midnight . . . You have to leave for the hospital before dawn . . ."

It's later than I thought. The shadows outside are evening shadows already.

"Mandy, I want you to hear this, as well, okay? Now, listen. You can't be late." She looks at me. "He's got to leave before the sun's up," she says.

"Or what?" I ask.

"Or he'll be late."

The big garage door is open and I watch as Belén helps him along the narrow path allotted to him, turning sharply in the alley, helping him home. I should close the door. But the neighbors seeing the clutter is the least of my worries, isn't it.

Belén is back shortly, already making calls to someone unspecified, calls so one-sided that I'm not sure if she's leaving voicemails or whether there's anyone listening on the other side.

"Where are you?" she says.

She calls again, or she calls someone else: "Where are you now?"

For a moment, I think I hear a movement upstairs. Less than a movement. An attentiveness, maybe, as if Sam might get up again, and come back downstairs, and begin again. She glances up.

"Lots of mercury in his bone marrow, which doesn't help," she says.

When I check, he's on the landing, in the dim light from the night-light in the hall upstairs.

"You wanted something," he says.

"I did?"

"Something there. You wanted there to be something."

The blue candle keeps burning, the way it's been burning this whole time on a perfectly round saucer stamped with a maker's mark on the bottom: Kobayashi China, right there, on the underside, where I didn't think to look. Now I see with shock the pearly glimmer of cataracts in both of Sam's eyes.

Then Belén is suddenly back, flipping her phone shut, stowing it in a pocket.

"Go back to bed, Sam," she says, wearily.

She sounds tired—whatever their relationship is, or was, they're entering a different phase now—but maybe I can't see clearly because he's sleeping in Jandine's room. And I'm remembering that on the day Jandine and I left this house together for the last time, she didn't remember that she was moving. I hadn't made the arrangements covertly. But there had been little point in reminding her, not when it surprised her, every time, and upset her, even though she liked the place. The live-music events. The rosebushes and fruit trees in the courtyard. Other people her own age. But later, when I came home without her, I had to close the door, on the evening of that first day. Because I couldn't bear to see the bed the way she'd casually made it, pulling the blanket up, before we left the house that morning, at an hour when she'd lived here still.

Belén is rolling pink silicone earplugs between her palms to soften them, like candy, and giving them to Sam to press into his ears.

He's sitting on the edge of the bed like an impossibly older version of the man who'd arrived . . . when was that? How many days ago? Now he wears clothing from the storage cubes in the garage, garments I bought for Jandine that she never had time to wear. The basic all-gender uniform of comfort, soft pants with elastic, a T-shirt that's loose, but not loose enough to catch on anything. A pair of no-skid socks. When I'd first shown these clothes to Belén, to see if he'd want them, saying he could have them, she'd said he wouldn't want to accumulate anything. *He travels light*, she'd said, sourly. *It's part of his practice.*

At some point, Belén must have reversed the doorknob to the guest bedroom, so that the flimsy privacy lock is on the outside, but I don't remember this happening.

She looks at him from the doorway.

By bedside lamplight the room sinks down into a better version of itself, and so does Sam. Belén waits until he lifts the blanket and gets in under the bedding. I'm moving away, down the hallway. These are not moments that need an extra witness.

"I'll be all right," he says.

She sighs, and nods.

I don't know how much he can see, or hear, but he says, "Thank you, Bethlehem."

I remember really seeing her for the first time, standing with some kind of physical confidence, a runner, or a yoga instructor, or a swimmer, wearing a green sundress. Sandals. That date with Jeff. She had been looking over here, at this house, then looking across, to TK's house, and I had wondered then if she had a feeling of being watched. But she'd been assessing factors. Who knows what. Maybe seeing which rooms seemed empty and available for what was now happening, or maybe tracking routes of waterlines under pavement and grass. It sounds batshit, even to me. But did I know she was familiar, even then? She's been around longer than I think, hasn't she? Since before the Bain de Soleil day. All last summer, maybe. The year before, maybe? I'm trying to remember the last time Jandine and I went to the pool, and whether Belén had been there, even that long ago.

"That's it," she says, back downstairs. "Your friend checks into the hospital early tomorrow."

She sits on the couch, and now, finally, she is visibly exhausted. She gets up again, taking soft steps on the bare wood, and returns opening an old bottle of brandy from the pantry cupboard. I've never seen her drink. She pours herself a tumbler, and one for me, and she sits. The phone in her pocket vibrates. She glances at it, puts it back.

How many days has it been again? Since I've had a drink?

"There's more to say about Hadley," she says. And she lifts the glass of brandy. To Hadley? To Sam? No, she's just looking at it. She sets it down without drinking.

Her phone buzzes, and she braces herself to look at it. Relaxes slightly, and answers.

"Hey," she says; she sounds different. "Hey, Jeff," she says.

I want to hide. As if Jeff can see me. That's just how it is.

I'm gathering to go—where? My office, I guess? She puts up a hand, and I wait, and her eyes tick up at me, at first in the unfocused way that someone's eyes always pass over your face when they're talking on the phone and they're half elsewhere. But then she looks at me deliberately. Jeff seems to be offering to come and, I don't know, support, help, whatever. Whatever. Her eyes drift away again, as she is saying, "No, no, that's all right . . . A family situation . . . occupying every minute of every day." Which is all true.

Oh, no: If she's breaking up with him I don't want to hear it. I stand again to leave and again she blocks me; I might climb over the back of the couch to get away from this—Jeff is a separate issue. One I'll end up thinking about more later.

"Let's be in touch," she says to him. "There's no rush."

She gets a text. Reads it, snaps the phone shut, and says, "Right. Help me in the kitchen for a moment. I want to show you something."

In the kitchen she removes a plastic clamshell container from the fridge, stickered with prices marked all the way down to clearance and surely well past its pull date by now. Her voice has a bright, hard edge.

"Mandy, come here please, and look at this. Would you agree that this smells like it's starting to ferment?"

I say, "I don't need to smell it. That looks terrible. But that's what happens when sugar decomposes."

"Yes, it's fermenting all right," she says. "Can you take me to the grocery store?"

"Um, sure," I say. "Right now?"

I don't want to say it, but I'm probably too tired to drive. I mean, really. Too tired to make reasonable decisions.

"Yes," she says. "Because of the fermentation. Sam can't ingest it like this."

In the car, once we're out of the complex, she glances in the rearview mirror, and says, "Mandy, I've got a problem. I need to ask you for another favor."

I'm driving as carefully as I can, both hands on the wheel, taking side streets. It's not far. That's how I try to justify it.

"I have to go back to Sam and Hadley's house."

"When?"

"Tonight. I can't find the cash and papers he put somewhere, and he needs to have them in hand, like, tomorrow."

This seems ominous to me. That his treatment day is the same as TK's surgery.

"Okay," I say.

"I need to tell you what to do for him, in case I get delayed on the way back. Can I ask you to give him his meal tomorrow, if I don't make it back in time?"

"I don't want to," I say. "But I will."

"Here's what to do," she says. "You're not supposed to pay for what you get for him, but you can collect it growing wild, or from someone's yard, or from a dumpster, whatever, any way of getting fruit and vegetables that doesn't include stealing. You can buy it as a last resort, but he'll pick up on it, if you do, because he'll ask you to tell him how you got it. And he'll want details. The important part is that he can't get it for himself. Because it would be spiritually abasing. I don't want to debate the finer points of what he's into," she says. As if I do?

"How does he live?" I say. "If he can't feed himself, I mean."

"He knows some people, from his—church. His organization. They work like interns, but they agree to it. So that people like Sam can do their part." She almost laughs. "So that he can do his important part. Let me tell you what to get." She's shaking her head. "If you have to get anything, find foods that are full of light—melons, he prefers. I'll tell you what I've been doing. You don't have to duplicate this, but it's what he'll expect. Once a day, on normal days, I'm supposed to tell him that I did the best I could, to get it for him in a blameless way, and then I ask to be forgiven, by him, for the harm I've inflicted in the world by doing whatever I did to bring it to him."

"Seriously?" I say.

She nods.

"I'm sorry," I say. "That sounds fucked up."

"I know. It's not the only fucked-up part." At this, despite herself, she does start laughing. And then it seems less mandatory, all of this. Just a passing thing. "Okay, so then he forgives me and then I leave the room so he can eat by himself because they only eat when they're with one another or when they're alone. By the way, do you want to know why? Because it's their holy work on Earth. They digest the light out of plants to send it back to where it belongs."

She waits for me to react.

"I don't think I'm following," I say.

"The elect do their work, by separating the divine sparks out. By metabolism. You might make the same unpleasant assumptions I did, but he is adamant that they don't merely flush the sparks back down into the sewers of this world . . . Yes," she says. "That's why I'm not in the house during the day. If you provide a meal, you're not supposed to be around when he goes to the bathroom later."

"Oh my god," I say.

"I know," she says. "I know. I can't even describe what he's doing without it sounding like a joke," she says. "It's so fucking pretentious . . . To be clear, terrible persecutions were visited on the people who practiced the real religion, originally. In the ancient world. And now he's got his own version, this nice, flexible practice. Bathing rituals, and drinking water rituals. Prayers, and mealtime rituals. I'm sorry. But I find it disgusting."

"Did you really want the grocery store?"

"Yes, fuck it—yes. Thanks. I'll collect some stuff. Hopefully you won't have to deal with it at all. But there's something else. I wanted to tell you this outside of the house."

What happened, I wonder. Something must've happened. I mean today.

"Remember what I was saying about the books they collected? That whether the instructions are meant literally or not doesn't matter, because somebody at some point will have tried it?"

"Yes."

"I think he's up to something," she says. "They had friends. Normal friends. I mean, they were Unitarians. But now he's doing this thing with this group of people he and Hadley had known for a long time, but they're people Hadley didn't like. She didn't trust them. And I think they're working those old protocols. Which would be fine, I mean it could be fine, except I think what they're trying to re-create is not . . . valid. I think that they're taking on descriptions that were written by people who hated and persecuted the original sect. It's perverted. Not just ethically. But actually. Metaphysically."

"Maybe it feels real to them."

She covers her face with her hands for a moment.

"Have you ever in your life heard of anything so hypocritical?" she says. "Retired people on a spiritual path of congratulating themselves for doing nothing but eating, sleeping, shitting, and talking about ritual?"

We're about to turn into the parking lot of the store.

"Do you know how they actually let the sparks out? The divine sparks?"

"Oh," I say, "I probably don't need to know details . . ."

"He lets them out by talking," she says. "The divine sparks are supposed to fly out of his mouth and ascend."

"Is that what I've been listening to?"

"Yeah. Congratulations on listening. You've done your part."

It takes me a moment to process this.

"Not here," she says. "Pull around back, to the dumpsters."

"Can I just buy it?" I say. "I realize you're not supposed to. But I could."

"No," she says. "This is the way he likes it."

I turn off the engine, to wait. Immediately the interior of the car is too hot, even with the windows down. I'm expecting someone, a security guard, a manager, to come out of the back of the store and tell us to leave, but the only other people I see are a loose group of two or three people bedded down on the gravel median that separates the back of the grocery store from the back entrances of a strip mall on the other side. It's uneven ground. But maybe the rockery is cooler, after the heat of the day. Cooler than cement, or asphalt. And with fewer sprinklers than a patch of grass would have, turning on automatically overnight or before dawn.

She brings back a cantaloupe with sunken areas the size of dimes, and a dripping container of cut watermelon.

"Is something bad going to happen to TK?"

"I hope not," she says. "I'm trying to find out. So keep your phone where you can see it. I'm going to let you know, if something seems off."

I say, "What more does Sam want?"

"I don't know anymore," she says, shaking open a plastic bag from her pocket. "I thought he was looking for a way to be all right without her. I thought that was the reason he was so involved. I assumed it was probably a good thing."

She stops before getting into the car to wrap the watermelon more carefully, so that it won't spill. Like something she's done many times before.

"Listen," she says. "Just make sure your friend and his mother get on the road safely by dawn. I don't think anything is going to get in their way. I don't expect your friend to refuse to go. But don't leave those two on their own."

I remember this, with my mother. That sometimes situations that seemed serious brought on a lot of pressure, and then things would fall apart. She would get angry with me, if I made a suggestion or request that belonged to a time that was over. Like the mail. "Please. If something official comes, I need to see it. This is important." And she had been angry with me. Because, as is obvious to me now, she was afraid. But all that showed was the fury. "What do you want me to say? Do you think this is about you? Don't you think I'd do things right, if I could? How do you think I feel?"

Belén gets back into the car. "Keep your eyes open," she says. "A lot of people want a little bit of what your friend is carrying."

"Wait," I say. "The tumor? That's what's going to fix Sam?" I say. And I'm mad at myself. Because of course it would be something like that.

"Yes," she says.

I carefully put on my turn signal, waiting until there are no other cars around to leave the parking lot. Blinking my eyes, to try to sharpen up my night vision. "They can just have it. Right? Sam can just take the—medical waste? Because he knows the surgeon. That's the plan, right?"

"I thought it was the plan."

"What's the actual plan?" I say.

"I'm realizing I'm not privy to the exact plan," she says.

"But what's happening?" I say, with my hands tight on the wheel.

"Take a breath," she says, as we're already in the alley, about to turn into my garage and park.

And then what is there to do except drop it. For the moment.

Chapter Fifty-Eight

Back at my living room she takes out a bag of filters, or chokes, or capacitors, or something in the form of small metal boxes that she plugs in at intervals between the fish-tank lights and the outlets, after asking my permission. I don't know what they are exactly, and I plan to remove them once she's gone. But I'll admit that afterward, the whole house feels better. As she does this, she talks, continuously, conversationally. So normally that I feel like I might be hallucinating the conversation in the car. About the sparks.

"I hope this will help," she says. "I mean, I hope it will be helpful for you. Sam and I live without this kind of interference. And I notice that your friend," she says, "your friend has been keeping his house pretty quiet."

"I've never been to his house," I say.

"I don't mean just quiet," she says, "I mean he's not watching TV, he's not listening to music. The power's on, but he's not using much. Maybe he's unplugged everything. Maybe he flipped some breakers in his fuse box, but he's not doing anything over there. I mean, nothing that leaks any traces."

"You've been checking?"

She makes a dismissive gesture.

It seems so invasive. But maybe only as invasive as an ultrasound, or the ground-penetrating radar at an archaeological site.

She says, "His mother watches TV all night and she's on her phone. Her computer. She cooks and does normal things. His aunt always goes to bed early and the other two houses are unoccupied."

I say, "I know Paloma collects mail for some empty units."

"There are lamps on timers in the empty ones. But he's obviously the kind of guy who turns everything off. Probably even unplugs things."

"He talks about power strips a lot," I say. "He likes to turn appliances off that way."

"When I walked over there with him earlier it was different," she says. "His house must be lit up behind the drapes. Everything must be on. His aunt's place is noisy, too, all of a sudden. Fluorescent lights. Washers and dryers running, AC cranked. Wireless all over."

I can imagine him all too well, drifting through rooms, during these hours of waiting until it's time to go to the hospital. Filling time as best one can. Checking and adjusting the exact time on the digital clocks on the oven, on the microwave. Resetting the AC for all the hours he won't be here. Scooping ground coffee, just getting little things lined up, then remembering he's not allowed to eat or drink. Do they still allow black coffee? Isn't that, along with plain water, just about the only thing left?

She's readjusting the cords around Pinky's tank.

"I don't have a lot of electronics on," I say. "Do I?"

"Yes, you do. Fish tanks," she says. "Filters, pumps, those lights that mimic daylight."

By now I'm seeing heat mirages, here and there. Or, water mirages. Or something.

"There must be a reason he chose to come here," she says. "To your house."

One of her phones gets another text. I wonder now where all the old devices ended up. I wonder if Jeff has any of the old email passwords from Terry's computer, or his BlackBerry? I'll never get over discovering, after Jandine's death, that everything in her inbox and everything in my old inbox, everything I'd kept, all the emails she'd ever sent to me had been deleted when I didn't log into that account for a year. I was so preoccupied and so busy, when she was sick, that I just wasn't thinking about checking that old account. She hadn't written to me in a very long time by then, and I just assumed I would always have those years of correspondence to go back to. I was looking forward to that. To hearing her written voice, from before she got sick. Losing all the years of emails back and forth with Jandine is the reason

I feel about Yahoo a bit the way I felt about the doctor who let the horses die.

She gets another text, reads it, and flips the phone shut, and the sound is so familiar. Nostalgic, even. An old familiar sound from the turn of the new millennium, years ago. She looks up at me.

"I don't want to do this." She's got a handful of her own hair, bunched on top of her head, The way you do when you're trying to dampen your thoughts?

"And you're sure it's not something you can replace without going back?" I say. "Maybe a payday loan? It's not ideal. But maybe under the circumstances."

And she snorts. That's new, the snorting. It's a little bit like the laugh-to-keep-from-crying strategy that my mother recommended.

"I'm off-grid, most of the time. And he doesn't even have any backup ID on him. He used to. But I don't know what he did with it.

I bite my tongue instead of suggesting that maybe he shouldn't be carrying his own ID. These things are hard. It's hard to know what to do. And when. And she did say she expects him to be better soon. It's a delicate conversation to have.

She's looking at a map on her phone.

"Oh, I don't want to be there after dark," she says. "But there's no way around it now. So I have to leave here soon. I'll turn around and come right back. Though I guess that depends on how long it takes me to find where he's keeping his papers," she says. "And more of his cash."

"You should sleep for a couple of hours before you go," I say.

She looks up at me, surprised. "Probably so," she says. "Good idea. Thanks. That's going to make it very tight. But you're right." She goes unsteadily up the stairs and into my room, and shuts the door.

But she's back down a few minutes later, with her phone in her hand.

"TK's surgeon is not cleared to do surgery in Nevada yet," she says. "I just found out."

"Who told you that?"

"One of Sam's people," she says.

I don't know if this is funny, or not funny, or what.

"Ask if Sam's traveling surgeon friend will be in network," I say.

"Your friend got a Medicare supplement. He'll be covered."

Instead of going back upstairs, she sits.

"I'm sorry about leaving him here, with you," she says. "But I can't take him with me—he may decide he doesn't want to leave the house again, if I do."

"It's okay," I say.

But she looks troubled. She says, "If he got away from me he'd be lost. Their house is on five acres, at the end of a long driveway. There's one neighbor, somebody he knows from his church, who can see the lights through the trees at night. They hadn't seen any lights in a while, and when they went over to see if he needed anything, there was no answer. So they got in touch with me."

Why didn't the neighbor call in a welfare check, I wonder.

"He pulled the house phone out after Hadley died and there's spotty cell service at their place, so it doesn't mean anything if he doesn't answer. Otherwise I would have just called to check in with him."

"You went by yourself?"

She nods.

"The gate was unlocked, and there were some tire tracks, more than just his and the neighbor's who checked. It didn't feel right," she said. "Too quiet. I rang the front bell, and he didn't answer. So I walked around the house. There's a ravine in the back but it's easy to get up to the library window. I used to do that as a kid. You know how it is."

"Habit kicks in," I say.

"Yeah," she says. "He was home with me during the days when Hadley was working, and he usually locked himself in the library, so I would climb up there, to see what he was doing. There's a window on one side and a skylight on top. I figured maybe I'd see if he was on the floor or something. It was surreal, that I was checking to see if he was dead."

She's been frowning, but suddenly she laughs a little, at the thought. The way that you can laugh about a thing like that as long as the person you love was not in fact lying dead on the floor. Like the way my mother had uncharacteristically gone into her room at memory care for a nap on the day of her first hospice evaluation. She never took naps. I had waited in the lobby for the visiting nurse, and when we went to Jandine's room we found her in bed. She looked like a corpse. She didn't react when the nurse called her name softly. Her hand was daintily placed between the pillow and her check, and I could see that she was holding something against her face, but not what. I hadn't thought she'd even qualify for hospice, and seeing her like this was a shock. Before I really panicked, the nurse put a light hand on my arm, and stepped me out of the room. She let me know that this was not uncommon. A sudden downturn. I answered her questions at the table in the sitting room of the residence, and she explained hospice care, and what to expect. Fifteen minutes later, when the nurse was gone, I went back to check on Jandine again and found her wide-awake, sitting in the chair by the window with her legs crossed at the knee, nibbling on a Valentine's Day sugar cookie that she had apparently been sleeping on, to judge by the heart-shaped mark on her cheek. It's funny now because that was three years before she died, and because she had looked truly ghastly that day she got to enjoy visits from friendly hospice nurses twice a week, though they had to cut her off after six months for being too healthy.

"He was slumped over the reading table and there were a dozen books lying face up on the floor," she said, and it takes me a moment to readjust, to remember that she's describing the day she followed her muscle memory up over the cedar shingles to look down into the private library that Sam and Hadley spent years acquiring. "His cheek was against the vellum page of the last book he'd been reading, but it didn't look like a heart attack in the middle of an ordinary day. He and Hadley always wore cotton gloves when they handled the books," she says, "and they used archival weights if they needed to hold the pages open. The reason they didn't let me spend very much time in the library was because they thought I wouldn't be careful enough with the books. And now suddenly he's got them lying on the floor."

"That's what they said, anyway," I say.

She looks confused.

"I mean, they said that's why you couldn't go in. Maybe there was more to it."

"Yeah, well, I don't know."

"So he was just asleep?" I say.

"I got the impression he was not asleep."

"You can tell when something's not right," I say.

"I think he was listening to it," she says, flatly, like she's putting something distasteful on the table for a second opinion. "To the vellum page."

"That's weird," I say.

"Yep," she says. "I tapped on the glass. Plexiglass, whatever. I tapped, and then I knocked, and he didn't react. I couldn't tell if he was ignoring me, or what. And the more I watched, the more I thought I could see him moving a little. I thought I could see him breathing. His eyes were open. But he was there for so long that I started thinking maybe I'd imagined it."

Her mouth is pressed shut in a thin flat line.

"So I watched, deciding how long I might be willing to sit up there and wait."

"He must have let you in eventually," I say.

"I knew how to get into the house in an emergency. But it meant following an underground access."

"A tunnel?" I say. "You had to go through a tunnel?"

"The entry is out in the trees and then it opens up inside by the door to the library. I wanted to check on him, but I didn't know if there was anybody else in the house. I put off deciding until it was starting to get dark. And then I didn't want to go look for that entrance in the dark. I hadn't been there in a long time. I just couldn't decide what to do."

"That's reasonable," I say.

"I got down the same way I'd climbed up, and I walked around to the front of the house. I was going to try the doorbell one more time. There are no windows in the front of the house, just the cameras, and I was going to look into the doorbell camera to make sure he knew it was me, and give him one more opportunity to answer. But then as I was walking around the house, I thought, no, I'm not too sure about doing that."

"Because what if it's not him that opens the door," I say.

"But when I got there, the front door was slightly ajar."

"No," I say.

"Yes," she says.

"He got up? He went and unlocked it when he saw you leave the skylight?"

"He didn't know I was there," she says.

"Fuck," I say. "What did you do?"

"I decided there was probably nobody in the house with him at that moment. I decided that if there had been somebody inside, they probably left after I rang the bell, after they would have seen me heading around back. So I went in, and I found him at the table in the same place he had been all day."

"How did it feel inside the house?"

"It felt like he was there alone. It was a mess. It looked like he wasn't able to keep things up."

"What was he doing with that book?"

"He had his face pressed to it. His eyes were open. He was awake. I had to lift his head. His face was a little more humid than is good for the books, I would guess. I had to kind of . . ."

She makes a gingerly motion with her fingers.

"I had to almost peel it off his face. Then I sat him up, and a minute later, he was more or less as he is currently."

"He put his face on that book on purpose," I say.

"That's not the weirdest part," she says. "He had a legal pad open on the table, and his hand was lying on it, holding a pencil. I'd seen that from the skylight, but I didn't see that the pencil was still upright, in a writing position. And up close I saw his muscles move a little. The pencil twitched. And then I saw it happen again. But it was so slow. At that rate, the half a page he'd filled might have been a week's worth of the kind of movement I saw."

"What was he writing?" I say.

"I don't know. He was writing with a mechanical pencil," she says, "with a very fine lead in it. Whatever he was writing was so small and the lines were so close together that I couldn't make it out."

"How long do you think he'd been at the table?"

"I don't know," she says.

I don't ask any probing questions. About the physical state he was in. Bodily functions. And so on. Instead, I say, "What was the book?"

"The book? That he had been reading?"

"The book on the table," I say. "The book that was on his face."

Something in the expression on her face clicks shut.

"I don't know," she says. "I don't remember. I helped him up, and then when I came back, there were so many books open on the table that I wasn't paying attention."

"Do you remember what the other books were?"

"They were grimoires."

"Did you note the pages?" I say. "Before you put them away?" But the question seems unwelcome.

"I didn't put them away. They're all right where he left them." There is a small satisfaction in the way she says this.

I don't particularly want to know what he was doing, in that house in the middle of nowhere, with the steep ravine behind and the square skylight darkening overhead. But it seems like it might be important.

She seems too restless to wait, and in a few minutes she's ready to leave.

"Just be aware," she says, looking upward, to where Sam is. "Just keep your eyes open. Make sure your friend and his mother make it to the hospital in the morning."

"I will," I say.

"You kept saying he wasn't your friend. So then why did you let him into your house?"

"I needed help," I say. "That's kind of his thing. Being helpful. I appreciated it."

I give her the car keys. And a bottle of water. And some apples, and a bag of walnuts, and she opens the garage door, carefully backs out, and drives away.

She's right, though: There was a little more to it. Last year, last August, I'd been out walking. It was hot and shrill. The sky revolving overhead, like you see in movies when someone goes walking through this world on a sheet suspended over nothingness. I was going to take my afternoon walk around the complex, but I was pulled by cicadas in the silk tree, and then by a globe cactus in the landscaping. Such a small thing. In such a small corner of the landscaping. And on that day it was blooming beneath a crown of purple flowers.

It can happen so fast. Like camera angles in the 1970s, when a shot of the blue sky would shatter into a prism as a way of showing heat, or delirium, or mysticism, or an acid trip. All it might take is knowledge of even one earthly life collapsing, under the weight of the sun, while still putting forth a crown of purple flowers. I saw it and I thought, How much longer? How much longer do I have to keep doing this?

"Hey," he'd said, standing in the front door of his town house, with a folded newspaper in one hand, lifting it as if he were a neighbor hailing me from another decade. "Hey there," he said, stepping out. "Hey, are you okay? Listen—I'm glad I saw you. I wanted to tell you something . . ."

I didn't really know him, but it was clear he was trying to

think of something to say, anything to say. I knew it like a dull thud, but I couldn't feel a thing. Later, though, I realized he must have seen something from his chair by the window. Something in my face.

I remember a shirring movement in the trees, the sky. So much sound, in a hot, bright funnel, almost overtaking me.

He'd plunged out of his door without shoes, but he couldn't stand like that on the burning pavement of the path.

He said, "I wanted to ask you something—tell you something, I was going to tell you that I saw something, at the store—you know the flooring they have? All the flooring at the salvage-supply store is half off. You were looking at flooring, weren't you?"

Had I been? I did not see then what a valiant effort it was.

"Thanks," I said. "Thanks for that." I was turning away already.

"Hey," he said, "hold on a sec—I also wanted to ask your opinion on something."

He was speaking so loudly.

"Do you have a second?" he said. "It's right here. Right around the corner. I'm just going to open the garage door—if you can wait a minute and tell me what you think—"

He'd walked through the grass as far as he could and then hotfooted over the asphalt to the corner of his garage, where he dropped his folded newspaper and stood on it long enough to enter the code on his number-pad garage lock.

I could feel every ripple in the atmosphere as I looked up at one tree, then the next. I couldn't see where the cicadas were, but I might have known the code he'd entered just from standing there, in such an otherwise empty afternoon.

"Let's see . . ." he said. "Come take a look. It's . . . It's this," he said, fixing on a dining room chair, one of a set of four. Compact, and neatly made. "See," he said. "These chairs. Nice chairs, Drexel, butternut, pretty nice. I think. What do you think? I mean, that's a chair. That's a good chair, isn't it?"

"Yes," I said. "That's a good chair." Because he was right, it was a good chair.

"How do you suggest I go about refinishing it?" he said. "I've never been into furniture." He gestured at a few projects in progress, and his old Dodge pickup truck. "Paloma said you're the one to ask. I don't want to strip it. Do I have to?"

The bright day hung at my back.

"Here," he said, "stand in the shade." But without trying to get me to go into the garage, necessarily. Just to stand at the margin. He was putting on a pair of old shoes from the back of his truck. Work shoes. Sockless. I think he was reluctant to leave me there and step into his house for other shoes, in case I disappeared as soon as he was out of sight.

I told him what to use. The easiest way.

"Okay," he said. "I've never used that. What is it?"

"It's easy," I said, turning again.

"How long does it take?" he asked, to slow me down.

"Not long," I said. "Take TSP and some fine steel wool to clean the wood. Then the stuff to restore. Wipe off the excess after half an hour, wait, buff it with Orange Wax, and you'll be done in an afternoon."

"What are you doing at the moment? Going for a walk?" he said.

I was looking at the seat of the chair now.

"This is a new kind of project for me," he said.

"You'll want to replace those seats," I said.

"Oh, I don't know," he said. "There's still some life in that upholstery yet."

"That's not upholstery. It's vinyl. Waterproof. You'll need new foam, I'm sure."

"What do you mean?" he said. "What's wrong with the seat?"

These were the thoughts that flashed through my mind: Everybody ends up incontinent. That's the prize you get for living a long life. Me, you, everyone.

"The vinyl was probably for someone's grandkids," I said, because I didn't know him. "Get new plywood, cut new foam to fit, wrap it in a new cover, and staple. It's not a big deal. They'll be really nice."

He was staring down at the seat. "Guess I might have to rethink this," he said.

"I have urine destroyer," I said. "You can try it on the wood, if you want."

He didn't ask why I have urine destroyer.

"Older cats," I said. "Enzymatic cleaners."

"That's great," he said. "That's great," he said again, "that's good to know. If it's okay, I'll borrow some of that. I guess. For the . . . Yeah."

"Okay," I said.

"I appreciate it," he said. "This is new to me," he said. "I appreciate the help."

"That's okay," I said, and what I mean was, *You don't have to talk like that. You don't have to try to make me feel useful.*

"I'll come tomorrow for the enzymes?" he said.

"Sure," I said, turning away.

"Tomorrow?" he said. "I'll come tomorrow? For the enzymes?"

"Okay," I said.

He said, insistently. "You'll be there?"

"Yes," I said. "Okay. I'll be there."

PART SEVEN

In saying this, I went to sleep; and saw a sacrificing priest standing before me, above an altar in the shape of a bone ash bowl used for testing the purity of precious metals. The altar had fifteen steps to climb. The sacrificing priest stood there, and I heard a voice from above that said to me: "I completed the act of going down the fifteen steps, by walking toward darkness, and the act of climbing the steps, by going toward the light. It's the sacrificing priest who renews me, by rejecting the dense nature of the body. Thus ordained out of necessity, I became a spirit."

Having heard the voice of the one standing on the altar, I asked him who he was. And he, in a reedy voice, answered me in these terms: "I am Ion, the sacrificing priest of the sanctuaries, and I have suffered unendurable violence. Somebody came suddenly this morning, and attacked me, cleaving me in two with a sword, and dismembered me, following the rules of combination. He took all the skin from my head, with the sword he held; he mixed bones with the flesh and made them burn with the fire of the treatment. This was how I learned, by the transformation of the body, to become spirit. This is the unendurable violence." As he went on, compelled to continue speaking to me, his eyes became like blood, and he vomited up all his flesh. And I saw that he was a small man made in opposition, tearing himself apart with his own teeth, and collapsing.

Filled with dread, I woke and thought: "That was the chemical composition of water, wasn't it?" I was convinced that I had understood; and I went to sleep again.

ZOSIMUS OF PANOPOLIS, *Collection des Anciens Alchimistes Grecs, Vol. 2: Comprenant, Les Œuvres de Zosime: Texte Grec et Traduction Française, Avec Variantes, Notes et Commentaires* (TRANS. CHARLES-ÉMILE RUELLE)

You can trust the unconscious.

MILTON H. ERICKSON

Chapter Fifty-Nine

I watch the aquariums like windows, even though it's not yet time for dawn inside their acrylic walls. But I can't sit still. I guess I'm waiting for whatever happens next.

My ringer is off but set to vibrate, for when Belén calls. And when someone does call, a short time later, it isn't Belén, but TK.

He says, "Mandy, I just saw the time, and I'm sorry. I didn't mean to call so late."

"It's okay," I say.

"I don't know why I'm calling."

He doesn't sound confused, exactly. Perplexed, I would say.

"Is everything all right? Is your mom there with you?"

"She's at her place. She's sleeping. To tell you the truth," he says, and then there's a long pause. "I don't have the heart to wake her," he says.

I say, "Would you like me to—to wake her?" I almost say, *To check on her.*

"I think it would be all right if I drive myself there," he says. "To the hospital."

"Let her sleep a little while longer," I say. "You still have a couple of hours before you have to leave, right?"

"Right," he says. He hesitates. "That's right."

"I'll come over, if you'd like," I say; it's not a question, is it. More like an observation of how these circumstances are playing out. From him now I almost expect some equivalent of rapping on the top of my car, giving me a thumbs-up, and turning away.

"If you could," he says instead.

I turn off the light switch in the kitchen that controls the motion-activated lights outside, and slip out through the back door and across the patio. I don't know that anyone is listening, but if they are, they might hear the garage door, so instead of pressing the button I'll disengage it from the track overhead and lift it manually, quietly, just high enough to step out into the alley. If anything she says is true then I guess I can navigate by the light of the blue candle, as I'm waiting to see how this Kobayashi story might wrap itself up at dawn. But then again it sounds like she grew up inside a Kobayashi story. So while I don't know if I need to be careful, it feels only correct to slip out of the house quietly like this, into the night. Well before the earliest dog walkers appear on the paths.

All around me I feel the atmosphere of every early-morning airport trip, and at some distance, the memory of Jandine in the kitchen making coffee, and of myself, sleepy, maybe even still asleep upstairs in my old room. Nothing is in the expected time and place, and my car is gone. I know Belén took it, but I hadn't known the open unlit place in the garage without it would seem so unreal that I'm not sure I could walk through without my body turning of its own accord, conforming to the habit of the cramped and narrow spaces that aren't there. I turn back to look through the security door between my garage and my patio, just to see the unlit rectangle of my own kitchen window and be sure that Jandine isn't somehow in the kitchen here even now, somehow still making coffee. I know she isn't. But it feels as if she could be. The window is empty, of course.

Something flutters up beside me in the dark, startling but gentle—there's a hummingbird moth with me. I'm about to urge it through the bars, out to the baskets of hanging petunias and tomato blossoms. But a slight movement in the dim window across the patio stops me from moving. There's nothing to see, at first, and then Sam is surfacing there, like something drifting up from the dark. Maybe he heard me after all. The moth on the security door closes its wings into brown and blends away in the shadows, and I freeze, too.

The recessed light above the sink faintly illuminates the top of his head, the sharp parts of his face, the tops of his shoulders. I can't see his hands in the sink, out of sight below the window frame, but I feel like I'm getting a glimpse of preparations above a small stage before a puppet show. Until he lifts a small glass of water and drinks it, fastidiously. And then I'm afraid that when he's done and as he passes back through the living room on his way back upstairs he'll notice that I'm not asleep on the couch.

But then he's back, drinking water again from the tiny glass, again leaning forward over the kitchen sink. And I'm surprised that even now my impulse is to go back inside and help him back upstairs to bed. It's almost as if I'm not even a person at all.

He turns and goes away again, and this time I slip out to the alley and around to the side of the house, so that I can try to see what Sam is doing in the living room; under ordinary circumstances my blinds would never be left open, not even a crack, I hope, but now I suppose it's luck, or coincidence, or lucky coincidence that there's a space at the bottom, as I left them, in case I needed to look out.

There are so many opportunities inside for divination using reflective surfaces.

Sam had said to me, apropos of little: A house full of vessels is full of divination by reflection, and I thought he was speaking generally. But maybe he was also talking about the aquariums placed around the room. Or maybe that's crazy. But just in front of my face on the window glass there's a spiral of lacewing eggs. It is not strange to see them. Lacewings are everywhere in spring and summer. And also fall, and even winter. But it is strange to see them here, an inch from my face, as if I am supposed to see them, and then behind them through the window see that in my living room Sam is reaching behind the light bar of the big tank, one hand lifted in the air as if for balance, holding his little jelly-jar glass with the other and letting it fill from the waterfalling outlet of the algae scrubber. A nice clean catch. The kind you're supposed to collect in a urine specimen jar at a doctor's office.

That's good, I guess, because if he were dipping the glass into the tank he might contaminate it with faint soap residue.

Or his fucking mouth residue. And then in a blink I'm angry. When he turns and goes back to the kitchen I retrace the way I came, through the garage and into the patio. When I open the security door the moth slips out, as if it had been waiting. Before I open the door to my kitchen, I realize Sam is sitting at the cluttered kitchen table, motionless beside the hospital tank, as if waiting.

The hummingbird moth returns, a fluttering weight moving across my chest with a light touch that slows me down, before it disappears among the hanging petunias, moving like a night self of the hummingbird in daylight. Unrelated, except by the names that we've given. Many moths are falling through the air among the hanging baskets, like small pinches of silk, easy to lose in the dusk until they open their wings, and flutter, the color of coral.

When I say his name he looks up. The jelly jar of aquarium water is in one hand, and in the other he holds an ancient flip phone that I haven't seen him with before.

"To Mandy," he says, lifting the glass, and then he drinks, as the flip phone disappears into the pocket of his new soft pants. He looks at his empty glass, as if the taste of the water wasn't what he expected. And then he says, "Do you know what American astronauts on the Apollo mission said about the moon?"

"I'm sure they've said many things about the moon."

I just want to get this over with.

"They said it smelled of gunpowder. It smelled of spent gunpowder, and charred steak. What does that tell you?"

"Are you ready to go back upstairs?" I ask.

"It tells me we've got a limited library of metaphors to work with," he says. "Up here." He taps his temple. "And so, if the shoe fits . . ."

His hand is light, his fingers cool around my wrist. At the top of the stairs he recognizes the room where he sleeps. The birds outside in the silk tree are stirring and we hear them even through the closed windows as I lift the linens and hold them open so that he can slip under. Then he points to the door and makes the motion to lock it behind me. I don't lean in. He reaches up and takes my wrist and his fingers are moving lightly. Like he's counting.

I look down at his hand, and then under the bed I can see the edge of something poking out, because there is always something hidden under the bed, isn't there? Every bed, in every story? It's the corner of a book and I get it out, with my foot: *In Search of Ancient Gods: My Pictorial Evidence for the Impossible*, by Erich von Däniken. Open, lying face down. When I pick up the book I see that he's written in the margins in that same tiny wave in blue ink, illegible, and on the open page he's starred a quotation von Däniken included from the Babylonian Etana epic, taken from a clay tablet in the library of the Assyrian king Ashurbanipal. He's made a notation next to the second line.

> The eagle said to him, to Etana:
> 'My friend, I will carry thee to the heaven Anus,
> Lay thy breast on my breast,
> Lay thy hands on the pinions of my wings,
> Lay thy sides on my sides.'

I assume it's my eyes playing tricks, or my brain skipping. Then I realize it's on the page, a typo, where maybe an apostrophe got dropped, because Anu is a god. Anu is the incarnation of the holy sky, in ancient Mesopotamia, I think. Whereas this is, as written, is an invitation to fly to the anus of heaven.

There have always been mistakes in these books, big ones but also little ones and medium-sized ones, images captioned wrong and left uncorrected in later editions—I'm spending too much time on this; I have real things to get to—but even if something here is supposed to be possessive, or even if something here is supposed to be plural, what is this supposed to mean?

Actually, I'm pretty sure it just means Sam saw it, and then folded it too literally into his parable of biology and gravity, because he's probably not reading carefully at the moment.

Or maybe he is. Since I see that he's also changed the word *pinions* to *opinions*, with what looks like a soft lead pencil. And I assume he probably took in a detail I missed at first glance, which is that the king's name, translated from cuneiform into the Latin alphabet, is given here by von Däniken with the common German spelling, not the standard English one. So while *Assyrian King Assurbanipal* isn't wrong, necessarily, in this context it's got to be a choice, doesn't it? Even if not deliberate, it can still carry meaning.

He makes a motion. "Mandy," he says. "I just remembered what I wanted to tell you most."

I don't want to listen. But I don't want him to pick up on how anxious I am to leave, either, because I don't want him to try to follow me downstairs.

"What is it, Sam?"

He gestures for me to sit on the edge of the bed. I do. But only for a moment.

"This is important, given your interest in brain research."

I remember reading in the newspaper, decades ago, about a blessing being done at a new research facility in Washington, where head injuries would be inflicted on primates. I've always remembered that. Because of course we should acknowledge the seriousness of doing such things. And who are we? That we do both? I have never forgotten it. The premeditation, on all fronts.

"No thanks," I say.

"It's about pigs," he says.

I'm already getting to my feet, as he speaks.

"Everybody knows that pigs are one of the most similar animals to humans," he says. "And not just physically. Not only for heart transplants. Did you know pigs are as smart as a three- or four-year-old human child?"

"Yes," I say.

"Hadley used to say they're the fifth-most-intelligent animal in the world," he says. "You can look that up, if you'd like."

My thoughts sound so mechanical, even to me. But I don't know how he can keep talking. And how I can just stand here, hating him this much.

"Mandy, this is important work, with the potential to do a lot of good. It might even help people facing what your mother experienced. And although I don't expect you to like the fact that the work is being done at all, I hope you'll be reassured to know this research makes use of brains collected from slaughterhouses."

"I'm stepping out now, Sam," I say. "I don't want to hear any more."

"It's a delicate process. As it would have to be, to restore any brain that had been traumatized and deprived of oxygen for so long. Which should be impossible, right? Because the cells start to die almost immediately after the animal's death. That's what we all assumed. But reviving a brain from that state has been possible for years. Mandy, I know you don't care. But you understand," he says. "I know you understand me."

He's perfectly calm, meeting my eyes like he's counseling me over some minor mishap that he, older and wiser, sees with a greater perspective than I do.

"The people who pioneered this work were careful to suppress the electrical activity in the brain. To use anesthesia and other drugs to make sure that a brain revived outside the body doesn't ever have to return to consciousness."

I can feel something crawling away from my stomach, outward in many directions. My blood, redistributing itself. Because what he avoids saying outright is that it must therefore also be possible to do the opposite.

"It's a repeatable miracle. It's been done hundreds of times, with no sign of pain. And the creatures that contributed were not killed for the purpose. Mandy, I understand that it would be hard for you to accept, if they had been. But they were already dead. They were already nothing but meat. Some day, knowledge gained this way will benefit you directly, and you might as well just make peace with accepting that help."

He's reclining against the pillow. Gently stroking his beard, in a way that suggests he finds some novelty in the way it feels. Touching his hair, and appreciating his own face, perhaps looking forward to the time, soon, when he'll be well again. Thinking of himself, and not of the other lives he'll spend like petty cash along the way. I have no idea what Hadley's real work may have been, and I don't want to know.

"Sam," I say. "I think I preferred your allegories."

He says, "Everything's allegorical."

"Even the pigs?" I say.

"I apologize," he says, after a moment. "I should not have told you that."

I don't know if he actually sleeps or not. But I'll leave him to it.

"You can lock the door from the outside, if you like," he says, and I do.

It feels like the soles of my shoes are rounded and soft, like I'm moving along a corridor inside a rolling ship. I lock the door of the guest room behind me, because I don't have the bandwidth now to do otherwise. My mental processes are slow; I can actually feel them. I stand for a moment in the hall, listening to make sure Sam doesn't try to follow. I check my phone. Nothing from Belén. I send her a text.

On my way to TK's house now. Sam's in bed.

And then: *He talked about bringing brains from slaughtered pigs back to life for research. It was upsetting. I can't listen to him anymore.*

The sprinklers will begin hissing in the grass any time now. So many birds, in the trees, waiting for the strange humidity. So much to off-load, out of my mind. I step into the alley, and listen. I don't know when the birds sleep, or if they sleep because every hour all night long they sound like the beginning of dawn, and I almost don't notice the familiar cluster of yellow globes somewhere behind my patio wall, right above the woodpile, until Jandine says, "Look!"

She's at the picnic table at the farm; it looks like the farm, but does it feel like the farm? I remember when the table was painted, and Jandine looks too young to be sitting there before it was painted that shade of buttercup.

It's my own imagination, isn't it? My own active imagination? Like the movie about the little French girl whose mother dies in a car accident, who wants to see her mother so badly that of course her mother appears, sitting overhead on a branch in the tree their car ran into. That's what I remember. That's what I always knew, that it might be my own making, if I do get to see her again.

"Someone must have forgotten to bring the ladder," she says. "I guess one of us will have to climb up on the wall."

I wondered even at the time whether she was always looking at that tree to avoid looking at me for some reason. Always at that point in the path on all those evening walks. Or whether it was just something about that curve. Even if only because the first time we'd walked it, there had been something there, and so there would always be the echo of something there.

I could easily forget what I'm doing.

Once that I remember, a grapefruit grew low enough for us to pick and we washed it at the sink of the kitchenette in her residence, very carefully because there were birds in those trees, and I saw a small puncture in the skin of the grapefruit, probably from a branch, but it seemed just in the realm of possibility that a wasp might be inside, and I held the grapefruit gently, trying to feel whether anything was moving within. They don't keep sharp knives in the kitchenettes at memory care but I found something with enough of an edge to cut away the peel and see that there was nothing sleeping, nothing hiding under that little hole in the firm pliant surface. But it had seemed so possible, in the moment, and I had been afraid.

This brief cool hour before dawn. And how the air felt getting out of Jandine's car in front of the elementary school in Tacoma in the last week of school in June when it was finally possible to risk not bringing a jacket. How amazing. To be walking in this cool soft air.

She had a cardigan the color of cinnamon neatly folded on the back seat. I know it's still neatly folded, someplace.

"Why won't you look at me?" I ask.

"I will," she says.

TK's check-in time is still hours away. Depending on how much time is passing now.

She is looking up, at the grapefruit.

"Mom," I say.

And she says, "I will, honey. I will."

I take the long way around, because of the sprinklers.

Jandine had liked driving home in the twilight through the fields, after an occasional shift at the cannery. To buy new school clothes. Or to pay for books, in college. Raspberries, in peak season. Then maybe green beans. With the car windows open. With the radio playing back when she was fearless, either driving alone or maybe with a girlfriend or two, or maybe he was there, my father, picking up the same shift on purpose when they were in high school, to ride there with her. To ride back together, to their neighboring houses. She loved that feeling of open windows and empty roads and the sky tilting toward dawn. Or toward dusk. The same reason she never minded going to the airport in the small hours of an early morning, always dropping off someone else who was taking a trip. A good excuse to be alone on the freeway, as the sun came up, on her way home after. It all moves along with me, and then away, through the air, and then it's gone.

Chapter Sixty

As I pass the parking area I feel the presence of a white car parked in the spot that TK dislikes for being out of the range of the security camera. He likes to block it off with traffic cones, but cones can be moved aside. I think it's funny, usually. TK's house has different colors of lantana growing by the door than mine, and a different welcome mat, and though it's the mirror image of my own front step it's also nothing like it. I ring the camera doorbell and I also ring the old bell, small, yellow, the size of a dime and backlit. He doesn't answer either, and I reach for the doorknob to let myself in.

His living room has the same shape, reversed, and the feel of a house about to be put on the market, or a house newly sold. Lots of open space. He's sitting on the couch, calm, composed, bathed, shaved, dressed in clean clothes. Other than sitting like this in a dark room, he appears reasonably pulled together, with a clean bandage in the middle of his forehead. But the moment I step over the sill, I feel a wave of the kind of nausea that precedes the arrival of bad news you've always half expected.

I step backward, over the sill, to the front step. I feel a little better outside.

"Sorry," I say. "I'm still getting some air, or something."

He nods. "Something is a little off over there, on your side of the lawn."

"I know," I say. "It's getting fixed this week."

It's been a while since I've seen him out in the world the way a stranger might. And maybe this is what everybody else has been seeing, the whole time.

"May I?" I reach in and flip the light switch and a velvety green swag lamp glows in a far corner of the room. He winces at the weak light. I should turn it off again, if he's that light sensitive. But I just want to see the room first. Even for a moment. He's seated on a gold-and-brown mid-century sectional couch, and on the wall there's a triptych of oil paintings of a bridge in a candlelit city and pontoon boats waiting in the shadows. Right where my sixty-gallon tank should be, there's a fireplace.

"It's nice in here," I say. "Are the dimensions different?"

"I think so," he says. "But only a bit."

There's blue painters tape on the moldings and baseboards. By my feet, a sealed five-gallon bucket. I tap it with my foot. It's full and heavy. It's paint, I remind myself. It's not aquarium water. I'm astonished to realize that it's not a bucket of river stones, either. The front door doesn't have a gas tube overhead, trying to pull itself shut, but I can feel the pressure anyway, of something trying to nudge me over the sill.

He says, "There's no end, once you get started."

Such a feeling of helplessness. I had it every time I walked in through the tall front doors and saw the perpetual motion of Jandine, revolving in and out of rooms, and Terry in his chair, not moving.

"Do you think your mom is all right?" I say.

Tired isn't a comprehensive enough word. I might be hallucinating, in fact. There's another swag light behind him, bolted to the wall behind the couch. In the style of an old-fashioned reading light. It's on, and I don't see how I missed it a moment ago.

"I used to have one of those," I say. "It belonged to my grandparents. I gave it to charity."

"Funny coincidence," he says. "Mine belonged to your grandparents, too. She's all right. Just overtired. She took half a sleeping pill."

He stands, and crosses the room unsteadily, but seemingly with little or no hesitation over waterlines. Maybe he shut the water off at the main. Or maybe that was only true across the way, only in my house. I don't think it was bullshit, not entirely. He touches another switch and in better light I can see the corners of the gold carpet pulled away from the tack strips, the electrical outlets without faceplates, leaving margins where the emptiness inside the walls and between the walls and floors can be glimpsed. It looks like I've interrupted a search for hidden valuables.

The birds outside continue.

He says, "I don't want to leave it a mess. I mean, if anything happens to me."

Everyone always says that. But everybody always leaves a mess anyway.

"The foundations here are shifting all the time, I'm sure you know that," he says. "In a perfect world, they wouldn't. But they do. That's why most people go with carpet. Carpet hides a lot of problems."

"That's disgusting," I say.

He's moving toward the downstairs coat closet. Getting ready to leave, I assume. He's got a stack of loose papers under one arm, a manila envelope in one hand.

"What's that?" I say. "What do you have there?"

He stares down at what he's holding. "My intake papers, I guess. They told me to fill out the medical history."

"You can do that online," I say, though it's too late now.

"I don't think that's any easier. Not easier for me, anyway. I need to have the paper in my hand, or I'll worry about losing it. Same with plane tickets. I miss those long paper tickets for the whole itinerary. My wife . . . She took care of those things. Call me literal minded, maybe," he says. "But what's to stop the electronic boarding pass from disappearing before we get to the gate? I probably sound silly."

"No," I say, "it doesn't sound silly."

"She thought it sounded silly," he says, and he smiles. And then I don't know what to say. It doesn't seem right to contradict her, after all. It's his own memory he's talking about.

"Before we go, I need to show you something."

When he turns back to see if I'll follow, the center of the bandage on his forehead is damp. His hand drifts up, toward his face. I want to tell him to go wash his hands. If he's not going to stop doing whatever he's been doing up there. He gestures at the coat closet, under the stairs. Where in my house I keep pool noodles that I never use. And those spare boxes of laminate flooring that I thought I might need some day.

"I used to see you around more, looking at things. That seems like a long time ago now."

"It was a long time ago," I say.

"You were shopping for doors, I thought."

"I don't think I was," I say. "But here we are."

"That's right," he says. "Here we are."

It's not like I've never had to wonder whether I should be afraid of another person. I'm sure most people have. I'm certain all women have, at some point. You have to listen to your gut, but you also have to put that unease on hold sometimes, even just to live an ordinary day, full of moments that remind you of how much we don't know about other people. I think I see some iteration of this playing out on his face. And I also see something every time he uses the pronoun *I*, some funny little jolt of an expression that appears momentarily, as if the word seems wrong to him, or imprecise. It's like a secret signal. He's slipping an arm into a jacket now, moving slowly, carefully, as if his balance isn't good. He precariously shifts what he's holding, to shrug into the other arm of the jacket.

"Mandy," he says. "Could you get the door? The closet door."

"No. You open it," I say. "I'm sorry. That came out wrong."

He gets the jacket on, straightens his lapels, and then opens the door wide. A little motion-activated light blinks on inside.

"I'll go on ahead," he says. "But please do come see this."

"Okay," I say. "I'll try."

He steps into the closet. I give it a moment before following. The motion-activated light inside reveals a narrow pocket doorway in the back wall, pretty newly cut, judging by the drywall dust still scattered in the carpet underfoot. He's on the other side, waiting, with his hand on the knob of the next closed door. If this were my house, he would be standing in the closet under Paloma's stairs.

"You installed a sliding door?" I say.

"I did. For some reason, they just kept coming up. I found this frame kit at the salvage store," he says. "It was new, still in the box, and seventy percent off. I had to buy it."

He slides the door out from the wall, slightly, to demonstrate.

"A new gray door," he says. "To pass through."

It's an ashen shade of oak, a dull color, one I noticed popping up everywhere in the last decade or so. For me, it's the background color of years in public places, years that passed in a grinding, distorted blur, like the waterproof laminate flooring in new or expanded neurology practices, physical therapy clinics, emergency room waiting areas, government offices. In elevators on the way down and out of medical buildings. That washed-out gray even appeared in the common areas of memory care, after the corporate takeover, in spaces that had been so cheerful, before, but not until the color was already dated.

"Is that your neighbor's house?" I ask.

"Technically, yes," he says.

I try to make a remark about technicalities, but can't think of one, and suddenly I feel a bleak hatred for him so intense that it stops me from moving.

"You shouldn't have wasted your time doing that," I say.

"This was the only time I had," he says, as if we're discussing a normal project. He lifts his hand toward his forehead again.

"Stop it," I say. "Get your finger out of your forehead."

He turns the knob, but doesn't open it yet.

"Mandy," he says quietly. "We can't talk here. Not in my house, and not in yours."

Now I understand. It's time to change rules and follow them as if they're real, for as long as they seem to work.

"I think you're going to need to close that door behind you," he says.

"I don't think I can do that," I say.

"I'm going through this one," he says. "Do whatever you think is best."

Closet doors in moments like this are usually louvered, aren't they? Not solid. Because everything is scarier when you're looking out through narrow gaps.

I feel carsick again. My face breaks out in a sweat.

"Keep moving," he says. "I think it's worse if you don't keep moving."

He opens the door into the living room of a house that feels immediately like the occupant has passed away with no next of kin, longer ago than you might realize, until you turn on the overhead lights.

"You're doing great," he says. "This won't take very long. But I do want to show you something, real quick." He's now speaking in a bright unsettling voice, though he's not looking back at me. Then he goes into the living room, and I advance to the place where he was just standing. He's waiting for me just beyond the brassy transition strip that separates the carpet of the living room from the area of tile just inside the front door, at the foot of the stairs.

"You'll be in the living room," he says, as if we're touring the place. "I'm already in the vestibule."

This must be the home of the air force officer's widow. I barely knew her, except in the distance as a lovely, petite lady, always in a casual skirt suit, until she fell, went to the hospital, and didn't come back. Her remote control sits in a ceramic dish on the coffee table, between two stacks of magazines that look current from here. The magazines have a certain end-of-summer look to them. A Labor Day atmosphere. Vaguely coastal. They must keep arriving, and he adds them to the pile. Or Stacia does. The sadness of this stops me.

"I know," he says. "It doesn't feel right just passing through. But we have to keep moving."

He's already walking up the floating stairs.

"This is a different floor plan than the end units," he says. I almost respond to say I know, I've been in Paloma's house. But then I don't. Because it moves Paloma closer to the day somebody here will remember her as the lady who wore bright colors, and took her little dog everywhere, seen in the distance.

"When you're ready," he calls from the top of the stairs, "I'll show you the closet in the big bedroom."

I won't let him go to the hospital alone. I don't think I should let Stacia take him. Though I don't know what I could possibly do to help, if someone comes for him. Sam's people. Or what I would be able to do if it turns out they're waiting outside. Or if a slow pursuit is already underway.

"We need to—" I start to say, a reminder that we need to leave by dawn. But maybe that's not something I should be saying too loudly. Just in case.

I want to be aware, as aware as possible, of the spaces around us that we can't see. This thought makes me shut the closet door behind me and then I want to bound through the living room and up the stairs, quick as I can. Like I used to. Because whatever had been at Terry's house had a heavier presence near the doors, which I knew without recognizing it until I saw photos online, when the people who bought it from Jandine put it on the market a few years later. There was new paint on the walls and a lot more light from the windows after the spruce trees were gone, and I could still feel the knowledge of something at the slate entryway and by the door to the garage. Around the sliding glass doors. I don't know about the basement door, because there were no photos. Which seems odd, to leave such a large finished basement out of the photos entirely.

At the top of the stairs I catch a glimpse of TK at the far end of the big bedroom, with a balcony view of the swimming pool behind. This is the closest I've ever been to Paloma's bedroom. He's sliding open one of the big floor-to-ceiling mirrored closet doors, four in a row, in heavy gold frames, before stepping in.

"They might seem a little gaudy for today," he says, from inside. "But I like it. I've always liked the fact that regular people can expect to have beautiful things here. That's Las Vegas," he says. "To me, anyway." I hear him pushing a dozen hangers along the rail.

"When you're ready," he says.

The closet is wide, but shallow. He's cut an opening into the wall and hung a sheet of six-millimeter black plastic taped like a curtain, rustling a little against the raw edges of the cut drywall.

"No asbestos," he says, quietly. "Don't worry. I paid to have the walls and ceilings tested."

"Great," I say.

"I didn't have a chance to finish any of it very well. I'm sorry about that."

He holds aside the flap of hanging plastic, and I feel the air pressure change a little.

I remind myself that the work he's been doing here wasn't done for me, it was work he needed to do to keep the wheel of time moving, as if he was waiting to find out what to do next. The insulation is exposed. Seeing old insulation always gives me the shits, because fiberglass is a warning that you've broken through to an area that somebody before you intended to seal permanently.

He's waiting for me, a shadow in a bedroom on the other side.

"Whose house is this?" I say, following.

"A neighbor who died," he says, "a long time ago, now. And then her next of kin died. We don't know whose house it is now. But it feels wrong not to hold onto the spare key."

You have a key, but it felt right to cut through the wall, I think. But I guess that will be easy enough for somebody to plaster over, someday.

"I'm going downstairs," he says. "And then I'm going to step out onto the patio. If you follow, we'll go over together."

He doesn't turn on any lights, but there are night-lights here and there, enough to see that the rooms are empty. I don't recognize the floor plan. This is a different house, smaller, more symmetrical, concealed in the center of every row of houses here that I've been walking past for years. I follow TK closely down the stairs, into the darkened kitchen, waiting while he finds the key on a full key ring. On the patio, there are eight-foot slump-stone walls on either side, and on the one that must be shared with Stacia it looks like there's a short area standing only a couple feet high. I wish the patio light had a motion detector. Or maybe I don't.

He says, "The neighbor who lived here had a pomegranate tree that had grown through the boards of the original wooden fence, and when the fence had to be replaced, neither the neighbor nor my mother wanted to see it cut down. They're supposed to live a long time. Everybody thought it would be there forever."

"What happened to the tree?"

"I don't know," he says. "It got sick and it died."

I should check the time. But he's leading me to step over the low spot in the wall that marks the spot where the tree used to be, waiting on the other side with a forearm proffered, in case I need to steady myself, and I don't have the heart not to put my hand lightly, briefly on the sleeve of his jacket. A good thing, because I nearly stumble when the light over Stacia's back door turns on automatically. Her patio is full of succulents and colored metal ornaments, and a café table with four matching chairs. I assume we're on the way to wake her. Instead he points to the far patio wall, and then he's leading me through a little wooden gate in the cinder block wall between Loretta's patio and Stacia's. A cute little painted gate. I can imagine what it might have been like, here, a few years back. How social and sunlit those years might have been. And now, in the whole row, there is only Stacia and TK left.

He's got so many key rings. But he finds the one to unlock Loretta's back door easily.

Is it possible the sun won't come up at all? It feels that way.

"Just this," he says. "Then we'll go."

So I step inside after him.

"You remember Loretta," he says. "I mean you know Loretta. You know her."

I do. I know Loretta's sunny yellow bedroom now, after being here alone, briefly, gathering clean clothing on the day she left.

"I set this up last night," he says, and he turns on the coffee maker. "It seemed like a good idea at the time." The machine begins to creak, as it heats up. And suddenly the kitchen starts to warm up with the atmosphere of morning, instead of the quiet inert quality of night in a kitchen.

"In the living room," he says. "The floor. That's what I wanted you to see."

"Wait," I say, because I want to ask him what happened, what happened to Loretta's hand, on that day, on the Fourth of July? Had he been there? I had forgotten that I still don't know. Briefly, I hear the sound of water in the pipes, overhead, somewhere.

"I keep forgetting to fix that," he says, looking up at the ceiling, again in the bright strange voice of the awareness of possibly being overheard and not wanting to tip one's hand. "Must be a toilet running somewhere."

He probably doesn't have time for all of this. Though now, with the coffee brewing, it almost seems like he does. Like a normal morning.

"She lives here alone, you know," he says, moving toward the living room.

"I do know," I say.

There's a NuTone intercom set into the kitchen wall, and I stop.

"Is that what you wanted to show me?" I ask.

"That? No," he says, turning to look at it, as well. "My mom has one in her kitchen, too. That's the intercom she and Loretta used, before cell phones."

It's weird. Isn't it weird?

"I didn't see it when I was here before."

"It's been here a while," he says. "Loretta's husband bought it to install in a house they were having built."

"But he didn't," I say.

"He died early, long before the house was done. Loretta had these out in the garage, until my dad finally installed them. That must have been . . . I don't know when it was, exactly."

"We had an intercom like this," I say. "At my stepfather's house."

"Just like this? No kidding. Same model?"

"It looks the same," I say.

"They're great," he says. "Haven't been used in a while, though. Loretta wanted to get the radio working again, so I was looking for a manual online, and I found out this model is the last of the vacuum tube intercoms. A hybrid, with vacuum tubes and solid-state components. It must have cost a fortune."

He pauses, looking at the intercom, and this feels like a moment in which I should realize something. Like that maybe it was unwise to follow him through a row of empty houses where nobody will think to come looking for me. Or maybe I'll suddenly realize what we're up against.

My phone chimes. A text arriving.

"But you can't just turn on an old radio," he says. "Even if they look fine, they might short out, because some of the components are so fragile. Did you know some antique capacitors made out of paper are still working? Waxed paper caps, sixty years old, still functioning. That's incredible. But you can't predict when they're going to fail. From what I looked up, you could start a fire. Just from turning it on."

"I don't know what a capacitor does," I say.

He's looking at me now. "Maybe it doesn't matter," he says. "But some of the old ones were sealed with beeswax. I knew you'd like that."

That would explain why some old radios smell so nice.

"They sound warmer," he says. "And older. Everything sounds older, like it's coming from farther away, even when it's a song you know."

"Because it has beeswax inside," I say. "And paper."

"I don't know. But I'd like to think there's beeswax and germanium inside."

"Germanium?" I say.

"Germanium transistors," he says.

He doesn't look good, suddenly. I almost tell him to eat something, drink something, but it's too close to check-in and of course he's fasting.

I say, "Let's go now."

His face has the look of a cold sweat. If he's going to pass out—

"I'm okay," he says. He flips the closest light switch.

The gathered and tucked upholstery of the settee and occasional chairs in the living room look like ball gowns on display in a museum. That's what I used to think, whenever we would go to Ursula and Warren's house, where the furniture was not entirely dissimilar. On one end table there's another big remote control, and when I toggle the switch something flickers somewhere behind my back, where channels change with the audible thunk of an 8-track-tape player inside the dashboard of a wood-paneled Country Squire station wagon. Loretta must have sat here alone, often. Watching TV by herself.

He says, "That remote doesn't work."

Around the corner there's a dining area, a rectangular dining table covered by a full-length tablecloth. All damask tablecloths are pretty much the same, but somehow it's the most unsettling thing in this room.

"What did you want me to see?" I ask, because I can hear the birds outside, more clearly than before. "It's almost time to wake up your mom."

"Thank you," he says. "Yes."

I don't feel dizzy anymore. I've hit the stage of exhaustion where everything is sickening and it feels like my skull is full of helium. Which is good. Because it's keeping me awake.

"I'm not proud of the work I've done here," he says. "But I have to call it a day."

I don't know whether we're still talking about renovations. Or whether we're talking about everything else. He's looking up at the ceiling again, listening. Maybe I was guessing wrong, about the static, the feedback, whatever it was that made me feel so terrible those other nights, when TK turned up. Maybe it wasn't proximity to him, with his—with whatever we're calling it. I can't remember who was where, at what times. I realize I'm reaching. But everybody's always reaching.

"Listen," I say, "I have a strange question . . ."

I'm trying to figure out what I'm even asking.

"You know Sam? The one staying at my house this week? Belén's . . . godfather?"

He's looking at me blankly, and maybe he didn't really see Sam? Because Sam did go upstairs, out of sight; he had to stay away until he knew if TK was alone. Or until he knew if TK was . . . networked? Something like that?

"You felt unwell, at my house," I say.

"Sometimes," he says. "Sometimes, yes."

Maybe Sam hadn't been upstairs, in the room; maybe he'd been waiting on the stairs? Would that make any difference? These are ridiculous questions. I feel like there are rules that are eluding me. But maybe he felt ill when Sam was too close. And I felt ill, too—this is a form of the unsolvable cookie experiment. For now, what matters is that we should leave. This is the test, I guess. But he's resting his hand on a small, substantial-looking piece of office equipment on one of the walnut side tables.

"Do you remember desktop intercoms? They were everywhere on TV, in swanky places and mansions. Or offices, when the boss needed to call somebody in."

He twists the dial and a small red light glows.

"FM wireless, it says. Three channels to choose from. See this button? That's the call button. You press that to get the other person's attention. Then they press the button and you can hear them."

"I'm familiar with intercoms," I say. "We were just talking about the one in the kitchen."

"That's right, we were," he says. "When I was looking for videos about how to fix that one, I came across an unboxing video about desktop intercoms. Do you know what NOS means? Of course you probably do, but I didn't. New old stock. A vintage set, never opened. So I watched some of that. And the very next day, I found this one. I've never seen one of these out in the world before. Never come across one. And there it was, on a shelf in a junk store. The timing was so strange."

"Maybe you've seen others, but they weren't on your mind, so you didn't notice."

He's shaking his head, a little.

"I don't think so," he says. "You plug them into an AC outlet, and the sound goes through the wiring in your house. I thought that was really neat. That's why I stopped to watch the video. I would have noticed."

The desktop intercom is well-made, and looks like it has a lot of life left in it, and suddenly I remember the Ray Bradbury story. The one about the foghorn, and the creature.

"But of course you need at least two. So I looked for another one online."

He turns it over.

"It's like this brand never existed. This model number, on the bottom? That should help, you'd think, right? But it doesn't."

"Some things just get lost," I say.

"It wasn't that long ago!" he says. "This can't be more than forty years old, and there are people selling antique and vintage online all the time, and yet there's no trace of a whole company. Did you know there are people on YouTube smashing answering machines? And electric typewriters? Using sledgehammers to break up electronics that are full of perfectly good components."

The bandage on his forehead is oozing again.

"You seem like a nice person," he says. "Can you just tell me? What's going on?"

I almost laugh. Only almost. "I wanted to ask you that question," I say.

"Something isn't right," he says.

"I know," I say.

"One night, a few weeks ago, I was out somewhere and I wanted to go home, and then I suddenly found myself in my patio, like you do when you're driving, and you kind of wake up in your driveway and realize you don't remember the last ten miles. I was looking at my back door. And then I realized it wasn't my back door, and there were other people inside, because I could see them moving, in the light, behind the curtains. It was like a dream. I knew it was bad, but I didn't feel anything."

"I'm sorry that happened," I say. "I'm sorry you felt like that."

"To be honest, when they told me there was something on the scan, I was relieved. I was glad to have an explanation. I felt like having a party. It's not great news but it beats standing at your back door and realizing you have no idea where you are."

I say, "I should have asked you how you felt."

"Oh, no, Mandy. That's okay."

"But I knew something was happening."

"I didn't want to talk about it. I just wanted to stay busy."

And he's already waving it away.

"Listen, I want to show you the floor, and then I'll be ready to go. But you're going to have to bear with me, because I don't think I can describe what I mean. I know that's nonsense. But I just can't put it into words. Anyway," he says. "That's why I want to show you what it looks like."

He lifts his hand up, as if he's going to touch his head again.

"Don't touch your head," I say.

"I feel like I have to," he says.

I hear something then. A sound at the front door, maybe? Maybe not, but it fills me with the cold feeling that we have fucked up. We're taking too long. He realizes this, too. But he's already down on one knee, in an awkward crouch.

"You bought several boxes from surplus—that lava stone tile. From Italy. With a beautiful reactive glaze. Am I right?"

I remember looking at some.

"That was you," he says. "Wasn't it?"

"Yes," I say. "I probably got it for the powder room."

"Have you started yet?"

"No," I say. Does he not know he was just in that room, for days?

He pulls up one corner of the thick olive green carpet. It's not tacked down; he must have already tried to pull it up and scrape the old carpet pad away from the concrete subfloor.

He says, "Do you see that?"

"See what?" I say.

"Can you hold this?"

So I do, I set my bag down and reluctantly kneel, taking the edge of the carpet and holding it out of his way. He lifts the flattened carpet pad in one piece, gently, but it crumbles in his hands when he tries to fold it back on itself. He brushes the dust of it aside and points to a fissure in the concrete. It's about a quarter of an inch wide, and one side is higher than the other.

"If this is your subfloor, then you'll have to address this problem before putting something new over it." When he looks up at me, his eyes are so bright. So bright they remind me of what some people who have sought out trepanation now say about the way it feels, after. As if drilling into the skull has let the light in. Which is different from the library books I'd seen as a kid, which only seemed to mention letting the demons and evil spirits out.

"You'll want to grind this down, until you have a level surface to work with. Self-leveler isn't too difficult," he says. "It's tedious, but not that hard."

“I know,” I say. “I did that. Before I put in the laminate floor.”

“Good,” he says. “I thought you’d know what I meant. The next step is important. You should install a decoupling membrane. Do you know what that is?”

“Sort of?” I say. “It’s an underlayment for tile?”

“Yes,” he says. “Given what’s going on under the floor, you need the uncoupling.”

“Uncoupling? Or did you say decoupling?”

“What’s the difference?” he says.

But by the way he says it, I know he’s telling me that there is a difference, and he’s drawing my attention to it. But I don’t know what it is.

“Look,” he says. “Just put down a good undecoupling membrane.”

“Wait,” I say. “That’s a double negative . . .”

“If you want to throw in some screed, do it. You’re entitled. Then you can put the membrane over, and proceed.”

He’s sweating now, and the forehead—I can’t look.

“Screed? I don’t know what that is.”

“Screed,” he says. “Screed is a layer of gritty sand.”

I’m looking at him, trying to square all of this.

“Otherwise, Mandy, you’re going to keep feeling that movement under your house.”

“Can I add decoupling membrane under laminate?”

“No,” he says. “I know you don’t want to have to pull up the floors you just put in. It was a lot of work, I know. You did a good job. But I assume you don’t want to keep experiencing . . .” And he makes a gesture. “Sometimes, you have to start over. And tile is the strategy I would try, if it were my house. I don’t know how much I mean that. But it’s true.”

“Okay,” I say. “Thanks.” Because I’m not taking up my floors.

“I think the other option is to add mass. If it’s a problem with vibration, or some kind of low-frequency noise, you might be able to dampen it with stuff. It sounds like your parents went that route. Wood furniture, heavy drapes, pillows, couches, rugs, those can all absorb some of the vibration. I lifted one of the two end tables you put out for bulk pickup," he says. "That wood was saturated. It was completely full of heat."

"It's Las Vegas in summer," I say. "Everything is full of heat."

He shakes his head. "Wood absorbs sound waves, which get converted into heat. You know what resonance is?" he says. "I don't know anything. But my wife played the piano. Someone told her wood emits waves, too, when it comes into contact with other sound waves. Supposedly wood is in conversation with other things. Maybe that's why it helps."

"In conversation with things like what?" I say.

"I don't know," he says. "I didn't ask."

I hear something again at the front of this house.

"I think there's someone out there," I say.

"Listen," he says. "Try to stop the low stuff from getting in here in the first place." He gestures, but it's not clear if he means in here, the house, or in here, my head.

Somewhere, I think I hear the sound of an alarm clock going off.

"There's so much pressure, when the ground moves," he says. "There's nothing you can do to stop a monolithic slab from moving when the ground moves, from reacting to pressures that are out of our control. It's brittle. Eventually, it's going to crack. I'm not talking about stopping it from cracking, I'm more concerned with stopping the vibrations from doing any more damage inside your house, because you still need to live there. Make sure what you put over that slab is flexible enough to absorb that pressure before it gets to you. That should work. That should count for something."

"Okay," I say again. "Thanks."

"I have to figure it out over here, too."

"What kind of foundation did you say?" I ask.

"That's a foundation and floor in a single piece. These town houses are built on big monolithic slabs. You and your neighbors, me and mine, we're all on the same slabs."

The movement outside hasn't repeated. If in fact I heard it at all.

"Well. That's all I wanted to show you," he says. He flips the carpet back into place.

"Much appreciated," I say.

We both listen. All I hear outside are birds. One, then another, then another, in sequence.

He takes a deep breath, and gets to his feet.

"After you," he says.

Chapter Sixty-One

On our way out, he stops to turn off the coffee maker. He fills two travel mugs for the drive. But even though he puts the lid on mine for me, I am so tired that when I try to hold it my hand seems weak, and nerveless. I drop the mug and black coffee spreads over the tile floor.

"It doesn't matter," he says. "I'll get that when I come back."

But I am paralyzed for a moment, watching the dark liquid running along the grout lines.

"Really, it's okay," he says. "Leave it."

I guess it could be a kind of anchor. Something left undone, a task for him to come back here and finish on the other side of surgery. Maybe that's not the worst.

He retrieves the fallen cup, pours half of his coffee into it, and hands it to me.

"Good enough," he says. He's got yet another set of keys in his hand. "We'll take my wife's car. It's parked in Loretta's garage. Since Loretta doesn't drive anymore."

"Are you sure it'll start?" I ask.

"Oh yes," he says. "I come over and start it regularly. For the battery."

He holds up a heavy brass key chain, the kind that will always feel like a presence in your purse, the kind you don't leave behind because when you don't have it with you, something doesn't feel right. A big brass initial: V. And I realize I don't even know her name.

"It's still Valerie's car," he says.

I need to be careful, or I might end up standing here forever, in the grip of something. Either distraction, or a pattern, or so many patterns that they combine to distract me, like the fruit at the bottom of the bowl, in the Ray Bradbury story of the same name in which a murderer has killed someone in their home, and then tries to leave the scene of a crime, but stops to wipe his fingerprints off one thing, and then another, and another, until he is compelled to wipe everything, including the fruit at the bottom of the bowl. And by then, he's lingered too long.

I turn and follow TK out. It's still dark, but not for long. In the garage I take a step, but something catches at the sole of my shoe. I look down, and see that the garage floor is cracked, riddled with long dark branching fissures that are wider than the one inside, and more uneven. Like we're seeing it in between rolling movements that take place with geologic slowness.

"Look," he says. "See what happens?"

The bulb overhead is dim, but the floor appears to be clean and dry. The widest of the cracks runs across the garage, disappearing under a square upright chest freezer against one wall, with a tarp tucked over the top.

"I didn't even know there was a freezer out here," he says.

I feel a flutter at the base of my throat, my heart, skipping half a beat. Because you see how easy it might be? To assume that everything is as it should be?

I don't want to look around, because it feels to me now like something awful hangs in the corner behind me, where Terry's waders would have been.

Valerie's car is a Buick Skyhawk, the color of wine.

I look back down at the fissure under my feet, and kneel, to get a closer look. I set down the tumbler of coffee he gave me.

"What are you doing?" he says.

"I don't know," I say. "Where's your phone? Can you shine the light?"

He has that look, that empty look.

"Phone?" he says. He touches his pockets, looking for it.

I can feel the urgency, the need to leave. But also that too much is happening out of sight for normal clock time to matter the way it usually does.

It would be so much easier, if I knew what was happening. If I could put a name to this.

He pats himself, slips a hand into the pocket of the jacket

he's wearing, and then between two fingers he's holding out some matchbooks. He looks at them like he's never seen them before. Maybe it's not his jacket. Or maybe it's his, but from some other time.

He offers the matchbooks to me the way a magician might hold cards, aloft, between two fingers. I can't see well enough in the dark to choose so I take one at random, and I strike a match, and then think of the attic scene in *The Cabin in the Woods*, after the group of friends finds an attic full of antiques but before they know that choosing one will set the invisible machinery that surrounds them in motion. Still in his hand: Dunes, Sands, Stardust. I'm holding Monte Carlo. A roll of the dice.

There is a gleam in the fissure. I light another match and hold it close. In the moving, wavering light my hand is strange—the scabs and scrapes, the wrinkles of my knuckles. I recognize it, but I've already dropped the match, which disappears into the fissure with a tiny damp hiss as it's extinguished. We don't see the smoke, but we smell it. Not incense. Not hallucinogenic vapors from underground. But something. It's faint, almost sweet. Mild and a little burnt. It's a pleasant aroma, but that doesn't mean we should be leaning into it.

"My papers," he says, suddenly. He puts his hand back into his pocket, though the pocket is of course too small for the envelope he had earlier. "My papers," he says.

He could probably fill out duplicates at the hospital. But he won't want to, and I realize I don't have my bag. It must be where I set it down, to look at the floor under the carpet in the living room. I'd rather not go back inside, but someone has to.

"My papers," he says again, with a note of escalation in his voice.

"I'll get them," I say. "But I need the house key."

He hands me a heavy ring of keys, singling out the one I'll need to get back into Loretta's house. Before I can suggest otherwise, he gets into the driver's seat of Valerie's car, and I don't stop him. The window is down, and I lean in.

"Stay in the car," I say. "Please."

I leave the door to the garage open behind me. I'm listening for any sounds from the alley, from the other side of the wall. In the kitchen I step over the spilled coffee to collect my bag from the living room floor, and find his envelope, and I'm turning away when I hear something at the front door—possibly the sound of someone lifting a little brass door knocker? I freeze, but the front drapes are closed, and nobody can see in. And the front door has a chain lock in place. That's good, I think, that's something. I hear the sound again, like a brass knocker being lifted. Which can't be right, and can't be real. Nobody would lift the knocker, and lift the knocker again, without knocking. But this time, close by, I hear a small, labored movement, like a metal part tapping a hard plastic casing. I'm almost to the kitchen when the knocker lifts again, and a small metal part clicks inside the yellowed doorbell chime box mounted on the wall, so close to my head that it startles me and I drop the keys. It's still tapping, tapping at a bell that isn't there when I shut Loretta's back door quietly behind me. I can't lock it. I don't know which key to use. As I cross the patio, back to the garage, I can see that the sky overhead already looks a little lighter than it did.

The security door to the garage is closed now. Even before I put my hand out, I know it won't open for me. I rattle the doorknob. The way you always think will help, in movies.

I can hear birds, and other small sounds, here and there. My arms feel like floss, floating. Insubstantial. Through the bars of the security door, I can see TK sitting in the driver's seat of his wife's car, faintly illuminated by the interior lights.

I don't think I have a key to this door. What else do I have to work with? All I have is a memory of Jandine, locked out, having lost her key. Her parents are still at bingo. It's possible she told me this story, once. She's seated on the picnic table, with the old transistor beside her, and in her dreaming state, she turns toward me and her face changes. "I knew I'd see you," she says. She's so young.

I have to split myself in two, because I can't turn away from her, and I can't turn away from the garage. I have a searing memory: a phone call from memory care one afternoon, the receptionist asking whether I was in fact coming to pick Jandine up. She said she had been offering to call me, just to check, but Jandine had been adamant not to bother, that I'd be there soon. But by then she'd been sitting in the lobby for an hour.

I should have gone there that day. I don't remember what I was doing, or why I thought I couldn't, and now all this time later, out of all of the things I thought I wanted to tell her, it feels like this is the only one that matters now.

"I'm sorry that I kept you waiting," I say. "I should have come to meet you."

"You did come to meet me," she says. "I just got here first."

"I mean, that day. I'm sorry."

She says, "It was a long day. And you were there for almost all of it."

I have sometimes wanted to know whether she ever tried to leave, whether she knew those doors to the memory-care courtyard were locked, and, if she ever did try them, whether she remembered afterward. And even if she didn't remember, whether the feeling of being locked in had stayed with her. I hope not. I don't know what to do. I can't prioritize anything.

I say, "There just isn't enough time."

There's a coldness and a quietness, a pulling; I understand now why we always call it a chill, I understand the metaphor by which we recognize the presence of absence.

You do your best. That's all you can do.

Am I? Doing my best?

You work with what you have to work with at the time.

In the light from the dashboard, I can see that TK is still sitting in the driver's seat, one arm propped along the car door, elbow out. It looks like he's listening to the radio, but I don't hear it. I don't hear anything. It's so quiet that I don't dare call his name or try to get his attention.

It's not my right hand holding the camera that shakes, it's the left, with the infrared illuminator, so to keep from dropping it I loop the cord around my wrist, quickly, everything quickly. I point the illuminator through the iron bars of the door, and hold my breath; the power button doesn't make a sound. At first I don't see anything, I can't even tell if the illuminator is on, until I remember to look at the camera screen. The flat, unnatural light beyond the visible spectrum makes it only a foot or two into the darkness. I try again, with my eyes, without the camera. Nothing. I look back to the screen and there's something there, just on the other side, something with a texture like wrinkled fabric. I think I've been looking at TK over someone's shoulder, and I move the illuminator up, to where the face should be, and thank god, I don't see one. I hope that means whoever it is, they haven't seen the illuminator yet.

I try to see whether TK has noticed anything. But I can't make him out as clearly, now. I see the dashboard lights, but they're haloed.

I go quietly back into Loretta's house as quickly as I can move, grateful that I didn't lock the bars behind me, whatever the reason. I pull them shut, lock the door from the inside. I should try to leave by the front door, that's the best option, right? Wake up Stacia. Call 911. Get the garage door open. Or get the garage door open first? I don't know why it doesn't occur to me to call 911 now, from here. But there's probably nobody waiting at the front door, because they're after him. Not me. And as I touch the metal of the doorknob, reaching for the lock, I remember the white car parked in the blind spot, like the white car in the *X-Files* episode in which Scully notices something in the corner of the windshield of a white car in a photo of a crime scene and they zoom in, using the grainy low-res tech of the time, zooming in, zooming in, and it matters, because what she sees is a caduceus, the medical symbol, and it helps them figure out whom they should be looking for: a doctor. It's not much to go on, but it's something. And I have always known, haven't I, that there would be somebody sitting in a car concealed in plain sight. I need to remember to tell TK that he was right to have misgivings about that spot. Or maybe I don't get all the way through that thought. Maybe I only get as far as, I hope I'll get to tell him, before I see something flicker between the peephole and the faint light on the path outside. And when whatever is blocking the light steps away, I know there's still someone there, right outside the front door.

I run up the stairs, up the stairs quickly, quietly, and I guess I'll try to get out one of the upstairs windows? I'm trying to remember which side the little balcony is on, but there's no little balcony. I'm in a version of my own house, and yes, obviously I don't have a balcony. But still, I'm confused by the opposites, the reversals. It would be easier, almost, if it were less familiar. At the top of the stairs, with all of the bedroom doors closed, I'm just disoriented enough that I don't remember which door leads to the bedroom that I want. I don't remember which room I thought would help me. I keep reaching for the walls, feeling for a switch that isn't there. And then the door closest to me moves a little, in the frame.

I am working with the worst combination of conditions for problem-solving. Nothing is clear, except that I don't need to open that particular door. The doorknob is faintly warm, and turns soundlessly. This is the bathroom, of course. And there is my own reflection in the vanity mirror. I know it's the outline of my silhouette, but for a moment it's also something that isn't me.

A drop falls from the faucet and lands in a sink already full of water.

I turn on the light. The stopper of the sink is closed, the basin full, and in a different story, the next drop might break the spell. But here the drain-overflow outlet maintains the water at an even level, and on the reflective surface I see some of the ceiling, and some of the wall opposite, and on the wall, there's a small dark shape. I turn to look directly, and find a paper wasp, with its wings spread, not in repose, but in stasis. And now I'm in stasis. I know I need to move, but I can't.

A drop falls into the full basin of the sink, and nothing happens.

In the center of the ceiling is the plastic housing of the bathroom fan, over a vent—or under a vent?—that probably doesn't open directly to the sky. It's likely the wasp got here through a series of turns that it couldn't reproduce in reverse, making this room, for this wasp, into a trap it couldn't leave. It's been sitting in total darkness for some unknown length of time. How long has it been, since Stacia left? It might still be alive. And if it lives, I think, then we all live.

What's the most direct way out of this house? Out of my house? I close the bathroom door, softly. Down the hall, to the window of the big bedroom, a version of my own. I slide open the old window and pop out the aluminum frame, gritty, lightweight, abrasive. I don't know what I'm doing, or why. I need something, and something comes easily to hand—TK's envelope? It's in my bag, and I return to the bathroom and I open the bathroom door, and I slowly raise the envelope, gently, making the surface available to the wasp while keeping it as flat as I can. At first the wasp doesn't move. Then it notes me. It adjusts itself, minutely. Acknowledges. Steps slowly onto the paper, and I slowly lower the envelope, and I go slowly down the hall, to the bedroom. I'm afraid there will never be enough time to do these things in the order they want to be done. I lower the envelope to the windowsill. The wasp steps off. The open air is there, but the wasp waits for telemetry before it turns, by increments, to face me. I feel it memorizing my face, and I hear a voice in my mind, on a delay, asking it to wait, asking it to be all right, again to wait, the window is coming, and I realize I'm hearing my own voice from a moment ago, as I was carrying the wasp down the hall, to this window. A new memory consolidated, maybe. Or a recording that was already there.

This window faces due east. I can see in the sky that it's almost time.

The moment before the sun is visible, a signal comes, either from the wasp, or for the wasp.

To move east. To go.

The wasp launches backward, still facing me, and waits. It hangs in the air, and my unchosen choices fall around me, landing on the carpet like ash. I don't hear anyone on the stairs, moving quietly, but I know that what's coming next is the sound of someone appearing in the hallway, stepping softly, and then in a few more moments someone I don't know will step into the room with me.

I hear the car engine start inside the garage, and I know the time is over.

In split-second decisions you don't decide so much as defer to a balance of something like your life filtered through present conditions. In front of me I see the flimsy lattice top of the patio cover, the slump-stone walls on either side, and the flat top of Loretta's garage. Across the alley are the flat tops of the neighboring garages, and another set of town houses laid out facing away, with bedroom windows full of blackout curtains. Beyond and above, the sunrise. I'll make it to the garage if I can carefully step down from the window and then, with a little luck, walk along the double header beam at the edge of Loretta's patio cover, where it transitions into Stacia's. I'll be stepping on the lattice. I probably won't be able to see the beam through it, but if I can walk a straight line I'll make it to the roof of the garage. From there, I'll try to pull the silver ventilation fan out of place. Before I step through the window, I slide TK's envelope into my bag, and my phone chimes. There are missed calls from Belén, and six texts that say:

ANSWER YOUR PHONE

PICK UP

PICK UP

PICK UP

PICK UP

MANDY, PICK UP

The seventh says:

HE WAS READING THIS, FROM THE PICATRIX

The eighth and ninth are longer, and I try to scan quickly, but I can scarcely focus, and I have to start over.

They only ate what grows on land such as plants, vegetation and grains. Additionally, they washed themselves everyday in the hours of the ☉ and the ☽. Some of them washed seven times a day in the hour of planets.

I wonder whether she typed this, or pasted it from somewhere.

If we cover all the strange things they have, this book will be too long. One of these is 'the head' which a generation of their clergy believe in. They set it next to the dragon's head. Then they pick a hairy, bluish, black-eyed man with connected eyebrows. They lure him with things he likes until they get him into the house of temples, and then he is undressed and placed in a basin full of sesame oil that covers him up to his neck. They close the basin leaving his head sticking out of the lid of the basin. They nail the cover and seal it with lead leaving the head out while the rest of the body is submerged in the sesame oil. They feed him with a certain amount of dry figs soaked in sesame oil and burn incense next to his nose and face. They do this for forty days without giving him any water. This process will render his bones flexible, his joints loose and his veins will flow abundantly; he becomes as flexible as a candle. At the conclusion of the forty days, they get together and discuss things among themselves. Then they burn incense, grab his head and pull it from the first vertebra. Pulling the head out of the body, his veins will be stretched until they all separate from the first vertebra, thereby leaving the body in the oil. Subsequently, they place it on an arch on a layer of screened ashes of olive and surround him with fluffy cotton. They perfume it with a special incense of theirs, and consequently, it tells them about fluctuation of prices, the overthrow of governments and what takes place in the world. His eyes will remain open and it will remind them if they miss any of their worshipping sacraments to the planets, prevents them from doing certain things and tells them what will happen to everyone personally. If they ask it about knowledge and art, it will be able to answer their questions. Afterwards, they bring out the rest of the body from the basin, extract the liver and slice it, and they will see the signs which they are looking for. The bones of his shoulders and his joints will tell them about what they want, as well. Also, they do not cut their hair, eat or drink except in his name.

Chapter Sixty-Two

"Careful," says Jandine, as I step along, and now I'm glad the brightening line at the horizon is obvious. The flat top of the garage is filthy in the way of hot fire-retardant places nobody ever goes. I hear the engine of the car running below. The ventilation fan is old, aluminum. I'm afraid to lift it, afraid in case a sudden wind, or any movement at all, moves the fan blades against my fingers. But luckily the anchor screws pull out of the dry wood under the roofing shingle easily when I kick, and kick again.

None of this is the fault of the fan. But the things of this world suffer damage. Two of the corners come loose, and the other two lift enough to pull the fan up and lay it on its side, out of the way, exposing a square hole. And from there, it's simple enough to drop down to the top of the car in the familiar carport. And when Tineke pulls the screen door open I know that sound so well, and when we finally step inside I know the faint rattle of the dirty white plastic compost bucket, sitting just inside the door. And I'm about to ask, *Why is the compost bucket always white? Why on earth?* But it's a question that drops away. There's a hot waffle iron in the house, and now there's a hole in the wall near the ceiling where once upon a time the kitchen had the woodburning cookstove before the electric one, and someone hung a pretty tin pie plate over the hole, because it was exactly the right size and shape. What a thing to do. What a thing to forget. What an opportunity for a draft; tell me somebody insulated that?

She tightens her grip on my arm. I hope, as I sometimes do, that I'm not having a stroke. Because I feel something throbbing. Maybe just the well water throbbing under everywhere. I know this is almost the last time, but I don't know what I mean by that, and then I hear Tineke.

"Jake!" she says. "Jacob!" The light hits the movement around my grandmother's hand as she turns to reach, a happening like the blur of hummingbird wings, a sight so different once you slow it down in photographs to a series of stills. The way we have to. I lean forward, slightly, and around her hand I see a prism in too many layers to count and the edge of many hands. And the room is so large and so small that I can't turn my head as far as the window in the living room to see. But I can feel the presence of the big ficus that Tineke fed occasionally with a spoonful of milk. And the potted rubber tree that she polished with a dab of mayonnaise on a soft cloth. These plants are older than I am. And so is the big armchair where my grandfather spent so much of the retirement he certainly earned.

The television in the living room is a flat green-gray and I can feel the 1975 inside, but it's fleeting. So is 1977 . . . 1979. Then nothing.

"Are you all right, pet?" asks my grandmother.

Footsteps at the back door, and now he stops to change his work shirt before stepping into the kitchen. He stops short, looking at me. "Oh," he says, "oh, Mandy." Because we were always afraid he might catch pneumonia again, after breathing wood flour at the mill for years. And the other house is outside, in the setting sun, a golden butternut in the long grass, glowing, but empty. When I turn back they're looking at me. At rest, I think, but attentive to the moment. Like everyone is at the end of a Shakespeare play, waiting to be heard from no more, behind the lights, to slip out of character, to be actors, not merely players.

"You can't really answer me," I say, "can you."

They love me, but they'll wait until the play itself concludes. What did I miss?

"Dead?" I say. "I'm not dead yet, do you mean?" Because, as Jandine would say, *You can always change your mind. Until the day you die.*

I realize how slow they are, now that they see that I've really seen them, like birches in the winter, and just like that, color falls away and I flicker out by the woodstove reading that the dead are merely shadows of themselves in the afterlife descriptions of the ancient world. In one library book after another, all that year. Jandine's hands were soft and very heavy, during the long days and nights when she was dying, and in the years when I slept on the floor of her room, the hospice nurse gently touching her feet under the covers, to see how cool they might be, to know how close she was then to the end of a life, drawing away from her body with the steadiness of a tide, falling back and slowly taking her.

I say, "I don't have to go."

My grandmother had asked me every time I saw her for years how school was. Even when I was not in school.

"I'm done with all of that," I say.

"Oh, chicken," says my grandmother.

"You'll be late," says my grandfather.

"Rush hour," says Tineke. "You know about I-5, and if you don't leave now you'll barely have enough time . . . But you'll see us again in the morning, pet. And Ritchie will be here, too."

"But where's Jandine?" I say, but I can't finish.

My grandmother is touching my hair, and she and my grandfather bow their heads down close around me, and for a moment I think they're going to toss me right out the door, but in the flutter there's more than I remembered: red corduroy, so small, tied with a white satin ribbon and a set of canvas lawn chairs and a tent unfolding in the sun, and the smell of yellow paint for the walls of the brooder house. Gravenstein apples and gooseberries. And the chicks. Including how to hold the littlest ones. Which were soft in the palm of your hand. Weightless, warm, and alive.

I cross under the shadow of the carport, over the gravel driveway, to Jandine's Ford Galaxie. Open the door and find the seat pushed too far back; Jandine's legs were so long. Pull the lever and slide forward. Find the tank half full of gas.

"No," I say. But they're waving, from the porch, as the car pulls away.

Chapter Sixty-Three

The HOA lane takes me right to the airport, and by the time I get there I realize that I don't know if I'm arriving or departing. But I'm taking a trip, or taking more than one, or all of them, all at once. And when I'm there in the terminal it feels as if my flight has already arrived, like I had no reason to stay inside with all the busy people coming and going to their gates. You know how that goes, at the end of a day of travel. Passing everyone still trying to make their connecting flights, hauling carry-ons, shepherding children. Standing with one hand slightly curled, lightly touching a child's hair, protectively, as everyone pauses to look up at the big arrival and departure screens.

By now I'm walking through the almost-deserted baggage-collection area, not quite closed down for the night, nobody guiding the enormous canister polisher over marble floors in the distance behind chrome stanchions and retractable-belt barriers. Anyway. It's getting late.

This was travel. Nobody waiting, nobody knowing where I am except me, regrouping before walking out through automatic doors into evening twilight.

I pause at a row of joined seats around one of the empty baggage claim carousels. It's all so quiet, in this long space, under soaring glass ceilings. Especially after years of flying home to the airport in Las Vegas—Reid, now, it's Harry Reid International now—where you can hear the slots dinging as soon as you're off the gangway. Where big screens above the baggage carousels show images of aerial circus performers moving continually and fountains rising and falling, and the flames of gas burners in pristine restaurant kitchens rising and falling, as well. I loved all that. I really did.

I loved this, too, though. Only a screen or two lit among the dark signs that would, and will, announce incoming-flight baggage-collection details. Which I don't need at the moment.

I set my bag down and turn to check the Weather Channel. That's safe, isn't it? Just a straightforward stream of information about the material world, if you want it. The temperature, wind chill, humidity, dew point, barometric pressure. The wind speed, visibility, and precipitation for the month so far. The time of day with the seconds slowly rolling. And the date. But somehow not the year.

Conditions at Sea-Tac Int'l Airport:

Partly Cloudy.

Information rolls in the moment of calm, while I wait for whatever I sat down to find out. The conditions of the world are passing, but if I miss them, they'll repeat in a while, on the eights, reliably.

Today . . . Partly Sunny. Highs Around 70.

Winds Light and Variable.

A blue background, a utilitarian white font like a phone book for the weather, and now you know how much you loved all of that, too, without ever knowing this was part of the mostly invisible background that propped up everything else. Such moments of calm. Like the early-morning hours on public radio on the drive to one job or another, working as a temp, the endless school semester and early drives to the airport, and the feeling of continuity, the promise from the Weather Channel that the day would always continue. I become aware of the Weather Channel music, playing softly, but audibly, even though I might also be inside the Tacoma Mall, the lower atrium, gone now, but with a fountain and a wall of—brick? Or maybe it was green tile, and a tile pool, with a scattering of copper pennies? And I may also be waiting inside the ferry terminal, without knowing where I'll wake up tomorrow. It's a good place to sit down for a minute. In the suspended conditions of the atrium, the foyer, the departure lounge, the platform, the gate, the lobby. Where I can hear myself think.

"Did I get here first?" she says. "I knew I was supposed to wait out front until you got here." I can see her outside. I can see Terry, behind the tinted car windows, pulling away to circle the airport again, so that he can pick us up on the next pass.

Jandine wears a pretty viscose dress, in a soft neutral color with a small floral print, and with shoulder pads, lacy lapels, and a line of small gold buttons. A matching belt and smooth leather flats.

"You have bangs," I say, into the flip phone. "And look—you're my age."

A treasure is gently handed off. Something I've been responsible for, and that I've been carrying all day, and now I can set it down. Something so fragile and at times so heavy that I have barely been able to lift it, much less protect it as well as I should have.

"Is that—what is that?" she says. "Are you an organ courier now?"

It was only late, only when Jandine was already very ill, that she no longer seemed pressed, or rushed, and no longer seemed to feel like she had to change her way of doing things to make other people happy. She didn't have to struggle then to keep things organized, and hopefully she didn't remember the feeling of trying not to disappoint. I can't imagine her ever saying to others—family, coworkers, strangers—that we were disappointing her, as well. While on every real TV, in every direction, there was the suggestion of a leviathan stirring. "How would you and your family prepare for disaster? Join us tonight at six for a special report on what to do . . ."

It's obvious now that we were watching the beginning of the end on all those screens. And standing there in the field, across the way, looking at the house but as people who don't live there, I wanted to ask: Did it help? Not to accuse her of anything, and not to blame anyone. Did it make anything less painful? But it wouldn't have been fair, to ask her then, on the day we left. But it also didn't seem fair to ask her now. Because I didn't want her to feel it again, whatever it had been like.

I can see her outside in the passenger-pickup area, holding

her phone a little awkwardly, like someone who rarely uses a cell phone would have. She's looking up and down the empty lanes, as if she thinks I'm arriving from outside, rather than from inside the airport. Almost as if she thinks I'm the one picking her up.

"I wanted to tell you about it," she says. "But we were hurt so badly. It took such a long time."

I've never been so grateful for the quiet around me.

"The thoughts that go through your mind," she says. "It's true. Time does slow down."

I'll wait. She'll tell me as much as she wants to.

"Before we hit the tree I saw every combination settling into place. How the future would unfold if you died and we survived the accident without you. But also how it would be if you were the only survivor. If we all died, or if any of us were injured, I saw all the combinations. The car was already spinning. It was spinning so slowly but I couldn't change anything."

As she is saying this I almost remember it myself. She turned away from the driver's side at the last minute, away from him, toward the passenger-side door. I knew the starburst of broken glass in the passenger-side window. The breach in the glass where she'd hit her head, that center of her concussion, and of so much that followed.

A moment like that? How could any moment like that just disappear?

Her face is serene, and so distant. I have almost never seen Jandine cry.

She's slowly walking up and down the empty unloading area. The breeze is light, and it moves her hair, slightly, and ripples the hem of her dress. "It was only a few seconds, but long enough to know that you don't get to make decisions. You realize you're living out the decisions you've been making all along."

"I'm so sorry," I say.

"He took the impact. I know how this must sound. But in that moment, he made a choice."

The glass wall is tinted, and now it's getting dark. Even with the lights above.

"How old were you?" I say; I know this, but still.

"He was twenty-five," she says, softly. "I was twenty-four."

"Why?" I say, but it's hard. "Where were we going?"

She has turned, walking slowly back. Her face is still calm. "We were going to the hospital. You were coming."

I did know that. She must have told me.

I can barely get the words out. "Were you . . . okay?"

"No," she says. "No."

And now I'm afraid that she might continue saying this, and feeling this, and remembering only this much. Because changing focus, that's an executive function like all the others.

"Can I ask you something?" I say.

"Of course."

"Are you going on a trip?"

She laughs, lightly. "I always say that looking forward to the trip is the fun part," she says. "Anyway, no, I'm just back from one. Terry's picking me up at the airport."

I say, "You dropped us off. He picked us up."

"I think he's here," she says, looking down the length of the lanes, to where cars enter, and line up, preparing to collect people.

"Okay," I say. It's hard to say anything.

"Call me when you get there," she says, and then she seems confused.

"I will," I say. "Will you answer your phone?"

"I have to let you go now," she says.

Terry is pulling up, opening the door, popping the trunk, walking around the side, and I can barely see him, behind the dark glasses, under the ball cap. Loading something? Does she have bags with her? I can't see what he's doing, and then she's in the passenger seat, adjusting the seat belt, and I see her carefully holding the phone away, as if to keep it safe, the way we did when phones were new. And then they're gone. But when the phone rings again it goes right to voicemail: "I think we got cut off?" she says. "So I guess I'll see you in the morning?" And again, she's gone.

I don't want to go back through security, back through the concourse, board a plane, why should I? But it looks like this place is closing, drawing down into darkness, and there's only the walkway back through, to concourse A, where it seems I'll have to go.

But on the way I stop in Tacoma from a winter-break night in college, out with friends at nearly the turn of a new year and when I get home Jandine and Terry were asleep already, and Jeff was presumably still out at a party. New Year's Eve, 1993. So I did the usual: locked the front door behind me and turned to go unobtrusively up to my bedroom without even stopping for a glass of water from the kitchen. I braced my shoulders. Kept my eyes low and neutral. The same feeling as always, of something waiting and just about to lean into the back of your neck, but at the same time never changing in any way that would let you get a bead on it.

Whatever moved at night always began downstairs, in the dark basement, over the burnt orange carpet, surrounded by wood paneling, moving near the stairs with a faintly hollow reverb. I thought I knew all about it by then, though never what it was. I knew it moved slowly. And that it had never been human. And that knowing it was there felt like hearing a heavy foot in a heavy shoe, set down with deliberate quiet, in a house in which you were supposed to be alone. A step, followed by a long wait. No real effort to conceal itself; the hesitation seemed more like a pause to assess whether or not the right step had been taken. Maybe, I thought, each movement was only potentially a step closer to us. Maybe with every step it navigated intangible tumblers of possible combinations leading into the house from elsewhere; maybe between steps some quantum tunnel would reset itself again and again. Maybe instead of progress up the steps, with every pause the odds went whirring back to indifference. And all the versions of the house, paper-thin, would fold again into other paths through other places.

In that case whatever was there was constantly having to start over. Which might take so long to make any progress that it was never able to actually reach us. If the odds were infinite, then it would never get here. But it might? I couldn't untangle these thoughts. Because on the one hand, granted, I'd been snapping bong hits all night but I could also recognize the shadow of the mathematical sublime blotting out my ability to imagine the infinite dimensions through which something might be carefully trying to get here. For what, I didn't know; my mind was too overwhelmed by magnitude.

Midway up the stairs, I thought, What am I doing?

You know how it is; a little knowledge is a dangerous thing, and a psychology module and a philosophy seminar can make the world deceptively easy to diagnose. The more I blocked it out, the stronger it would get. The basic math of psychology, more or less.

I was starting to think by then that residual hauntings might happen all by themselves if conditions were right, with no more intelligence left behind than in a photograph or a videotape. An emotion or event imprinted like a negative, leaving a trace in the wood, the wires, the stones, to then replay independently on a loop before fading. I'd begun to think either what I heard could never reach the house . . . or, that whatever was there was residual and not intelligent. Either way, not really present.

And so, either way, nothing to be afraid of.

But for years, I'd been petrified.

I stopped, midway up the stairs, just to see how it would feel to be unafraid.

Jeff was awake, and he heard me and hollered up from downstairs, his voice muffled by the closed basement door, and I nearly went upstairs without answering, just to let him imagine he'd heard something and see how he liked it. But instead I went down, turning on the den lamp, faint and yellow against the dark wood paneling. I heard Jeff's voice again, and I opened the basement door and leaned down to answer.

"What?" I said in an annoyed stage whisper.

The big TV was flickering at the far end of the room with the volume off. Jeff's bedroom light was on, he was probably sprawled in a beanbag on the other side of the pool table, on the floor in front of the TV. He was still in high school and it sounded like he was on the phone, talking to a girlfriend. So I withdrew, but before I closed the door I heard him call me again.

I recognized a sibilance then; there was a record on the turntable, still turning, after the music must have ended. The needle kept skipping, skipping, a slinky loop of a sound that wasn't quite anything. The flickering TV screen was irritating enough to make my brain itch and I made a sound of exasperation and shut the door, going back upstairs.

Halfway up, though, I felt bothered. Probably by the knowledge that he was going to fall asleep there and leave the record turning, turning. He would leave the TV flickering and I would know it was flickering. I blamed the bong hits. But I knew it would still bother me.

Also, he'd called me, hadn't he?

So I went back, all the way down this time, walking behind the dry bar to lift up the hairy-sounding needle. Jeff wasn't on the floor watching TV, and by the light of the kitschy orange lava lamp on his nightstand I could see that he was in bed, with the silvery phone cord stretched from the other side of the room, gleaming a little against the carpet.

"Jeff," I said, and he didn't answer. Which was irritating, but a little concerning. Or was he messing with me?

"Jeff?" I said again, without getting any closer. "Are you passed out?"

Something shifted in his room then, behind the half-open door, something so close to the gap between the hinges that I didn't recognize it as the silhouette of someone watching me from the shadows. Maybe not watching—maybe just standing there. Just waiting. My head was ringing so loudly, and I thought: That's only a pattern of light and shadow. It's the lava lamp's fault. The amber light was slow, lugubrious. Then the shape stepped behind the door, out of sight, and I couldn't get a breath of air into my chest until I think it also moved behind me, and then I screamed. Jeff kicked frantically as he woke, disoriented. I spun around—nothing behind me, nothing visible—and then I fell into his room, where Jeff was up and out of bed now, wild-eyed and brandishing a baseball bat with both hands. "What the fuck!" he was shouting. "What the fuck!"

"Someone's in your room!" I said. "Behind the door, behind the door!" I moved back as Jeff slammed the door shut, trapping us in the room but ready to bring down the bat on whatever he found there. But there was nothing, nobody. He threw the door back open.

"What the fuck," he said again, looking at me in disbelief. "There's nobody in here."

His eyes slipped past me, and he took my arm and pulled me away with him down the length of the basement and up the stairs. He slammed the basement door behind us. He was flushed, and I could smell the stale booze boiling off him, aerosolizing out of his pores. His eyes were bloodshot, and staring.

"What was that about?" he demanded.

"A man," I said, "behind your door, I saw a man hiding."

"Yeah, I looked behind the door," he said. "There was nobody there."

I said, "But you saw—"

"I didn't see anything," he said, "and all I know is I was completely asleep and you came in screaming bloody murder—"

At this, we remembered that Jandine and Terry were asleep upstairs and we paused, listening, because surely Terry would be on his way down, surely he'd have pulled a pistol out from under the bed—surely they heard me screaming, and the tumult of us running up the stairs? The doors slamming? Jandine must have called the police, but in the quiet we could hear the distant drawn-out buzz of Terry, still snoring.

Jeff opened the door and went back downstairs.

"Wait," I said. "We have to make sure there's nobody down there."

"Don't ever do that to me again," he said, tossing the bat onto the beanbags as he passed.

"I'm sorry," I said, hating myself for apologizing.

"I don't want to hear your bullshit," he said, and went into his room and closed the door.

So I went through the den, up the stairs, to the entryway. Looking up more stairs, to the hall that would lead to my bedroom at the far corner of the dark house, deciding on that night that I would never stay overnight again if I could help it, the only question being whether to leave now, or whether to go up, as usual, as ever, to at least see Jandine in the morning, to let her know I couldn't stay here any more. But it's a Friday, I realize. Is it Friday? We're going to Bellingham. The whole drive, again. The same as ever. In the end, I'll be back at the farmhouse.

My grandfather is glad to see me, and he's also dismayed.

"You're so young," he says.

I look down, expecting to see myself eleven years old again, but I'm not, I'm as I last saw myself, in the mirror, with the wasp. I don't know why, but my eyes are watering. Or tears are running down my face.

I'm not, I mean to say. *I'm fifty-four years old!*

Instead, I say to him, "You're so young. Look at you."

I did not have enough time with him. Not nearly enough. I already knew this, but now I see it, and I feel it. He was working. He worked every day. That's not the kind of thing a child knows about, not at the time.

"You'll stay longer, next time," he says. And he's not solemn. I think he's reaching back to take a work shirt off the nail near the sink in the mudroom and change, the way he used to, the way he did, when coming in and coming out of the house. Instead he opens the fuse box. I hear the click as he cuts the power. The house is cast in twilight, colors running out, underfoot, in all directions, like a wash of soapy water to the baseboards, sinking out of sight.

"No power, no pump," he says. And there's a moment of absolute silence. And only then do I realize how breezy it was, the sound of that place. Air moving gently all around, all around the corners of the house.

"Ticky," he says, to my grandmother, standing now behind me. "Power's out."

I feel her hand on my arm. The rough skin of her fingers, catching a little. And I put my hand over hers, my full hand, my adult hand.

"It'll be on again soon, though," she says.

He says, "It will."

But they say it like a promise, not like a threat. And I cannot remember the sound of their voices, already. In the shadowy living room, or dining room, wherever we are in the dark house, I realize there's someone else. Other people, there are other people here. It's like I've arrived too early. Hours before the birthday party is supposed to start, or the baby shower. It's only Friday night still. And the plan is to meet for Sunday brunch. I feel Jandine coming slowly, from the other room, materializing out of the shadows, pale, and indistinct. I feel her hand, searching for mine, and her fingers are cool, and hesitant.

Oh no, I realize. She isn't here yet.

I can feel the pump, under the house, waiting to be restored. To be imminently restored, already almost shuddering back into motion.

"Time to go, kiddo," says my grandfather, and he puts his large hand over the top of my hair, and it makes me laugh, I don't know why, exactly, except that it's so strange, when an adult touches your hair gently with a big hand, and someone else's hand is on my shoulder, more than one, everyone gently but firmly pressing me down, like they're pushing me on a tire swing that instead of arcing out into the air drops downward, suddenly, and so fast that I know they gave me a good push before I could protest, and before I feel their hands release me I feel someone else catching at me from below, one hand closing firmly around my ankle, then another around my other ankle, and all the others fall away, and I feel my grandfather's big hand, last to release me, and when he's gone, I feel pain at the back of my head instead.

Chapter Sixty-Four

Belén's grip is firm around my ankles as she drags me out of the garage and into the alley behind TK's house. I know it's her, but I try to kick her hands away anyway, and I have never hated anyone so much. She checks my pulse with cool fingers, moving quickly, efficiently. It takes a heavy effort to close my eyes, or to open them, I mean. But then I remember that someone was lying in wait, to take TK. As he sat in the dark, in the car of his late wife, alone.

"Who else is here?" I say. My pulse is thundering in my chest. In my throat and head. I try to sit, or at least to prop myself up, but there's no strength in my arms and I melt back down to the asphalt of the alley.

"Was that intentional?" she demands. She looks exhausted.

"What?" I say. "Was what intentional? Where is he?" I try to sit up again. But it's like the flu. First the disbelief of seeing yourself so weak. And then the weakness itself, catching up.

"He's okay," she says. "He's fine. I need you to concentrate, Mandy, because I'm not sure this whole misevent is over yet."

She glances around, tucking her hair out of the way; it's dirty, I see, with surprise.

"Let me give you the basics, okay? Mandy, are you listening?"

Her voice begins to stretch, and I'm afraid I'm now where I think I am.

"He'll survive," she says, "and he'll go for surgery, with real doctors. I knew you came over here to check on him. So I also checked and it's lucky someone did."

"Why are you talking like that?" But at the same time, I assume it's me. My brain. Something wrong. The feel of asphalt on my bare arms is sickening. She helps me up, moves me off the pavement. My legs fold under me a moment later, but at least I'm on cement. I can see TK lying on his back in the grass.

"Mandy, listen," she says, dropping down beside me. "Please. This is important."

She keeps scanning the alley from one end to the other. Including the roof. And the shadows in the open garage. And then back up and down the alley.

"I was not privy to the plan," she says. "I did not know."

"I don't even know what we're talking about," I say. My eyes are burning, and I don't have anything to wipe them with, so I cover them with my arm, to get away from the light, even for a moment. She hands me a bottle of water.

"Rinse your eyes," she says. "And your face. All I knew was that Sam always needs more of the calcifications your friend has. And that your friend needs to have them removed anyway. That's all. There was nothing nefarious, it was just a lucky break that I spotted what was happening to him. I only meant to leave Sam at your house for a day or two while I tried to find his money. But he must have made plans I didn't know about. You were right, about checking what he'd been reading. I sent you a translation of the page open on the table when I found him. Did you see that?"

I say, "There's sesame oil spilled in the garage."

She turns away from checking the ends of the alley, staring at me. "Your garage?"

"No, this one."

She exhales.

"And I saw somebody," I say. "In the garage with TK."

Her eyes slide back to the open garage, where Valerie's car sits with the driver's-side door open.

"Somebody locked me out of the garage just as we were getting ready to leave. I'm going to throw up, I think," I say, surprised. The sun is hot already.

"They started the car," I say. "That could have killed him."

"I doubt that was the plan," she says. "They need the operation done carefully, by somebody who knows what they're doing, and who knows what Sam wants."

"I guess it's possible he turned it on for the air conditioning, without thinking."

"And you're sure it wasn't you?" she says. "You didn't start the car?"

"Me? No. When I heard the car start I nearly broke my neck getting back into the garage. You should have seen what I did. I went out the window."

I'm aware now that I'm slurring my words, and that I sound inebriated.

"It was stupid," I say, "but it was amazing."

"I should have known something wasn't right," she says, "and I'm sorry." She's got her eye on TK, and when he moves, she jumps up to help him roll onto one side, in case he throws up again. When she returns I realize she's sweating. She's still wearing the same clothes she had on when she left, and it's clear she hasn't slept.

"I drove all night," she said. "Drove to their place, got in, found money to replace the cash Sam lost, then realized payment was probably the holdup with your friend's surgeon getting cleared to operate here. I still don't know what Sam did with the other money. Check your house," she says. "If you find it, you should keep it. Buy the new iron bars with it."

I have two thoughts: I don't want it, and also, how much money are we talking about?

She says, "You texted."

She stops, like she's finding the right words.

"He was talking about severed heads?"

"About brains," I say. "About taking the brains of slaughtered pigs, and restoring them back to life but not to consciousness. Then keeping them in that state. Tell me it's bullshit," I say.

"No," she says. "It's real."

My throat is closing, and I won't be able to say much more. My head hurts. And I am having trouble keeping these things out of my mind.

"When I saw the text from you, it fell into place," she says.

"Wait," I say. "You said they want the surgery to go well.

Doesn't that mean TK was always supposed to go to the hospital this morning?"

"Of course," she says.

"Then what was the weird ominous shit you said about leaving at dawn?"

"I said to get him to Sunrise. Sunrise Hospital."

"But that awful description—the oil? They weren't going to do that to him? I mean, there's sesame oil, spilled in the garage."

She's looking at me the way I'm sure I've looked at other people, when realizing we're not on the same page. It's not exactly like I'm holding the blue candle. But not unlike it.

"No, Mandy," she says. "Your friend would have been fine."

"Then why send me that horrible description?" I say. "I can't get it out of my head." I swish my mouth with water from the bottle she gave me, and spit. My mouth and nose feel full of poison.

"I thought you understood me a minute ago," she says, almost sharply. "They were setting up for you. That oracle plan was for you."

"I'm not a man with a unibrow," I say.

"I told you, he'll do what works in the moment."

Like the virgin who isn't a virgin in *The Cabin in the Woods*, I think. You have to improvise.

"Nobody gave me what I like," I say. I'm trying to remember what else was in the text. While also trying to forget it. "Nobody gave me anything."

"Maybe Sam thought he did."

That sucks, I think.

"Somebody needs to make this right," she says. "To put things back into alignment. I know there are people who failed in their responsibilities to your mother. Mandy, anybody in your position would want to see that rectified. You don't have to think about this now, but evening that score would be suitable. That's heavy enough to matter. It's also serious enough that you won't tell anyone anything about it."

I'm pretty sure she's talking about something she clearly wants for herself.

"Nobody's responsible for what happened to my mother," I say.

"I hate people like that," she says. "I hate people who don't answer for their failings."

She's looking away from me.

"I know you tried to go through the proper channels. There was an administrator who fucked up. At the memory-care place. Right?" she says.

I don't answer.

"I did go through your papers. I apologize. I had to look absolutely everywhere that Sam had access to, every place he might have hidden that envelope. I saw your notes. I know you met with the ombudsman, to follow up on a complaint you made, about the care director whose job it was to prevent your mother's head from hitting the floor when you weren't there."

Suddenly I feel sickened again, by a clothes dryer nearby venting hot air and chemical perfume into the alley. It's too close. And I can't believe she looked through all of that.

"They didn't even tell you, the last time your mother fell. They concealed it. Am I right?"

"Two staff members told me what happened afterward," I say. "Separately. They would have lost their jobs if anyone knew they told me."

We hear the sirens arriving at the entrance of the complex and shutting off before turning in. A moment later the fire department emergency vehicle appears at the far end of the alley, silently pulling their flashing red lights along all the closed garage doors on either side. They drive through the cloud of floral detergent, scattering it, bringing diesel fumes.

"I also saw your—how shall I say this? Your Switzerland file?"

She must mean the bottom file drawer, where I keep all Jandine's medication, everything I'd bagged up to take for responsible disposal. Various pain meds left over after her surgeries. Too many bottles. Which I've kept, just in case.

"Assisted suicide is legal in more places than just Switzerland," I say.

But obviously it's not just the legality. There's the cognitive element, the way the ice gets slippery for anyone who doesn't want to live with dementia. The aperture of perspective: I have to assume it closes pretty quickly. I don't know if missing the window of legal opportunity and then appearing to forget Switzerland was ever an option might be nature's way of protecting you, as Jandine might say. But I have to consider that Tineke had Jake and Jandine to help her. And then Jandine had me. But I'll have nobody. And I know what that would mean for me because I saw what it was like for her, even when I was there advocating. Even when I was doing everything I could.

In the weeks I spent alone with her in the house in Tacoma, Jandine said she felt anxious, and I offered some guided relaxation visualizations to listen to. I burned them onto a disc, and gave it to her in an old CD Walkman with a piece of red tape over the start button, to make it easy to push. *What do you think?* I'd asked, after a few days.

I wasn't sure if I should tell you or not . . . but my mind kept wandering. My thoughts kept drifting . . .

That happens to me, too.

She'd laughed. Light, quick, genuine.

I thought it was just me, she said. *I thought I was doing it wrong.*

It's like a conversation overheard from a distance, and I want to put my hands on either side of her head, I want to press my forehead against hers, because within just a couple of years that kind of conversation would be impossible. I had music on an MP3 player for her, and in the last weeks I got a splitter so that I could plug two pairs of headphones in, one for her, and one for me, so that I could hear the music she'd loved as she was hearing it, or so I'd imagined, so I'd hoped. And now suddenly I am within ten years of the age when my mother's first symptoms became visible. Though I only saw it in retrospect.

There is more happening now, and a second emergency vehicle arriving. I'm sure the invoice will say ambulance. But they're also kind of like small campers. Belén is kneeling in the grass, leaning over TK with what probably looks like pure concern, and I'm sitting alone propped up against the stucco. My fingernails, I notice, are still violet. Red violet. For those who remember the precise name of the color on the paper crayon wrapper.

"Are you family?"

"We're neighbors," she says. "We called you."

"Do you know if he has a hospital preference?"

They are always handsome, the EMTs here. Always.

". . . Benign brain tumor," she says.

A blue plastic pulse oximeter appears on his finger, and then another appears on mine.

"Hospital?" someone asks him. He doesn't answer. She leans down, as if to listen.

"Sunrise," Belén says. She straightens up and stands with her arms folded across her chest like someone who will agree to stay until Stacia comes out but who doesn't know what medications he may be taking . . . or that I might be taking . . .

She says, "Amanda Vandervelden." She spells it.

". . . You, too?" asks an EMT. "Amanda? How long were you in there?"

"Yes, she was also there," says Belén, a hand on my back, leaning me forward. Because people need to be told what to do. Because she looks so much like my friends and I did back then, in the nineties, the droopy Levi's, and the Hanes pocket T-shirt, the long smooth hair. The way we were before we got old. Before it happens without any time passing at all.

A handsome Henderson EMT slips the blue plastic pulse oximeter back onto my index finger from where it fell in the grass.

"You're good in a crisis," I say to him.

"Yes, ma'am," he says.

Belén is explaining, pointing, looking up at the window that must be Stacia's, and the curtain moves and then Stacia is bursting out through a patio door and appearing in the grass beside him, and at some point, Belén slips away. Other neighbors come out, and people will be talking about this for a while.

Recent trouble . . . When two residents of a town house community in Paradise were taken to the hospital early this morning after nearly succumbing to carbon monoxide fumes in an unfinished garage. Both are said to be fine, but one is still in the hospital, due to complications from an unrelated preexisting condition.

That's scary stuff.

Very scary stuff . . . Always trouble in Paradise, isn't there?

. . . Action team have compiled a list of what to look for, if you think your home might be making you sick. . . .

"Oh, god, this again?" says Paloma, seeing a trail of blood on TK's face. "Just stop taking so much fucking baby aspirin!"

Stacia goes with him in the ambulance. When they take me, nobody rides along, and I tell them I don't care where we go.

Chapter Sixty-Five

Someone once told me, when I first arrived in Las Vegas, that a surprisingly high percentage of injured people run away from EMTs here. Because, you know, insurance issues. But I still have my job, as far as I know, and they take me to an ER that's slightly familiar because I think I've been there before, after one fall or another, with Jandine. I couldn't stay awake. But I'm fine. I'll be fine.

Later, Paloma takes me home. "Where are your shoes?" she says, looking down at my feet in the fleecy hospital no-skid socks they've given me.

"How should I know," I say.

She brings the car right up to the circular pickup area and the orderly helps me into the passenger seat of her Lincoln Town Car.

"Are you going to throw up?" she says.

"Anything's possible," I say.

"On a scale of one to ten?"

"Two," I say.

She hands me a plastic bag, just in case. "No offense," she says.

"Is he okay?"

"Yes, but no surgery today. He didn't quit the blood thinners—he didn't follow any of the pre-op instructions, I don't think." She's shaking her head. "And he's got the biggest canker on his head I've ever seen."

"But he's in good hands?" I say.

"How would I know?" she says. "Stacia's still there, though."

"Did you see his doctor?" I ask.

"I did not," she says. "I wasn't at Sunrise. I was here, waiting for you."

The vapor lights along the dark stretches of Henderson are a different color. At a stoplight we sit idling in a wash of tinted pavement. Peach, maybe. Sort of amber.

"What does your shirt say?" I ask her, in a voice that croaks as if I haven't spoken in a long time. "Your T-shirt."

"I forget," she says, wrestling with a three-on-the-tree gear shift under the steering column. "We'll look at it when we get home."

It's a smooth, quiet glide back to our part of town. Fewer cars on the road than I'd expect, at any hour. Fewer and fewer people. People die in sequence, maybe a random sequence, or maybe not, but isn't that the way? The person who lives longest will have fewer people from the past at their funeral. That's the math of it. Paloma will hold on to the mailbox keys, one by one, as people she's known a long time pass away, just in case any mail slips through the mail-forwarding orders that divert the mail to family in other cities. She must have a system for what to do with all the ephemera. I've never thought to ask. A system in place until she's gone, and Stacia's gone, but in the meantime everybody agrees to let these details continue to matter.

She parks in her garage and comes around to help me out of the passenger seat.

"I'm fine," I say. At eye level, her shirt says, *Tempus Fugit*.

She tries to help me into my house, but now that I'm alive again I don't want her to witness the state of the cat box. Or Sam, if by some chance he's here. And when I think of Sam, I wish I hadn't gone into the house alone.

He's not. The house is as tidy as it ever is, or a little more so. The floor has been swept and there's a new bin liner in the kitchen trash can; Belén has, characteristically, taken out the trash.

Once I scoop the cat box and take the contents out to add to the bin I can see, through the thin white plastic, the blue-and-red checked pattern of Sam's shirt. His pants are probably in the bag, as well, and probably the hat. Maybe even his cane. I wheel it all out to the alley, and leave it for pickup, tomorrow.

TK is discharged home in a week or so with a scar at the base of his skull and a shaved head. In another week after that he'll be back in my house, pointing up at the big tank, and though he doesn't have whatever he means to say quite handy yet he likes the fancy guppies. They're a new and unruly mob, all male, and all beautiful, and Goldie is beautiful again with them. Stacia rang the bell medium too early this morning and when I opened it she handed me a brown paper bag.

"He wanted to come over," she says. "Is it all right? Paloma and I have an errand and I can't leave him yet." She looks a little defensive. He stands on the lawn, waiting, and when I look up he raises a hand in a greeting, a question. He looks older, but maybe that will pass.

"I don't know what kind of sandwiches vegetarians eat, but these are peanut butter and jelly, and there's one for each of you," she says. "Here, I hope it's all right. Is it all right?"

Jandine had sometimes packed my lunch in pastel paper lunch bags. When she saw them on sale somewhere, discontinued, she bought as many as the store had in stock. A whole school year's worth. How can every single thing still be so painful. I take the sandwiches, and I thank her, and it's the small tremor in her hand that slays me.

"He'll just watch TV," she says. "You really don't have to entertain him or anything."

It's a year and a day now, and a little more. *How can it be a year already?* Jeff texted. I just can't think of an answer.

I'll empty the storage cubes and donate the clothes from memory care, the comfortable pretty things I spent hours finding in thrift stores. I've got a pair of embroidery scissors to cut out the garment tags inside where I wrote her name in permanent marker to keep track of them in the laundry. Then I'll send them back to where they came from. TK watches me cutting out tags, and because his hands are restless on his knees I offer him a tobacco can full of mixed nails and screws and washers, in case he wants to sort them, no pressure. No pressure. But he does, why not. It's something to do. It's still early and cool enough to sit outside, for a little while longer, and he divides the metal bits by size into piles on the patio table. He recognizes them almost without looking, by the weight or shape.

"Metric," he says, about some, pushing them to one side.

The small wound on his forehead. Another small wound on the back of his skull. As if something passed right through him. And for what? Why did that happen to him? Why does any of it have to happen at all?

I get out the big jar of buttons, too, not because they'll ever need to be sorted particularly but in case he wants another task. Instead of waiting he reaches in and scoops out a handful of miscellany to add to the sorting pile. I'm halfway hoping that he'll find the gold teeth. Just to see his reaction.

The bully hummingbird had lifted abruptly when we first stepped outside, but now he settles in again, staying close to his perch by the feeder. He's continually checking the air, checking the sky. His head turns in one direction, then another, ready to defend the sugar by which he lives. From time to time he glances back at us. I plan to add two more feeders in places he can't also defend without giving up the first feeder, after reading somewhere that this is how to thwart the sight lines. How to relieve him of so much unnecessary pressure.

Under the UV fabric, in the cross breeze, TK sorts and sets aside individual buttons and beads and hazy sea glass, all the bright things Sam also sorted and then dumped back into the container. He holds something up to scrutinize, a little thing that, like Odradek, seems both whole and incomplete, like a small bullet with three stiff end wires standing out like a tail.

"Transistor," he says, and starts a new pile for it on the table.

The hanging plants are in bloom. The small birdbath with a solar pump turns water over under the motionless wind chimes, and ancient Jasper stretches across my lap for decades. The hummingbird watches the sky. His hanging copper perch vibrates with the work of his vigilance; inside the red glass jar is the root of his heart, and it is everything.

The parable of my own heart is this: My seventh-grade

English class had been given a take-home test on writing transitions, in the form of a two-page description of the entryway to paradise. No generalizations, just describe in great detail everything you see around you while you're there. Pearly gates? A velvet rope? A ticket window? A drawbridge? Just describe it all, everything as you find it. Simple enough? Most of the class wanted to write about heaven. Yes, that's fine, as long as you describe the actual details that you can see, touch, hear, smell, etc. If there's a gate, how does it open? Are there hinges? Is there a lock? Do you have to wait in line? Be detailed! No people, though. Focus on the place.

One kid asked if he could write about the gates of hell.

Just follow the assignment, said the teacher, who no doubt already regretted the entire conceit.

For the test I carefully described a large vaulted chamber of stone where I expected to someday stand before the animal-headed deity who would weigh my heart the day after my death on a set of scales made of shell suspended on brass chains; on one side, a large beautiful ostrich feather. On the other, my heart. Following the prompt, I described the piles of evidence against me, against everyone; the mountain of dirty, broken, stained, empty things left behind. I'd ridden along to the dump in Bellingham enough times that I could extrapolate about the way it felt there, and the way the air smelled. About the sound of the weight of it settling, all around, even if I couldn't see it. The witnesses gathered behind me, out of sight, an assembly of the creatures we've hurt in this world by way of flesh, skin, laboratories, dead fields, charnel ocean dragnets, so many wounds inflicted. And hopefully, I wrote, there will be a smaller corner somewhere reserved for the creatures we loved and who loved us, from childhood until the end, summoned as character witnesses who knew us better than we knew ourselves.

Is this really your idea of paradise? the teacher had written, in red ink. There was an 83 = B in the corner. *Very creative*, the note said, *but be sure to follow the instructions*.

I'd hung around after school, hoping to explain about the entry into an afterlife in the field of reeds. That in order to possibly get to the field of reeds, we first go through this test first.

She said, *Are you a hundred percent sure that's not a description of the gates of hell?*

I said, *It's the moment when you know the truth about yourself.*

She reached over and added a + to the big red B. Then, seeing my face, she added another.

I stared down at it. B++ was my grade? Based on the weight of my heart, the actions of my soul?

You forgot to include the positives, she said, and I walked away through the empty hallway, accepting that I must have misunderstood some detail so obvious that it hadn't been included in the assignment.

At home, Jandine found a red pen and changed the grade, carefully making the 83 into a 93. *That doesn't count*, I'd said.

It counts, she said.

From one of the containers, TK has drawn out a long wire and then a second long wire, both gleaming copper in the sunlight. He sets them down, pushes them to one side, with the other piles of unknowns, and continues sorting. And I pick them up, because they're Belén's dowsing rods. The first spins in my hand, a quick 360 degrees, as if looking for the other rod and when I have one in each hand they lean together briefly, a quick click, and then they point forward, all business, like two sheepdogs who've been ready since dawn. But I don't know what to look for. Because I've sort of had enough of looking at anything, for the moment. They spin, and revolve around to point at the wall of my garage.

A text arrives from Paloma: *Stacia found your shoes, your broken flashlight, your blank mail and your jacked-up camera. I don't know why you haul so much useless shit around but I'll bring it by later.*

I send back the thumbs-up.

She sends back a martini-glass emoji.

TK looks at the rods.

"They're . . . funny," he says.

They want to go into the garage, apparently, so I stand, and he gets the security door. In the garage the rods seem to take a moment, like they're adjusting to the shadows, or maybe I need the moment, and then they're indicating that I should go right, which I can't, really, because the cars are in the way.

I lean down, then kneel, to look under the cars.

"Stop, you're recuperating," I say, when TK stoops down, as well.

He clicks on a flashlight.

"Where did you get that?"

He shrugs as if to say there are flashlights everywhere.

There's a storage container wedged tightly under the Buick, and the side says, *Fragile—Ceramic Tiles.*

It takes a minute or two to move my car, and to not be a jerk I move it to the lot, instead of leaving it in the alley, by which time I'm pretty sure I'll come back to find I misread the container, but I didn't. Then it takes some doing, to get it out from under the car. I consider leaving it there, now that I know where it is. But I can't.

TK wants to help wrestle it out, but I do not let him, I do it myself, and then I cut the tape and shift the lid out of the way. There are newspapers, dating from the end of the time in Tacoma, and for a moment I want to stop, to look to see what was happening then. I have no memory of anything outside of the house. But I don't, I move the papers aside, too. We're sitting in the empty half of the garage, where my car would ordinarily be, and this has the feeling of a discovery. And so, okay. Let it be a discovery. Packed away in a lot of newspapers.

Jandine had been valiant about losing track of the date, and for a long time as she realized she had no idea what day of the week it was she would say, *Well, when you retire, there's no reason to keep track!* Or, *That's why I still get the newspaper delivered—otherwise, I might never know what day of the week it is!* Said with good cheer and the kind of self-effacing lightness meant to take the sting away from even something so frightening. She was brave, she would wade in to make the horror normal—not just normal, but somehow almost naughty. Like the first girl on a 1959 school trip to kick off her shoes and run into the cold surf, something they were not supposed to do, until she did it, making it easier for others, even for the others who kept shoes on for that moment. She was laughing and she was pretty because she was happy, making a splash, but not making a scene, and again, naughty, almost naughty, and also nice. So very sweet, she was.

"What do you see?" TK asks, waiting.

Treasure. One album is the color of coral, the other of turquoise and lapis lazuli. Positioned just so, each labeled in script of gold.

"Wonderful things," I say.

A Note on Sources

The opening reference to Night, Chaos, and Erebus is from *Mythology: Timeless Tales of Gods and Heroes*, by Edith Hamilton. Mandy's speculations about accessing old memories come from the work of Dr. Wilder Penfield; her college textbook passages are from *Visions, Apparitions, Alien Visitors: A Comparative Study of the Entity Enigma*, by Hilary Evans. Old Jumbo and other whittling references are from *You Can Whittle and Carve*, by Amanda Watkins Hellum and Franklin H. Gottshall, and the Egg Frog and Decorator Tool are paraphrased from *The Fine Art of Garnishing: From Radish Roses to Watermelon Whales*, by Jerry Crowley. The wasp and rosewater recited by Belén are from *Picatrix: A Medieval Treatise on Astral Magic*, translated from the Latin by Dan Attrell and David Porreca, and the passage about the man submerged in sesame oil is from *Picatrix (Ghāyat al-Ḥakīm), or, The Goal of the Wise*, translated from the Arabic by Hashem Atallah. The observation of forams selecting a single red stone to complete their tests is described by artist, writer, and interdisciplinary researcher Claire Beynon, in her article "Nature's Little Masons: Seven Meditations on Two Antarctic Seasons" in *Junctures: The Journal for Thematic Dialogue*. The verse from the Etana epic is reproduced as it appeared in Erich von Däniken, *In Search of Ancient Gods: My Pictorial Evidence for the Impossible*, translated by Michael Heron (Corgi Books/Transworld, 1974). Chalcidius was a fourth-century Roman philosopher and scholar whose translation of the first part of Plato's *Timaeus* was the best version available to readers of Latin in the west for eight hundred years. The female chalcid wasp whose image graces the cover of this book was captured in a Malaise trap in Aranda, ACT, Australia, in 2022. I translated into English the quotations of Zosimus of Panopolis from Charles-Émile's Ruelle's French translations from the Greek.

I am indebted to Dr. Milton H. Erickson's pioneering work in therapeutic hypnotherapy. Nothing in this novel represents the empathetic core or ethical standards of Ericksonian hypnotherapy, but Sam has learned to pick out narrative and conversational hypnosis techniques for covert use, like storytelling, anecdote, metaphor, wordplay, and analogy, while adapting Erickson's confusion technique, My Friend John technique, strategic number references, and others to misdirect a listener's conscious mind and initiate non-consensual contact with the unconscious.

I am also indebted to Dr. Raymond Moody's writings and public conversations about the psychomanteum he built, inspired by the Oracle of the Dead at Ephyra, to research visionary encounters with deceased loved ones as a tool for resolving grief. His descriptions of mirror gazing and other techniques at his John Dee Memorial Theater of the Mind, as well as the underground tunnel architecture of ancient sites, played a part in the writing of this novel.

My layperson's appreciation of chaos magic has been informed by the writings of Peter J. Carol, Phil Hine, Alan Chapman, Duncan Barford, and Andrieh Vitmus. The works of C. G. Jung gave me an appreciation for alchemy as a symbolic framework, as well as a vocabulary for understanding the nigredo stage in psychological alchemy and a heightened awareness of synchronicity. I discovered the research into reviving the brains of pigs in the published writings of Dr. Nenad Sestan and his co-authors and team members, including their careful attention to the ethical dimension of the work.

Finally, I am grateful to voices who brought me new perspectives on the past I kept returning to while writing this, including John A. Keel, the original investigator of the phenomenon; Whitley Streiber, whose bravery changed the zeitgeist; Art Bell, holding airspace in the sleepless hours; Bob Fischer, whose *Fortean Times* article "The Haunted Generation" gave me an extra piece of the puzzle of my early life on the border of Anglophone Canada; and, at the eleventh hour, Caroline Fraser, whose book *Murderland: Crime and Bloodlust in the Time of Serial Killers* startled me with an uncanny portrait of my hometown and an explanation for the heavy atmosphere I once assumed was the normal state of the world.

Permission Acknowledgments

University of Nevada, Las Vegas press releases are reproduced with permission from the UNLV Office of Media Relations.

The passage about the barrel of sesame oil is from Majrīṭī, Maslamah ibn Aḥmad, *Picatrix: Ghayat al-Hakim: The Goal of the Wise*, translated by Hashem Atallah and edited by William J. Kiesel (Ouroboros Press, 2001). Reprinted with permission from Ouroboros Press.

The quotation from Plato, *Ion*, translated by Paul Woodruff, appears in *Plato: Complete Works*, edited, with an introduction and notes, by John M. Cooper. Copyright © 1997 by Hackett Publishing Company, Inc. Reproduced with permission.

The quotation from *The Collected Wisdom of Milton H. Erickson*, edited by Ronald A. Havens (Crown House Publishing, 2005) is reproduced with permission from Crown House Publishing.

Excerpt from *VALIS* by Philip K. Dick copyright © 1981. Used by permission of the Wylie Agency LLC.

Acknowledgments

I would like to thank the New York Public Library's Dorothy and Lewis B. Cullman Center for Scholars and Writers, where the alchemical process of researching and writing this novel began. My time at the Cullman Center was also the inspiration for making Mandy's local public library a sanctuary, as well as for her daydreams of an adult life spent in a vast library at the crossroads of the world. Thank you, Jean Strouse and Marie d'Origny.

Thank you to everyone at Blue Sky Memory Care: I'll never forget your kindness. Thank you to the Lou Ruvo Cleveland Clinic Center for Brain Health, and to Karen Coltin and the caregiving staff who worked in Red Cottage at the Cottages of Green Valley. Thank you to the nurses and all the good people at Harmony Hospice. Words cannot express my gratitude.

Thank you, Aldema Ridge, Dr. Mike Brinkman, Elee Oak, Peggy Bacon, Keith York, Nicole LaVigne, Dawn Gordon and Aaron Horner, the Writer's Block Bookstore, everyone from the Henderson Veteran Writers Group, and Matt Hume, Tom Hume, and David Gala. Thanks to Rene for telling me about her mother's Christmas cactus. Thanks, Riley Wargo, for the sunshine. Thank you to The Beverly Rogers, Carol C. Harter Black Mountain Institute, past and present, and to Richard Wiley, my fellow writer from Tacoma, for a shared sense of place, good advice, and so many Tacoma stories. Thank you, Maritza White, Cindi Reed, and Joe Langdon. Thank you to David Armstrong and Drew Cohen, for listening to my early attempts at summarizing this novel. Thank you to Jeb Haley and Alyse Burnside for help with research. Thank you, Aaron Mayes, for being part of so many happy times and ensuring they'll be remembered. Thank you, Beverly Rogers, for celebrating what it means to hold a rare book in both hands. Thank you, Alissa Nutting, for having lived in the townhouse depicted here, and for treasuring the original Jasper, whom we knew as Little Gray Kitty.

Thank you to my sister, Danielle, especially for the time in Las Vegas with Mom, and for the fact that her life here was amazing, and full of love, music, and new experiences. Thank you to my father, Landy, and my stepmother, Libby, for reading drafts over the years and worrying just enough about my many missed deadlines. Thank you, Dominic Biondi, for listening to ten years of revision plans and morbid material. Thanks to my aunt, Diane, for answering endless questions about brooder houses, hen houses, egg houses, outhouses, and other details of the farm. Thank you to my stepsister, Shannon, for keeping the beloved dead present in spirit. Thanks to my cousins, Sue and Jim, for the inside scoop on Vegas HOAs, and also to family members who don't realize they helped me want to write about Bellingham: Boyd, Randy, Betty, Elaine, and more.

Thank you to those at UNLV who supported and wished me well over the years of writing this novel, which were also years of caregiving, chronic illness, and Covid. Thank you especially to my creative writing colleagues, and to the creative writing students, past and present; I remember the cups of tea and manuscript conversations, even when I'm slow to stay in touch. Thank you to all the friends I haven't seen in such a long time, while I have been on this long orbit. I look forward to coming back to Earth, and to reconnecting. Thank you, Megan Becker, for your support and guidance, for the revelation of theory, and for hooking me up with incense from a three-thousand-year-old tradition. Thank you, Doug Unger, for supporting and checking in about the novel over these years, for being the model of a generous writer and colleague in the good work, and for amazing Bellingham stories.

Thank you to those who have gone on ahead. To Carol Harter and to Dave Hickey; I have thought of you both so often, especially while writing about moving to Las Vegas and discovering that I loved it here. Thank you to my stepfather, Ron Evans, for so much, including keeping the doors open for all the animals. Thank you to my stepbrother, Shawn Evans, for such optimism, and for the magic tricks. Thank you to all of my grandparents; I wish I could go back to know each of you much more than I had the opportunity to, in this life. Thank you also to all the creatures, past and present, great and small.

Thank you to Lynette, my kind, funny, beautiful mother, for everything.

Thank you, everyone at Graywolf Press, for being patient with me for so long as I finished this book, and for all the support now that it's here.

Thank you, Jim Rutman, for ensuring that this book made it into the world and for the incredible gift of your correspondence after my stepfather died, during a dark time when I felt like an astronaut knocked off course; while I was staying in the house depicted herein, you kept the channel to the world open by email.

Thank you, Ethan Nosowsky, for your wisdom and guidance in reshaping this work of many years, especially your attention to rebalancing the past and present, avoiding the tropes and expectations that were important to me to reject, and reducing the bulk by nearly half, which I could not have done alone. I am grateful to you for being the *frater mysticus* of this novel: witness, stabilizer, anchor, and, to paraphrase Jung, the guarantor who prevents the work from descending into mere subjectivity. I can't thank you enough.

MAILE CHAPMAN is the author of *Your Presence Is Requested at Suvanto*, short-listed for the Guardian First Book Award and a finalist for the PEN Center USA literary award in fiction. She holds an interdisciplinary BA from the Evergreen State College, an MFA in fiction from Syracuse University, and a PhD in English from University of Nevada, Las Vegas, and has been a fellow at the New York Public Library's Dorothy and Lewis B. Cullman Center for Scholars and Writers. She was an ASLA-Fulbright grantee to Finland, researching hospital and institutional architecture, and has facilitated medical-humanities and creative-writing groups for health care workers and veterans. She is a past editor at *Witness* magazine and other publications, and was also a kindergarten teacher on the campus of DESY (Deutsches Elektronen-Synchrotron) in Hamburg, Germany, a renowned center for research in particle physics, astroparticle physics, and accelerator physics. Her stories have appeared in *A Public Space*, *Best American Fantasy*, *The Dublin Review*, *Boston Review*, *Granta*, and elsewhere. She teaches creative writing and American literature at the University of Nevada, Las Vegas.

Graywolf Press publishes risk-taking, visionary writers who transform culture through literature. As a nonprofit organization, Graywolf relies on the generous support of its donors to bring books like this one into the world.

This publication is made possible, in part, by the voters of Minnesota through a Minnesota State Arts Board Operating Support grant, thanks to a legislative appropriation from the arts and cultural heritage fund. Significant support has also been provided by other generous contributions from foundations, corporations, and individuals. To these supporters we offer our heartfelt thanks.

To learn more about Graywolf's books
and authors or make a tax-deductible donation,
please visit www.graywolfpress.org.

The text of *The Spoil* is set in Caecilia LT Pro.
Book design by Ann Sudmeier.
Composition by Bookmobile Design & Digital
Publisher Services, Minneapolis, Minnesota.
Manufactured by Friesens on acid-free,
100 percent postconsumer wastepaper.